making of a warlock

A WARLOCK'S BEGINNING

DOMINIC ANAGA

HILDE
BRAND
BOOKS

an imprint of W. Brand Publishing

NASHVILLE, TENNESSEE

Copyright © 2026 Dominic Anaya

Publisher's Note: This is a work of fiction. Names, characters, places, and incidents are a product of the author's imagination. Locales and public names are sometimes used for atmospheric purposes. Any resemblance to actual people, living or dead, or to businesses, companies, events, institutions, or locales is completely coincidental.

This book does not represent personal or political views. It was written for entertainment. regardless of race, religion, or country of origin.

All rights reserved. No part of this publication may be reproduced, distributed, or transmitted in any form or by any means, including photocopying, recording, or other electronic or mechanical methods, without prior written permission, except in the case of brief quotations embodied in critical reviews and certain other noncommercial uses permitted by copyright law.

Hildebrand Books an imprint of W. Brand Publishing
j.brand@wbrandpub.com
www.wbrandpub.com

Cover design by JuLee Brand | designchik
Magical Artifact Icon designed by: Ayda Rose

Making of a Warlock: a Warlock's Beginning – Dominic Anaya first edition

Available in Paperback, Kindle, and eBook formats.
Paperback ISBN: 979-8-89503-040-0
eBook ISBN: 979-8-89503-041-7

Release date: March 12, 2026

Library of Congress Control Number: (applied for)

Contents

Chapter One 1

Chapter Two... 11

Chapter Three 17

Chapter Four 27

Chapter Five 35

Chapter Six 43

Chapter Seven 51

Chapter Eight 59

Chapter Nine 73

Chapter Ten.. 81

Chapter Eleven 89

Chapter Twelve 99

Chapter Thirteen 107

Chapter Fourteen 117

Chapter Fifteen 125

Chapter Sixteen.. 131

Chapter Seventeen... 137

Chapter Eighteen 143

Chapter Nineteen... 149

Chapter Twenty 157

Chapter Twenty-One... 165

Chapter Twenty-Two 175

Chapter Twenty-Three.. 181

Chapter Twenty-Four 191

Chapter Twenty-Five 199

Chapter Twenty-Six 207

Chapter Twenty-Seven 219

Chapter Twenty-Eight 229

Chapter Twenty-Nine 241

Chapter Thirty 251

Chapter Thirty-One 263

Chapter Thirty-Two 269

Chapter Thirty-Three 279

Chapter Thirty-Four 291

Chapter Thirty -Five 303

Chapter Thirty-Six 315

Chapter Thirty-Seven 325

Chapter Thirty-Eight 333

Chapter Thirty-Nine 341

Chapter Forty 349

Chapter Forty-One 359

Chapter Forty-Two 367

Chapter Forty-Three 381

Acknowledgements 387

About the Author 389

To my late mother

Theresa Anaya

1957 - 1996

You will always be my biggest cheerleader

CHAPTER ONE

"We are in preparation for landing in New Orleans. Please make sure your seatbelts are fastened, seatbacks are upright, and tray tables are secured. We're coming through the cabin now to pick up any items you would like to dispose of. We will be landing soon."

Victor gazes dreamily out the airplane window at the New Orleans skyline. The sun gleams brightly, casting reflections off the downtown buildings and areas below as the plane glides overhead. It's Victor's birthday weekend, and plans are to spend it in New Orleans with his friends. The hope was that this trip would cheer him up. Victor's boyfriend of five years, now *ex*-boyfriend James, had just broken up with him. And right before Victor's birthday. What an ass.

"Earth to Victor," says one of his friends. Victor doesn't seem to hear his friend calling out to him. "VICTOR!" Victor snaps back into reality.

"Huh?" Victor responds indifferently. His friends stare at him with some concern.

"Are you okay, Vic?" asks Elliott with a bit of worry in his tone.

Victor shrugs his shoulders, "For the most part." He turns his attention back toward the window. He tries to hide the pain in his eyes behind his sunglasses.

Elliott and Frank are two of his closest friends. All three met when they started training to become flight attendants almost 10 years ago. Elliott is tall and muscular, and he likes to dress as though he's still in college, wearing simple T-shirts and jeans, even though he's in his early thirties. When out of work, you can always catch him wearing one of several favorite baseball hats. Elliott loves to eat, but you wouldn't know since he's at the gym almost every day.

Frank is lean and toned like Victor, but a couple of inches taller and likes to dress more stylishly in designer collared shirts. He's not afraid to brag about his handbags, or his "murses." Frank loves to be the life of any party and hosts one at his place at least once a month. Even out in public, he is your typical social butterfly, always talking to strangers. He likes to say, "A stranger is just a friend you haven't met yet." He also says he cares about Victor more than anyone else, but Elliott will dispute that argument.

This breakup has been hard on Victor, and they wanted to make sure their friend enjoys his weekend. Elliott and Frank were both by Victor's side when the break-up happened. While Frank wanted to slash James' tires, Elliott wanted to be Victor's emotional rock. These two friends have always been at Victor's side whenever he needed them.

Frank sits in the aisle seat and leans over Elliott in the middle seat to speak to Victor. Elliott gives Frank an annoyed look, but Frank doesn't care. "Come on, Vic," Frank says, "we are going to have a good time. Your birthday is on Fat Tuesday this year. Mardi Gras, baby!"

Elliott pushes Frank back into his seat. "Do you mind?" Elliott snaps. "It's bad enough that I'm stuck in the middle seat between you two skinny bitches. You won't even share the armrest with me."

"You know how this game works when non-revving," Frank responds sarcastically. "If you don't check into the flight on time, you get what you get. You snooze, you lose."

"Will you two shush already? I'm tired of your voices right now." Victor's other friend, Amber, calls out from the row in front of them, where she's sitting with her girlfriend, Lupe. "We're here for Victor."

Amber met Victor a month after she finished her flight attendant training over seven years ago. They both hit it off on their layover in Seattle, where she brought Lupe. Ever since Victor met her, she's always had a pixie haircut. Her favorite hobby is kickboxing, which sometimes scares Victor when he watches her in action. Although Amber is athletic, she occasionally dresses up as a girly girl. Sometimes it shocks Victor when he sees Amber in a dress.

Lupe isn't a flight attendant, but she definitely enjoys the travel benefits. She is a little shorter than her girlfriend. Compared to Victor and his friends, Lupe is the shortest of the group. Her hair is a long braid of silky, dark hair draped over one shoulder. Lupe lets Amber be the spitfire of the two because she knows no one is safe if Amber blows a gasket.

"Babe, just let the boys bicker," Lupe tells Amber.

"If it weren't for my air pods dying, I wouldn't give a crap about them," Amber responds to Lupe as she holds her hand.

Lupe smiles too cheerfully and gently squeezes Amber's hand. "I told you to make sure everything was charged before we left."

Amber narrows her eyes at her girlfriend, "And I told you to put the cords in your backpack, not the checked bags. Yet here we are."

"Who invited her?" Frank asks Elliott.

"Who knows? I think it was this dried-out husk of a man sitting next to me," Elliott responds as he nods to Victor. Frank and Elliott look at Victor with worried, sad expressions. Elliott places his hand on Victor's upper back and gently rubs circles between Victor's shoulders.

"Are you sure you're okay?" Elliott asks Victor.

"Mmhmm," Victor responds without turning away from looking out the airplane window.

As the plane lands and parks at the gate, Elliott gently shakes Victor. "Hey, Vic, you ready to get off the plane?"

Victor looks over at his friends. His heartbreak was masked behind his sunglasses. "Yeah," he says unconvincingly.

It had been only a couple of weeks since Victor's *ex-boyfriend* James broke his heart. Victor didn't even want to go on this trip. All he wanted to do was stay home, eat ice cream, and stream sad movies. But everything for his birthday weekend was planned and paid for before the breakup happened. As Victor's friends make their way off the plane, he stays behind for a few moments before he collects his belongings and walks off.

Victor falls behind the group as they make their way through the airport terminal. He doesn't have the energy to keep up with his friends, who are excited to start partying. Elliott slows down and waits for Victor to catch up.

"Hey, did you want to get some beignets to take with us on our way to the hotel?" Elliott asks, pointing to the *Café Du Monde* kiosk on their way to the exit.

"Yeah, sure. Why not?" Victor answers in a monotone.

"Come on, Vic. I don't like seeing you like this," Elliott comments as he steps in front of Victor.

"Like what?" Victor asks without looking up at his tall friend.

"Like you don't give a crap about life," Elliott says concerningly.

"I do give a crap," Victor responds, but the inflection in his tone says something different.

Elliott grabs Victor's shoulder and pulls him to the side, out of the way of other passengers walking through the terminal.

"Victor, can you please cheer up a bit? For me? I really don't like seeing you like this."

Victor lets out a deep sigh as he lowers his head. "I'm sorry, Elliott. I can't believe that James did this to me. What did I do wrong?"

Elliott pulls Victor in for a firm bear hug. Victor responds by placing his hands on Elliott's back while he rests his face in Elliott's chest. "James is an asshole. He's the one who did something wrong. And that was breaking your heart because he couldn't handle you being a flight attendant."

Victor lets out another deep sigh as he pats Elliott's back to release him from the hug.

"Come on, let's catch up with our friends." Elliott tips Victor's chin up to look into his eyes through the sunglasses. "And don't worry, this weekend I will do everything in my power to get James out of your thoughts."

"Getting blacked out drunk won't solve the problem," Victor responds.

Elliott smiles back at Victor. "Hey, it's helped me with a few of my breakups."

Victor cocks an eyebrow. "And how did that work out for you?"

Elliott shrugs his shoulders. "Who cares? They aren't on my mind now." Victor rolls his eyes, and they start walking down the terminal.

Once Victor and his friends arrive at the rental car area, Amber and Lupe head to the counter to collect the keys as Victor, Frank, and Elliott find a bench to sit on. "I'll be right back; I need to go pee," Victor says as he hands his bags over to Frank and Elliott. He turns and walks away without a response from the others.

As Victor uses the restroom, he stares blankly into space, ignoring everyone else around. While washing his hands, he takes his sunglasses off and stares into the mirror as thoughts rush through his mind.

"You look like a total dumpster fire. Why the hell did you even agree to come? You should have just taken the hit and not gotten your money back for canceling at the last minute."

While Victor splashes his face with water, trying to drown out the thoughts on his mind, he doesn't pay attention to the man standing next to him. The man is slightly taller than Victor, with dark brown hair and hazel eyes. He's wearing fitted khaki slacks and a fitted button-up shirt that hugs his toned figure. The man looks at Victor in the mirror but never speaks a word.

The man walks away just before Victor looks up again to dry his face. There is a sudden feeling Victor gets, as though he should have been paying attention. Victor smells the fragrance of leather and sandalwood from the man's cologne. He looks around to see who's wearing the stimulating aroma, but he's no longer there.

Wait a minute. Who was that guy? And why was he looking at me like that? Victor asks himself, just realizing someone was next to him. He walks out of the restroom to look for the man. As he looks around, the man he thought he saw is nowhere to be found. Victor shakes his head and shrugs it off, just thinking to himself that it is just a coincidence.

As Victor returns to his friends, Amber can be heard arguing with the rental car agent. "What's going on over there?" he asks Elliott and Frank.

"Apparently, they messed up on the rental," Elliott responds before sipping his frozen daiquiri.

"Where the hell did you get a frozen daiquiri?" Victor asks with a perplexed look.

Elliott points to a small stand about 30 feet away. "Over there."

"Seems pretty reckless having alcohol next to where you rent cars," Victor judges.

"I'm not the one driving," Elliott says as he takes a big gulp of his frozen beverage. "Ahhh fuck, brain freeze." Elliott keels over, pressing his thumb against his temple.

Frank laughs at Elliott's pain. "Dumbass."

Amber and Lupe walk over to the boys, keys in hand. "Finally!" Amber expresses aggravated exhaustion. "Let's get going before traffic gets bad. I need a drink after this."

Elliott points towards the stand. "They have frozen daiquiris over there."

Victor shakes his head while rolling his eyes. He turns his attention to Amber. "So, what happened?"

Lupe looks at Amber, cocking an eyebrow. "She used her charm to get us an upgrade. Even though she paid for a smaller car."

Amber sports a shit-eating grin. "What can I say? I know how customer service works. Come on, I got us a nice SUV."

Victor sits in the back of the SUV and stares out the window, lost in thought. All he can think about is getting to his hotel room, closing the curtains, and sleeping all weekend. *Will my friends notice if I don't show up tonight?*

"No!" Elliott slaps Victor on his leg. "Don't start thinking you can wallow and stay in your room all weekend."

Victor looks over at Elliott, holding back his surprised expression. "I wasn't thinking that."

Elliott glares as he points his finger in Victor's face. "I know you, Victor. Here's the plan: you're going to shower, put on something sexy, and we're hitting Bourbon Street."

"I don't have anything sexy," Victor responds softly.

Elliott smirks as he continues holding out his finger. "I packed your bag, so I know what outfits you have."

Lupe turns around in the passenger seat. "Elliott, let Victor relax. If he needs to be alone with his thoughts, just let him. Don't try pushing him to do something he doesn't want to do."

Elliott sits back and huffs, "He's been this way for over two weeks. He needs to get out of this funk."

Lupe cranes her neck around and looks at Victor. "He'll get out of it in time. Perhaps we'll just go out for dinner tonight. I know this cute café just a few blocks from the hotel."

"Why on earth would we want to go to a café?" Elliott protests. "We should hit the bars first."

"Second that thought," Frank responds from his seat in the back.

Amber looks at the boys in the rearview mirror. "You two need to behave yourselves. This is Victor's birthday weekend."

Victor isn't paying attention to what his friends are saying. He looks out of the window and asks, "Does anyone know if Lucas and Jon are coming?"

Lupe shifts to better see Victor sitting behind her. "I got a text from them before we took off. They'll be here tonight."

Victor nods and checks out from the conversation around him. His friends try to involve him, but he doesn't hear them. All he wants to do is get to his hotel room. As they pass by a familiar street corner, Victor is reminded of a time when he and James went to a restaurant down the road. He lets out a deep sigh, trying to hold back the tears from forming.

Amber turns onto Canal Street and a few minutes later pulls into the entrance of the Marriott hotel. Victor opens his door and looks up at the tall building as he steps out.

"I haven't stayed at this hotel in a while," Victor says. "Looks like they finally updated their lobby."

"That was three years ago," Elliott comments as he helps Frank grab everyone's luggage from the back. "You haven't had a layover in New Orleans since then?"

Victor shakes his head as he collects his luggage and enters the lobby. As they wait in line, Frank and Elliott excitedly talk about which bars they want to hit while Amber and Lupe look at places to visit on their phones. When one of them asks Victor a question, he vaguely replies with shrugging his shoulders. When Amber shows him something on her phone, he simply smiles and nods, agreeing with her so she will let him be.

Once it's Victor's turn, the clerk at the front desk greets Victor. "Welcome to the Marriott. May I have your name, please?"

Victor lifts his sunglasses and places them on his head. "Victor Russo."

The clerk smiles cheerfully. "Welcome, Mr. Russo. I have you confirmed in a one-bedroom suite on the concierge level. Let me get your welcome gift for being a Platinum Elite member with us." Before she turns around, she looks back at Victor, "Would you like me to get someone to help you take your things to your room?"

"No, no, it's okay," Victor interjects. "Is there any way I can have a standard king room instead?"

The clerk tries her best not to frown. "I'm sorry, Mr. Russo. We are all booked up for this weekend. But you get to enjoy free breakfast in our concierge lounge every morning during your stay with us."

Victor sighs deeply. "That's okay. Thank you, though."

The clerk smiles and hands Victor his welcome gift and key card. "Here's your key, Mr. Russo. Would you like to set up a turndown service?"

Victor shakes his head and thanks the clerk as he heads to the elevator. He doesn't pay attention as his friends are waving their arms. He just heads to the elevators and up to his room. He knows he's going to get an earful about it later, but all he wants is just to be alone for a while. As Victor exits the elevator onto his floor, he looks down as he walks, almost bumping into a man.

"Excuse me," Victor mutters without really looking at him.

The man doesn't say anything but has a sly smile as he steps into the elevator and watches Victor walk away. "You're excused, Victor," the man says softly as the elevator doors close.

Victor pauses in the middle of the hallway when he recognizes the scent of the man's cologne. It's the same scent of leather and sandalwood from the airport restroom. Victor twists around but doesn't see anyone in the hallway. Victor shakes it off and proceeds to his room. He unlocks the door and looks around the giant room.

Victor takes a deep, long sigh. "Well, happy birthday to me."

CHAPTER TWO

Victor is curled in bed, hugging a pillow, staring at the wall. The curtains are closed, so he cannot tell how late it is without looking at the clock. His bags are still in the living room of his suite, just where he left them. The television is on and muted, still on the welcome screen with his name and the caption "Happy Birthday" in bold white letters. The sounds of traffic on the streets below are low, yet still audible, providing subtle white noise as Victor lays still. As he stares off into space, there's a knock on his door.

"Victor? It's Lucas."

Lucas has been Victor's closest friend since high school; they have been stuck at the hip since the first day they met. They even worked together at a very popular theme park before Victor became a flight attendant. Victor was also Lucas' best man when Lucas married Jon. Even though Victor has moved around the country the past several years, they have always remained close.

"Victor, can you please open the door?" Lucas says on the other side. Victor doesn't move from the bed. "Don't make me call security to open the door," Lucas comments jokingly, even though he is serious about the threat. Victor begrudgingly gets out of bed and walks over to open the door, groaning all the way.

"Hey, mister. How are you feeling?" Lucas asks as he enters Victor's room.

Victor turns and heads back into the bedroom, "Fine, I guess. Just watching my shows."

Lucas cocks an eyebrow as Victor heads back to the bedroom. "Your shows? What are you, 40?" Lucas closes the door behind him and follows Victor.

"I just turned 32; that's practically 45 in gay years," Victor responds.

When they enter the bedroom, Lucas looks over at the television and notices it is still on the hotel's welcome channel. "I see you're watching some trashy dating competition," Lucas jokes.

Victor crawls back into bed, and Lucas takes a seat next to him. "Everyone's been trying to get a hold of you for a while," Lucas mentions, turning on the nightstand's light. "They're starting to get worried."

"Just tell them I'm fine, just dead inside." Victor pulls the comforter up to his neck and rolls onto his side.

"Come on, get up. Let's get you into the shower." Lucas gets up, goes over to the window, and opens the curtains. Victor hisses dramatically when the curtains open, letting in the remaining daylight. "We're taking you out to dinner. Get ready."

Victor pulls the covers over his head. "You guys go celebrate without me."

Lucas glares over at the bed. He storms back over and forcefully pulls the covers off Victor, "I didn't fly all this way to see my best friend, whom I haven't seen in almost two years, hide away in his room. Now get your ass up, shit, shower, shave, and let's go."

Victor resentfully complies. "Ugh! You're the worst," he moans.

"And that's why you love me," Lucas says as he walks to the bedroom door. "You better be downstairs in an hour." Lucas leaves the suite as Victor gets up and heads into the bathroom.

Victor freshens up and steps out of the shower. As he dries his hair, he steps up to the sink and takes his towel to wipe the foggy mirror. "You look like a dumpster fire covered in glitter while being pulled by a unicorn," Victor mutters to himself.

While brushing his teeth, he starts to zone out, staring down at the faucet. Suddenly, something catches his eye in the mirror. He stops brushing to look over at the spot in the mirror but doesn't see anything. Victor shakes his head, then bends to spit and rinse his mouth.

When he looks back into the mirror, the man he passed by while exiting the elevator stands in the foggy background. Victor turns around in a panic; no one is behind him. He looks back in the mirror, only to see his reflection. His heart still racing, he assures himself, "There's no one here. You're just seeing things because you're tired and hungry. Let's go downstairs and meet your friends."

Victor and his friends arrive at the restaurant where Lupe had made reservations for dinner. The restaurant is packed. The aroma of Cajun food fills the air as the group walks over to their table. A band in the corner plays lively jazz as a few couples take the floor and dance to the rhythm. Victor takes a seat at the head of the table while his friends sit on either side. He can't stop thinking about seeing the mystery man in the mirror while getting ready. As a result, he doesn't notice when the server asks for his order.

Jon snaps his fingers in front of Victor's face, causing him to pay attention. "Everything okay, dude?" Jon asks as he and Lucas give him a concerned look. "You looked like you were a thousand miles away."

Victor looks at everyone, looking back. "Sorry, I was just thinking about something."

"Do you need another minute to order?" the server asks.

"Yes. No. Sorry." Victor shakes off the thought and looks up at the server. "I'll have the jambalaya, please," Victor orders while pointing at the menu. "And I hate to be a pest, but is there any way to not make it too spicy? My stomach is acting up."

The server looks down at Victor as though he's an idiot, "I'll see what we can do for your upset tummy." The server jots a couple more notes on her pad before walking away. Moments later, the server returns with everyone's drinks and shots for the table.

Elliott holds up his shot glass, and everyone follows suit except for Victor. "Here's to the man of the hour! Happy Birthday, Victor!"

"HAPPY BIRTHDAY!" his friends shout around the table.

Victor smiles a little and downs his shot. It helps cheer him up a little, but he doesn't engage in idle conversations around him. At first, Victor was thinking about James, but now, his attention returns to the man in the mirror. He doesn't talk about it because he doesn't want his friends to worry. He still thinks he was seeing things, but the man was all too real.

As soon as the food arrives, he cheers up even more. He's been looking forward to eating the best jambalaya in New Orleans; at least, that's what Lupe mentioned. As Victor starts eating, he begins to talk more, which makes his friends happy to see their friend finally emerging from the funk he's been in. Victor lets out a little chuckle here and there, still trying to engage, even though he would prefer staying in bed for the weekend.

Toward the end of the meal, the server brings over a slice of cake with a scoop of ice cream on the side and sets it in front of Victor. This is the part Victor hates. Everyone sings "Happy Birthday." It's not because everyone is singing off-key; it's because everyone is giving him attention he didn't ask for.

Afterward, Victor and his friends leave the restaurant and head down to Bourbon Street. Everyone is talking about which bar to go to first, while Victor walks in the middle of the group. Along the way, they stop at several shops to check out beads and masks. As Victor looks down the crowded street, he is startled when Lupe adorns a set of beads around his neck with a large birthday cake dangling at the bottom. Lupe places a kiss on Victor's cheek as he rolls his eyes.

As they continue down Bourbon Street, Victor stops in front of a bar and looks inside. "They're playing '80s music. We must stop here first." Victor says enthusiastically.

They walk inside and head to an open spot along the wall. Lucas and Jon head to the bar to buy the first round. Victor starts lip-syncing to "Take On Me" as Frank and Elliott sandwich him while dancing to the music.

Lucas and Jon return with two trays of shots, and Victor's eyes open wide.

"Oh fuck, you're going to kill me," Victor mentions as the shots are handed out. "This is how my life ends, in a seedy bar on Bourbon Street due to alcohol poisoning."

"Drink up, bitch!" Jon cheers, forcing a shot glass into Victor's hand.

Victor rolls his eyes and takes a shot with his friends. Then another, and another. By the fourth shot, he shouts, "WOOHOO!! IT'S MY FUCKING BIRTHDAY, BITCHES!" All his friends, including the entire bar, start whooping and cheering.

"There she is!" Elliott shouts, pulling Victor in for a tight bear hug. "About fucking time you got out of your funk."

Amber kisses Victor's cheek, "Happy Birthday, my Lesbro."

After a couple more drinks and singing at the top of their lungs to every song played, they leave the bar to walk to one of the local gay bars Frank suggested.

"Onward! There are shenanigans afoot!" Victor shouts, pointing down the street.

Frank puts his arm around Victor's shoulders, "You're drunk."

Victor smiles back, "And you're sexy."

As they laugh, they don't notice a woman standing just a few doors down on one of the side streets. She's a tall woman with sepia-colored, reddish-brown skin. Her long, tight braids drape past her shoulders. She leans against a post while smoking an old-fashioned tobacco pipe with her arms crossed. The woman delicately brings her pipe up to her mouth as her deep brown eyes watch Victor and his friends cross the street.

Jon looks over and notices the woman. He gently nods while keeping up with the group. After Victor and his friends are no longer in sight, the woman looks over her shoulder as the mystery man steps out of the shadows.

"Is that him?" she asks the man in her thick Creole accent.

"I believe so," the man responds softly, his soothing Brazilian accent evident. "I wouldn't have followed him from Arizona if I didn't think so. But we won't know for sure until you talk to him yourself."

The woman takes a puff from her pipe and blows a small cloud of thick tobacco smoke in the air. "He seems a bit old."

"Not everyone we find is a spring chicken." The man puts his hands in his pockets and turns to walk away. "Are you sure he'll want this life? He's technically been off our radar for years."

The woman doesn't look back, responding, "I think he'll come to enjoy it. And maybe he will surprise us." She takes another drag from her pipe, "Besides," she exhales the smoke and looks deeply into the cloud, "he doesn't have much of a choice."

CHAPTER THREE

Victor finally crawls out of bed the next day around midday, still in his clothes from the night before. With one eye open, he looks around the room and sees Elliott and Frank spooning on the other side of the bed. He gets up and walks into the bathroom, groaning all the way. When he turns on the lights, he realizes it was the worst thing to do with a hangover.

Shuffling over to the sink to wash his face, he looks into the mirror and sees a woman with tightly braided hair smoking a pipe in the corner. Victor freezes, unsure he's hallucinating. The woman smiles back and gives him a wink. He turns his head, but no one is there. Victor looks back in the mirror and sees the woman smiling back at him before she turns and leaves the bathroom. He rushes into the living room of his suite, but no one is there. Lastly, he checks his door, and everything is locked.

Victor rubs his face as he says, "I really need to stop drinking after 2 a.m."

"Who you talking to?" Elliott asks, rubbing his eye with the heel of his hand.

Victor looks around the room, "No one. I was talking to myself."

"Well, could you keep it down?" Elliott groans, rolling back over to spoon Frank. "I'm trying to get some sleep." Suddenly, someone knocks loudly on the door. "Oh, who the hell is banging on the door?"

Victor slides over to open the door. "Amber?"

Amber looks inside, "Why aren't you boys up?"

"Because someone wanted to get me drunk last night," Victor responds, looking over his shoulder at Elliott. Elliott gives Victor a smug smile.

"Well, you boys need to get ready," Amber demands. "Lupe has the afternoon all planned out, and you know how prompt she is with her schedule."

"But it's my birthday," Victor smirks, resting against his arm on the door.

"And it's my fiancée. Do you really want to upset her?" Amber asks.

Victor shakes his head, knowing how Lupe can be if you're not on time. "No, no," Victor responds. "We'll be down shortly." Amber walks away before Victor closes the door. As he walks back into the bedroom, he flops back down on the bed.

"What did she want?" Elliott asks, his face buried in Frank's hair.

"Lupe has the afternoon planned. We need to get up and get ready."

"Can't we sleep in a little longer?" Elliott whines.

"Why is everyone yelling?" Frank groans as he tugs Elliott's arm to hold him tighter.

Suddenly, the phone rings in the room. All three of them cry in agony. "Make it stop," Elliott cries out.

Victor reaches over and answers it. "Hello?"

"You boys got 15 minutes," Lupe says on the other end.

"Got it." Victor hangs up and lays back, looking up at the ceiling. "We got 15 minutes before Lupe breaks down the door."

"Ugh! Who invited her?" Frank moans as he struggles to get up. "Why did she make plans knowing full well we were going out drinking the night before?"

"It's Lupe. Just take a quick shower, drink some coffee, and meet them in the lobby," Victor mentions as he walks over to the bathroom, undressing along the way.

"Hubba! Hubba!" Elliott jokes.

"Knock it off, and get ready," Victor orders, tossing his shirt at his friends.

In the lobby, Victor and his friends gather while Lupe excitedly tells the group, "So, I got us booked on this Voodoo tour."

"Hard pass," Amber protests. "Why did you do that? You know I don't like stuff like that."

Lupe nudges Amber with her shoulder, "Come on, babe. It'll be fun. I read up on it, and it talks about the history of Voodoo in New Orleans and the Voodoo Queen." Lupe takes out a pamphlet and opens it for Amber. "They even take us to the graveyard where they say the Voodoo Queen rests."

"I think it'll be fun," Victor responds. "I don't think anything will happen to us, and I've heard that Voodoo is misunderstood."

Amber gives Victor a pointed look, "I'm a good Christian woman. I don't think we should go." After a short pause, everyone begins to laugh.

"You are far from it, my friend," Elliott says.

"Come on, Amber, where's your sense of adventure?" Victor asks.

"I left it back home because I thought this was just going to be a weekend of drinking and flashing my boobs for beads," Amber responds as she dramatically turns up her nose.

Lupe playfully caresses Amber's shoulder, "I got some beads if you show me your boobs."

"Eww! Gross!" Frank gags, holding his hand over his mouth, pretending to be disgusted.

Victor wraps Amber in his arms and nuzzles his face against hers, "Please, for me? It *is* my birthday, after all."

"It'll be fun, Amber," Jon reiterates. "And if you need someone to protect you, Lucas volunteers."

"I do?" Lucas questions, unsure if his husband is joking or not.

Amber grimly gives Victor a side-eyed glance, "Your birthday was yesterday," Amber groans as she pushes Victor off her. "Fine. But if I get cursed, this is all on you, birthday boy."

Victor gestures to Amber to take his arm. She wraps her arm around his, and the group walks out of the hotel to tour the city and the oldest graveyard in New Orleans. Forty minutes into the tour, they arrive at the graveyard. As their tour guide walks them through, she explains why the graves are above ground and how the term "graveyard shift" originated.

While walking around the tombs, the woman with the tight braids appears, walking down another aisle of tombs parallel to Victor and his friends. She has her braids in a bun on top of her head and is wearing a green and purple flowy dress. She keeps her distance as she watches Victor.

Victor doesn't notice her right away as he listens to the guide and reads the names on the tombs. He stops to read the names on one of the larger tombs. When he turns his head, he makes eye contact with the woman. She gives a bit of a mischievous smile.

Victor taps Lucas on the shoulder. "I think this lady is looking at me funny."

Lucas looks over, "What lady?"

Victor turns his head back, and she is no longer there. He blinks a few times and looks around. "Nothing. I must still be drunk."

Lucas tilts his head, pondering his friend's mental state. "Are you sure you're okay?"

Victor lightly nods and mutters, "Yeah."

Jon looks over at Victor and Lucas and asks, "What's going on?"

"He's just seeing things," Lucas responds.

Amber jumps into the conversation, "Who's seeing what? I told you this was a bad idea."

"Babe, calm down," Lupe comments subtly. "Don't make a scene where I have to drag you off."

"Oh, please do," Frank encourages. "I always enjoy a good lesbian catfight."

Lupe rolls her eyes, "I'm about to drag you off, Frank."

Victor interjects, "Guys, I'm still hung over because of Elliott."

"You're welcome," Elliott says proudly.

"Let's just finish this tour and get something to eat. I'm getting hungry." Victor's friends agree and catch up with the tour group. Before Victor walks away, he turns back to where he saw the woman.

Later that night, the friends leave a diner and walk toward Bourbon Street. Victor slows down and stops to look down at one of the streets. "Let's go this way," he suggests.

Frank leans back on one leg to look down the street. "There are no bars down this street," Frank responds.

"I know," Victor replies. "The streets are like a grid. We'll make it there eventually. Besides, I want to check out the architecture of the buildings."

To their surprise, they enjoy the scenery and the small shops along the way. When Victor comes upon one of the avenues leading to Bourbon Street, something tells him to walk down it. Unbeknownst to this action, Victor gestures to his friends to follow. As they walk down the avenue, they come across a painted sign offering tarot and palm readings.

Victor is intrigued and turns to his friends. "Let's check this place out."

Amber hesitates, "I don't know. I've never liked the idea of having my palm read, let alone having cards tell me my future."

"They don't tell you *your* future," Victor comments. "That's a misconception about tarot. It's more of a guide. You take it as you will."

"You talk as if you know how to read tarot," Lucas comments.

Victor shrugs, "My grandma used to read tarot cards. She did it mostly as a hobby."

As Victor reaches for the door, Jon stops him, "Are you sure you want to go in there?"

"Why not?" Victor asks.

Jon looks over at Lucas with a worried expression, and Lucas shrugs in response.

"No reason," Jon says as he steps back to stand beside Lucas.

The friends walk inside. The smell of incense and tobacco lingers in the air. As they look around, tapestries and a couple of stuffed cats are on the walls. Black metal light fixtures hang from the ceiling and look like they haven't been dusted in months. Around the corner, they can hear cards being shuffled. Over the shuffling, they hear a woman's voice.

"Come in, *chers* and *chères*."

When they turn the corner, the woman Victor has been seeing is sitting behind a large round table. Five empty seats are already waiting, plus two more seats behind them. Victor stops in the doorway, the hair on his arms and neck standing on end. *She is real.*

The woman gestures for everyone to take a seat. "Welcome," she smiles. "I've been expecting you." As Victor's friends gather around the table, Victor hesitates to approach her. The woman locks eyes with Victor and smiles softly.

A tobacco pipe sits on the table next to her. A plume of smoke hangs over the pipe as it slowly evaporates into the air. She keeps her eyes on Victor as she continues shuffling the tarot cards.

"I hope each of you are enjoying my hometown," she comments, finally acknowledging the rest of the group.

Victor blinks a few times before he walks over to the table. "We are," Victor responds as he takes a seat directly across from the woman, as his friends pair off to the other empty seats. Jon and Lucas take the seats in the back, keeping quiet as the woman speaks to the others.

"We're celebrating his birthday," Elliott comments, gesturing his thumb over to Victor.

The woman smiles and clasps her hands together while still holding the cards. "Well, happy birthday, *chéri*. How many times around the sun have you been?"

"I turned 32 yesterday," Victor responds shyly.

"Well, I hope the locals are making your birthday memorable." She sets the deck of cards down and holds out her hands. "I am Madame Jeanette, and this is my home. I've been living here for over 50 years. But you can't tell, can you, huh?" She gives a little wink.

"I love your accent," Lupe says.

Madame Jeanette smirks as she picks up her pipe to take a puff. "Well, *chérie*, I enjoy my accent too." She reaches over to grab Lupe's hand closest to her. She turns Lupe's hand over and examines the palm while puffing on her pipe. "I see great things for you, *chérie*. Lots of love is in your life. Maybe marriage?" Madame Jeanette smiles with her pipe as she looks at Amber.

Lupe perks up and gets a little bashful, "I just proposed to Amber a couple of months ago." Lupe looks over at Amber. The two giggle and lean against each other's shoulders.

Madame Jeanette smiles at Lupe and Amber, "Congratulations, you two." She then turns her gaze over to Frank and Elliott sitting next to her. She takes Frank's hand and studies his palm. "A strong soul, very loving, and cherishes family. But a bit stubborn."

Elliott giggles, "She read you." Frank jabs Elliott with his elbow.

Madame Jeanette sits back in her seat and starts shuffling her cards. "Who would like to go first? Ladies maybe? Or what about one of you handsome gentlemen?"

"I'll go," Frank answers. "Why not see what my future holds?"

Victor rolls his eyes as Madame Jeanette starts placing a few cards in front of her. "Well, looks like someone is biting off more than he can chew." She points at a reversed "Lovers" card and the "Six of Pentacles". "You like the enjoyment of spending money on others, but don't want a commitment."

Victor snickers, "He doesn't spend money on anyone but himself."

Frank bites back, "Hey, I've been spending money on you."

"Yeah, only because it's my birthday. But when it comes to dinner with that guy you've been seeing, you ask to split the check," Victor argues.

"Which guy are you talking about?" Frank asks, crossing his arms. "I've had many."

Madame Jeanette takes the cards back and then shuffles again. She looks over at Victor and flips over three cards: "The Devil", "Death", and "Judgement". Three powerful Major Arcana cards of the tarot. Victor looks at the three on the table. "The "Devil" card is upside down, and the other two are upright. Madame Jeanette turns over one more card. The " Wheel of Fortune." Upright. Victor remains silent.

"Is everything okay, *chéri*?" Madame Jeanette asks, letting out a puff of smoke.

Victor finally looks up into Madame Jeanette's eyes. "Yes, everything is fine." All the while, he thinks, *What in the flying fuckery is this? Her cards didn't read properly to Frank, but my relationship is spread across the table in front of everyone.*

"Are you sure?" Madame Jeanette knowingly looks deeper into Victor's eyes. She knows her cards sparked something inside him but needs him to admit it. "Well, if that is all, my fee is twenty. But for you, my handsome birthday man, I'll give you a discount of ten."

Victor looks deeper into her eyes as she holds out her hand, waiting for payment.

Victor shakes his thoughts out of his head, "Sure, here." He places the money into her hand. She winks with a sly smirk on her lips. "I guess I'm good, thank . . . thank you, Madame Jeanette." Victor doesn't quite know how to react. He knew how to interpret the cards, but for them to be so specific about his breakup?

As soon as he stands up, Madame Jeanette draws two more cards, the "Six of Swords" and "Eight of Swords." Victor takes a long moment to look at the cards before he turns and walks out without a word. Confused by his reaction, his friends thank Madame Jeanette for her time. Lucas and Jon take a moment to look at Madame Jeanette. They remain silent as if they know what the other is saying. Lucas and Jon look at each other before taking their leave.

As they leave, Madame Jeanette leans back into her seat and takes a long drag from her pipe. "They're gone."

The mystery man walks out of the shadows. "So, what do you make of him?"

"I'm interested. I can see he knows a thing or two about the cards. That could help him find what is hiding inside."

The man sits next to Madame Jeanette and hands her a neat glass of bourbon. "He seems to be . . . broken. Maybe lost."

Madame Jeanette takes a puff from her pipe. "He just suffered a breakup. I'm not sure he'll be ready at the moment. But I have a feeling that he'll return to me."

"Will he be alone?" the man asks.

Madame Jeanette takes a long puff from her pipe. She exhales and investigates the cloud of tobacco smoke. "I may be seeing him much sooner than we think."

The man sits back in his chair, swirling the liquid in his glass. "Should we tell the others?"

"Not right now, *chéri*." She takes a small drag from her pipe. "Let us wait until he returns."

CHAPTER FOUR

Over a week has passed, and Victor is working with his friends Amber and Elliott on a flight to New York. Their coworker is lazy and complains about everything. While Amber and Elliott had to work in coach with the grumpy flight attendant, Victor works in the front as the lead flight attendant.

While Victor cleans up the galley after finishing the meal service, Amber comes up to help him. Amber grunts as she walks into the galley. "I swear to God, I can't wait for this trip to be over already. I don't know how much longer I can deal with her." Amber says aggressively.

"You want me to tell her the wrong pick-up time for tomorrow?" Victor jokes.

Amber ponders Victor's question a little too long. "I'm pretty sure she's smarter than what she lets on. But she has been flying for 25-some-odd years."

Elliott walks into the galley and closes the curtain behind him. "*FUCK!*" he groans softly enough so the passengers don't hear him. "Are we there yet? I don't think I can deal with that bitch in the back. I can't even get around the galley because she's got shit all over the place."

"This is why I don't cross the cabin line," Victor smirks.

"That woman is getting on our last nerves," Elliott continues. "I had to hold Amber back before we started to service."

Amber nods, "Oh yeah, I was about to shake her like a British nanny just to get her to pay attention to what the hell she was doing back there. You should have seen the galley before we took off. She had the soda drawers and snacks everywhere."

"I was about to punch her in the thyroid," Elliott moans as he crosses his arms and leans against the counter.

Victor chuckles a little. "Don't worry; we have another hour at the most. Just try your best to avoid going back there."

Suddenly, they hear footsteps coming up the aisle, which weren't coming from a passenger. These footsteps are a disgruntled woman going through menopause who has a sense of entitlement. She flings open the galley curtain, pushes her way into the galley where Victor and his friends are standing, and proceeds to open the carts while ignoring them.

"Can I help you find something, Cheryl?" Victor asks as politely as he can muster.

Cheryl huffs, "There's no more food?"

Victor cocks his eyebrow at the spectacle in front of him. "Everyone ate. So, no, there isn't anything left over."

She gives a disgusted look as she huffs and puffs and leaves.

Amber has a look as if her eyes are about to pop out of her head, and she gestures with her hands, expressing her frustration. "This is what I'm talking about! How are we supposed to deal with her for one more day?"

Victor continues to put things away, "We only have one last flight tomorrow with her. And it'll be a quick early morning flight. Once we get home, we can go day drinking at drag brunch."

"Tomorrow isn't getting here quickly enough," Amber responds as she leaves.

Elliott looks down the aisle as Amber walks away. "So, what happened back in that tarot reading place?"

"What are you talking about?" Victor asks, busying himself by wiping down the counter in the galley.

"You know what I'm talking about," Elliott insists. "That Madame Jean or Jeanette was reading your fortune, and you just froze. You didn't say a word when you looked down at the cards."

Victor tries to come up with a response to Elliott. "It was nothing. I think I was getting a slight headache from all that incense and tobacco smoke. I just wanted to get out of there."

Elliott gives Victor a side-eyed glance, moving out of the way of Victor's cleaning, "I'm not so sure about that. You saw something."

"I don't know what you're talking about," Victor says.

Frustrated, Elliott lightly slams his hand on the counter. "Oh, come on, Vic. Don't act dumb. I know you can read tarot. What did you see?"

"It was nothing," Victor snaps back. "She acted like she knew how to read cards but was doing parlor tricks to freak out tourists."

Elliott sighs in annoyance toward Victor. "Seriously, bro? You're going to act like you don't know what you saw?" He moves closer to Victor and lowers his voice. "I remember you froze and paid close attention to what was laid out. Then she laid down two more cards without saying a word. You tried your best to hold back your expression, but you saw something."

Victor slams one of the carts shut while looking at Elliott. "Look, just let it go. I was annoyed, that's all."

"If you say so," Elliott says begrudgingly as he leaves the galley and heads back to coach.

A few days later, Victor lies in bed in his hotel room. He hasn't been able to fall asleep all night and will need to wake up in an hour to get ready for his flight home. As he tosses and turns, trying to get comfortable, he lets out a disgruntled sigh. The conversation he had with Elliott the other day continues to weigh on his mind. He knew Elliott was right about his reaction to the cards. But Victor was too stubborn to admit it.

Victor reaches over and grabs his phone off the nightstand. Bored out of his mind, he looks through Facebook and Instagram to see what annoying posts his fellow flight attendants are ranting about.

"They sent an email about that two days ago," he says out loud. "Read your emails, and maybe you won't rant. But then again, someone's going to bitch about it."

Once annoyed with Facebook, he starts looking to see if he can trade any of his upcoming trips. Scrolling through the trade board, he notices a trip available with a layover in New Orleans. Victor pauses for a moment and stares at his phone. He scrunches his face while scratching at his beard as he contemplates the trip. Something inside is telling him he needs to go back to New Orleans. Another part is telling him he should just forget about it and move on.

Victor stares at the screen for a few minutes before he makes a decision. He taps on the trade button, adding the trip to his schedule.

A week later, Victor arrives back in New Orleans at the Marriott with a crew he's never flown with. While in the elevator, one of the male flight attendants asks, "Hey Vic, we're going to head out tonight. You want to join us?"

Victor turns to acknowledge him, "I'm good. Thank you, though. I'm not feeling well. I think I will order room service and call it an early night."

Luckily, Victor's room is on a different floor from the rest of his crew. He leaves the elevator and heads to his room without looking back. After quickly changing out of his uniform, Victor makes his way back down to the lobby.

He quickly dashes through the lobby, hoping not to run into anyone on his crew. The man is on a mission, and that is to meet up with Madame Jeanette.

As Victor walks down the streets, retracing the steps he remembered to where Madame Jeanette resided, a tall Latin man rests against a post outside a gift store. He has a masculine jawline, a five o'clock shadow, and thick, dark, wavy hair. He's wearing tan khaki shorts and a light green button-up shirt with the top half open enough to expose his lightly hairy chest and tattoo. The man pretends to be tapping away at his phone as he observes Victor walk down the street. Victor is so preoccupied with remembering where to go that he doesn't notice the man.

Victor finds his way and approaches Madame Jeanette's door. The door opens a crack as soon as he is about to touch the doorknob. The door creaks as he lets himself in. The bell on the doorframe rings when the door hits it. Victor looks around as the scent of incense fills the air, causing him to crinkle his nose.

"Hello?" Victor says loudly as he walks deeper into the room.

As he looks around, he notices that many more candles are lit, and the lights are dimmer than the last time he visited. Before he could close the door, a light breeze passes by Victor, causing the candles to flicker and the door to slam shut. Victor jumps slightly from the slamming door, and the wind chimes in the little shop off to the side clank loudly.

Victor calms himself and clears his throat as he continues further into Madame Jeanette's place. "Hello? Madame Jeanette?" Victor calls out into the empty room. There is no answer, but he walks farther inside. The sounds of cards shuffling slowly grow louder as Victor gets closer to the room with the table. He turns the corner and sees Madame Jeanette with cards in hand.

Madame Jeanette doesn't look at Victor as he approaches. "Well, hello again, birthday boy. What brings me the honor of this visit?"

Victor pauses for a moment before he walks over and takes a seat at the round table across from Madame Jeanette. "I don't know why I'm here. But something keeps going around in my head about the day my friends and I were here."

Madame Jeanette takes a puff from her pipe and exhales. "Are you talking about the cards?" she asks suspiciously.

Victor swallows a little. "Yes."

Madame Jeanette finally turns to Victor and smiles wickedly, "Well then, why don't we talk about the cards?" She turns to a credenza behind her and removes another deck of tarot cards from the drawer. As she turns around, she slides the deck over to Victor. The deck stops just inches from Victor.

Madame Jeanette removes her pipe from her lips and rests her elbow on the table. "What would you like to know?"

Victor looks at the deck. "I was wondering . . ." he pauses, still entranced by the box, ". . . why was my reading so accurate but my friends' weren't?"

She gives him a little smirk, "Whatever do you mean, *chéri*?"

"You read my friends' palms correctly; I'll give you that. But when you started reading their cards, you were misinterpreting them." Victor breaks his trance and looks up at Madame Jeanette. "When you looked at me, however, it was like you immediately knew what was happening in my life. And as I was leaving, you threw down two more cards. The coincidence of those two appearing the way they did is improbable."

"Why don't you tell me what you saw? Or better yet, why don't you read my cards?" She gestures to the deck, still sitting in front of him. The box looks untouched and new. "You seem to know your way around the tarot. Go on. Try them out. They've been waiting for someone to touch them."

Victor hesitates as he reaches for the deck. "I . . . I don't lay the cards out the way that you do."

"That's fine, chéri. You read them however you feel is right to you." She smiles at Victor as she takes another drag from her pipe.

Victor opens the box and slides the cards into his hand. The edges are smooth, and the cards retain their glossy appearance. "These are new. Am I the first person to use them?"

"That you are." Madame Jeanette leans back while delicately holding her pipe to her lips.

Victor hesitates, "I don't know; these are your cards. I shouldn't be touching them."

"Go on, feel the cards in your hand," Madame Jeanette advises. "Let them be shuffled and start enjoying what lies inside them."

Victor starts shuffling while focusing his attention on the cards. Then, he looks up into Madame Jeanette's eyes. He starts feeling something, but he doesn't know what it is. He feels his stomach start turning. But he keeps shuffling.

Victor begins laying the cards on the table as he continues looking at Madame Jeanette. He places the first two cards down, one crossing on top of the other. He then places one card on each side of the first two, one above and one below. He sets the rest of the cards aside. Victor notices that the "Death" card is on top of "The Devil" card. Many people would come to their own conclusions as to what these two cards represent. But Victor knew, by the thumping of his heart, that those interpretations were correct.

Madame Jeanette leans forward on the table and asks, "Do you fear something, *chéri*?"

Victor blinks a few times before he answers, "I . . . I don't understand the question."

"Do you fear something?" She repeats. " I can hear your heart beating out of your chest. What is it that you see? Are you afraid of me? Are you afraid that this was a mistake? What's making you afraid?"

Victor can't speak at this point. The words are in his mouth, but he can't let them out. He doesn't feel afraid, but he's unsure of himself right now. He wants to run, but he doesn't. He wants to cry, but he can't. He can't decide if he wants to leave and never come back or to stay and learn more.

CHAPTER FIVE

Madame Jeanette leans over and keeps eye contact with Victor. Victor doesn't move until a cat jumps onto the table. He breaks eye contact and looks over at the feline. The cat is a tabby with black and gray fur and white mitten paws. Victor feels the tabby's grayish-blue eyes peering into his soul. It sits close to Madame Jeanette and starts licking one of its front paws.

"Hello, my little Beignet," Madame Jeanette smiles as she collects her cat in her arms. "Were you expecting a black cat?" she asks Victor as she starts to pet the cat's head.

"To be a little honest, yes," Victor responds as he keeps looking at the fluffy feline.

"Not all cats have to be black," she giggles and makes small kissing noises while scratching the cat's chin. "This is Beignet, and she is very special to me. She came to me one night when I felt alone, and she helped me find my way back to the living."

"Back... to the living?" Victor asks with a crack in his voice.

Madame Jeanette giggles again as she picks up the cat. "I was in a dark place many years ago. I felt lost and broken after many loved ones had left me." Madame Jeanette nuzzles her cheek against her feline. "She came to me in the middle of the night, just meowing outside my window. I opened my window, and she just made herself at home. And she hasn't left my side ever since."

Victor looks down at the cards and sees the "Tower" on the left. She did have a tragedy in her life. The "Wheel of Fortune" is at the bottom. Victor begins to realize that her reading is similar to his. Unlike Victor, Madame Jeanette isn't afraid to let her troubles be out in the open.

Victor tries to look at the other two, but his eyes start to go blurry. He rubs his eyes, trying to get them to refocus, but it doesn't work. He rubs them again, hoping this strange feeling will subside. When he opens his eyes, the cards are no longer in front of him. He blinks a couple more times, trying to make sure he isn't hallucinating.

When he looks back up, he's startled when the Latin man from earlier is sitting next to Madame Jeanette. He gives Victor a corner-of-the-mouth smile as his hand is placed on top of the cards, gently rubbing his thumb against the side of the deck. He holds a neat glass of whiskey in his other hand.

The man is now wearing a dark charcoal vest with matching slacks. His shirt is pale green, with the sleeves rolled up past his elbows. The top buttons are undone because he isn't wearing a tie. Victor somehow remains calm, even though this stranger appeared out of nowhere.

After a moment of staring at each other, the man speaks with a Spanish accent. "Hello, I am Eduardo. But everyone calls me Eddie."

"H-Hello, Eddie," Victor answers with a bit of hesitation.

"I am very impressed with your reading skills. Why don't you try reading my cards?" Eddie slides the deck back over to Victor.

Victor stops the cards with his hand. "I don't understand."

Eddie sits back in his seat, crosses his legs, and clasps his hands in his lap. "Tell me, what do the cards tell you about me? Show me what you find."

Victor picks up the deck and starts shuffling. He looks between Eddie and Madame Jeanette.

"Focus on me and not her or the cat. You should know this about tarot," Eddie remarks.

Victor starts to put the cards down; the first card is the "Emperor."

"Ahh!" Eddie says gleefully, slapping his leg, "A strong card. That's definitely me."

Victor places the "Moon" on top of the Emperor. Madame Jeanette giggles. "Looks like you're acting a little cocky, ah, Eddie?"

"Would you like me to continue?" Victor asks.

Eddie scratches his chin and then takes a sip of his whiskey. "I think you're good. But not ready."

Victor is confused, "Ready? For what?"

"Where do you live, chéri? Do you still live in the desert, or is your heart elsewhere?" Madame Jeanette asks without hesitation.

Victor is baffled by her question. "What do you mean?"

Eddie snaps his fingers. A maroon business card with silver writing appears. He tosses it to Victor, and it stops perfectly before him. "When you get home, call this number."

Victor picks up the card and studies it. It only has a number written in silver foil font, no name or address. The border has an elegant design. Victor looks at the back and sees nothing. He is confused by what was given to him. When Victor looks up, only Madame Jeanette is sitting before him. She rests her chin on her clasped hands while giving an almost devilish smile on her lips.

Victor is so focused on Madame Jeanette that he doesn't notice Eddie appearing beside him. Eddie blows some black powder into Victor's face. Victor coughs a little as he inhales the odorless powder. Victor's eyelids start to flutter as he slumps over into his seat, knocked out from the powder. The mystery man appears from the darkness of another room.

Behind him stands a slender Japanese woman with shoulder-length, straight black hair, wearing an asymmetrical, bright red dress and matching red high-heeled shoes.

"Boys," Madame Jeanette starts as she puffs her pipe, "take him back to his hotel room. And make it look like he never left. We don't want to startle him right away."

Victor sits up quickly in his bed. His entire uncovered naked body is covered in sweat. He looks rapidly around his dark room, breathing heavily. *What happened?* he thinks to himself. *Was it a dream? Did that actually happen?* He turns on the lamp, reaches for a bottle of water on the nightstand, and starts chugging away.

When he finishes drinking the water, his breathing and heart rate start to slow down. The room no longer feels like it's spinning. He continues to look around, but no one is present. Victor gets out of bed and heads to the bathroom. He walks over to the sink and proceeds to wash his hands and face.

As he dries off his face, he looks into the mirror and sees the slender Japanese woman standing behind him. He makes eye contact with her piercing blue eyes. She looks up and down at Victor's naked body and gives him a smile and a wink.

Victor turns around and sees no one there. He looks back and forth between the mirror and where the woman stands. He takes a deep breath to try to calm his nerves. "I really need to stop coming to New Orleans."

Back at Madame Jeanette's table, Eddie sits to her right, and the mystery man is to her left. The Japanese woman sits across from her. Another older woman and a man smoking a cigar sit in the other seats. Madame Jeanette is now dressed in a tailored suit, as the rest of the audience.

"Well, what did you think, Chiyo?" Madame Jeanette asks the Japanese woman across from her.

Now dressed in a bright red suit, Chiyo taps her matching red fingernails on the table, "I can sense a lot of magic coming off him. It needs to be trained soon." She turns to Eddie, raising an eyebrow. "He was a little startled when I saw him naked."

Eddie snickers, "I took him for a guy who likes to sleep naked. And I was told to make it seem like he never left his hotel."

Chiyo rolls her eyes. "I'm saying he has much potential. I can sense there are many avenues he can take and accomplish each of them."

Madame Jeanette holds her pipe close to her lips and mentions, "He knows his way around the tarot. That is perfectly clear."

"Do we know if he is part of a coven?" Chiyo asks.

The mystery man places a folder on the table. "He is not. However, many of you might remember his grandmother." He opens the folder and slides it over to Chiyo. "It was such a shame she never got to pass on her teachings to her daughter and grandson."

Chiyo picks up the folder and examines its contents. "Do we know what *really* happened to her?"

"She died from cancer," the man responds. "At least that's what the autopsy will say. But we know it was more than that."

Chiyo looks over at Eddie and hands him the folder.

"What about his mother?" Eddie asks as he looks over the files inside. "I remember when she was young but never heard if she kept up with her lessons."

"His grandmother died before she could pass anything of great value onto his mother," The mystery man responds. "But that was because his grandmother pulled his mother out of her studies at an early age. His mother then passed away before she turned 40. He was barely 13," the man stated with a hint of sorrow. "He's practically been off our radar since his birth. How that was possible, your guess is as good as mine."

Eddie hands Madame Jeanette the folder, and then Madame Jeanette gives the folder back to the mystery man. "I remember his mother and grandmother," Madame Jeanette says. "His grandmother was an amazing witch. I wish Victor were able to learn from her. Do you think you will be able to guide him?"

The mystery man returns the folder to his satchel, "I believe so. He definitely has a gift that needs to be tapped. I could feel the strong energy coming from him during my encounters."

Madame Jeanette takes a long and heavy puff from her pipe. She exhales the thick smoke around the table. The smoke starts to curve into a dome. The others cannot see anything in the smoke while Madame Jeanette sits back, examines, and informs them what she sees.

"Victor seems to have great potential; that is correct," Madame Jeanette begins. "But we must proceed with caution when we engage with him. He is already tightly wound up from our encounters." She looks over at the man sitting between Eddie and Chiyo. "He is not afraid but will question every step of the way. He might struggle and lose focus, so we must be patient." She brings her attention back to the cloud. "He can accomplish so much, possibly more than his grandmother. But is Victor the one we need?"

Madame Jeanette looks to the woman sitting next to Chiyo. "What say you, Akisha?"

Akisha is a dark-skinned woman of African descent with short silver hair. She grew up in London after her family immigrated there when she was three. Her eyes are intense, seeing many great things, but more tragic. She is the eldest at the table and is respected among the covens. Many covens come to her for approval or guidance even though she does not hold the official title of "Superior" or "Elder" within her own coven.

"I vaguely remember his grandmother. What I do recall about her is she was mighty. She never wanted to be feared because of this. She was kind and generous in her teachings. It was a tragedy when she was taken away. If Victor holds anything in his blood like his grandmother, we must ensure he is on the right path and will not be persuaded onto another."

"Are you sure the council will approve his training? Being that he is not part of a coven?" Eddie asks.

The man sitting next to Eddie looks deeply into the smoke on the table, even though he can not see anything beyond it. "Let me handle that part," he says in his Texas drawl. "In the meantime, let's keep all this to ourselves for the time being. Victor has been off our radar for a reason. If it was something his grandmother did to keep it that way, we must proceed carefully."

Madame Jeanette turns her attention to the mystery man. "Well, looks like he will be yours soon enough. Keep an eye on Victor and take care of him. If we play our cards right, he will be the warlock we hope he can be." She looks back into the smoke fading away on the table. "But if we lose sight, he could be our worst nightmare."

CHAPTER SIX

Victor returns home after a couple days of flying. He opens the door to his apartment which feels empty, even though it's fully furnished. He's still not used to living alone again, having been with James for almost three years. Honestly, he doesn't miss James as much as the dogs. He would like to get a pet, but as he's away from home so much now, it wouldn't be fair to the animal.

Victor closes the door and walks deeper into his apartment. He doesn't turn on any lights on the way to the bedroom. As he walks into it, there is a hint of tobacco; it smells like the same tobacco Madame Jeanette smokes. He slowly looks around. He calls out to his Amazon Echo to turn on all the lights. He looks over his shoulder into the living room but is all alone. He shakes his head and plops his suitcase onto his bed.

Victor unzips his suitcase, collects his dirty clothes, and walks over to the hamper, but doesn't notice that under those dirty clothes is the pack of tarot cards that Madame Jeanette handed him. As he gets undressed, he turns on his Bluetooth to listen to his playlist and then turns on the shower. While in the shower, he tries to clear his thoughts from the past couple of weeks. This is the first time he is alone with his thoughts.

He's been so busy with friends and work he hasn't had much time to decompress. It is in that moment that it finally hits him. His knees buckle a little, and he lowers himself into the tub. He cups his hands on his face and lets it all out. He cries for what seems like 20 minutes as the pent-up emotions can finally be released.

The break-up with James. The heartbreak when James started seeing someone else. Victor keeps telling himself that James was insecure and couldn't handle him being away from home for days at a time. But he also feels he could have done more to keep the relationship afloat. The move back home was rough since he didn't want to live with his parents, even though his folks told him he should for the time being.

After what seemed like an eternity, he gets on his knees and washes the tears off his face. For once, he feels a sense of clarity. He needed this good cry alone, with no one telling him how to act or feel. He slowly picks himself up so as not to get dizzy from standing up too fast. His legs are still a little weak, but he is starting to regain his strength. Victor finishes his shower, puts on some comfy pajama bottoms and a shirt, and stands in the doorway to his bedroom.

After a few moments to collect himself, he pulls the hamper behind him, Victor takes the first load of laundry to the washer. When he walks back into the bedroom, he reaches for his suitcase. He is about to set the suitcase on the floor, then freezes, noticing the tarot cards tucked under his clothes. His hand shakes as he reaches to pick them up.

I thought it was a dream. How did these get here?

As he picks up the box, he notices it is the same one Madame Jeanette handed him. But now, it is tied with a small ribbon, which he unties and opens the box. As the deck slides into his hands, a small piece of paper drops with them. "A gift for you, *chéri*" is written in gold lettering.

He feels a piece of cardstock on the bottom of the deck. He turns the deck over to reveal the maroon business card. Looking at the card, he realizes it wasn't a dream.

Victor sits on the side of his bed, taking the card in his other hand. He looks back and forth between the business card and the deck of tarot cards in his other hand.

Victor takes a deep breath and sets the deck down. He reaches for his phone and dials the number. He hovers his thumb over the call button and hesitates to tap it. His breathing is calm, but his heart is racing and his hands are shaking. After staring at his phone for several moments, he takes a dry gulp before finally calling the number.

Victor brings his phone up to his ear as it rings. It rings several times before someone answers, but they don't speak.

"Hello?" he asks the person on the other end.

Silence.

"I was told to call this number." Still waiting for an answer.

The call disconnects. He pulls the phone away to look at the screen, unsure of what happened. When he returns his phone to the charger, a text message comes from an unknown number.

I'll see you soon. -L

Who's L? Victor asks himself.

While Victor ponders the text he receives another text message.

"Trade request approved?" Victor is perplexed. "I don't remember submitting a trip trade request." He opens up his schedule to see that he is now working a flight to São Paulo, Brazil. "And I'm the Lead Flight Attendant? When did I put in this request?"

Five days later, Victor is working in First Class on his way to São Paulo. His passengers have just finished dinner and are drifting off to sleep on the long flight. He dims the lights in his cabin and gathers any dirty dishes or glasses from his sleeping passengers.

One of the flight attendants approaches him. "The gentleman in 11D would like to talk to you."

"Do you know what he wants?" Victor asks as he places the dirty dishes on the counter in the galley.

The flight attendant shakes their head. "No, but he specifically said your name."

Unsure of the request, Victor walks into business class. When he approaches 11D, he stops and sees the mystery man sitting there reading a book. He's dressed in matching dark blue slacks and vest. His maroon shirt is a few shades lighter than his maroon tie. Victor stands a few feet away for a moment.

The man looks up from his book and gives Victor a gentle smile. "Good evening, Victor," he says in his Brazilian accent.

Victor snaps out of his trance and approaches the man. "Hello, sir. I understand you wanted to speak to me?"

The man closes his book and sets it in his lap. "Would you like to take a seat?" He gestures to the ottoman on the other side of his business class suite.

Victor hesitates at the offer. "Is there something I can do for you? Was there something wrong with the service?"

The man smiles and holds his gesture. "No, no, my friend, please have a seat."

Victor cautiously takes a seat in front of the man. "I'm sorry, I didn't have time to look at your name before I came over. My flight attendant made it sound like it was urgent."

"My name is Leopold Oliveira. But you can call me Leo. And it's not urgent at all."

"How may I be of assistance to you, Leo?"

Leo takes a sip from his cocktail and keeps his hazel eyes on Victor. After a few small drinks, he finally asks, "Are you feeling any better?"

Victor seems confused and concerned but maintains eye contact with Leo. "I believe so. Why do you ask?"

"Well, I understand you've been dealing with some difficult life changes. Honestly, he was an asshole, and you deserve better." Leo winks at Victor.

"Are . . . are you asking me out?" Victor is unsure where this conversation is going.

Leo chuckles, "I'm here to answer your call."

Victor sits back, leaning against the wall behind him. "My call?"

"Yes, you did call, didn't you?" Leo smiles whimsically.

Victor becomes puzzled. "What call are you talking about? I didn't call you."

"Of course you did, about five days ago," Leo pauses, letting Victor connect the pieces. "Do you know how tricky it was to get on this flight? Unfortunately, all the first-class seats were booked, so I had to settle with business."

"Was that you who answered the phone and didn't speak?" Victor ponders.

"No, that was an assistant. But I was informed as soon as they hung up. I felt it was more proper to speak in person," Leo explains as he sets his book down.

As they are talking, two flight attendants walk past them. Victor notices another attendant walking down the other aisle, trying to be inconspicuous. Victor knows they are hoping to listen in on their conversation.

"Do we have to talk about this now?" Victor asks softly. "I have a feeling my crew is trying to listen in."

Leo notices another flight attendant trying to get a good look from behind a wall and smirks. "We can talk more while you're on your layover."

Victor cocks an eyebrow while he presses the tip of his tongue against one of his canines. "I have a feeling you already know where I'm staying in São Paulo?"

Leo tries to hold back his grin. "Of course I do. I used to live there as well. I'll take you to breakfast at my favorite cafe near the hotel." Leo finishes his drink and holds out the glass for Victor to take. "For now, I'm going to take a nap. We have a long day ahead of us tomorrow."

Victor stands up, takes the glass from Leo, and smiles to give his crew the impression that the conversation was good. He walks back into first class, where most of his crew awaits him when he turns into the galley. "Shouldn't you be taking care of our passengers?" he exclaims. "And shouldn't half of you be on break?"

"Well, what did he want?" asks one of the other attendants.

"It was nothing," Victor responds quickly. "We went to high school together. It took me a moment to realize who he was."

"Are you going to meet up with him?" asks another with a smile. "He's really cute too."

"Will the four of you please get back to work or go on break?" Victor says, dismissing their inquisitions.

They begrudgingly leave the galley, hoping for more juicy details, but Victor knows he can't talk about what has happened to him over the past few weeks.

After an exhausting flight and a long drive to the hotel, Victor finally walks into his room, completely spent. He starts getting settled and unpacking when he receives a text message from Leo with the cafe's location. Victor sits at the foot of the bed, then falls back. *The café is close by. I just need to shut my eyes for a moment,* he thinks. An hour later, he is awakened by another text message.

Are you on your way? I just ordered for you.

"Shit!" He quickly changes his clothes, puts his phone in his pocket, and heads out to the cafe.

When he walks around the corner from the hotel, he sees Leo sitting on the cafe's patio reading the same book he was reading on the plane. He is dressed casually in a button-up shirt with the top two buttons undone and light blue shorts.

"Wow, he wasn't joking about it being close to the hotel," he says aloud to himself. He walks up to the table and takes a seat across from Leo.

Leo looks up from his book and smiles at Victor. "*Bom dia.* Happy to see that you made it. Our food should be . . . there it is."

As soon as the words leave Leo's mouth, the server sets down two plates and places a glass of orange juice and a glass of water in front of Victor. Leo picks up his cup of coffee and toasts, "*Provecho.*"

"I didn't think Brazilians said '*Provecho*,'" Victor comments as he picks up his utensils.

"Well, you are Mexican, aren't you?" Leo asks.

"I'm half. The other half is Sicilian," Victor responds, taking a bite of his food.

Leo picks up his juice and asks, "So, is your mother or father Mexican?"

"My father," Victor answers with a mouth full of food.

"Really?" Leo ponders for a moment. "Russo isn't a Mexican last name."

Victor takes a drink of his orange juice before responding. "My parents divorced while my mom was pregnant with me. When I was born, she gave me her maiden name. It was a little awkward when my father started to come back into the picture a few years after I was born. He wasn't too happy when he learned I wasn't given his last name."

Victor takes another bite and swallows before he continues. "When my mom passed away, I moved in with my father and stepfamily. He wanted to change my last name, but because I was already 14, I was given a choice: Russo or Fernandez. Russo was easier to spell. Plus, it was my mom's and grandma's name, and I had no other family. It only felt right."

"Were you close to your mother and grandmother?" Leo asks.

Victor fiddles with his food, reminiscing about the past. "I didn't really get to know my grandmother. She died after I turned five. But my mother was my world, as I was hers. I was an only child and didn't have that many friends or family growing up. When she died, I felt like I was lost. Something was missing in my life, and it wasn't just my mom; it felt like something more."

When Victor finishes talking, he begins to tear up. He tries to cover it up. "Sorry, I think I got something in my eye."

Leo reaches out and places a hand on Victor's. "It's okay. You don't need to excuse yourself." He pats Victor's hand as he leans back into his seat. "I lost my grandmother at a young age too. I miss her every day. But I know she's still with me."

Victor takes a deep breath to compose himself as he sips water. They finish their breakfast in silence. When the check arrives, Leo hands the server cash before Victor can say anything. The server walks away, thanking Leo in Portuguese.

"Wait, you don't have to do that," Victor explains.

Leo smiles at Victor as he puts his wallet away, "I invited you, didn't I? Are you ready to go?"

"Where are we going?" Victor questions.

"Come with me. There's something I want to show you," Leo says mysteriously as they exit the cafe.

CHAPTER SEVEN

Victor and Leo walk through the streets of São Paulo. Leo points out some points of interest from growing up in the city. They walked by some boarded-up stores where Leo used to get candy as a child and a restaurant that had once been an arcade where he would hang out with his friends after school. They stop in front of the *Museu de Arte de São Paulo Assis Chateaubriand*.

Leo looks over the building as memories of his childhood return. "This is where I came on my first date. Well, sort of. I was 16, and there was a boy I liked in my class. I didn't know if he liked me back. We came here on a field trip, and when it was time to find a buddy, I made sure he was mine. We never really spoke in class and didn't exchange words during the tour. I was so nervous, I couldn't think of what to say.

"He finally broke the silence when he made fun of an art piece we were looking at. I started to giggle. Then I pointed out how funny a painting looked, which made him laugh. We ended up enjoying each other's company. We got in trouble with our teacher when she overheard us making fun of a piece resembling a penis.

"Eight months later, he brought me back here, just the two of us. It's when I discovered his love for art. He gave me a private tour, discussing his favorite pieces on display. It was quite charming watching his eyes light up when we arrived at his favorite painting."

Leo turns around and nods for Victor to follow him across the street. They walked past some street vendors and into a park. "We came to this park after the museum and sat on that bench for lunch," Leo says, pointing to a bench in the shade of a lush tree. "He got a couple of bags of *pão de queijo* from a street vendor that used to be on that corner. This park was also where we had our first kiss. He told me how it took him so long to get the courage to ask me out because we always had other friends whenever we hung out.

"We started dating secretly, since no one knew we were gay. After we finished school a year later, he wanted to join the U.S. military because he wanted to leave Brazil and move to the U.S. He knew joining the military would help with his immigration. I decided to stay for a few more years and go to university."

Leo stops in front of the bench and looks down as he continues, "We kept in touch for almost a year while he was on tour in Southeast Asia, and then I couldn't reach him. I thought the worst, but I kept telling myself everything was okay. It had been almost three months since his last letter arrived when I received a letter from one of his military friends.

"His friend told me that my boyfriend's platoon had been attacked. They lost several soldiers, including him. I cried for days, but my family and friends didn't know I was in a gay relationship. It was hard for me to talk about him because he was my first gay lover.

"A little over a year passed, and I started dating someone from my university. We were together for almost two years. He was too afraid to come out, but I wasn't anymore. I was going to tell my parents I was gay, but he didn't want them to know we were dating. So, he broke up with me."

Victor and Leo take a seat on the bench when Leo had his first kiss. "Why did you choose to share this with me?" Victor asks.

Leo looks down at the bench as he moves his hand across the smooth, but still rough surface. "Because I can tell that you are still in pain. And I wanted to share with you some of the pain I've had in my life." He looks up at Victor and says, "Sometimes, the pain is what helps us move forward. We shouldn't fear it. We should embrace it. It's what makes us stronger and helps us learn and grow. It's only harmful if you don't learn from it and let it repeat itself."

Victor looks off into the park in deep thought. Many people are enjoying their day. Kids are running around in the play area. Couples are holding hands, and elderly couples are sitting together, feeding the birds. Victor places a hand down on the bench to lean on it. He doesn't realize he brushed his hand against Leo's. Victor gets startled and jerks his hand back. He looks up and makes eye contact with Leo, but they say nothing.

After a moment, Leo finally breaks the silence, "So, what did you think of Madame Jeanette?"

Victor is caught off guard by Leo's question. "You two know each other?"

"We do," Leo nods. "Also, I want to apologize if I scared you the other day in your hotel room."

Victor's eyes widened. The realization of everything that happened since his birthday was not a dream. Everything he saw, smelled, and felt was real. "So, I wasn't seeing things? You guys were looking at me." He is shocked by his subsequent realization. "I was naked! You and that Japanese woman both saw me naked!"

Leo couldn't hide his laughter. "That's right, Chiyo visited you too. Our apologies. We didn't mean to startle you or see you naked. It was just a coincidence that it happened."

Victor crosses his arms, clearly upset. "You could have just introduced yourselves and not remained silent. At least made sure I was dressed before you appeared."

Leo smiles, "You know you're cute when you're angry. Also, we were technically looking at you through the mirror. So, we didn't know whether or not you'd be clothed. Also, you have no idea how tricky it was to make sure I placed a rune in the right room."

"Wait," Victor pauses, "you walked into the elevator when I was heading to my room, and I could have sworn you were standing beside me in the airport restroom. Why didn't you say anything to me then?"

Leo straightens up and smooths out his shirt. "I was asked not to engage with you, only observe. Jeanette wanted to have a look at you first. She knew you would visit her while in New Orleans." Leo crosses his legs and leans back on his hand. "After your second encounter with her, she and a few others determined I should officially introduce myself to you."

Victor begins to calm down, but keeps his arms crossed as though he is guarding himself. He looks into the distance and asks, "So, what is going on? Why am I being looked upon, and why did you have to wait to introduce yourself?"

"How much do you know about your grandmother?" Leo probes.

Victor looks back at Leo with a raised eyebrow, "Why are you answering my question with a question?"

"Why don't you answer mine first so I can give you the proper answer to yours?" Leo winks, giving Victor a sly smirk.

Victor lets out a deep, aggressive breath through his nose. "Fine," he says pointedly. "I don't remember much about her. She loved her little family and wanted to ensure we embraced our traditions."

"What about her tarot cards?" Leo pries.

Victor gives Leo a look of confusion and uncertainty. "Her tarot cards? She never had tarot cards. My mother did."

"But were those her cards?" Leo implies.

Victor looks down and ponders his answer. "My mom wanted to learn about Tarot. I remember one day when I was younger, she had them laid out on the kitchen table. She was reading a book about each of the cards. But I didn't think anything of it."

Victor starts to recall a memory. "A cousin on my dad's side mentioned that my grandma used to read tarot. She knew my grandma more than me."

Leo takes a slow and deep breath as he prepares to answer Victor's questions. "What I'm about to tell you will come as a shock. You will likely experience a mix of emotions, including confusion and anger. But I want you to take what I say and process it."

Victor looks over at Leo, and after a moment, he nods.

Leo inhales deeply, "Your grandmother was a powerful witch. She was a lot older than you remember. She was well known among others of our kind."

"Our kind?" Victor inquires.

"Witches. Warlocks. Sorcerers. Wizards. Magicians. Whatever you want to call us," Leo explains. "She was excellent at reading tarot cards and was an empath. She was very proficient in other forms of the magical arts. Sadly, your grandmother died before she could get an opportunity to pass down her teachings to your mother."

Victor doesn't know how to process what he's just been told. "Did you know my grandma or mom?"

Leo shakes his head, "No, I never met either of them. But I've heard about them in passing conversations. I think Jeanette and Akisha met your mother before she disappeared. Your grandmother's death was a tragedy and a mystery."

Leo uncrosses his legs and smooths out his shorts. "As you know, she died from cancer, but most of us think it was a cover for what actually happened. There is also speculation about what happened to your mother. But we don't have any clear evidence to make a proper determination."

Victor stands up and wraps his arms around himself. "I need to go for a walk. It's a lot to process right now."

"Would you like me to join you?" Leo asks as he stands. Victor nods, and they make their way down a trail in the park. They remain in silence for a while.

Victor finally speaks, "So why am I being told about all this after all this time? Why wasn't I told when I was younger?"

Leo shrugs and places his hands in his pockets. "Well, you've been off the radar until recently. We thought when your grandmother died, so did her teachings. You didn't come to our attention until about two years ago. We didn't even know about you." Leo pauses for a moment, "Well, Madame Jeanette knew."

"What do you mean?" Victor inquires.

Leo looks forward down the path. "Well, your mother met Jeanette before you were born. But she doesn't remember the conversation because your mother put a memory spell on her."

"Then what did I do to draw your attention?" Victor asks.

"It was a tarot card reading you did on someone who was a warlock. He was impressed by your reading and mentioned it to Jeanette," Leo replies.

Victor cocks an eyebrow and looks at Leo from the corner of his eye. "I only read tarot cards at parties. I've never read them professionally."

"It was good enough," Leo responds. "Jeanette wanted to know more about you. When we did some more digging, we realized who you really were—the grandson of Maria Russo. We needed to make every effort to bring you to us, so it wouldn't seem like we were coming to you. Akisha explained that we never looked for you because your mother decided to fall off the map."

Victor stops and turns to look at Leo. "So, was my trip to New Orleans planned?"

Leo looks at Victor and smiles. "It was a happy coincidence. But also, Jeanette has the ability of premonitions. She also teaches the formal practices of necromancy."

Victor stops in his tracks. "Necromancy?"

Leo gives Victor an assured look, "Don't worry, it's not what you think."

"That would explain why when she had me do her reading, both "Death" and "The Devil" appeared right away," Victor proclaims.

Leo tilts his head, pondering, "You're not wrong. But unlike other necromancers, she ensures that her powers are used appropriately. She hates it when it's used as Dark Magic. Well, it *is* Dark Magic, but she teaches it as though it's not."

"So why are *you* telling me all of this?" Victor questions.

Leo turns to face Victor, "I'm kind of like a mentor. I was picked to help you along your way."

"What if I choose not to?" Victor queries.

"Then I guess we will let you be. But you might change your mind after you discover that untapped energy inside you." Leo gently tilts his head to the side, gazing deeply into Victor's eyes. "You seem to be taking this pretty well. Most people we find who discover they have magic as adults experience mixed emotions, become scared due to their religious background, or are overly excited. But you seem very calm about everything I told you."

Victor pauses for a moment, then licks his lips before he responds. "I guess subconsciously, I've always known there was something different about me. Like, how could I read someone's tarot and understand it without being taught? Also, my mom did have some lovely necklaces that I now realize could mean something."

Victor looks down at his watch. "I need to head back to the hotel and get some sleep. I have to fly back out tonight. I hate these short layovers." He pauses for a moment before he continues. "How much time can I think all of this over?"

Leo puts his hands on Victor's shoulders. "Take all the time you need. But I would appreciate it if you don't take too long." He takes a maroon business card with silver writing out of his pocket. "When you're ready, call this number. And this time, someone will answer."

Victor takes the card from Leo, and then they walk back to the hotel in silence.

CHAPTER EIGHT

Two weeks have gone by since Victor spoke with Leo. During this time, he has been lost in his thoughts. He dropped two trips so he can be at home during this time. His memories of his grandmother and mother feel fragmented, as though he is trying to remember his childhood the way he wants to remember it. But could there have been more he overlooked? Was there something about his past that was kept hidden from him?

Late one afternoon, he's in his living room, looking through a family album sitting on the coffee table. The TV is on with the volume down low as he strolls down memory lane. Pictures of him as a baby, in his grandmother's arms, nothing out of the ordinary. A picture of him when he was four, sitting in his mother's lap. A memory he knows is authentic, as his mother always took photos of them twice a year before he was 10.

As Victor turns the page, he sees something appear out of the corner of his eye. He looks over to his dining table, and Akisha is sitting in one of the chairs. She looks at him without saying a word. Victor doesn't seem startled this time, mainly because he's not naked like the other times. He notices a hint of translucency, which tells him Akisha isn't there.

"Can I help you with something?" Victor asks. She doesn't respond. "I guess when you guys astral project, you're unable to talk."

"No, we can talk, as well as hear. With the right training," Akisha responds, which surprises Victor. "I just wanted to see you for myself this time. I'm Akisha. Leo might have mentioned me."

"Well, Akisha, you've got to look at me," Victor comments.

She takes a moment and gazes at Victor. "You have your grandmother's eyes."

"I was told I had my mother's," Victor quickly replies.

Akisha scoffs with a smile. "And she had her mother's, so in some retrospect, you have your grandmother's."

Victor stands up and walks to the dining table. "Did you know my grandmother?"

"I did. She was an amazing person. Kind and generous. I never worked alongside her, as we were both in different covens. But the times I did meet her, that's what I got from her."

Victor takes a seat across from Akisha. "What was her specialty?"

Akisha sits back as she reminisces. "She was very talented. She could melt metal and keep it cool to the touch while manipulating it into an elegant design. There's a beautiful metalwork tapestry hanging over my coven's fireplace that your grandmother gifted to a former superior. It inspired my coven's emblem that we use today."

Victor leans back and clasps his hands on the table. "I have a feeling you are wondering why I haven't called Leo yet."

"Empathic," Akisha remarks. "Even with someone who's astral projecting, it's very impressive. You do seem to take after your grandmother. What else can you feel?"

Victor focuses on Akisha. He doesn't know what to say, but instinct sets in to answer her. "You're nervous, and you're also expressing mixed emotions about me," Victor asserts.

Akisha nods with approval. "Very good. I won't lie to you, but you do make me nervous."

Victor grows confused. "Why? What is it that makes you nervous about me?"

Akisha doesn't hesitate to respond. "You don't understand the great power that runs through your veins. It's sad that your mother never got to experience it. Now, you have an opportunity to carry on your grandmother's legacy."

"I'm part of a legacy?" Victor questions.

"Yes. You have so many untapped magical abilities. I'm still amazed you've never known about any of this." Akisha crosses her legs and places her hands in her lap. "It is a shame. You are old enough to teach young people to discover their magic."

"So, is there a school I need to attend? Do I need to go find a wand or something like that?" Victor asks.

Akisha laughs, "No, you don't need to wait for an owl to send you an invitation. We normally teach a group of children at the same time. But because of your advanced age, all your teachings will be one-on-one."

"Advanced age?" Victor implies.

Akisha ignores Victor and continues talking. "And Leo will be your mentor as you learn. I must go now. Leo is still waiting for you to call him." And with that, she vanishes as Victor blinks.

Victor sits at the table, curious about Akisha's comment about his grandmother. After a moment of wondering, Victor looks for the maroon business card Leo gave him. He retrieves his phone just as he receives a notification.

"What the?" he says to himself. "Why is scheduling emailing me?"

> Flight Attendant Russo,
> Your request for a one-year academic leave has been approved. Your travel privileges will be maintained during this period; however, please note that you'll be responsible for any related charges (e.g., international taxes, extra luggage fees). If you require additional time, please submit a request at least one month prior to your planned return date.
> Best wishes for your education journey, Crew Planning

Victor chuckles, "Looks like they already knew my answer before I even called." He dials the number, but there is no ring back tone. Curious, he looks at the screen, and it's already been answered. "Hello? Is this Leo?"

"He's not available right now, Mr. Russo, but he wanted me to inform you to meet him in New York City. The sooner you can get there, the better. Pack light." The call hangs up.

Victor pulls the phone away from his ear and looks at the blank screen. "Well, I'd better pack and head to New York," he says.

Victor arrives at the JFK airport the following day. As he heads to baggage claim, a woman wearing a black chauffeur's suit and dark sunglasses holds a black sign with his name in white calligraphy letters. When he approaches her, she turns and walks away.

"Good morning to you too," Victor says as she walks away.

Victor follows her out to the curb and sees a very shiny black Cadillac 300. The trunk pops open as the woman gets into the driver's seat. "And it looks like I have to put my luggage in the trunk." After he does just that, he takes a seat in the back, and they drive off. Victor would like to ask her a few questions, but the privacy divider is up. "Guess you're not very talkative, are ya?" Victor sits back and looks out the window as they leave the airport and head toward the city.

A short time later, they pull up to a tall building in the garment district of Manhattan. Outside the window, Leo walks up and opens the door for him. Leo is wearing the same blue suit he wore on the airplane, accompanied by a matching blue jacket.

"Welcome," Leo smiles. "I hope the drive over wasn't that bad."

Victor glances over to the driver, still sitting in the town car. "I might have a few comments to post online later." When Leo closes the door, the car drives off. "HEY! My stuff!"

"Don't worry, she's taking your things to the hotel," Leo comments as he places a hand on Victor's back. "First, we need to get you fitted."

"Fitted?" Victor questions.

Leo leads Victor into a tailor shop outside the building. When they walk inside, Victor looks around, unimpressed. "This looks pretty ordinary," Victor observes.

"Were you expecting something fancier?" Leo smirks.

"I was, actually," Victor says with disappointment.

Leo giggles, "Then I don't want to disappoint."

He guides Victor further into the shop and leads him through a door at the back. As they walk through, they enter a store that resembles a 1960s department store. A giant crystal chandelier hangs in the center of the store. Several racks of jackets, slacks, and shirts are in their designated sections. Shelves along the walls are filled with shoes and rolled-up ties. Glass cases throughout hold wristwatches, pocket watches, and small daggers.

The other side of the store houses more feminine attire. Long evening gowns hanging on racks. A wide range of styles and colors of high-heeled shoes decorate several tall shelves. Various glass cases display custom jewelry, ranging from bracelets to tiaras. It's a treasure trove for those who want to be a princess.

Victor looks around the store, mesmerized, letting out a low whistle. "This is very impressive. Are those daggers in that glass case?"

"As well as other little trinkets and weapons that can be used," Leo mentions as he walks toward the center of the room.

Victor follows behind, mesmerized by the wide variety of items.

Leo stops in the center and spins around with his arms wide. "Welcome to our first stop of this long journey that you are starting. This is *Magi Scriptor Sartor*. A Magician's Tailor. This is where all people of magic shop for their outfits."

Leo tugs at the lapels of his jacket. "This is where I got my suit. And this is where we will have one tailored specifically for you. There are several tailor shops like this around the world, but I like coming here more. They always have the latest fabrics that help enhance our magic." As Leo mentions magic, he flicks his wrist, and a ball of blue fire appears in his hand.

Victor stares in awe, mesmerized by the flicker of the blue flame. "So, is your specialty fire?"

Leo grins as he lightly spins the ball of flame. "Yes, and I can also manipulate water. I've also done some dabbling in Air and Earth Magic. I'm not fully versed in other avenues, but I keep trying." Leo flicks the fireball over to a rack of jackets, and the ball extinguishes once it hits the jackets. "See? These fabrics help protect us from Fire Magic. Fire Magic is a very popular and powerful specialty. So, the elders and superiors of many covens wanted to ensure that what we wore could protect us from it."

Victor examines some shirts next to him. "These feel as smooth as silk."

Leo takes a sleeve and slowly feels along the length. "And they breathe like Egyptian cotton," Leo drops the sleeve and circles the rack. "You could be in a full suit in the middle of the Sahara and not overheat. What's also fascinating is that you can be stranded in the Arctic and not get frostbite. Our suits are fashionable and durable."

Victor looks around and notices Madame Jeanette walking a few aisles away. She smiles when she spots them and starts walking over. She is wearing dark plum-colored slacks and a matching jacket, with a cream-colored blouse.

"Madame Jeanette, you look different," Victor says when she arrives.

"I clean up good, no?" Madame Jeanette responds. She gives each of them a double-cheek kiss. "I am happy to see you here, chéri. I was beginning to worry that you were not going to come. Have you been fitted for your suit yet?"

"He hasn't," Leo answers. "We just arrived, and I'm showing him around."

"Very good. Whatever you do, avoid Monsieur Clarence. They can be pretty intense." She gives Victor an air kiss on the cheek, "*Au Revoir, chéri.*"

When Madame Jeanette turns and leaves, a flamboyant individual walks in their direction. "Looks like she jinxed us," Leo mentions as he notices them.

"Who is he?" Victor inquires.

Leo's focus remains on the person approaching them. "That is Monsieur Clarence. And *they* have been expecting you."

Clarence has a fire in their step as if walking down a runway. They are wearing black with white pinstripe slacks, a powder-pink cummerbund around their waist, and a white shirt with frills at the cuffs and down the middle. A tomato pincushion is around their wrist, and a tape measure hangs around their neck like an open tie.

Clarence has little makeup on, but it is still noticeable. Their eyes give zero fucks at what you think because they know they look good. They stop three feet away from Victor, cross their arms, and place an index finger at the corner of their mouth. Clarence lightly purses their lips and studies Victor.

Victor holds out his hand, "Hello, I'm Victor Russo. I understand you are Clarence."

Clarence doesn't speak immediately, but they look at Victor, which feels almost judgmental. Victor slowly lowers his hand back to his side, pondering what Clarence is thinking about him.

"Strip," Clarence finally says in their Essex accent.

"Excuse me?" Victor asks with some confusion.

"Strip," Clarence orders.

Victor looks over at Leo, who shrugs his shoulders.

"Hello, I'm over here," Clarence demands while snapping their fingers. "Don't look at him; look at me."

Victor directs his response to Leo, "She wasn't kidding about them being intense."

"Are you going to remove your clothes, or will I have to do it for you?" Clarence says aggressively.

"Okay, okay," Victor responds as he slowly pulls his shirt over his head.

"Oh, for fuck's sake!" Clarence pulls Victor's shirt off and throws it on the floor beside them. They take a few steps back, puts hands on hips, and look up and down at Victor's bare torso. "Very good. Now, the pants."

"I'm sorry?" Victor interjects.

"Pants, now," Clarence demands once more.

"I don't know who you are, but I'm not–" Before Victor can finish, Clarence pounces on Victor and tries to undo his belt. "The fuck, Dude! What's your problem?!" Victor shouts.

Leo places one hand on Victor's shoulder and holds up the other hand toward Clarence to make them back off. "Victor, would you please take off your pants?"

Victor looks at Leo with disgust. "Seriously? I've already removed my shirt, and now you want me to take off my pants? Am I going to get dinner out of this?"

"If you play your cards right," Leo winks.

"I need to see what I'm working with here," Clarence barks in frustration.

Victor takes a deep breath and growls in the back of his throat. "Fine." He unbuttons his pants and forcefully drops them to the floor.

"Nice, nice. Turn for me," Clarence requests as they twirl their finger. Victor slowly turns around with his pants around his ankles while Clarence starts to *mmhmm* under their breath. "Good, good. Nice frame. Broad shoulders. Great legs and ass."

"Thank you?" Victor questions, unsure how to respond.

"This way," Clarence gestures to a stall with floor-to-ceiling mirrors.

Before Victor follows Clarence, he removes his pants from around his ankles. He feels a little awkward walking around in his briefs, but no one seems to care. When Victor steps up, he's caught off guard when Clarence begins taking measurements. Victor wants to comment, but instead, he submits and spreads his arms and legs.

Clarence's hand gets much too close to Victor's family jewels once or twice. When Victor thought it was over, Clarence starts taking other measurements. They measure the distance between Victor's nipples, and then he wraps the tape around Victor's ass and crotch. Victor looks at Leo in the mirror, and Leo shrugs his shoulders.

"Are all these other measurements necessary?" Victor asks Clarence.

Clarence looks at Victor in the mirror. "You want your suit to fit well, don't you?" When Victor nods, they go back to work. After three questionable minutes, Clarence finally stands up and steps behind Victor. "What colors do you like?" Clarence asks Victor.

"Well, I guess . . . " Victor starts before he's interrupted.

"Don't guess; just tell me," Clarence commands.

Victor shrugs. "I don't know. Blues, purples, maybe red."

Clarence steps down and tosses a robe over to Victor. "Put this on. Don't get dressed right away. I'll be back shortly."

Victor puts on the robe and gives Leo a look of frustration. "Was all that really necessary?"

"You'll see why I prefer to come here rather than the other tailors," Leo answers as he places his hands in his pockets and leans against the wall.

"I just feel so . . . violated. How are they still working here?" Victor grimaces.

"You'll soon find out." Leo nods to Clarence as they walk around the corner with a couple of suits. They are carrying a dark blue suit, a charcoal gray one, and several shirts and ties in various shades of blue, orange, and yellow.

Clarence hands Leo the shirts and ties when they return. "First, which suit do you like more?" Clarence holds up the two suits for Victor.

Victor looks between them, "Is there any difference?"

Clarence steps up and looks Victor in the eyes. "Your suit is your armor. But it also represents who you are as a warlock. The vibe you give off tells me that you're strong, but you're not there yet." Clarence holds up both suits. "You need a suit that helps you control that, as well as to be able to take on powerful attacks." Clarence holds both suits up higher. "These two suits can do that."

After a moment, Victor points at the charcoal gray.

"Very good," Clarence says, tossing the blue suit onto a chair against the wall. Clarence gestures for Leo to come over with the shirts and ties. "You said you like blue, purple, and red, but that's not what I'm getting. The only color I'm feeling is blue. But sometimes orange or yellow might fit."

Victor looks over the shirts Clarence holds out for him. "I like this shade of blue."

Clarence ponders Victor's choice as they look into Victor's eyes. "Are you sure?"

"Yes," Victor responds.

"This is the color that calls out to you more?" Clarence clarifies.

"Yes, I like this shade," Victor explains.

"Why blue?" Clarence probes.

Victor is slightly confused by Clarence's question. "Why does it matter?"

"It matters," Leo answers.

Victor takes one of the blue shirts and a tie, a few shades darker than the shirt. "It was my mother's favorite color. And it's mine too."

Clarence folds the other shirts over their arm. "That's good enough for me. Now, get dressed in room four. I also left several pairs of shoes for you to try on." Victor gathers the garments and scurries over to the dressing room.

Several moments later, Victor emerges dressed in his new suit and shiny new black shoes.

Clarence nods with approval, and Leo is in awe.

"What do you think?" Victor asks.

"You look stunning," Clarence responds as they snap their fingers. The snap sounds like a crystal chime in the air.

"Now, I see why you took all those other measurements," Victor comments as he looks at himself in the mirror. "Who knew I could have a snatched waist?"

Clarence walks over to Victor and takes a lint roller to the suit. "Tell me your cock and ass don't feel like they're floating on a cloud in this suit."

Victor looks at Leo in the mirror. "What do you think?"

Leo snaps out of his trance. "You look great. I got a couple of gifts for you while you were getting dressed." He hands Victor two boxes: one is a small, square box, and the other, a long, slender box.

Victor opens the small box, revealing a black and silver watch. "Thank you, Leo."

"You're welcome," Leo smiles as he helps Victor place the watch around his wrist. "This watch not only tells time but helps you keep track of your energy when you start to use magic. That way, you can learn how to conserve energy but still throw a powerful attack. This will be a great tool for your lessons."

Victor opens the long, slender box. "A dagger?" He picks up a small, silver dagger with a blue handle and a sapphire gem embedded at the end of the handle.

Leo pulls a sheath with a clip on the side from the box. He opens Victor's jacket and clips the sheath inside one of the pockets. "You'll learn that sometimes blood will be needed, so you will need something to prick your finger or slice your hand. It's also useful if you need to open letters or defend yourself from an attack."

Leo closes and buttons Victor's jacket, then smooths out the sleeves. He pulls out a solid silver tie clip from his pocket, attaching it to Victor's tie, and pats it. "There, that looks good."

Clarence and Leo take a few steps back as Victor turns back to the mirror.

Victor looks at himself in the mirror. "I know I wear a suit while working, even though it's a uniform. But this feels and looks different."

"That's because you feel and look different," Clarence mentions. "No other suit will ever look or feel the same now that you start wearing this. And I'll select another shirt and tie to complement your dark blue suit. Take both, and remember to dry clean, don't wash."

Clarence walks away while Victor keeps looking at himself in the mirror. "You ready to go?" Leo asks.

"Where are we going?" Victor responds to Leo in the mirror.

Leo steps up next to Victor and smiles back at him in the mirror. "Well, you mentioned that you should get dinner for getting undressed the way you did. So, let's go have dinner."

CHAPTER NINE

Leo takes Victor to a fancy restaurant. Victor feels confident in his new custom- tailored attire. When Victor walks inside, he looks around. "I feel like I need my credit checked just to walk in here," Victor comments.

The restaurant is the typical upper-class style you would find in Manhattan. Victor's eyes adjust to the dim, artfully arranged lighting, revealing plush velvet banquettes, dark wood accents, and polished marble floors. A low hum of sophisticated conversations and the clinking of delicate silverware. Waiters in crisp, black-and-white uniforms glide silently between tables, carrying meticulously presented dishes that look more like works of art than food.

Leo laughs and places a hand on the small of Victor's back, leading him over to a table waiting for them. When Victor looks at the menu, the cheapest item is twenty-five dollars.

"I don't know if I can afford any of this," Victor says dismally. "I might make good money, but I don't make $50 steak dinner money."

Leo chuckles, "Don't worry about it. We're not going to be paying a dime here."

Victor looks confused and asks, "Are we going to dine and dash or something? Do you have a company credit card?"

Leo laughs while glancing over the menu. "No, no. This entire restaurant is catered to people like us."

"Gay?" Victor questions.

Leo's laugh echoes around the room. "Yes, well, no, but yes, I suppose. Everyone here, including the servers, are people of magic."

"Question, why do you say, 'People of Magic?'" Victor ponders.

The server sets down two glasses of bourbon and small ramekin of marinated olives. Leo reaches for a drink as he explains. "Well, it's just like those of us in the queer community. We all prefer to use either gay, lesbian, nonbinary, or queer, for example. The same goes for magic wielders. Some prefer to be called a sorcerer over a warlock. There are even some witches who prefer the term 'magician' or 'wizard'. So, I use the term being inclusive without offending someone."

"So, what do you identify as?" Victor asks as he takes a sip.

"Gay and Warlock," Leo answers, popping an olive in his mouth.

"So, if this place caters to us, and we're not going to pay, then why do the menus have prices on them?" Victor inquires.

Leo finishes his bourbon and sets his menu down. "This restaurant is in the middle of Manhattan. We could've created an illusion spell for the mundane, but we're greedy and like money. So, we charge these outrageous prices to the mundane. And they pay for it! The food is great, don't get me wrong, but the steak is not worth $50."

The server returns with a refill for Leo and takes their orders. Leo orders an eight-ounce filet mignon with mushrooms and a red wine sauce. Victor selects a ten-ounce sirloin topped with garlic butter and steamed vegetables on the side. Once the server leaves, Victor looks around the dining room. He starts to notice a vibrant array of different colors swirling around. Then he realizes these colors are hanging above the other patrons.

"I . . . I think I can see the auras coming off other people here," Victor remarks, trying not to overreact to this newfound scenery. Victor remains calm, as if this is second nature to him.

Leo looks around and smiles. "I see your new suit is starting to enhance your empathic abilities. Empaths can see auras better than others who try." Leo looks around the dining room,

"I'm not empathic, so I can't see what you see. But I bet it's incredible, almost like you're looking at the aurora borealis with the number of people here."

"How do you know that I'm empathic?" Victor questions as he continues looking around.

"Your grandmother was an Empath. It's been known that this ability is passed down the bloodline."

Victor is in awe as he looks around, then over at Leo. He starts to study Leo. "What do you see?" Leo asks as he takes a drink.

"I see hints of orange, yellow, and blue," Victor responds.

Leo blots his lips, "Sounds about right. Do you know what the colors mean?"

Victor shakes his head. "I never looked that much into it. I just angled on the emotions more than the colors of someone's aura." He keeps looking around, noticing other forms of energy around the lamps and tapestries hanging on the walls. "I know non-living things don't have auras, but I'm seeing something coming from everything else."

"That's still part of your empathic tricks," Leo comments. "That will help you when you need to look for another energy source when using your magic; for example, those candles behind me and around the corner."

Leo nods behind him, directing Victor's view over his shoulder. "We didn't see them when we walked in, and can't see them from where we're sitting, but I can sense them because of my fire specialty. So, if I need a bump, I can hone in on those candles and use the flame's energy."

Victor gives Leo a questionable look. He gets up and looks around the corner. Two candelabras, each holding five candles, sit on a table against the wall. Victor shoots Leo an impressed look. Leo returns it with a wink as he takes another drink. As Victor sits back down, the server returns with their salad course.

"So, how long have you been a warlock?" Victor asks as he starts to eat.

"I've been practicing magic for about fifty-eight years now," Leo responds without hesitation.

Victor almost chokes on his salad. "How old are you?"

Leo swallows his food and smiles mischievously, "How old do you think I am?"

"I would have guessed in your late 20s or early 30s," Victor responds questionably.

Leo looks up at Victor as he's about to take another bite of his salad. "Try mid-60s."

Victor chokes on his food again. He starts to cough profusely and needs a drink of water.

"You okay over there?" Leo chuckles.

Victor nods and holds up his index finger as he takes a drink of water. Leo snickers some more as he takes another bite.

"Did you just say mid-60s?" Victor asks once his airways are clear.

"Sixty-six, to be exact. But you would never know it," Leo winks.

Victor blinks a few times, comprehending the information given to him. "Damn, you look really good for your age. I need to know your secret."

Leo pushes his finished plate to the side. "When you start to use your magic, you'll realize that it starts to slow down your aging process. It's partly because you begin to use the life energy from other sources," Leo explains.

"For me, it's Fire and Water. Even though they aren't technically living creatures like you or me or those stray dogs outside, they still give off a source of energy. When you absorb that energy, it helps preserve your life. Magic always comes with a price."

"And because of that, necromancy has a bad reputation," Victor remarks.

Leo clicks his cheek and shoots a finger gun at Victor as if he were saying, *"You got it."*

The server comes back and sets down their steak dinners. Victor and Leo start to eat in silence. After several moments, Victor begins to get a tingling in his shoulders and arms. His vision starts to go in and out of focus. He tries to blink but still has trouble seeing.

Leo is about to take a bite but stops and looks concerned. "Is everything all right?"

Victor starts to look around but has difficulty keeping his eyes open. "I . . . I don't know. There's something . . . off. It's hard to tell, but my vision is getting blurry."

Leo sits up, alert as he starts looking around the dining room. He notices another empathic witch who is also alert. Leo sets his napkin on the table and stands up. "Stay here."

Victor is trying to see where Leo is going, but his vision is still blurry. He can barely see Leo talking to the witch. The room starts to spin around Victor. He braces himself by holding the sides of the table. There's a ringing in his ear, so loud he can't hear any commotion that erupts.

Suddenly, a huge flame heads toward Victor. All he can see is a blurred orange and yellow object coming his way. Out of nowhere, another warlock grabs Victor and drops him to the floor. Dazed and confused, Victor looks up and sees a blurry Leo blocking the flame. A witch on the other end intensifies the spell she's casting.

Leo does his best to absorb the blaze with his Air Magic, but it's too much for him to handle. He tries to counterattack with his Water Magic, but the fire is still too intense. Two other warlocks try to defend Leo but are knocked out of the way.

"Hand over the melee warlock, Leopold!" the witch shouts.

Leo pulls one of his hands out of the inferno and holds it to his side as he tries to grab something with a claw-like gesture. He struggles as he tries to turn the claw into a fist. The flame glows brighter, blinding Leo. He continues struggling to conjure another spell. When Leo finally makes a fist, the witch starts choking.

She tries to keep the spell going while she struggles to breathe. Leo uses his Air Magic to suck the air out of the witch. She grabs her chest and scratches at her throat. When she drops down to her knees, the flame extinguishes. Her eyes grow wide with fear as she's gasping for air. Leo holds his fist out as he walks towards her.

Victor starts to regain his vision, and the room is no longer spinning. He sees Leo's aura swirl around as if Leo were inside a tornado.

"Leo!" Victor shouts. But Leo doesn't hear him. "LEO, STOP!"

A flash pulses off of Victor and breezes by everyone. The lights flicker, and the candles are blown out. Leo lets go of his fist, and the witch falls to the floor, gasping as she can breathe again. Leo looks over at Victor as a couple of warlocks are helping him up. He looks down at the witch as two witches pick her off the ground and use a binding spell on her.

"Who sent you?" Leo aggressively asks the witch.

She sneers as she tries to hold her head up to look at Leo. "As if I'm going to tell you, pole jockey."

Leo lifts her head by her chin. "Take her to my Superior. I'm sure he'll love to interrogate this one."

The two witches drag the attacker away while everyone else in the dining room returns to their seats. One of the servers flicks her wrist and snaps her fingers, lighting all the candles. Everyone returns to normal, except Victor, who looks on at Leo, befuddled and bewildered.

Leo stops in front of Victor and places his hands on Victor's shoulders. "Are you okay? Were you hurt?"

Victor shakes his head. "N-No. I'm fine." He takes his seat as Leo pushes the chair in for him.

Leo tries to smooth out his shirt with his hand as he takes his seat. "Are you sure? I understand it will be a lot to process what happened just now." Leo clasps his hands and rests his mouth against them as he studies Victor. Victor looks down at the center of the table. "Would you like to go?"

Victor looks up and makes eye contact with Leo. He can see that Leo is concerned. Victor notices Leo's aura is now a mixture of red and green, hovering around him like an aurora borealis. He takes a deep breath before he responds, "Let's finish dinner first. And then we can go."

A server sets down new plates for them and a couple glasses of water. The two finish their meals in silence. But Victor's mind is racing. *Maybe this was a mistake,* Victor thinks to himself. But why did the witch want him? Victor wants to get a few answers but doesn't want to spoil dinner by going down the rabbit hole.

CHAPTER TEN

Leo and Victor are in the town car, driving through the streets of Manhattan in silence. Leo knows they should talk about what happened at dinner, but he doesn't want to pry, letting Victor process this new reality at his own pace. A short time later, they stop in front of a hotel. Leo gets out of the car first and then offers to help Victor out of the vehicle. Victor steps out and looks up at the hotel, which he doesn't recognize.

Victor finally speaks after almost an hour of silence. "Where are we? I don't recognize this hotel."

Leo looks up at the hotel and responds, "That's because, unlike the restaurant, this hotel has an illusion spell. To the mundane, it appears as a regular business building. This hotel is only for us, hence why we can see the hotel."

"How come I've never seen it before?" Victor asks. "I'm not mundane. Well, not anymore."

Leo taps his finger on Victor's tie clip. "This hotel is also protected by those who don't carry this metal. As long as you have this clip or another variation of the same metal on you, you can see protected things that are hidden from others. If we were here before the attack . . ." Leo stops before he can finish.

Victor finishes the sentence for Leo, "If we were here before that witch attacked us, we would have been safe."

Leo slowly nods. He lets out a sigh and then smiles at Victor. Leo nods to the entrance, and they continue into the hotel.

When they walk in, Victor is amazed at what he sees. The lobby is exquisite, with pristine white-and-black marble floors. The walls are painted white with thin vertical lines of gold. Gold and silver trimmings along the crown molding. Large crystal chandeliers hang down from the tall, vaulted ceilings. In front of the elevators, a waterfall flows from the ceiling. The air is filled with light floral fragrances of rose and lavender, with the added crisp scent of fresh water from the waterfall.

Several golden animals run around the lobby's shelves, providing enjoyment to the children sitting around while their parents are chatting and enjoying a drink from the lobby bar. Golden birds of different varieties fly around, singing a beautiful melody. Musical instruments play by themselves as they hover over a platform off to the side. Victor can feel the magic in the air while he looks around.

The concierge acknowledges Victor and Leo as they approach the front desk. "Mr. Oliveira and Mr. Russo, welcome. We have your rooms ready. Only the best for the two of you."

"Thank you," Leo responds as he approaches the counter. "Have our belongings been delivered to our rooms?"

The concierge smiles as they slide the keys over the counter. "Yes, sir. Including the few packages that arrived about an hour ago."

Leo thanks the concierge again as he grabs the keys and turns to Victor, handing him one of the keys. Victor cocks his eyebrow as he holds up his key. Hanging on a placard with the room number is an old-fashioned brass key with an elegant design.

"What are we in the 1950s?" Victor smirks.

Leo snickers and gestures a nod toward the elevators. "Come on, we have rooms overlooking Central Park." They walk up to an elevator whose doors open as they approach it. A bellman stands inside and greets them as they enter.

"Floor 13, please," Leo requests as he and Victor step to the back.

"How appropriate," Victor chuckles under his breath.

"What do you mean?" Leo asks as he continues to look forward.

"We're staying on the 13th floor," Victor mentions.

"Well, this hotel only has 13. I don't understand what you're getting at," Leo remarks.

Victor rolls his eyes as he chuckles to himself.

When they reach their floor, they exit the elevator and head to their rooms. Halfway down the hall, Leo stops in front of the door to his room. He looks at Victor, gives him a wink, and walks into his room. Victor opens the door and is amazed by his room.

It's a large suite with floor-to-ceiling windows. Sure enough, he has a terrific view of Central Park. An oversized lounge chair sits beside the window, and a huge flat-screen TV hangs on the wall. The wet bar is stocked with his favorite snacks. Of course, they would supply his favorite snacks.

When he walks into the bedroom, he notices the king-size bed faces outward to enjoy the view on the other side of the window. The TV rises from the cabinet at the foot of the bed. He walks into the bathroom. The shower and tub both have a view of Central Park. The shower itself is so large that it could hold eight people.

There's a knock at the connecting door to Victor's room. He opens the door, and Leo is on the other side holding two glasses of brandy. He's already out of his suit and into more casual clothes.

Leo smiles gleefully and asks, "So, what do you think of the room? I'm sure you don't get views like this on your layovers."

"Not at all," Victor answers as he steps to the side, to let Leo enter.

"Why don't you get out of that suit and into something more comfortable?" Leo suggests.

"You're probably right," Victor responds, looking down at his suit. "I almost forgot that I was still wearing my suit. You weren't kidding about how comfortable it is."

As Victor disappears into the bedroom, Leo takes a seat on the couch and turns on the TV. "Anything you like to watch?"

"No," Victor responds from the bedroom. "Do they have any streaming services?"

"Did you really ask that question?" Leo responds, selecting the menu for every streaming service available.

Victor walks back into the living room as he pulls his shirt down. He's ready to relax, wearing a T-shirt and cotton shorts. Victor takes a seat, and Leo hands him a glass. They clink their glasses together. A delicate crystal chime rings around them. Victor snuggles into the couch to relax. Leo puts his free arm across the back of the sofa behind Victor and kicks his feet onto the coffee table.

Leo points at the TV. "*The Warlock*, season two is available."

Victor giggles as he raises his glass to his lips. "I'll have to watch season one again and start commenting on how inaccurate their magic is."

Leo smiles as he looks at Victor. "Someone seems to be in a better mood." Victor shrugs his shoulders. "Would you like to debrief about dinner?" he asks Victor.

Victor decides to knock back his drink, then nods. "Do you know who she was?"

"Her name is Magenta," Leo responds in his glass, gulping down his brandy. "Her coven is always up to no good. Since the last time I fought her, she's been able to increase her Fire Magic."

"You two fought before?" Victor asks.

"About ten years ago. She lost, of course, but I never would have killed her. It's not who I am," Leo states while looking at the television.

"You looked like you were about to earlier," Victor comments without looking at Leo.

Leo side-eye glances at Victor before he answers. "I almost did. But then you stopped me."

"About that . . ." Victor sets his empty glass on the coffee table and then turns to give his attention to Leo, ". . . what happened back there?"

"What part?" Leo asks as he watches TV.

"The part when this flash of light came out of me." Victor keeps his attention on Leo, ignoring the scene playing on the screen.

Leo sucks in his lips and then puckers them, making a kissing noise as he ponders his answer. "That was your empathic energy being set free. That's the best way I can describe it to you without going into confusing details."

Victor sits back, calculating Leo's response. "So, in other words, I can extend my empathic abilities onto others?"

"In a sense," Leo replies, nodding. "But it's more along the lines of being able to shut down the emotions of others, which is what you did to me. I couldn't hear anything or anyone around me because of the rage ringing in my ears. I couldn't hear Magenta gasping for air as I took it from her. I didn't hear anything until you yelled stop."

"So . . . it's like a failsafe switch?" Victor questions.

Leo scrunches at the stubble on his cheek and nods. "I suppose so. I never really thought about it like that."

"She called me a Melee Warlock," Victor remarks. "That sounds like something out of D&D. D&D, right? I never played, so I'm spit balling here."

Leo smiles with pride, "Who do you think created the game? A bunch of warlocks."

"So, why was she after me?" Victor asks as he leans back against the armrest.

Leo looks at Victor and says, "Because you're special. You have something more rare than other people of magic. I don't think you understand the full potential you have within you."

Leo adjusts his body to look at Victor better. "Akisha told me she visited you yesterday. She mentioned that you told her she was nervous. But what she didn't tell you was that you were absolutely correct. You have untapped magic that can be a blessing or a disaster. I'm here to make sure that it's a blessing. Magenta wants it to be a disaster."

"How did they find out I was alive?" Victor inquires. "From what you mentioned back in São Paulo, I was off everyone's radar. I just started walking into this, and now it feels like I'm already being fought over."

Leo looks away as he responds, "I don't know. But we'll find out soon."

Victor slumps his shoulders. He looks up at Leo for reassurance. "Should I be worried?"

"No." Leo places his free hand on Victor's shoulder. "As long as you're with me, you'll be safe."

Victor and Leo maintain eye contact in silence. Without a word, Victor leans in and kisses Leo. Leo embraces Victor's affection. Leo places his glass on the side table without breaking his kiss with Victor. He then wraps his arms around Victor to pull him in closer.

Victor can feel Leo's tongue massaging his. Victor almost forgot what kissing someone with so much passion was like. He hadn't felt that way in a long time, even with James. After a few passing moments, Leo breaks free, and they rest against each other's foreheads. They breathe heavily.

Leo licks his lips, knowing the kiss was a mistake. "As much as I enjoyed that, we should stop. I'm supposed to be your mentor."

He looks into Victor's eyes, and deep down, he wants to kiss those lips again. Leo stands up and walks toward his room. "I . . . I should . . . I think we should go to bed. We have a long day tomorrow." Leo stops at the doorway and looks over his shoulder, "Have a good night, Victor."

"Good night, Leo." As Leo closes the door, Victor puts his fingertips to his lips and keeps looking at the door. A moment later, he turns off the TV and walks into the bedroom, closing the door behind him.

CHAPTER ELEVEN

Victor is curled up in his bed. He slowly wakes up and stretches his arms. His phone starts chiming rapidly from multiple notifications. "For fuck's sake, who is it?" He struggles while crawling to the side of his king bed. When he picks up his phone, the notifications are from his friends in their group text. He sighs heavily, "Well, fuck. How am I going to play this off?"

> Elliott: Where are you???
> Frank: I'm right here!
> Amber: Not you, you noob . . . Vic
> Elliott: Why isn't he answering?
> Frank: Maybe he just found out Menudo broke up
> Elliott: LOL
> Amber: LOL
> Victor: LOL
> Victor: I'm sorry, guys, I've been busy
> Elliott: THERE SHE IS!!!
> Frank: Where the fuck are you?!
> Victor: NYC
> Amber: WHAT?!?!?! And no invite?
> Elliott: Rude!
> Frank: So rude dude
> Victor: LOL I'm sorry guys; it was a last minute thing
> Frank: What are you doing in NY?
> Victor: Just hanging out with a friend
> Amber: You have other friends besides us?
> Victor: Yes, I have other friends

Elliott: You have other friends besides us

Elliott: Oh, Amber got to it before me

Victor: Yes, I have other friends besides you guys. Don't worry, you will always be my favorite.

Frank: See, we're still his favorite

Amber: Red it again numbnuts, he said it in singular form.

Elliott: So who's your favorite?

Victor: ;-)

Elliott: Ass

Victor: I am what I eat >D

Amber: GROSS!! (vomit emoji)

Frank: Did you just type out vomit emoji???

Victor: She did

Amber: Yeah, so, all of us were supposed to fly to Lima next week and I saw you're no longer on the flight.

Frank: WTF BRO

Elliott: WHAT?!?! I thought we were rainbros!!!

Victor: I'm sorry guys, something came up. I came to help my aunt because my uncle is having knee surgery.

Elliott: I thought you were hanging out with a friend

Victor: I am right now. My aunt is at the hospital with my uncle. His sugry is today.

Victor: *surgery

Amber: Hmmmmm, don't lie to use

Amber: *use

Amber: *USE

Amber: FUCK ME!!

Amber: US!!!!!

Elliot: LMAO

Victor: ROFL

Frank: JAJAJAJAJAJA

Amber: Fuck you guys >:-(

Victor: Listen guys, I need to get going. My aunt just called and asked me to take something to her at the hospital. I'll message you later. Love you! Mean it!
Elliott: Love you too
Amber: TTFN
Frank: Besos

Victor sighs deeply as he just lied to his friends. He knows that he can't come out to them. "Wow, I have to come out again! But this time, as a Warlock. Should I tell them?" He looks at the time; it's only 9 a.m. "What the fuck are they doing up at this god-forsaken hour?"

"Maybe they worry about you?" Leo comments as he leans against the doorframe.

Victor is startled and pulls the covers over himself because he's naked underneath. He looks over to the bedroom door, and there's Leo in a robe, holding two mugs of coffee.

Leo chuckles as he enters the bedroom. "I'm sorry. I didn't mean to startle you."

"It's okay," Victor says as he sits up against the headboard. "I was just texting with my friends."

Leo takes a seat and leans against the headboard as he hands Victor a mug.

"Thank you," Victor mentions, taking the mug from Leo. They sit in silence for a few moments while they sip their coffee. Victor turns on the TV, and the weather report comes on. They look onward at the TV until Victor breaks the silence.

"Leo, about last night . . . "

Leo holds up his hand to stop Victor from continuing. "It's okay. Don't worry."

"I just don't want to seem like I overstepped," Victor says.

"You didn't," Leo explains while watching the weather report.

"Okay," Victor responds as he takes another sip of coffee. "So, what are our plans today?"

"We are going to review some books," Leo answers as he gets up from the bed. "Why don't you freshen up, then meet me in my room?"

Leo is about to leave the room when Victor asks a question. "Does anyone know?"

"About our kiss?" Leo asks, turning back around.

"No, about you being a warlock," Victor clarifies.

Leo walks back over and sits back down on the side of the bed. "My family are also magic wielders. But the only friends I have are fellow witches and warlocks. I don't have any mundane friends. At least, not anymore."

"What happened?" Victor asks as he crisscrosses his legs.

"Remember, I'm 66, but look in my 30s," Leo mentions. "My mundane friends are already in their 60s and 70s, and they look it too. One died recently, and I hesitated to go to his funeral. But I did it against my better judgment." Leo takes a moment, remembering his friend's funeral. "I acted like I was visiting another gravesite to not seem like a mysterious person in the shadows."

Leo sips his coffee before continuing. "I believe you should cut your losses with your friends soon. I don't mean to sound like a total asshole about it, but as soon as you start using your powers, it will only be a matter of time before you look like you have stopped aging while you see all your mundane friends grow old.

"And before you suggest necromancy, remember how Anakin became Vader? He gave himself over to the dark side. And if you don't know how to avoid the temptation of necromancy, you'll lose yourself in it. I watched one warlock attempt to revive a dear friend of his. He had to fight his friend and take him out." Leo stands up and walks over to the door. "Now, freshen up. I ordered room service, and it should be arriving any minute. We have a long day ahead."

Victor walks into Leo's room in regular clothes. He notices Leo is still in his robe as he looks over a few books from a box on the couch. Two more boxes are on the lounge chair. Breakfast is already set on the small table near the window in the far corner.

Leo looks up and smiles at Victor. "Come on in. Eat. I'm just looking for the right book to give you first."

Victor takes a seat and uncovers his breakfast. He sees an omelet made to his liking, a bagel with cream cheese and salmon on top, freshly squeezed orange juice chilling in the bucket on the side of the table, and a fresh cup of coffee. Victor is about to start eating when Leo sets a book in the center of the table. He looks at it and wonders about a few markings along the spine. He's never seen them before, but they look very familiar.

"I'm going to take a quick shower. Eat up, and we'll review this book when I return." Leo retreats to his bedroom. Victor looks over at a mirror that looks in. He watches Leo take off the robe, allowing him to see Leo's firm back and ass. He watches and hopes Leo turns around to see the front, but Leo walks into the bathroom. He's halfway through his breakfast when he hears the bathroom door open.

Curious, Victor looks in the mirror. Leo walks out, but he has a towel wrapped around his waist. Victor can see Leo's muscular and fuzzy chest. The hairs on his chest are dark against his tanned olive-colored skin. Leo doesn't notice Victor gazing in the mirror as he closes the bedroom door.

A moment later, Leo walks into the living room wearing a T-shirt, shorts, and flip-flops. "How's breakfast?"

"It's good," Victor answers when he finishes swallowing his food. "They cooked the eggs just the way I like."

"Of course they did," Leo smirks.

"Is food always going to be this way now? Where is it to my liking?" Victor asks.

Leo smiles and shrugs his shoulders as he sips his coffee. "So, have you looked at the book?"

"I was waiting for you," Victor says.

"Well, go on and start reading while I dig into my food," Leo advises.

"Isn't your food . . . " Victor stops when he sees Leo's hands glow red as he holds them above his plate. " . . . cold?"

"Not anymore. You forgot I can control fire," Leo says. He flicks the linen napkin, giving it a good snap before he takes a seat.

Victor reaches over to grab the book, giving Leo a playful eye roll. He looks at the writing in bold green letters. He reads the title out loud, *"The Waking of the Warlock.* Sounds interesting."

"It is," Leo says as he puts a forkful of food in his mouth.

Victor opens the book and reads the first page.

THE WAKING OF THE WARLOCK

BECOMING A WARLOCK IS A CHALLENGING TASK. THE PROCESS IS GRUELING AND LONG, BUT OH- SO-SATISFYING. MANY MEN, AND THOSE WHO IDENTIFY AS MEN, WILL TRY TO OVERCOMPENSATE, WHICH IS THEIR FIRST FAILURE. JUST LIKE A NEWBORN CHILD, A NEWBORN WARLOCK MUST BE ABLE TO ADAPT TO NEW ENVIRONMENTS AND LEARN TO TRUST THOSE AROUND THEM AS THEY LEARN TO BECOME INDEPENDENT ON THEIR OWN. IF YOU WISH TO SUCCEED, YOU MUST BE PATIENT AND NEVER GIVE UP IF YOU CAN'T MAKE THE SPELL WORK

ON YOUR FIRST ATTEMPT. DO NOT LET FRUSTRATION TAKE OVER. DO NOT BE AFRAID TO FAIL; THAT IS HOW YOU LEARN.

After Victor reads the first passage, he notices Leo has already finished his breakfast. "What did you do, unhinge your jaw and drop your food down your gaping hole?"

Leo laughs out loud, "That sounds so inappropriate. So, what do you think of the passage?"

"It's . . . interesting," Victor comments. "It sounds like the writer knows a thing or two about being a Warlock. If they are writing a book about it, they should." Victor looks at the author's name, "Clarence Waterlily? Their last name is Waterlily?"

"Yup," Leo says as he finishes his coffee. "You'd be surprised how talented a Warlock they are. Or witch. I think they go by either, depending on who's talking about them. Anyway, they are very talented, but they enjoy being a tailor. They like to size others up, no pun intended."

"Feel up, too," Victor says sarcastically. Victor looks back at the spine and examines the symbols some more. "Leo, what do these mean?" he asks.

Leo looks closer at the symbols. "I'm not completely sure, but they might be coven emblems. I think this one might be a rune. Why do you ask?"

"Just curious," Victor replies softly. "I just have this feeling that I might have seen these before."

"Maybe you have and not realized it. Your grandma might have owned something with one of them on it," Leo suggests. Leo leans in and looks closer at the symbols. "I think most of the books I got you have symbols somewhere on them. You should read this book first before moving to the next. They discuss what you can expect during your journey. But, before you do that, we need to get ready to check out."

"Why, where are we going?" Victor asks as he thumbs through the pages.

"We are going to Chicago to meet up with your first instructor. Your first course is Air Magic," Leo informs.

"Sounds appropriate, being the windy city and all." Victor looks up just as Leo rolls his eyes.

"Actually, his specialty is Water. But for some reason, he enjoys teaching Air Magic," Leo explains. "I guess it's because Air is very easy to achieve, and there's a demand for air instructors. Plus, he enjoys hearing himself speak. A lot."

"If I knew we would be traveling a lot, I wouldn't've packed light like you suggested," Victor remarks.

Leo finishes his juice before pushing away from the table. "Don't worry, everything we need, we can get where we're going. So go pack, and you can leave your things; someone will collect them for us. Can you be ready in an hour?"

"I guess," Victor answers as he gets up from the table.

"Good, meet me on the third floor in an hour. And don't worry about changing into your suit. We can do that before we go to your first lesson." As Victor walks away, Leo clears his throat. "Forgetting something?" Victor looks down and grabs the book before he heads back to his room.

An hour later, when Victor is about to leave his room, he peers into Leo's room. He's not in there, and neither are the boxes. When he walks to the elevator, the doors open when he approaches.

"Floor three, sir?" the bellman asks Victor.

"Yes, please. Thank you," Victor says as he steps to the back of the elevator.

Victor exits the elevator and looks around for Leo. The only things in the hallway are several large, wide mirrors attached to the wall. Victor cocks an eyebrow as he speaks to himself, "How original. Walking through a mirror to get to where we are going."

"Were you expecting a green portal?" Leo asks as he walks up behind Victor.

Victor jumps and gives Leo a pointed look. "I'm going to have to put a bell on you."

Leo laughs as he takes Victor's arm in his hand. "This way." They stop in front of the fourth mirror. Leo places his palm against the mirror. The mirror turns hazy. "Ready?" Victor nods, and Leo walks through. Victor takes a deep breath and walks through himself.

CHAPTER TWELVE

Victor emerges from the mirror and into a hallway that resembles the one in the hotel in New York. He looks around and doesn't see Leo right away. He looks back at the mirror, hoping he didn't mess this up. A couple of whistles came from down the hall. Victor spins and sees Leo peeking around the corner. Victor walks over to Leo and notices that the hotel looks exactly like one in New York. When they approach the elevator, the doors open, and the bellman seems like the one in New York.

"What in Pokémon hell is going on?" Victor remarks in confusion.

Leo gives Victor a puzzled look. "Huh?"

"You know, Nurse Joy from Pokémon? She was all over the place. They even joke about it as every nurse is Nurse Joy," Victor explains.

"I have no idea what you're talking about," Leo states.

"Then why does it feel like we're still in New York?" Victor questions.

Leo scrunches his face with more confusion from Victor's reaction. "We're not. We're in Chicago. Why would you think we're still in New York?"

Victor pinches the bridge of his nose. "How can you tell we're in Chicago?"

"Because our rooms face the water," Leo responds. "I don't understand the problem."

Victor looks over to Leo, slightly aggravated. "Really? Everything looks the same, down to the bellman."

"But this is Jerry. You saw Jerry in . . . " Leo finally realizes Victor's comments. " . . . Ooh, I see what you're saying now."

"If our rooms are the same number, I think I'm going to scream," Victor says, looking up at the floor counter.

Leo is silent as he looks forward and doesn't make eye contact. "Leo?"

Leo doesn't answer or notice Victor glaring at him. "Leeeooo . . . " Victor snarls.

Leo finally answers, "Here's our floor!"

Victor looks up and sees 14. "You got off lucky."

Leo jokingly whispers under his breath, "That's what she said." Victor narrows his eyes, causing Leo to snicker. Leo takes out a couple of key cards and hands Victor one of them.

They exit the elevator and walk toward the corner rooms at the end of the hall. When Victor opens the door, his living room window wraps around, giving him a panoramic view of the river and most of downtown Chicago. The decor in the room is different from New York. He barely has time to check out the rest of the room when he hears knocking at the connecting door. He opens the door, and there's Leo.

"What, no drink?" Victor jokes.

Leo walks in with two more books. "Not right now. I need you focused before we attend your first lesson later." He hands Victor the two books, "I need you to read the first five chapters in both these books before we meet up with Karl Landring tonight. In the meantime, I'm going to go get some items we'll need."

Victor examines the books. "Well, can't I go with you?"

Leo shakes his head and taps his index finger on top of one of the books. "No, because the first five chapters in this book are 50 pages alone. And I need you to be reading."

Victor slumps his shoulders and moans like a disgruntled teenager, "Why does this feel like I'm not getting time to do anything else?"

"What can I say? He was able to see you right away before he had to leave for his own lessons next week. But don't worry; you'll do fine." Leo walks out the front door and turns to finish talking to Victor. "I already programmed my number into your phone. Just call or text me if you need anything. Preferably call; I hate text."

Victor watches the door close behind Leo. "Who prefers call over text nowadays?" he says. He takes a deep breath, plops down on the couch, and looks at the books he was given.

The first book is titled: *"Air Bending: Not Your Ordinary Kids Show."*

He thinks to himself, *Seriously? Who came up with that title?* The second book is titled: *"The Air Within You."*

Almost as bad as the first title. But which one should I read first? Victor shrugs. *Meh, I'll go alphabetically since I don't know the Dewey decimals for these books.*

Victor opens the first book and then looks up to where his luggage is. They're gone. He looks around the room and sees nothing. He looks into Leo's room . . . nothing. He walks into the bedroom and sees an older woman.

"Umm, hello? May I help you?" Victor asks the stranger.

The woman has short, curly red hair and is dressed in a simple pale blue, knee-length dress with a pleated skirt and a light green cardigan sweater. She looks up and smiles at Victor. "Oh, hi there, Mr. Russo," She responds in her Midwestern accent. "I'm the maid assigned to you and Mr. Oliveira. Don't mind me. I'm just here to make sure everything is in order for your stay this week."

Victor tries to get a word in but can't.

"There will also be a couple of garment bags from that Clarence Waterlily fella. They sent one over for each of you. And I'm hoping a package that was sent for you arrives later today." She walks around the bed to the nightstand to place a new box of tissues. Victor tries to talk, but is still unable to get a word in.

"I made sure there was plenty of bottled water for you in the wet bar, and I supplied you with all your favorite snacks. If you should ever need more, there's no need to call. I have already anticipated your needs."

She walks around the bed again and heads into the bathroom. Victor still can't get a word in as she shouts from the bathroom. "I made sure there are lots of towels for you. If you wish to take a bubble bath after your lessons, I put a bottle of bubbles on the sink. There should be plenty of shampoo, and I found the hair products you like to use. But I also provided some that my grandson uses. He has the same hair as yours."

She starts to walk towards Victor. He moves out of her way as she enters the living room. "Lunch will be here in a couple of hours, so please don't fill up on snacks. I already know you had breakfast; it's the most important meal of the day, next to lunch, even dinner."

She stops talking and giggles but starts up again before Victor can speak. "If you would like turndown service, please let me know later today. I'm going to take your suit to be cleaned and pressed, so it will be ready before you leave for your lessons. Other than that, if you need anything, please give me a call." She exits the room, leaving Victor in utter silence and confusion.

Leo walks into a shop that sells magical artifacts. He looks inside a small glass case containing rings. He leans over, getting a better look at the variety inside. A woman approaches him and says, "Hello, is there a ring that tickles your fancy?"

Leo looks up and smiles. "Hello. I'm looking for a ring that can assist with Air Magic."

"I have a few rings to help those with air specialties." She reaches in and pulls out a small tray of rings. "I like this one." She holds up a silver ring with a large blue gem.

"Too gaudy," Leo replies.

"Well, how about this one?" She holds up a black ring with several tiny white gems wrapped halfway around it.

"No, I need something without gems. Like this one." He points to a metallic blue ring.

She gives Leo a funny look. "Well, this one is very plain. Are you sure this is what you want?"

She hands Leo the ring. "Yes, this will be perfect," he responds. "He is a strong empath, and the gems will either block his ability or intensify it too much."

The woman takes the ring back and places it in a small box. "You could have mentioned it was for an empath. I do have some other artifacts that could help." She walks Leo to the other side of the shop and stops in front of a tall glass case containing wands and swords.

"Everything in here is perfect for an empath and their specialties. If this is for someone learning a new skill, might I suggest this sword?" She takes out a small black sword with blue leather wrapped around the hilt. A round sapphire is attached to the top of the hilt, and a medium-sized pearl is embedded in the black metal. "This will be perfect for using their empathic abilities when defending against attacks. It will slice the magic in half like butter."

Leo takes the sword and examines it carefully. "What about Fire? I'm having a hard time seeing if the magic in this will prevent fire attacks."

She takes the sword and twirls it around with her wrist. "Throw something at me." She takes up a defensive stance as Leo looks at her. "Come on, throw something at me."

He takes a few steps back and twirls a blue fireball her way like a baseball. As it comes at her, she swings the sword and slices the fireball in half, causing it to extinguish. She twirls the blade with her wrist again, waiting for more. Leo tosses three more fireballs, more prominent this time. She swings the sword, connecting it to all three. They vanish just as soon as they connect with the steel.

Leo throws a green flame at her. She holds the sword up, and the sword absorbs the flame. The steel begins to glow a greenish color. She swings the blade to the ceiling and releases the green flame onto it. The magic protection of the ceiling extinguishes the green flame.

Leo nods, impressed, "I'll take it."

The employee smiles as she walks back behind the counter. "Would you like me to wrap it up for you?"

"Why not?" Leo smiles.

The clerk takes the sword and places it in a deep charcoal box. "You know, we do have some nice harnesses for sale," the clerk suggests, nodding to a rack with various harnesses for holding swords and other objects.

"Trying to upsell me?" Leo jokes as he walks over to pick out a harness. He finds a simple black one that slings diagonally across the chest. "I take it one size fits all?"

"If you're talking about the sword, yes," the clerk replies as she starts ringing up the items. "The strap is adjustable, and the sheath will fit the sword's size."

"That's what she said," Leo jokes under his breath. He walks back over to the counter and hands the clerk a dark maroon credit card. She thanks Leo as she hands him a bag with the items. As he exits the shop, he notices a maroon and silver bracelet in a cabinet. "What can you tell me about the bracelet?"

The woman smiles, "That will help with your fire specialty." He cocks his eyebrow and looks back at her, "I'll take it."

A short time later, Leo returns to his room and puts the bag on the coffee table. He takes out the ring box and walks into Victor's room.

Victor is in the lounge chair, reading the second book. There are three empty glass water bottles on the coffee table. He notices Victor's suit is hanging on the bedroom door.

"I see your suit has been cleaned and pressed," Leo comments.

Victor looks up at Leo. "That maid came in twice before that, and I couldn't even get a word in. When she came to drop off my suit, I didn't bother trying. She loves to talk."

"How's your reading?" Leo asks, walking over to Victor.

Victor sighs heavily, placing the book in his lap so he can rub his eyes. "I finished the first book while eating lunch. And I still have 10 pages to go before I finish this one. Good thing these books are small." He looks up at Leo, "Is it time to go?"

"Almost. You can finish the rest of the book in the car. Get washed up and ready," Leo orders.

Victor puts the book on the coffee table and walks into the bedroom. A short time later, he walks out of his bedroom in his new suit. Leo is standing at the connecting doorway and gives Victor a whistle.

"I've got something for you," Leo says as he tosses the ring box to Victor. Victor opens the box. "Aww, Leo, is this a proposal?" he asks sarcastically.

Leo laughs, "No, this ring will assist you with honing your empathic abilities while you channel your air specialty."

Victor slips the ring on his hand and approves. Leo gestures to the door, and they exit the room.

CHAPTER THIRTEEN

Victor and Leo sit in the back of the town car on their way to meet Karl for Victor's first lesson. Victor finishes the last chapter of the book. He sighs heavily, sets the book down, and rubs his eyes. "I don't know if I can read anymore."

"I'm surprised you did any reading," Leo comments jokingly.

"That's because you asked me to," Victor politely snaps back.

Leo snickers, "Well, I'm glad. Most new witches or warlocks I've mentored in the past tend to skip most of the reading. After about five lessons, they realize they should have read what I gave them."

Victor rubs the back of his neck. "So, I saw three boxes in your room. I take it they are filled with books?"

"That's right," Leo answers. "I hope you enjoy reading."

Victor lets out a disgruntled groan, "Why is there so much reading?"

Leo looks over to Victor and pats his leg. "Don't worry too much about it. I'm just having you read the important parts of the book. But make sure you find time to read what I give you."

Victor looks down at the book and slumps over in his seat. "I hope I don't need to read anymore tonight. My eyes are so tired."

"I think you should be good for tonight's lesson," Leo mentions as he takes the book away from Victor. "But I hope you enjoy reading. Because as soon as we get through those boxes, more will come."

Victor gives Leo a tired yet annoyed look. "How much reading is there for a warlock?"

Leo shrugs his shoulders. "Well, you're an empath. Therefore, you can expect a lot of reading in your future. But something tells me you might pick up things quickly. At least, that's what I was told about your mother and grandmother. Magic was practically natural to them."

"Why does being an empath have anything to do with it?" Victor asks.

"It has everything to do with it," Leo responds. "People of magic cannot become empaths, seers, or telepaths."

"There are telepaths?" Victor asks with astonishment.

"There are, but they are rare. Empaths and seers are just as rare. You see, unlike specialties that are taught, abilities are natural. Unless you were born with an ability, it cannot be taught or reproduced," Leo explains.

"You're saying I was born an empath?" Victor asks.

Leo nods. "That's correct. Remember at the restaurant? You saw the auras around you. Only empaths can see auras. Those who claim to see auras are merely projecting their own personal feelings onto that person. But empaths can see a person's true aura. That's why they are the best lie detectors."

Victor scratches his chin as he wonders, "Wouldn't telepaths be lie detectors too? Can't they read minds?"

Leo shakes his head and explains, "Although it's true that telepaths can read minds, some people of magic train themselves to trick telepaths with their thoughts. You can learn how to trick a telepath, but it's more difficult to deceive an empath. Your aura never lies, no matter how much you try."

"Can someone be empathic and telepathic, or have all three?" Victor inquires.

"I've heard it's possible, but *extremely* rare. I haven't met anyone with two or all three abilities," Leo responds.

"Does Madame Jeanette have an ability?" Victor asks. "I have a feeling she does."

"She's a seer. And she's the only seer I know. I thought I mentioned that to you."

"You probably did, but I forgot. Have you known anyone who tried to learn an ability?" Victor wonders.

Leo ponders Victor's inquiry. "I don't know anyone who has tried. But I have heard of the outcome of those who did. Some have tried making spells, but because it's all mental abilities, they went insane. We're talking chained up and placed underground for everyone's protection."

"Should *I* be worried about going insane?" Victor worries.

"Nah, those born with an ability live a normal life," Leo reassures. "But some do go a little mad initially because no one is around to teach them."

"I don't know anyone who is an empath. Should I be worried?" Victor asks.

Leo lets out a light snicker through his teeth. "You'll be fine. You're the third empath I know. Well, *now* know. There is nothing to worry about."

Victor still feels uncertain but changes the topic to help distract his mind. "Tell me about these '*Specialties*' I'm about to learn."

Leo shifts in his seat to get a better look at Victor. "There are three levels of specialties: *Basic*, *Medium*, and *Heavy*."

"Now, I hope you're paying attention," Leo suggests, watching Victor's confused expression. "Every person of magic has one, two, or sometimes all four Basic specialties. These specialties are *Air*, *Earth*, *Water*, and *Fire*. You can learn all four, but the more you learn, the harder it is to control each of them if you don't continue your studies and practice a lot.

Like, a lot. It's easy to create a fire tornado using Fire and Air, but lose control of it, and suddenly you're on the evening news."

"Did that actually happen?" Victor inquires.

"Yes. Thankfully, it was contained before any real damage happened."

"So, no Fire Tornadoes. Got it," Victor notes to himself.

"Medium specialties are *Light*, *Shadow*, and *Metal*. It's not common for someone to practice more than one, but it's more common for someone who practices one Medium and one or all Basic. For example, you can practice Air, Water, and Metal. However, practicing with Air, Water, Metal, and Light is very difficult. Medium specialties take up a lot of energy.

"Heavy Specialties are the most dangerous if not practiced properly. These are *Tarot*, *Stellar*, and *Necromancy*. Those who participate in Dark or Death Magic tend to abuse Tarot and Necromancy the most. Here's the part I hope you are paying attention to."

Victor holds up his hand as he comprehends what he was told. "Let me make sure I understand: Everyone who practices magic has at least one or more Basic. But it's rare if they practice more than one Medium or Heavy," Victor reiterates.

Leo nods in agreement. "Correct. The more specialties you practice, the more energy you use, which can become exhausting. However, for empaths like yourself and others with an ability, something about their ability allows them to excel in all specialties. We have yet to determine how this is possible since empaths are rare. It's a reason why some fear empaths. Some say it's because empaths can absorb the energy of others, giving them an endless supply."

Victor sits back and tries to decipher what Leo has told him. "So, you're telling me, I can be a powerful warlock?"

"That's why Akisha fears you. And that's why she worries that people like Magenta will try to convince you to join them and practice Dark Magic," Leo replies.

"Is there any difference between Dark Magic and Death Magic?" Victor inquires.

"They are one and the same. It's more of a generational thing. Younger people will say dark magic, but elders and superiors will say death magic. I think it's mostly because the older generation saw death more."

Victor looks out the window as they turn down a dark road. "I take it that I need to learn basic specialties before I practice the others."

"You're taking this very well for someone who just had their entire world turned upside-down," Leo says, noticing how calm Victor is.

"I guess deep down, I've always known there was something different about me," Victor tails off, gazing out the window.

Leo looks out the same window as Victor. "Looks like we're here."

The car pulls up to a warehouse. There isn't much light around, which makes Victor a little nervous. But as long as Leo's with him, he feels safe. Two muscular men in dark suits open the doors for Victor and Leo. Victor fixes his blazer, walks around the car, and stands beside Leo. The car drives off when a woman walks out of the warehouse.

The woman, dressed in a skintight black leather outfit and black high-heeled boots, greets them. "Hello, Warlocks. Wizard Landring is waiting for you inside." She turns to walk inside, and everyone follows. She pushes a sliding door to the side with ease. Inside, the center is well-lit, while all around, is dark.

Victor looks concerned as he looks around. "Is there a reason we need to be in an abandoned warehouse?" he asks Leo.

"Well, we can't practice in the open where the mundane can see us," Leo answers while walking further inside.

"Why didn't we walk through a mirror to get here?" Victor ponders.

"Karl doesn't like mirrors for some reason. Maybe it's because he can't stop looking at himself," Leo jokes.

As they reach the center of the warehouse, they see a tall man standing rigidly in a military posture in the light. He stands with his hands clasped behind his back, looking on with piercing blue eyes. He's wearing a dark green suit, a matching tie, and a light yellow shirt. He keeps a neutral face as he watches Victor and Leo approach him.

The woman gestures to keep moving forward. "Empath Russo, please meet Wizard Karl Landring."

Leo and Victor stop about six feet from Karl. "Wizard?" Leo asks. "Really, Karl? You're introducing yourself as a Wizard now? And what's with the fanfare?"

Victor looks confused as he sees Leo mocking Karl, but Karl doesn't move. He starts to worry until he notices Karl's orange and yellow aura.

Karl tries to keep his composure but loses it, revealing a cheerful expression towards Leo. "You son-of-bitch, I can't keep my stoic demeanor around you. How the fuck are ya?" Karl pulls Leo in for a bear hug.

Leo pats Karl's back as though he's hugging too tightly. "I'm good. It's been a hot minute since we last saw each other."

Karl has a big grin as he looks at Victor. "The last time I saw this guy was when I made the mistake of marrying that whore of an ex-wife. That was what, almost eight years?" Karl releases Leo from his grip.

"Give or take," Leo answers as he rolls one of his shoulders. "Karl, this is Victor, the empath warlock you've been hearing about."

Karl shakes Victor's hand much too firmly for Victor's tastes. "Ah, yes!" Karl responds. "You're the one Akisha and Jeanie keep talking about."

Victor tries to hold his composure as he feels the metacarpals in his hand breaking. "It's a pleasure to meet you, Mr. Landring. Or should I say wizard?"

Karl laughs gleefully. "Karl is fine. There's no need to worry about formalities here, especially in the presence of an empath."

Karl releases Victor's hand, and Victor tries his best not to see if his hand is broken. Victor gives Leo a confused look and mouths, *"What does he mean by that?"*

Leo notices and answers, "What Karl means is that Empaths are highly honored by those who don't fear them. Sometimes, they are introduced as Empaths, just as you were introduced a moment ago."

"Seems a bit overkill, doesn't it?" Victor responds.

"We're a bit traditional," Karl smiles widely. Using his Air Magic, he reaches for a chair, sliding it beside Victor. "Here, take a seat and watch for a moment. I'm going to show you your first spellcasting."

Victor gives Leo a baffled expression. Leo just smiles and shrugs, as if he were saying, *"Just go with it."* Victor takes his seat at the edge of the light. Leo moves to another edge of the light, directly across from Karl.

Karl takes his spot in the center and places his hands on his hips. "Tonight, my young empath, I will show you how to use Air to counter a Fire attack. Now, I know what you're thinking, 'Doesn't Fire need Air to survive?' The answer is yes. *But* what if you can take the Air out of the Fire?"

"Doesn't that seem a little advanced for him?" Leo queries. "This *is* his first magic lesson."

Karl shows off his pearly whites and replies, "He's an empath. He'll be able to pick up faster than you can say, *'Bitch better have my money.'*" Leo rolls his eyes at Karl's "impressive" dance moves.

Karl rolls his shoulders and cracks his neck. He looks over at Leo and gives a nod. Leo places his hands to his side and stands up tall. Leo keeps a blank expression as he focuses on creating a fireball. With a few hand and arm movements, Leo hurls a basketball-sized yellow fireball at Karl.

Karl raises his arms and spreads his fingers apart in front of him. Karl positions his hands with one palm facing upward and the other facing the fireball. As soon as the fireball is inches away, he flicks his hands above his head and spreads them shoulder-width apart, freezing the fireball inside a faded, cloudlike bubble.

Karl slowly lowers his hands, twisting his wrists. The bubble fills with smoke, engulfing the fireball. He brings his hands together, causing the bubble to pop and the smoke to evaporate as it's released.

Leo throws two more fireballs at Karl. Using the same hand and arm gestures, Karl adds a little twirl, as if he were dancing, to combine the two fireballs into one bubble. Then he pops the bubble. Leo takes a new stance and uses a flame-throwing spell at Karl.

Karl turns his body sideways and leans back, avoiding the flame flying by him. He opens his arms wide, along the length of the flame, and then twists his wrists and hands upward as if he's trying to lift a log. He creates the same faded cloud bubble that stretches the entire length of the flame, cutting it off at Leo's palms.

Karl twirls as he jumps and tosses the flame above his head. As the flame spins around in the air, Karl drops his arms and makes fists with his hands, acting like he's pulling down on a couple of ropes. The flame pops like a balloon. Karl turns to look at Victor and takes a bow. The woman and two men standing off to the side start applauding.

Leo lightly shakes his head and places a hand on his hip. "Show off."

Karl ignores Leo's comment and focuses on Victor. "These spells might seem simple, but it will take some time to perfect. Come, stand next to me." Victor walks over and stands next to Karl. "First, I want you to raise your hands as high as your shoulders and as wide, palms facing each other." Victor complies. "Now, I want you to focus on the air between your hands. I want you to see the molecules drifting by. Focus on it swirling around." Victor focuses as Karl starts to move behind him. Leo takes a seat as he watches.

Karl leans down and softly talks in Victor's ear. "Now, feel the air between your hands. As you feel the air, focus on pressing it together into a ball." Victor starts moving his hands closer together. Karl stops him and spreads his hands apart. "No, no. Instinct wants you to put your hands together as if you're making a ball with your hands. Don't do that. Use your energy to create the ball without moving your hands."

Victor nods as he clears his throat. He takes a deep breath and refocuses on the task.

Leo perks up when he sees something appear between Victor's hands. Victor keeps concentration as Karl smiles. "Good, keep your focus," Karl mentions. "Imagine a ball in your mind and manipulate the air into becoming that ball." Victor's hands start to shake. "Remain focused," Karl says in Victor's ear. A moment later, Victor drops his hands and exhales heavily.

Karl pats Victor's shoulder, "It's okay. I could see that you were about to create a ball. Could you feel how much energy you were using?"

Victor nods, "Yeah, it almost felt like my body was getting cold inside. Like it brought in the air through my pores, especially around my arms and hands. You know the feeling when a limb starts to fall asleep? But without the tingling."

"That's exactly what you're supposed to be feeling," Karl explains. "Every time you cast Air Magic, the part of your body you're focusing the magic on will have that feeling." Karl lifts his index finger. A tiny tornado begins to swirl around his finger. As it does, Karl's skin starts turning red from the chill. "You can also use Air Magic in your feet to jump higher or to kick a burst of air at your opponent. It's safer on your body than kicking and breaking a foot or leg."

Karl does a roundhouse kick and lets off a burst of air from his foot that knocks over a stack of boxes about 30 feet away. "See? But that lesson will come later. Do you think you are ready to try again?"

Victor nods and starts over, trying to create a ball of air between his hands.

As Leo looks on, his phone begins to vibrate in his jacket. He becomes annoyed when he sees who's calling and walks away to take the call.

CHAPTER FOURTEEN

Leo walks to a dimly lit corner of the warehouse. He looks over his shoulder to see if anyone has noticed he has stepped away. Then he takes a deep breath and answers his phone.

"I'm a little busy right now," Leo says harshly.

"Hello to you, too," the person on the other end says.

"What do you want, Derek?" Leo asks with annoyance.

"I don't understand why you're getting so upset talking to your husband. I haven't spoken to you in over a week," Derek says defensively.

"You know I'm mentoring someone right now," Leo remarks. "We just started training."

"Yeah, the empath. Is he cute?" Derek asks.

Leo squints, acting as though Derek is standing before him. "Why does that matter?"

"Because I want to know about my competition," Derek responds with a tinge of jealousy.

Leo looks back over to see Victor smiling. Karl pats Victor on the back, expressing his pride over a task. Leo knows he should be paying attention, but his husband is calling, which means he'd better answer.

"How long do you think you'll be away?" Derek asks.

"I'm not sure, Derek. He's an empath and in his early 30s. This could take some time since he has a lot to learn," Leo explains, doing his best to hold back his irritation.

Derek sighs, "I don't understand why they chose you as his mentor. Why couldn't they find someone else with more experience with empaths?"

Leo pinches the bridge of his nose. "I don't know, Derek. I've been a mentor for a while, and they probably figured I would be the best for his lessons."

"That damned council should give you a break. You're hardly home to be with me," Derek comments in a pouty voice.

Leo gives Derek an annoyed expression, even though Derek can't see it. "Derek, we don't even live together anymore. We haven't lived together for over three years now. I'm only still your husband because it's binding."

"That doesn't mean we can't still try, Leo."

Leo pauses and looks back at Victor. He takes a deep breath before responding, "Look, Derek, I'm in the middle of this lesson. I need to let you go."

"Fine, whatever. Call me back later." Derek hangs up before Leo can say goodbye.

Leo sighs deeply as he puts his phone back in the inside pocket of his jacket and returns to observe Victor's lessons.

After a few hours of practicing under the bright lights, Victor breaks a sweat. Karl looks cool as a cucumber. He notices the beads of sweat on Victor's forehead and casts a breeze to help cool him off.

Victor drops his hands to his sides. "I'm sorry, I just feel so tired."

Karl steps back and crosses his arms. "Not to worry. Let's take a break." He snaps his fingers, and the leather-clad woman walks over, pushing a dining cart. The men bring over a couple of chairs. The woman locks the cart in place and then lifts the metal covers off the plates. The smell of lemon and salmon fills the air around them.

"I hope you enjoy the dinner I've prepared for you," Karl says. His assistant rolls her eyes, knowing she was the one who prepared it.

The three of them sit and start eating while Karl's personnel stand off to the side with their hands clasped.

"Leo mentioned that your first specialty is Water," Victor tells Karl.

"That's right. That's how I got us salmon for dinner," Karl replies as he chews away.

"So why are you teaching Air Magic?" Victor curiously asks.

Karl finishes his big bite of salmon before he answers. "Air is the main ingredient for Water, Fire, and Earth. All three need Air to survive. Air is also easy to manipulate and can dilute several attacks when used properly. It's also easier to teach than Water."

Leo looks up as he's about to take a bite. "In other words, he's a show-off, and for him to always show off, he became an instructor in Air Magic since there is such a high demand for air instructors." Victor chuckles as Karl gives Leo a pointed look. Leo smiles as he takes a bite and winks at Karl.

"Wise ass," Karl huffs.

"Show off," Leo smirks.

"Why didn't you try to make Air your first specialty?" Victor asks.

"It's because my exams showed Water was my strongest," Karl replies.

"Exams?" Victor looks over at Leo, "What exams?"

Leo is caught off guard as he tries to finish a large bite of food in his mouth. "All those of magic have to go through a set of exams to see where they are to be placed."

"Why wasn't I given any exam to take?" Victor queries.

"Well, we're sort of doing things a little bit backwards," Leo answers. "I think the council wants you to start learning magic now. The exams will be later. We need to visit a warlock who can administer the exam for empaths. Right now, he's busy and needs time to prepare."

Victor looks between Leo and Karl. "Why am I learning magic before I know what I should learn first?"

"Those with abilities can control all forms of magic," Karl responds. "Empaths, in particular, can conjure more than one magic spell at a time. It's challenging for someone like me to achieve. I can conjure Water, Air, and Light. But it's difficult for me to conjure two at once. I've dabbled in Earth and Fire, but my magic can't handle them. So, I just focus on the three I'm good at."

"Which is why he's jealous that you are going to learn all of them," Leo comments, giving a sly wink to Karl.

Karl rolls his eyes at Leo and turns back to Victor. "So, what did you think of Jeanie?"

"Jeanie?" Victor questions.

"Madame Jeanette," Leo says without looking up from his plate with a mouth full of food.

"Oh!" Victor says as he puts his fork and knife down. "She's nice, but a little interesting. I think she likes me. And she does love her tobacco."

"That's her artifact to help with her seer ability," Karl comments.

Victor looks over at Karl and blinks a couple of times in confusion.

Leo notices and responds. "Jeanette uses the tobacco smoke to help with her premonitions. She's very good at it. Seers generally use an object to aid their premonitions, such as a crystal ball. Some of the best seers are traditional and use crystal balls as their artifacts. On the other hand, Jeanette figured out that the smoke from her tobacco pipe works for her.

"The pipe used to be her father's, who gave it to her before he passed. At her father's funeral, she took a hit from the pipe and noticed something in the smoke she puffed out. She believes her father fabricated his pipe to help her become a better seer."

Karl turns and looks at Victor. "And as an empath, you will figure out something similar. You might wear a piece of jewelry, like the ring you have on that's helping you with Air Magic. Which was a good idea, Leo."

"Thank you, Karl," Leo says with a smile.

Karl continues, "You might find a trinket, a coin, maybe even a pin that will help you amplify your empathic ability. Or it might be so natural for you that you might not need anything at all. You've probably already been told that empaths are rare. Not many people know what empaths need except for them. Most artifacts you will discover were created by empaths years ago, before the civil war between witches."

Victor ponders before he speaks. "You two say empaths are rare, but there was one in the restaurant the other night. And she didn't seem to know what to do."

Karl and Leo look at each other before Leo speaks. "She is an empath. However, she's older, like a lot older. Her abilities are starting to fade. She can still do smaller things like read auras or help with an investigation, but as for fighting, she's not someone you want to bring into battle."

"Abilities are very mental," Karl adds. "I once knew a telepath. But sadly, he took his own life when he reached 180 years old. He couldn't control his telepathic ability anymore. And since no one knew how to correct it or what artifact could help him, he descended into madness. Some superiors tried to contain him so as not to hurt himself or others, but he killed himself as they tried to bind him."

Karl becomes silent for a moment, lost in deep thought. He shakes his head and looks back at Victor. "I think you'll know how to help yourself and other empaths. You're younger than any of us here. Hell, I'm older than Leo by fifteen years and look like I'm in my early 40s. I'm still discovering new artifacts that aid me with my Water and Air Magic. Some work and some don't. And you'll do the same."

"You both have mentioned superiors. What are you talking about?" Victor asks

"A Superior is the head of a coven," Leo explains. "They are chosen by the elders and other high-ranking officers of the coven. My superior has been in his position since before I joined. You will meet him soon."

Karl and Leo wipe their mouths while Victor takes the last bite off his plate. As Victor puts down his utensils, Karl gestures to his staff to take the cart away.

Karl puts a hand on Victor's shoulder, "Okay, let's go back to practicing."

An hour has passed, and Victor finally makes an air bubble between his hands. He is pleased to maintain one longer than the others. "Damn, finally. I think I'm getting this."

Karl pats Victor on the back, "That's good. Now, concentrate on pulling the air out of the bubble, but don't pop it."

Victor complies with Karl's instructions. He can feel his hands growing cold as the pores in his skin inhale the air. The bubble starts to look cloudier than before.

Karl's smile grows bigger, and then he looks over at Leo. "Leo, toss over a small fireball."

"You sure he's ready?" Leo asks, uncertain about the request.

Karl nods and steps to the side. "Now, Victor, Leo will toss over a small fireball. I want you to catch it in the bubble."

Victor nods in response, trying to keep his focus on the bubble.

Leo stands up and flicks his wrist as he walks over to stand across from Victor. A small blue ball of fire appears in his palm. He underhand tosses the fireball over to Victor. Victor eyes the fireball and moves his hands and arms, catching it on his first try.

Karl crosses his arms and smiles proudly. "Nice job! Now, concentrate on the air that's inside the fireball. You want to pull the air out of the fireball just like you did with the bubble."

Victor looks at the fire inside the bubble. He doesn't notice that his breathing has slowed, and his heartbeat begins to slow down. All he can hear is the breeze blowing around his ears.

As Victor focuses on the fireball, Leo looks over and notices something. He's unsure as to what is happening.

Karl notices Leo's confused expression. "What's up?"

"I'm not sure," Leo answers as he slowly walks over to Victor.

As Karl makes his way around Victor, he jumps back. "What . . . what is this?" He twists his neck as Leo approaches. "Leo, what's going on?"

Leo shakes his head, "I have no idea. I don't know how to react." They look at Victor, who still hasn't noticed their confused and concerned expressions.

*Victor's eyes are **glowing white**.*

A moment later, Victor's eyes glow brighter. Then, the fireball is extinguished, and the bubble pops. A huge smile grows across his face. He looks up at Leo and Karl.

"I did it!" Victor says proudly. When he looks over at Leo and Karl, he notices the bewildered and startled expressions on their faces. He shifts his eyes between them, but they do not respond to Victor's joy. Victor turns around to see if there is something behind him, but there is nothing.

He looks back at them, his eye returning to normal, and begins to worry, "What's wrong?"

CHAPTER FIFTEEN

Victor looks at Karl and Leo, then turns around to see if there is anyone behind him. He looks back at them and realizes, "Why are you looking at me like that?"

Karl and Leo look at each other, then glance back at Victor. Leo opens his mouth but closes it when trying to figure out what to tell Victor. Finally, "Your eyes . . . they were glowing."

Victor's eyebrows pinch together as he tries to understand what he just heard. "Glowing? What do you mean? My vision was fine. I saw nothing shining in front of me except that blue fireball."

Karl pierces his lips together as he takes a deep breath through his nose. As soon as he exhales, he speaks. "I've never seen this before. Not with seers. Not with telepaths. And not with empaths. But your eyes *were* glowing."

Victor starts to feel uncertain and confused. "Has no one ever had their eyes glow before?" Karl and Leo shake their heads. "Not even elders or superiors?" Karl and Leo look at each other and stare before shaking their heads in unison. Victor starts to feel dizzy. Karl notices, uses his Air Magic, and pulls a chair over to Victor.

Victor takes the chair and sits down carefully. "I . . . I don't know how to process this." Victor stares off, trying to understand what just happened. He thinks to himself, *How could my eyes start glowing? I didn't see anything glowing in front of me. Is there something wrong with me?*

Karl conjures a water ball over his palm and offers it to Victor. "Drink some water." Victor doesn't know what to do with a ball of water. He leans in and starts to suck in the water as if drinking through a straw.

Leo pulls out his phone and makes a call. "I'll be right back," he says as he walks away.

Karl puts his free hand on Victor's shoulder as Victor slowly drinks the water. "How are you feeling?"

Victor pauses for a moment, "I think I'm okay. The room isn't spinning anymore." He looks into Karl's worried eyes. "Are you serious, though? You've never seen someone's eyes glow before?"

Karl slowly shakes his head. "No, my young empath. Never."

"I think I'm good with the water," Victor says, leaning back into the chair. Karl flings the water ball away, almost hitting Leo.

"Watch it!" Leo exclaims.

Karl looks over his shoulder. "Sorry about that."

Leo returns to Victor and crouches beside him. "We are going back to the hotel now. Karl, come with us."

As Victor slowly stands up, he becomes dizzy again. He holds onto the back of the chair until the room stops spinning. They slowly make their way outside and get into the town car. A quick drive later, they return to the hotel and head to their rooms. As they enter Victor's room, Akisha, Madame Jeanette, and another woman await inside.

"Akisha, Madame Jeanette, what are you doing here?" Victor asks.

Akisha stands and walks over to Victor. "How are you feeling, Victor?" She places her hands on Victor's shoulders and looks into his eyes.

"I'm fine," Victor responds. He looks at the third woman, who has whitish-blonde hair with touches of grey streaks and is dressed in a black-and-white suit and blouse. She wears a matching black necklace and bracelet, along with a diamond ring on each hand.

"Hello," Victor says to her.

"Victor, this is Superior Jackie Campbell," Akisha says. "She's heard about you from my superior and wanted to meet you."

Superior Jackie stands up and walks over to Victor. Akisha steps to the side to allow her to stand before Victor. "Good evening, Empath Russo," Superior Jackie says as she curtsies. "I hope that you are feeling well. I heard what happened during your lesson."

Victor is taken aback by Superior Jackie's gesture. He looks around and notices everyone's eyes are on him. "I-I'm fine right now, thank you. And you don't have to curtsy. I don't think that's necessary."

Leo steps up to Victor's side and speaks softly. "Superior Jackie is a traditionalist, and she respects those with abilities. Something to do with empaths is that they are superior to, well, superiors. Superiors do not bow or curtsy to anyone below them."

"It's almost like a monarch mindset, got it," Victor mentions to Leo.

Leo looks up to ponder and nods. "Sort of. We'll go over that later."

Superior Jackie clasps her hands in front of her as she speaks to Victor. "I heard that your eyes started to glow when you were casting a spell. Can you describe what was going through your mind?"

"Well," Victor starts as he looks around with everyone's eyes on him. "Karl was standing behind me as I was casting an air bubble. Leo tossed a small fireball, and I caught it in the bubble." Victor looks in front of him as he recalls the spell. He holds out his hands as he mimics the motions. "All I could think about was removing the air from the fireball. I could feel the heat and air being absorbed into my hands. I didn't notice Karl standing in front of me. I heard nothing else except the air blowing around my ears."

Victor lowers his hands and looks back at Superior Jackie. "As I continued to focus, the fireball extinguished, and then the bubble popped. I was excited because I felt I had finally accomplished something from my lessons. When I looked up, Leo and Karl were staring at me. They looked worried. That's when they told me my eyes were glowing."

Superior Jackie nods her head slightly as she *hmms* to herself. She slowly turns around and walks back to her seat. While pondering, she crosses her arms and taps her index finger on her chin. Superior Jackie momentarily stops in front of the chair she was sitting in before turning back and sitting down.

"What are you thinking, Superior?" Akisha asks.

Superior Jackie sits back and rests her arms on the armrests. "Well, I've heard something about this, but I have never experienced it myself. It was just tossed around like rumors or folk tales." She looks up at Victor and says, "Leo mentioned that you didn't see anything glowing in front of you."

Victor slowly shakes his head. "No. The only thing I saw glowing was the fireball."

"He said your eyes were glowing white. You didn't see anything white?" Superior Jackie asks.

"The only white I saw was the faded clouds surrounding the bubble," Victor responds.

Superior Jackie leans to the side and looks at Madame Jeanette. "What say you, Jeanette? Have you ever experienced something like this before, where your eyes glowed?"

"No, I am sorry, Superior Jackie. I have never been told my eyes glowed nor seen someone's eyes glow," Madame Jeanette responds.

"You saw nothing in the premonitions with Victor's eyes glowing?" Superior Jackie adds.

"No, nothing," Madame Jeanette replies.

Superior Jackie lets out a heavy sigh and looks at Karl and Leo. "Did anything happen to the two of you when this happened? Did you feel weak or dizzy, like energy was being taken from you?"

Karl and Leo both shake their heads.

Superior Jackie leans her elbow against the armrest and rests her chin on her fist. "Well, I'm going to need to research the archives and maybe speak to the council." She stands up and looks at everyone, "In the meantime, Victor will continue with his lessons. If anything out of the ordinary happens again, please let me know. I hope to have something soon."

Superior Jackie walks over to Victor and gives him a gentle smile. "I don't think there is anything to worry about, my young empath." She takes his hands into hers. "It's just, this is something new to us. To all of us. Plus, I have a feeling your lessons with Karl will be completed sooner than you think. I can sense that Air Magic will come easily to you." She lets go of his hands, steps back, and curtsies again to Victor. "Have a good night, Empath Russo."

As Superior Jackie exits, Akisha follows and stops at the door, looking over her shoulder. "Have a good night, boys. Keep me informed of any changes." Akisha holds the door open, waiting for Madame Jeanette.

Madame Jeanette walks over to Victor and kisses his cheeks. "Get some rest, *chéri*. You have a long journey." She gives Victor one more smile before she exits with Akisha.

Karl pats Victor on the back. "I better get going myself. As Jeanie said, get some rest, young empath." He gives Leo a nod before taking his leave.

As Victor and Leo watch the door shut, Leo notices a worried look on Victor's face. "What are you thinking?"

Victor takes a moment before looking at Leo. "Nothing." Victor tries to swallow, "I'm going to get out of this suit and go to bed."

Leo walks over to Victor and cups his hand on Victor's cheek. Looking deep into Victor's eyes, he says, "Everything will be okay, don't worry." He holds it for a few moments, taking in Victor's gaze. Slowly, he glides his fingertips along Victor's jawline to the tip of his chin.

Leo steps back, walks to the connecting doorway between their rooms, and closes the door behind him, but only halfway. Victor turns around and starts to get undressed as he walks into his bedroom.

After Victor takes a shower, he puts on some cotton shorts, crawls into his bed, and reaches over to turn off the lamp. He tries to fall asleep when he hears a door slowly squeaking open. Seconds later, there's a light knock at the door.

Victor looks up and sees Leo standing at the bedroom door wearing a sleeveless shirt and pj bottoms. "Hey, did I wake you?" Leo asks.

"No," Victor answers softly. "I can't sleep." Leo walks in and takes a seat next to Victor.

Victor looks up at Leo and asks, "Do you mind keeping me company?"

Leo nods and lifts the covers to slide into bed. Victor wants to be happy that he finally got Leo in his bed, but he has a lot on his mind right now. Victor scoots over to cuddle next to Leo. As soon as he places his head on Leo's shoulder, he starts to drift off to sleep. Leo lightly kisses Victor's forehead and falls asleep with one arm wrapped around Victor.

CHAPTER SIXTEEN

The next day, Victor and Karl are working on more air spells. They have taken off their vests and ties after hours of practicing. Leo and Karl's staff sit around a table playing cards. The staff are annoyed with Leo as he has a majority of the chips next to him.

Karl is impressed with how quickly Victor catches on with his air specialty. "Damn, I can't believe how much you have done today. Let's try doing some *'Jedi tricks.'*"

"You mean like a force push?" Victor snickers.

"That's the one," Karl answers as he throws his palm outward without looking in that direction. A gust of air knocks down a stack of wooden boxes. He starts showing off by throwing air punches, pushes, and kicks. Each time, he knocks down boxes all over the place. At one point, he kicks so hard that the gust of air breaks a box sitting on top of a stack. When he's finished, the two muscular guys annoyingly throw their cards down and start walking over to restack the boxes.

"Is he always like this?" Leo asks the female assistant.

"You have no idea," she responds with annoyance.

Karl creates a ball of water in each hand. He starts to drink one and then hands one to Victor.

Victor raises an eyebrow, asking, "Exactly how am I supposed to drink that without looking like you're feeding me from out of your hand?"

Karl winks and then starts to freeze the outer layer of the water, creating an ice cup. When it plops into his hand, he hands it to Victor. "This better?"

"Yes, this will work," Victor says, taking the ice cup. "I take it you used the air to freeze the water, or you froze the water itself?"

"A little from column A. A little from column B. Just a few tricks you'll learn yourself." Karl looks over and sees his staff finished placing the boxes back into stacks. "Okay, break time is over." As soon as Karl speaks, a small red fireball hits Victor's ice cup and melts it. Water goes all over the place.

"Really, Leo?" Victor shouts. Leo sits in his chair, giggling with a shit-eating grin.

Karl snickers while he escorts Victor to a stack of boxes about 20 feet away. "What I want you to do is throw a few punches. As you do this, concentrate on punching the air like you would do to a punching bag."

Victor nods as he tries to remember a boxing workout his gym trainer gave him and starts punching the air. He focuses on the stack of boxes as he throws punch after punch, but nothing happens. He keeps his focus and begins to feel something solid when he throws another punch. He throws another, and the solid form becomes harder. He starts to go faster, again and again. Air pulses are beginning to push away from his knuckles.

As the pulses become stronger with each punch, the boxes shift slightly. Out of nowhere, Victor throws a kick, and a pulse of air pushes the top box.

Karl is impressed. "Not bad, but just focus on the punching right now," he recommends.

Victor doesn't hear him. Victor punches and kicks. He moves around like an MMA fighter. He kicks, socks, and throws a knee in for show.

Karl becomes concerned. "Okay, now. No need to act like a street fighter. Just go back to punching."

Leo notices Victor showboating. "Vic! Just throw punches."

Victor is in the zone, however. He doesn't hear Karl or Leo calling out his name. Without him knowing, his eyes start to illuminate white again.

Karl starts to back away as Victor's movements become more intense. "Leo, what's going on?"

Leo walks over to Karl. "I don't know, but I don't think he can hear us like last time." When Victor spins around, he notices that Victor's eyes are glowing brighter than the night before. "Shit, I don't know how to stop him."

Victor starts throwing stronger air pulses, knocking down the remaining stacks. He throws his palm out to push the air. Victor begins roundhouse kicking, jump-kicking, and sweep-kicking. Then, before Karl and Leo can react, Victor begins to float. Karl and Leo start walking backward in shock.

"I don't even think I know how to levitate," Karl says in astonishment. "I can jump very high, but levitating, that's something I can't do."

"VICTOR!" Leo shouts as loudly as he can. "VICTOR, CAN YOU HEAR ME?!" There's no response from Victor. "I hate to do this but fuck it." Leo conjures a large fireball and throws it at Victor. Victor doesn't see the fireball coming but instinctively throws a backhand and knocks the fireball to the side, crashing into a couple of stacks of boxes. Victor remains levitating as he turns his attention to Leo and Karl.

"Well, fuck me," Leo mentions, as he knows what will happen next.

Karl's staff runs to the boxes and snuffs out the fire with their Water Magic. But Victor pays no mind to them. His targets are Leo and Karl.

Leo and Karl take defensive stances and start conjuring their magic specialties.

"He's using Air, and it looks like he knows what he's doing. We have to be creative with our attacks. I don't think your fire spells will work on him," Karl commands.

"Looks like we'll have to attack him with Air or Water," Leo replies, concerned.

Leo doesn't like the idea, but knows he'll have to take down the warlock he is supposed to mentor. Before Leo is about to throw an Air spell, Victor attacks.

Without physically hitting each other, Leo and Karl start throwing air pulses at Victor, who blocks and counterattacks. The two muscular men attempt to cast a couple of Water spells, but Victor stops their attacks and then goes after them. When Victor is about to throw anything at the two men, Karl conjures an air-roping spell to pull Victor back toward him. Because Victor is caught off guard by Karl's attack, Leo jumps in and throws a couple of fireballs.

That was a mistake.

Victor knocks the fireballs around, setting more boxes on fire. This time, the flames are much larger.

"What the fuck were you thinking?" Karl shouts at Leo. "Stop using Fire Magic before you destroy my warehouse."

Victor breaks free from Karl's spell and charges at Karl. Leo tackles Victor before he can reach Karl. They roll around on the floor. When Victor rolls on top, he uses an air push to fling himself backward into the air and throws a few air punches at Leo. Leo is lying on his back and covers his face with his forearms, allowing the bulk of the air punches to hit the sleeves of his jacket. Victor lands on his feet and looks at Leo.

The glow in Victor's eyes begins to flow outward from the corners of his eyes.

Victor then charges toward Leo. Leo takes a defensive stance to prepare for Victor to tackle him. When Victor is halfway to Leo, two large metal planks hit him. Outraged,

Victor looks to his side, and a large metal rod smacks him across the face. Victor is now surrounded by metal rods floating and circling him. He tries to throw air attacks and jump away, but the metal rods keep knocking him back down.

Superior Jackie and Akisha walk into the light. They flick their hands and wrists, controlling the rods with their Metal Magic. The rods lower, and Victor tries to fight back. The rods start to coil around his arms and legs. The more Victor struggles, the stronger the metal gets.

Akisha cautiously approaches Victor. She raises the palms of her hands, and they start to flash pulses of light, which look like Morse code. Victor flings his head around to avoid Akisha's hands touching him. Akisha lounges forward, cupping Victor's eyes. Several seconds later, Victor goes limp like a rag doll. His head rolls back, his eyelids start twitching, and then he passes out.

Superior Jackie releases the metal binds off Victor. Karl rushes over and helps Akisha catch Victor before he falls to the ground. They slowly lower Victor to the floor. Leo walks over, brushing off his sleeves.

"Are you alright?" Superior Jackie asks Leo.

"Yeah, I'm fine," Leo responds, using the back of his hand to wipe the corner of his mouth. "What did you do, Akisha?"

Akisha sighs while looking down at Victor. "Superior Jackie and I were able to find a technique in the archives that could help neutralize a magic-wielder when their eyes glow and they go into a rage. It looks like we arrived before things got worse."

Leo looks down at Victor's unconscious body. "Will he be okay?" he asks with concern.

Superior Jackie steps next to Leo and places a caring hand on his shoulder, looking down at Victor. "He will be. But right now, we need to take him back to his bed. I'm unsure how long it will be before he wakes up or how he will react.

But when he does, we'll be ready for a debrief over what happened tonight.

"Talk about perfect timing," Karl comments. "What brought you here? Besides the new empath raging out?"

"I wanted to see his eyes glowing for myself," Superior Jackie responds. She looks down at the unconscious Victor and says, "Like you said, Karl. Talk about perfect timing. I don't know what would have happened if we hadn't shown up. I can sense the power flowing within him. If he were any stronger, this warehouse might have been turned into rubble."

Victor bolts up on his bed in a panic. He looks around the room frantically, breathing rapidly, still wearing his suit. Leo darts into the room.

"Hey, hey, hey," Leo says as he jumps into bed with Victor and pulls him into his arms to help calm him down. "*Shhh. Shhh.* It's okay. You're back in your hotel room."

Victor begins to calm down as Leo holds him and strokes his hair while rocking back and forth.

Victor calms down but is still shaking. "How long was I out?" Victor asks.

Leo pulls away enough to look into Victor's eyes. "You've been out for two days."

CHAPTER SEVENTEEN

Victor steps out of the shower and puts on shorts and a T-shirt. When he walks into the living room, several people are sitting around: Leo, Karl, Akisha, Madame Jeanette, Eddie, Superior Jackie, and an older gentleman he hasn't met before.

The gentleman has a neatly trimmed salt-and-pepper beard and thick gray and black hair. He is wearing a gray and silver suit with a Western look. Instead of a standard tie, he wears a bolo tie with a deep blue sodalite stone with white markings. His boots are shiny black and gray, made out of stingray skin.

Leo approaches Victor, places a hand between his shoulders, and introduces him to the new guest. "Victor, I believe you already met Eduardo Leon, and this is Superior Charles Parker. Eddie is a Chancellor in my coven. Superior Charles is my Superior, and he is also-"

"*An Empath*," Victor interrupts softly.

Superior Charles remains seated, studying Victor for a few moments. Victor can feel the superior's eyes burrowing deep into him. He has always had a sense of someone watching him, but this is different. Victor can actually feel Superior Charles, even though they are ten feet away.

"Why are you scared, young empath?" Superior Charles finally asks.

Victor looks around nervously. "I'm not scared, Superior."

"Young man, you know you cannot lie to an empath," Superior Charles says in a husky Southern drawl. "After I heard about what happened, I felt it was necessary to meet you myself." He looks around the room, "Everyone but Superior Jackie may leave us."

With that, everyone makes their way into Leo's room. Leo makes eye contact with Victor and pats his shoulder.

"May Leo stay, Superior?" Victor asks. After a moment of silence, Superior Charles gestures to Leo to exit.

Leo gives Victor a subtle nod.

As he closes the door behind him, Leo looks at Victor and mouths, *"Everything will be okay."* He winks at Victor before shutting the door.

Superior Jackie sits on the couch and pats the seat beside her. "Please, have a seat, my young empath." Victor looks between the two superiors and then takes a seat. As soon as he sits down, Superior Jackie hands Victor a glass of water.

"Thank you, Superior Jackie," Victor says as he takes the glass. Victor feels like he's 10 years old and in trouble with his parents.

"Victor Russo, correct?" Superior Charles asks. "The grandson of the late Empath Marie Russo."

Victor nods, "That's correct. My grandmother's name was Marie Russo. Did you know her?"

Superior Charles snaps his fingers to create a small flame to light a cigar. He takes a few puffs as he slides the ashtray on the table closer to him. "She was an incredible witch. It was such a tragedy when I heard she left us. It's a shame you never got a chance to learn from her or your mother."

"Thank you, I think," Victor says sheepishly as he drinks water.

"Tell me," Superior Charles continues as he puffs his cigar, "what happened back at the warehouse?"

Victor looks down at his water glass, trying to recollect what happened. He takes a deep and nervous breath as he tries to answer the question. "I . . . I don't remember much."

"It's okay, young empath. Tell me what you remember," Superior Charles says while exhaling a puff from his cigar.

Victor looks at his glass a little longer before he looks up at Superior Charles. "The day was long. Karl and I were practicing several air spells. I was picking things up quickly. He decided to teach me some air-pushing skills. As I went through the motions, I started to get better and stronger."

Victor's gaze shifts away from Superior Charles as he continues. "I could feel the air around me. The air started to feel solid, making it easier for me to push around. Then, things got fuzzy. All of a sudden, I was floating in the air. After that, I don't know what else happened."

"You don't remember the fight?" Superior Charles inquires.

Victor pinches his eyebrows together, giving both superiors a look of confusion. "There was a fight? Between whom?"

Superior Jackie places a gentle hand on Victor's leg. "You attacked Leo and Karl, my dear."

Victor is shocked by the news. "*What?* Did I hurt them?"

Superior Jackie pats Victor's leg. "No, you didn't hurt them. However, Leo needed a new jacket. Akisha and I were able to stop you before things got worse."

Victor opens his mouth a little as he starts to remember more. He licks his lips, "I . . . I . . . "

"Yes?" Superior Charles responds.

"I remember cold metal wrapping around me. It was tight around my arms and legs. Then it felt like I could hardly breathe because something cold started wrapping around my chest and neck. There was flashing, like a strobe light. It was directly in my eyes. Then, I woke up in my bed."

Superior Jackie sits back in her seat. "Akisha and I had to use our Metal Magic to bind you. You were starting to lose control. Akisha used some Light Magic to knock you out. After that, you were on a 24-hour watch until you woke up. We didn't know what would happen when you did. Thankfully, after a few nights of rest, you returned to normal."

Victor starts to feel sick. His stomach turns as he tries to figure out what to ask next. "What happened to me?"

Superior Jackie reaches into her bag sitting on the floor and pulls out a thick folder. She opens it and hands the folder to Victor. "It's called *Rage*. It's an uncommon occurrence that happens to empaths. Empaths can channel and absorb emotions from others. But sometimes, those emotions can be 'poisonous,' causing an empath to rage out."

Victor looks through the papers in the folder Superior Jackie handed him. "So, someone was pushing their emotions on me to poison me?"

"Yes, for the most part," Superior Jackie answers. "We don't know who it was. By the time Charles got to the warehouse, the presence of the person who might have done this to you was no longer around."

"What about my eyes?" Victor asks as he looks at the two superiors.

"I can answer that one for you, young empath," Superior Charles responds, taking a drag from his cigar. "Some of the most powerful witches or warlocks with an ability will sometimes have glowing eyes, based on the specialty they are wielding. Your grandmother's eyes used to glow when she was conjuring a powerful spell."

"Do your eyes glow?" Victor asks Superior Charles.

"No. I'm not as powerful as your grandmother. You might be the most powerful empath warlock, even before me. That's saying something."

Superior Jackie takes the folder back from Victor. "Even though Charles is an empath like you and can control all the specialties known to us, you will become more powerful than him or me. You could become the next High Priest or even the Grand Warlock."

Victor shakes his head and bolts up from his seat. "But I don't want that. I don't want to be some superior. I don't even know how to be a warlock. I'm not even in a coven. I'm only 32 years old, much younger than both of you. No offense." He turns sheepish after that last comment.

"None taken, young empath," Superior Charles responds as he blows a puff from his cigar. He puts his cigar between his teeth as he reaches into the inside pocket of his jacket. He then starts patting around. "Where did I put it? Ah! Here it is." Superior Charles pulls out a silver metal card the size of a credit card and holds it to Victor. "Take this. It might help next time someone tries to give you their poisoned emotion."

Victor takes the card from Superior Charles. "Thank you. But won't you need this?"

"No, that's for you," Superior Charles answers, puffing his cigar. "It's an artifact I created for empaths. Keep it on you at all times. And if you're naked, keep it close to you. It will help repel emotions that are being forced on you, especially tainted ones." He stands up, as does Superior Jackie and Victor. Victor cranes his head as Superior Charles towers over him. "Once you finish your basic specialties lessons, come see me, and I'll assist you with your empathic ability."

Superior Jackie smiles gently while placing her hand on Victor's shoulder, giving a comforting squeeze.

"Until we meet again, young empath," Superior Charles says as he shakes Victor's hand. Leo opens the connecting door when the superiors take their leave. "Good evening, Superior Jackie, Superior Charles."

Superior Charles stops and speaks in a low, husky voice so only Leo could hear. *"Take care of our young empath."* Leo looks over at Victor, who has now sat back down. Superior Charles looks over his shoulder, *"He's going to be the most powerful warlock you've ever seen in your lifetime."*

Once the superiors exit the room, Leo walks over to Victor.

"Hey there, how are you doing?" Leo asks, placing his hands in his pockets.

Victor licks his lips and speaks softly. "I don't know how to feel right now."

Leo removes his jacket and vest and sits beside Victor. "The others left a few minutes ago. Would you like me to stay with you tonight?"

Victor nods and then rests his head on Leo's shoulder. Leo wraps an arm around Victor's shoulders and turns on the TV. Victor feels a little uneasy after speaking with the superiors. His mind questions why his grandmother kept all this hidden from him before she passed away. Why didn't his mother tell him anything? But Victor is still too tired, after the toll his body has been through the past few days. Victor can tell he needs to rest.

Victor and Leo watch the TV in silence until they retire to their bedrooms.

CHAPTER EIGHTEEN

The next day, Karl tests Victor on all the spells he's learned. Victor ensured he brought the silver card with him so he wouldn't rage out again.

"You're a very quick study," Karl proudly tells Victor. "And I'm happy you're not raging out today."

Victor stops his air throws to take a quick breath. "I'm sorry about that. I didn't know what was happening. I'm just glad I didn't hurt anyone."

Karl pats Victor's shoulder. "Hey, no hard feelings. It wasn't you that night. You shouldn't have to feel sorry for your actions." Karl looks over at Leo, "I think he's ready."

Leo gets up from his seat and brings Victor his jacket. "You sure he's ready?" he asks Karl.

Victor looks between Karl and Leo. "Ready? Ready for what?"

Leo tosses Victor his jacket. "Suit up. We're going to fight."

Victor gives Leo a confused look as Leo approaches his spot inside a circle. "I don't know if I'm ready for a fight," Victor states as he puts on his jacket. "What if I rage out again?"

Leo cracks his knuckles and neck, shaking his arms and shoulders to loosen up. "Don't worry about that. You've got your silver card on you, right? You'll be fine." Leo bounces up and down a few times, swinging his arms around him. He takes a deep breath and then prepares to fight. "I'll go easy on you." He gives Victor a wink.

Victor walks over to his spot in the circle, nervously thinking, *I'm not sure if I should do this.* Victor looks over at Karl, standing at the circle's edge with his arms crossed. Karl stands tall, with his muscular chest puffed out. Karl gives

Victor an assuring nod. Victor takes a deep breath and looks at Leo, waiting for the signal to start.

Karl opens his arms wide, his palms facing outward. Using Air Magic, he creates a dome. The clouds swirl around in the barrier like little hurricanes. Victor watches as the dome traces the circle on the floor and connects to the top. As soon as the dome is completed, Karl swings his hands into a loud clap, creating an air pulse from his hands as the signal to . . .

"*FIGHT!*" Karl's shout echoes around the warehouse.

"Why all the fanfare?" Leo comments to Karl.

Karl shrugs his shoulders and smiles brightly, amused by Leo's annoyance.

Leo turns his attention back to Victor and gives him a devilish smirk as he prepares for his first move. His hands start to glow yellow and orange, engulfed in flames. He throws an arm as if tossing a frisbee, and a fireball is flung toward Victor. Victor throws a palm outward and sends an air pulse to block the fireball, but it doesn't stop it.

Victor becomes worried, flings his hands out in front of him, and turns his face, anticipating being hit with a fireball. He slowly opens one eye and sees that he has captured the fireball in an air bubble. Before he could react, Leo throws another fireball, making contact, and Victor went flying back.

Victor coughs while laying on his back. "Ugh, Fuck! What the hell, man?" Victor groans as he struggles to get back onto his feet.

Leo flings another fireball, which Victor blocks perfectly. "I told you I'm not going easy on you, young empath."

Victor gets back on his feet and starts throwing air punches. Leo uses his forearms to block and knock them around. Leo then spins around and uses both palms to throw a green flame. Victor twirls his wrists together, creating a white tornado from his cupped palms. The tornado revolves around the flame.

Karl nods, his face very impressed. "Well, looks like I don't need to show him that move tomorrow," he says aloud.

The tornado sucks the flame in, causing the tornado to become the flame. It spins around between Leo and Victor. Victor pulls his arms back a little, then pushes his palms forward, tossing the spell back at Leo.

Leo flies back and gets knocked into the barrier.

Victor is shocked as he still holds the green-flamed tornado, "Holy Crap! I'm so sorry, Le–"

Before Victor can finish, Leo rolls a large red fireball like a bowling ball. The impact causes Victor to lose the green twister as he falls forward. As the green flame scatters throughout the dome, Karl quickly waves his hand across the air, conjuring his Water Magic to eliminate the flame before it causes any damage. Leo gets back on his feet and sees Victor face down on the floor, trying to get up.

"You let your guard down. You need to stop doing that if you plan to win," Leo shouts from across the circle. "And what did I say about fire tornadoes?"

Victor becomes upset with himself. He picks himself up as Leo gets ready to throw another attack. As Victor returns to his feet, he makes fists with his hands, and air swirls around them. He starts tossing air bubbles the size of basketballs and just as solid. Leo counterattacks and blasts the bubbles into smoke. He looks over at Victor and starts to get nervous. Victor's eyes are glowing.

"Um, Victor," Leo swallows a dry gulp, "your eyes."

Victor stops and stands straight. "Are you just saying that to declare me the winner?"

"Victor! Are you in there?" Karl shouts.

Victor looks confused at Karl. "Of course, I am. What's wrong with both of you?"

Leo takes a chance and starts throwing fireballs at a rapid pace. Victor snaps back into the fight and defends himself from Leo's attacks. He dodges the rain of fireballs and starts jumping and stepping on air-made steps under his feet, allowing him to move around the circle. When Victor gets a chance, he creates an air rope and lassos Leo's wrists together.

Leo looks down at his wrists and then at Victor, suddenly shocked. Before Leo can counteract the spell, Victor pulls Leo off his feet. When Leo is a couple of feet away, Victor throws his palm out and pushes Leo, slamming him to the ground.

When Victor lands on his feet, he looks over at Leo. Leo is not moving. The glow in Victor's eyes disappears, and he rushes over to Leo in fear.

"Fuck! Leo!" He runs over and drops down to Leo's side. "Leo! Leo, are you okay?"

Victor didn't see it coming.

Leo smacks a flame into Victor's face, causing him to fly back. Victor rolls around when he lands and finishes on his back.

Karl ends the fight. "Winner! Warlock Oliveira!"

Victor groans as he lies on the ground. As he opens his eyes, he sees the top of the dome starting to disappear. Leo looks down at him with his hands on his hips. Leo clicks his tongue against his teeth as though he is disappointed.

"What did I tell you?" Leo asks as he holds out a hand to help Victor up. "Stop letting your guard down." Victor takes Leo's hand and is lifted off the ground. "Let me take a look at you," Leo says as he examines Victor's face. He cups a hand under Victor's chin and inspects the damage. "Still got your beard and eyebrows. So, the flame wasn't as intense as I thought."

Victor pushes Leo's hands off his face. "That was pretty crappy what you did. Letting me think that I hurt you."

Leo laughs as he brushes the sleeves of Victor's jacket. "Maybe you'll learn your lesson next time you're in a fight. Never trust those who are on the ground. You don't know what defensive attack they have to slam in your face."

Karl walks over to Victor and Leo, smiling proudly. "I'm impressed, youth empath. I was also very impressed when you created that tornado. That was *very* wicked. Wicked in a good way. And I'm also pleased you didn't rage out when your eyes started glowing."

The leather-clad woman walks over with a brass tray with a bottle of champagne and three glasses. A small green box sits in the middle of the glasses. Karl hands Victor and Leo a glass and then pours them a drink.

Karl raises his glass and toasts, "To our young empath. Even though you might have lost the fight, you are a quick study. Here's to the next part of your journey."

They clink their glasses together. As Karl takes a swig, he remembers the box on the tray. "Oh, this is for you." He takes the box and hands it to Victor. "I got you something."

Victor hands Leo his glass and takes the box from Karl. He opens the box, revealing a silver bracelet encrusted with crushed celestite. As Victor removes it from the box, Leo puts their glasses on the tray and takes the bracelet from Victor. He then proceeds to fasten it to Victor's wrist.

Karl explains his gift. "Even though you have a ring to help you with your Air Magic skills, this bracelet should help with any rage issues. While you were passed out, I had my staff investigate what artifacts could help you."

Victor looks at the bracelet on his wrist and takes back his glass. "Thank you, Karl. I greatly appreciate it."

"Well, I was anticipating one more day of training, but I think we are finished here," Karl mentions as he takes another swig. "It's time for you to move on to your next specialty. Until we meet again, Empath Russo. And when it's time for you to join a coven, think of me when you do." Karl winks at Victor.

Meanwhile, in Madame Jeanette's home, she sits at her table with Superior Jackie and Superior Charles.

"Well," Superior Charles states as he exhales a puff from his cigar, "what do you see, Jeanette?"

Madame Jeanette takes a deep, long drag from her pipe and blows the tobacco cloud over her table. A few flashes of light look like lightning in a storm cloud. She leans back into her seat and strokes her chin as if she has a beard.

"We must be cautious with Empath Russo," Madame Jeanette explains. "Someone out there would like to see him be used under their power. If we do not stop them, we might be unable to stop Victor. And if we cannot stop Victor, then I feel it will be us or him."

She pauses and tilts her head in confusion. "His life could be in danger as well."

"So, whoever was at the warehouse wanted Victor to rage out," Superior Jackie comments.

"No necessarily," Madame Jeanette responds. "They might have just been trying to hurt him, as well as hurt those around him."

"Either way, we need to keep Victor safe," Superior Charles remarks. "The last thing we want is the council on our asses, having us answer questions we don't know. For now, let's just keep things to ourselves until we can figure out who is going after our young empath."

CHAPTER NINETEEN

Victor and Leo walk into Victor's room, laughing and celebrating Victor's first lesson completion. Victor notices his luggage is packed and sitting in the living room. Then, the maid walks out of the bedroom. Victor exhales a low, deep sigh because he knows what's coming.

"Oh, hello, Mr. Russo, Mr. Oliveira!" the maid says chipperly. "I have all your bags packed and ready for you to check out. If you like, I can have your suits cleaned for you before you go. I also packed lunch to take with you since it's going to be a long trip to your next lesson."

Victor looks over at Leo. Leo sees Victor's face in his peripheral vision, then pierces his lips together and lightly shakes his head as if to say, *"Don't ask right now."* As the maid continues to ramble on, Victor starts to tune her out. He drifts out of it, and then suddenly, he's no longer in his room. He blinks a couple of times and then starts to look around. *"This isn't my hotel room. Where am I?"* Victor says to himself. He looks around, and then he sees someone familiar. *"Amber? Lupe?"*

"Amber!"

"Lupe!"

Amber and Lupe are cuddling on the couch, watching TV. Amber looks disgruntled as she glances at her phone.

"Ugh!" Amber projects out. "That asshole isn't answering me back."

"Maybe he's busy," Lupe responds while watching TV.

"Victor isn't like this. He responds right away. It's been almost two days. I'm starting to get worried," Amber proclaims.

Victor walks up to Amber and Lupe on the couch. *"Hey! I'm right here!"* Victor starts waving his arms around and then stands right in front of them. It wasn't until he realized, *"Wait, you can't see me. What's going on?"*

"I think I should go check on him," Amber says, getting up from the couch.

"You're going to fly to Phoenix to see him?" Lupe asks, discouraged by Amber's overreaction.

"If I have to, I will," Amber responds as she heads to the bedroom. "Just call Elliott. He lives closer to Victor," Lupe suggests.

Victor tries to speak to them, but they still can't hear him. *"Guys, I'm right here. I'm standing right in front of you."*

"Elliott is on back-to-back trips right now," Amber mentions from the bedroom. "He won't be home until Thursday."

"Then ask Frank to go," Lupe offers. "Doesn't he live in Phoenix too?"

Suddenly, Victor is back in his hotel room. Leo is holding Victor by the arms; his face filled with worry. "Victor, are you okay?"

Victor shakes his head out of his trance. He notices the maid is gone, and it's just the two of them. "Y-Yeah. At least, I think I'm okay."

"You looked like you were a million miles away," Leo says with concern.

Victor still feels a little dizzy. He walks over to the wet bar and grabs a bottle of water. "For a moment, I was looking at Amber and Lupe. I think I was in their home."

Leo perks up. "You were visiting your friends?"

"I guess, but they couldn't hear me," Victor responds.

"Victor, you just had your first astral projecting experience," Leo smiles widely.

Victor looks at Leo with a perplexed expression. "What? I was astral projecting? I thought I was imagining things."

Leo grabs Victor's arms and squeezes with excitement. "No, you were there with them. How was it? Did you feel your body tingle all over?"

"No, I didn't feel anything. But I could hear them," Victor explains.

"Wow! That's not easy to accomplish on the first time," Leo exclaims.

Victor walks over to his phone and feels depressed. "I guess I'm just missing my friends. They are really worried about me. This is the longest I've ever been apart from them." Victor starts reading over the text messages, feeling lonely, even though Leo is there with him. He wants to respond, giving them some relief and not to call for a wellness check, but he doesn't know how to respond. Victor can't tell his friends he's a warlock, can he? Deep down, he knows he can't, but his friends are like his family. He doesn't like keeping secrets from them.

Leo walks up behind Victor and places a hand on Victor's shoulder. "I think you should start thinking about cutting ties with them. The sooner you do it, the easier it is to move on."

Victor shrugs Leo's hand off his shoulder and turns to look at Leo. "I've known these guys for a while. Elliott and I became flight attendants together almost 10 years ago. I've known Lucas since high school. How am I supposed to throw away all these years of friendship?"

Leo takes a seat on the couch and sighs. "The mundane won't understand, and it's natural for them to fear us. Need I remind you that we age slower than them? By the time you're in your 70s, you will still appear to be in your 30s. You will see your friends pass away before you."

Victor sits on the other side of the couch while Leo continues. "Do you know how old Superior Charles is? He's 147, but he looks in his late 50s, which is surprising, considering how much he smokes and drinks. Madame Jeanette is just over 100. She's lived in Louisiana her entire life. And she tends to keep to herself because that's the only way she can detach herself from society. Her ability makes it difficult for her to make friends, including with people of magic."

Victor looks down at his phone, seeing all his friends' social media posts. "When are we leaving?"

Leo sees that Victor is depressed and sighs deeply. "We don't need to go to your next lesson for another week. Tell you what, why don't we take a break? You go home and see your friends."

Victor lights up at Leo's offer. "Really? I can go home for a while?"

"Yes, but I'm coming with you. I need to watch out for you in case something happens," Leo explains.

Victor slumps his shoulders like a pouty teenage girl. "Aw, come on. Really?"

Leo stands up and buttons his jacket. "Yes, really. Make sure you get everything ready. I'll make arrangements for us to go to Phoenix."

Leo walks back to his room and closes the connecting door behind him. He is startled when he sees someone sitting at the dining table. "Damn it, Derek! What did I tell you about sneaking up on me?"

Derek is a cleanly shaved man with thick brown hair and green eyes. He is wearing a grey windowpane suit, a light pink shirt, and a dark pink tie. He looks at Leo as though he suspects something.

"So, you're going to Phoenix? When were you going to tell me?" Derek disputes.

Leo becomes more aggravated at Derek's appearance. "You know I'm Victor's mentor, and I will be with him until his lessons are complete. And why does that matter to you? We're no longer together."

"You're still my husband," Derek comments as he crosses his legs.

Leo rolls his eyes as he walks into his bedroom. "Did you astral project here to remind me of that? This could have been an email."

"I'm just wondering why you're going to Phoenix with that empath when he has no lessons there," Derek comments.

Leo returns from the bedroom with a garment bag. "Because I am to be with him the entire time. And after what happened the other day, it's safer if I stay with him."

Derek gets up and walks over to Leo. "I heard what happened to him. I guess it was a good thing you were there. Because we both know Karl couldn't handle the empath himself."

Leo glares at Derek, tossing his garment bag on the couch. "The empath has a name."

Derek shrugs his shoulders with a disgusted look plastered on his face. "I don't care. He's not superior to me."

Leo looks at Derek from the corner of his eye. "He's superior to all of us. And when he finally comes to terms with who he is, you will eat those words." Leo walks back into the bedroom.

"I don't give a damn who he is, and I'm not going to bend a knee to a homewrecker," Derek says with some hostility.

"Homewrecker?" Leo exclaims, walking back into the living room with his suitcase. "You're the one who cheated on me. With a throuple from what I remember."

Derek coyly looks over his shoulder, "Maybe you should have been home more often to ensure I didn't wander, Leopold."

Leo moves Derek away from the wet bar to retrieve a couple of water bottles from the fridge. "I can't wait until you're gone for good. Then I can be done with you."

Derek leans down to whisper into Leo's ear, "You'll never be done with me, sweetheart, unless you know what's good for you. Don't forget the oath you took when we got married."

Leo stands up, nose-to-nose with Derek. Even though Derek isn't there physically, Leo can still feel Derek's static coming off the tip of his nose and the warmth of Derek's breath. "Don't worry, I'm already looking into how to break that oath."

Derek kisses the tip of Leo's nose and gives a vicious grin. "Good luck with that." Leo becomes enraged, causing his fists to burst into flames.

Leo gets startled when he hears the door open. He quickly extinguishes his fists and turns to his attention toward the door.

"Leo?" Victor peeks into Leo's room. "Did you get everything ready for us to head to Phoenix?"

Leo looks back at where Derek was standing. Derek had vanished just when Victor appeared. Leo collects himself before responding to Victor. "Almost. Let's get a bellman to pick up our things."

Victor and Leo walk into Victor's apartment. Victor drops his suitcase next to the door and turns on the light in the entryway. "Welcome to my place. Sorry for the mess."

Leo walks further inside and looks around. Victor's apartment is neat and tidy. "What mess?"

Victor calls out to his Amazon Echo to turn on all the lights. He tosses his garment bag on the back of a chair at the dining table. "What do you want to order for dinner?" Before Leo could answer, there's a knock at the door. When he opens it, the maid stands there with a large bag in her arms. Victor's jaw drops when he sees her.

"Close your mouth, dear; you'll attract flies." She pushes her way in and goes to the dining room. "I wanted to make sure you boys have a nice meal tonight." She takes out two big to-go boxes. "Where are your plates, sweetie?" Victor's mouth is still open as he points to the cabinet where the plates are.

The maid walks over, closes Victor's mouth as she enters the kitchen, and gathers a couple of plates and silverware. "You like your steak medium-rare, correct? And Leo, you like yours rare. I remember that. Victor, I got you that chimichanga or chimichurri, whatever you call it. That herby green sauce you like to put on your steak. I remember that it's your favorite. I've never had it before. So, I tried it the other night, and I can see why you enjoy it on your steak. I think I'm going to start having chimichurro sauce with my steak now."

She walks back to the table and plates their food. Victor is still speechless as to what's going on. Leo chuckles behind his hand, trying so hard not to laugh out loud watching Victor's utter confusion. After a few more moments of the maid talking and gathering the discarded to-go containers, she says her goodbyes and leaves.

Victor stares at the door, "What . . . The Fuck . . . Just Happened?"

Leo laughs as he puts his jacket on the back of his seat and sits down, placing his napkin on his collar. "Don't overthink it and just eat."

CHAPTER TWENTY

A couple days later, Victor greets his friends at the door. "I'm surprised Elliott was able to make it."

Elliott pulls Victor in for a tight, bone-crushing hug. "The last day of my trip fell apart, so I was able to come home early." Elliott smacks Victor in the arm, "And where the fuck have you been?"

"Yeah!" Amber says as she pushes past Elliott and backhands Victor in the arm. "I've been worried sick about you."

"She wanted to fly out here to check on you," Lupe says, hugging Victor.

Victor looks over at Amber fondly. "Aww, Amber. You have a lady boner for me."

"Fuck off," Amber says aggressively as she pushes her way inside. "Where's the booze?" As Amber walks into the living room, she sees Leo sitting on the couch. "Hello?" she asks Leo while giving him a confused look. "Victor, who's the guy?"

Victor makes his way past his friends. "Oh, sorry. Everyone, this is my pal, Leo. He's visiting on a layover. Leo, these are my friends, Elliott, Frank, Amber, and her fiancée, Lupe."

"Pleased to meet you," Leo says, waving at everyone as they enter the living room.

"On a layover? Do you fly with us?" Frank asks.

Leo sees Victor behind his friends, pleading to play along. "No, I fly for Legacy Air," he responds. He glances over and sees Victor thanking him quietly.

"Oh, Legacy," Frank says in excitement. "I heard they just started flying to Johannesburg. I've been waiting for us to start flying there."

Leo crosses his legs and continues to play along. "Well, I'm based in San Francisco and don't feel like transferring to New York."

"So, Victor, how did you and Leo meet?" Elliott asks while giving Victor a sly look.

Victor starts to freeze up. Leo notices and answers for him. "We met at a layover in Mexico City. Our crews were checking in at the same time. My crew was discussing where we wanted to eat, and Victor chimed in, offering us suggestions. I invited him to join, and it ended up being the two of us. We hung out, exchanged numbers, and stayed in touch. When I told him I'll be in Phoenix, he invited me over."

"How come we've never heard about you before?" Elliott asks Leo while looking suspiciously over at Victor.

"It was a couple of months ago. And we're only pals," Victor says while trying to contain his nervousness.

Elliott squints his eyes and gives Victor an *"Mmhmm."*

Victor changes the topic by saying, "So, Amber, you mentioned booze?"

As the day passes, everyone laughs and updates Victor on their lives. Elliott starts pouring more drinks. Amber gently caresses Lupe's legs in her lap. Frank teases Elliott's ear. Elliott swats Frank's hand.

"So, how's your uncle?" Amber asks Victor.

"My uncle?" Victor questions with confusion.

"Yeah, the one that had knee surgery," Amber explains.

Victor almost forgot his lie. "Sorry, I thought you meant the one in rehab in Chicago. He's fine."

"Wait, you have an uncle in rehab?" Frank asks, almost snapping his neck to look at Victor.

"Yeah, that's why I was in Chicago last week. I thought I told you?" Victor's friends shake their heads. "That's why I wasn't texting all the time. It was a big ordeal. He almost OD'd. My dad couldn't make it out with some of the family, so he asked me to go." Victor starts to sweat, hoping his friends don't press for more information.

"So, Leo, how old are you?" Amber asks, changing the subject back to Leo.

Victor almost chokes on his drink.

"I'm 35," Leo responds.

"Where are you from?" Amber interrogates.

"São Paulo," Leo responds coolly. Even though he is not an empath, he can tell Amber is very suspicious of him.

"I'm going to São Paulo for the first time in a couple of days," Frank mentions. "You need to tell me the best place to eat. And your favorite bathhouse."

"Frank!" Victor shouts. "Why are you asking him that?"

"What?" Frank responds innocently. "I heard they're fun in Brazil. And one of the guys on my crew told me he wants to come with me. Pun intended."

Leo laughs, "I'm sorry, I've never been to one. But I hope you two can find one and have fun."

Daytime turns to night, and Victor says goodbye to his friends. They hug and give air kisses over each cheek as they leave. Victor plops back down on the couch next to Leo with contentment.

"Your friends are fun," Leo says.

"They are, huh? It was nice that they were able to make it. Too bad Lucas and Jon live in another city and aren't flight attendants, they might have joined as well." Victor turns his head and looks up into Leo's eyes. They look at each other in silence. Leo looks back and forth between Victor's eyes and lips. Victor licks his lips; Leo does the same. They start to lean into each other until they are interrupted.

"Ahem!" Leo and Victor are startled, thinking they were alone. They look over to see Derek sitting at the dining table. He's dressed casually with his legs crossed. He gives Leo and Victor a pointed look. "Am I interrupting something?" he asks with a touch of hostility.

Leo moves away from Victor and sits up. "What the hell are you doing here, Derek?"

"Seeing what the fuss was about," Derek responds in a sassy tone. "You've been here for a few days already, and everything seems fine. You don't need to be with the empath the entire time." He leans back far enough to get a glance inside the bedroom. "Or sleeping in the same bed with him."

Victor gives Derek a confused look. "I'm sorry, who are you?"

Derek holds out his left hand, showing off the wedding ring. "That warlock's husband."

Victor turns his attention to Leo. "You're married?"

"We're separated," Leo says as he walks over to Derek. "Why the hell are you spying on me? I could have you fined for invasion of privacy."

"I'm making sure you don't do anything you're not supposed to be doing," Derek replies.

"Oh, you're one to talk!" Leo becomes aggressive and crosses his arms. "Get your ass out of here and back in your own body."

Derek leans over the side of his seat and looks back at Victor. "You better be careful, empath. He took an oath in this marriage, and I would *hate* to see anything happen to him if he breaks it." He stands up and looks Leo in the eyes. "*Right*, Leopold? You wouldn't want to *break* the oath." Derek disappears like mist in the wind.

Leo's fists burst into flames as he groans aggressively. He lifts his head, closes his eyes, and slowly takes a deep breath. As he exhales, the fire around his fists extinguishes. He turns to look at Victor, who has his arms and legs crossed and a disapproving look on his face.

"Would you like to explain?" Victor inquires.

With another heavy sigh, Leo rubs the back of his neck. "That was Derek Hernandez. And yes, he is my husband. But we've been separated for over three years now."

Leo drags his feet back over to the couch, sits beside Victor, and slouches. "We got married back in 1982. I was 24, and he was 22. We met a few years prior as we began learning our Fire specialty. He would tease me as his way of flirting. Derek was also the third guy I ever dated. When our families found out about us, they figured it would be good for us to marry because their covens were at each other's throats on the council."

Leo looks down at his left palm and rubs it with his right thumb. "So, as part of the marriage to help keep the peace, we took a blood oath. I was young and stupid. I didn't think about the consequences. We enjoyed each other's company, but things started to go downhill after our 30th anniversary. The council approached me to become an instructor for Fire Magic. I think Derek got jealous because he wasn't asked. Five years later, they asked me to become a mentor. That's when things between us became difficult."

Leo leans back into the cushion and rests his head on the back of the couch. "I was gone for almost three years and mentored seven new witches and warlocks. One night, when I was free, I astral projected to check on him. That's when I saw him getting double penetrated and had his lips wrapped around a third member. I vanished before anyone noticed I was there. I was so furious that I went home right away. As he walked through the mirror, I stood on the other side, waiting for him. We got into a huge argument and almost burned our house down. I mentioned the blood oath we took, and then he laughed."

Leo focuses on his palm, where the knife cut his skin. "He then told me he never spoke the words correctly during the oath; only I did. I couldn't talk; I was so angry. I ran through the mirror so fast that it shattered. I sought out a seer who could see visions of the past. That's when I met Madame Jeanette. She helped me, and sure enough, only I said the words correctly. I was so upset that I went off the grid for a couple of months."

Leo starts fiddling with his thumb where his wedding ring used to be. "I returned to talk it over with Derek, and we tried to make things work. Little did I know, he was still seeing the couple. I moved out three years ago and got my place in San Francisco. But he keeps antagonizing me. When he found out about you, he's been on my ass, and not in a good way."

Victor calms down and starts to feel sorry for Leo. He is about to place a hand on his leg, but then he stops, not knowing if Derek will reappear. "I'm sorry that he's got you by the balls. And not in a good way." Leo gives Victor a broken smile, but then it fades as he knows he won't be happy for a while. "I'll get you some bedding for the couch. After this visit, we probably shouldn't share the same bed."

Derek walks out of the shadows and into a smoking lounge. The smell of tobacco and alcohol fills the air. Several witches and warlocks are dressed in all black, sitting in smokers' chairs and paying no mind to him. Derek walks up to a chair and stands to the side.

"I finally saw the empath in person, sort of. I think he's got something on him because I couldn't make him rage like last time," Derek informs the man in the chair.

The man's face is cloaked in the shadows. Derek can barely make out his features. The man takes a puff from his cigarette and blows it into Derek's face. "That's because you don't know how to push off your emotions while you're astral projecting, you nitwit." He takes another puff from his cigarette. "Do you know where the empath will be going next?"

"Kyoto, Japan, to learn Water Magic," Derek responds.

"Make preparations," the man orders. "It looks like Japan is going to be expecting a tsunami."

CHAPTER TWENTY-ONE

Victor and Leo arrive at the Kyoto Station by bullet train from Tokyo. As they make their way out of the exit, a woman in a black chauffeur's uniform holds up a black sign with their names in white calligraphy. Victor raises an eyebrow when he notices it's the same woman who met him at JFK Airport. Like before, she turns and walks away, making them follow her.

"Who hired her? She's a terrible chauffeur," Victor says to Leo.

"She's the sister of a superior, and she lost a bet. So, there's a sense of entitlement," Leo explains.

"So, can you please explain why we didn't just walk through a mirror to get here like we did to go from New York to Chicago?" Victor asks while placing his bags in the trunk.

Leo grins, "You didn't enjoy flying in first class, and the views from the bullet train? Besides, we needed to give your instructor time to prepare for your arrival." Victor gives him an unamused look. Leo's smile fades as he softly sighs. "There might have been a rumor through the grapevine that going through a portal isn't safe right now."

"Should I be worried?" Victor asks.

"Nah, we're good," Leo reassures.

Victor tries to use his ability to see if Leo is telling the truth, but he still isn't used to reading what he's looking at. As Leo loads the trunk, Victor focuses on Leo's aura. It swirls around, but Victor can't tell if it's a good sign or if Leo is deceiving him. Leo closes the trunk; the car drives off. Victor shakes his head in annoyance and then looks over at Leo.

Leo smirks with his hands in his pockets. "It's a nice day. Let's go for a walk." Victor raises an eyebrow, still annoyed over the situation, but complies and follows him.

They hop on a train and head to the Gion-Shijo station. After exiting the station, they start walking toward the Yasaka Shrine.

"I visited Kyoto a few years ago," Victor mentions as he looks around. "I came with my ex-boyfriend. We enjoyed our time, but unfortunately, it was raining most of the time we were visiting. We didn't see that many geishas walking around. But we saw a small performance at this center, not far from here. It was elegant."

They stop at a corner, waiting to cross. Leo looks down the street, which is blocked off to traffic. He places his hand on the small of Victor's back. "Well, you're in luck," Leo mentions. "We're going to see a tea ceremony."

"Oh?" Victor responds. He looks down the same street as Leo and notices several geishas.

As they walk down the street, many geishas stand outside, greeting patrons as they walk into the establishments. Halfway down, they stop in front of a tea house. A geisha wearing a light blue kimono comes down the steps and greets them.

"Mr. Oliveira, *irasshaimase*." She bows graciously. "We are pleased to see you again. This way, your favorite table is ready." Leo bows and thanks the geisha before they follow her inside. They take off their shoes and put on house slippers upon entering.

Victor and Leo follow the geisha to a table in the middle of the room, a few spots away from the stage. They sit on cushions, and another geisha kneels in front of them and pours the tea. When she's finished, she stands and bows before taking her leave.

Victor picks up his tea and inhales the aroma. When he takes a sip, the lights go down. The musicians start playing their traditional Japanese instruments. The air fills with the scent of cherry blossoms, even though it's not the season for them. The music feels as if it's surrounding Victor. As he looks onto the stage, two geishas start to perform their dance.

They move with poise and elegance. A few minutes later, another pair joins them on stage. The four perform an intricate dance with their fans. As Victor looks on, a bright red parasol opens in the back of the stage. It appears that no one is holding it. As the four geishas slowly make their way off the sides of the stage, the parasol moves closer to the audience. The parasol lifts, and a single geisha appears. The geisha is Chiyo Yamada.

Chiyo is dressed in a kimono in various shades of blue. The patterning resembles flowing water. Her obi belt is in various shades of gold, orange, white, and black, representing koi swimming.

Victor almost didn't realize who it was until he made eye contact with her, and she winks back. He was so mesmerized by her performance, he doesn't notice his tea floating. When he looks around, he sees water floating around like dragons flying.

Leo looks around and then over at Victor, who is amazed at what is happening. Leo smiles a little and can't take his eyes off Victor. He looks away right before Victor looks over at him.

Victor lets out a little chuckle, knowing Leo is trying to pretend he wasn't gazing at him before he looks back at Chiyo. The lights start to fade, and the music ends. The lights come back on, and Chiyo is gone. The audience applauds loudly.

Victor turns to Leo as a geisha pours them some more tea. "That was amazing. And I take it that everyone here are people of magic?"

"That's correct, my young empath warlock," Chiyo responds, sitting behind Victor and Leo, and has changed into a light red kimono with floral print, accessorized with a soft pink obi bow.

Victor jumps, startled, and holds his chest. "Why must everyone just pop up out of nowhere?" The geisha smiles gleefully as she pours another cup for Chiyo.

"I'm sorry, my young empath warlock, I didn't mean to startle you," Chiyo giggles as she takes a seat on the cushion beside Victor. "Did you enjoy the performance?"

"Yes, I enjoyed it very much. Everyone on stage was gorgeous, including you," Victor responds.

Chiyo bows her head with gratitude. "*Dōmo arigatō gozaimasu*, my young empath warlock." Chiyo and the geisha both bow their heads to one another before the geisha takes her leave. "I heard that you had visited Kyoto before. Was there any place you would like to visit again?"

"How did you know I was here before?" Victor asks.

Chiyo plays coy as she brings her tea up to her lips. "A little bird told me."

Victor side-eyes Leo, who shrugs. "Well, I don't know where to begin," Victor states. "I would enjoy being able to see it all again. I hope my instructor will give me some time between lessons."

"Well, I hope she does," Chiyo responds, setting her tea on the table.

"Victor, meet your Water Specialty Instructor, Chiyo Yamada," Leo mentions.

Chiyo gives Victor a wink. "And I never got to apologize about seeing you naked in your bathroom back in New Orleans."

Victor drops his smile and glares at Chiyo. "That's right, you appeared in my bathroom. Who else saw me naked?"

"I think only she and I," Leo responds. Then softly says, "Maybe Eddie." Leo takes a sip of his tea, looking away as Victor gives him a look of disgust and betrayal.

Chiyo leans over to Leo and speaks in Japanese. *"I bet you saw him naked more than once."*

Leo looks at Victor, holding back a coy smile, and responds in Japanese. *"Maybe a couple of times. Not on purpose, of course."*

Victor glares at both of them. "What are you talking about?"

"Nothing," Chiyo answers with a smirk while sipping her tea. "Have you started reading your books?"

"That's what he's been doing on the flight and train ride over," Leo answers.

Chiyo gives Leo a confused look. "You didn't go through the mirror?"

"No, we might have run into someone who may be after Victor and would pull him into the mirror realm," Leo informs.

Victor chokes on his tea. "I'm sorry? What did you say? You said I had nothing to worry about."

Chiyo and Leo look at each other. Chiyo gives Leo a nod to respond.

"We feel that someone is after you," Leo proclaims. "First, it was Magenta, and then when you raged out with Karl and me. If someone is after you, you would be most vulnerable walking through mirrors. There have been others that were captured in the mirror realm and never came back the same or never came back at all."

"So, does this mean we won't go through mirrors anymore?" Victor asks with concern. "Just for the time being. We are looking for protection spells and artifacts to protect us," Leo reassures.

"In the meantime, we took precautions at the hotel and where we will be training," Chiyo adds. "Just make sure you always keep the artifact from Superior Charles on your person at all times."

A couple of geishas walk up and set down bento boxes on the table. Victor's eyes grow wide with happiness. "Oh, this looks good." He picks up his chopsticks and starts digging in. As Victor eats away, he begins to feel dizzy. The room starts spinning around him. He remembers the restaurant in New York.

Fuck, not again, Victor thinks to himself.

Looking around with blurry vision, he sees that everyone is passed out. He notices two black figures walking his way. As they get closer, he feels water splashing on his face before he falls over and blacks out.

Victor sits up and looks around. He's no longer in the teahouse; he's in a glowing forest.

He notices he is now wearing a platinum silver suit. As he looks around, he can see the auras glowing around the plants, trees, and animals in his view. He gets up to his feet and starts walking around. There is no moon or sun in the sky. All he can see are the stars moving across the sky.

As he continues to walk through the forest, he spots a house in the distance. He tilts his head to study what he's looking at. It almost looks familiar, as though he's been there before. He keeps walking towards the house, but it keeps moving away. The closer he tries to get, the farther the house moves back. Victor stops and continues to look at the house. Suddenly, he thinks he hears a voice whispering to him. He starts to look around but does not see anyone.

"Victor?" Leo asks worriedly. "Victor, are you there? Come back to us."

Victor starts to moan as he opens his eyes. He sees Leo and Chiyo looking down at him. "W-where am I?" he says groggily. Leo helps him as he tries to sit up. Chiyo brings over a glass of water.

"You passed out at the teahouse, and we brought you to the hotel. You were out for like 30 minutes," Leo explains.

Victor takes the glass from Chiyo. "Thirty minutes? It felt like I was out for much longer." He drinks half the glass before he asks, "What happened? It was the restaurant in New York all over again."

Chiyo gently pats a damp cloth on Victor's face while she explains. "As soon as our food was delivered, everyone started to feel dizzy. When I started to notice, I gave myself a protection spell, but I couldn't get to you or Leo in time. I pretended to pass out in anticipation of an attack, and I was right."

"The two dressed in black," Victor comments. "They were after me, weren't they?"

Leo nods. "We believe so. Since I was passed out, Chiyo and her geisha took them on."

"I wish you could see it," Chiyo says to Victor with a little smile. She looks at Victor and clears her throat. "I mean, the two tried to knock out everyone. My geishas have artifacts in their hair to protect them from most spells. I laid there and waited for them to approach. When they got close enough, I attacked. As I fought them off, I saw Leo trying to crawl to you. He crawled on top of you to help protect you from any attacks."

"You tried to protect me even though you were passing out?" Victor asks Leo. Leo nods sheepishly.

Victor turns back to Chiyo and asks, "What happened to the two trying to come after me? Do we know where they came from?"

Chiyo uses her Water Magic to refill Victor's glass. "We are trying to figure that out. Apparently, they are as resilient as Magenta with the interrogation."

"So, we don't have any leads," Victor says, concerned. Chiyo and Leo shake their heads. Victor takes a deep breath and looks back at Chiyo. "When is my first lesson?"

Chiyo tilts her head, baffled by Victor's tenacity. "Are you sure you don't want to take a day off?"

"Nope, I'll be fine tomorrow," Victor responds. "Just let me know when and where."

Chiyo cheers up a bit. "Well then, get some rest. I have a tranquil spot, and the mundane won't disturb us." Chiyo gets up and walks to the door. She turns and bows to Victor and Leo, "*Konbanwa*, Empath Russo, and Leopold."

Once Chiyo exits, Leo gets up, but Victor grabs his arm. "Wait, I need to tell you something."

Leo sits back down with a concerned look. "What is it?"

"Where are my tarot cards?" Victor asks.

Leo tilts his head to the side. "They are in the top drawer of the dresser. Why?"

Victor takes note of Leo's curiosity. If he is to trust his mentor, he should inform him about everything that happens to him. "I guess I should probably tell you what happened to me when I passed out." He tells Leo what he saw while he was unconscious and goes into every detail he can remember.

Leo's face grows more and more worried. Leo turns away from Victor as he tries to comprehend what was told. He gets up and walks over to the dresser to take out the tarot cards. He remains silent as he sits beside Victor, handing him the deck.

"I think you should do your reading and see what the cards have to say," Leo suggests.

Victor hesitates a moment before taking the box. He takes a deep breath, removes the cards from the box, and starts shuffling. He focuses on his memory of the place he visited. The glowing forest, the moonless sky, the strange yet familiar house in the distance. Victor sits in silence as he sets the cards down and cuts them into three piles. Leo watches him return the three piles back into a single stack.

Victor starts flipping over the cards, and his eyes begin to tear. As he looks down at the six cards he set before him, his lower lip quivers. His eyes well up, knowing what he saw wasn't a dream.

Leo notices a tear running down Victor's cheek. He takes his knuckle to wipe it away. "What's the matter? What do you see?"

Victor takes a deep breath and licks his lips. He places his fingertips on the two cards stacked in the middle of all the other cards. The bottom card is "The Empress" and the card lying across it is "The Page of Cups."

"It's my mother. She's trying to speak to me."

CHAPTER TWENTY-TWO

Victor wakes up and stretches, as it's a brand-new day. He walks over to open the curtains and sees that his room faces Lake Biwa, which reminds him of his last visit here. Victor knows he is in Otsu, just outside of central Kyoto. As he takes in the beautiful morning view, he hears Leo knocking to come in. Victor smiles to see Leo, mainly because Leo has coffee.

"How did you sleep last night?" Leo asks as he hands Victor his coffee.

"Okay, I guess. I had trouble sleeping last night after I read the cards," Victor responds before sipping his coffee.

"I could hear you crying last night," Leo comments over the rim of his mug.

Victor looks up from his mug. "I was crying?"

Leo nods. "Yes. Whatever you were dreaming about made you sad. I wanted to crawl into bed with you and hold you, but I didn't know if it was appropriate."

Victor hides his disappointment. Regardless of what's going on in Leo's life, he would have enjoyed having Leo cuddled up with him. "If I was dreaming, I don't remember what it was."

"We can do a spell to find out," Leo suggests.

Before Victor could respond, there's a knock at the door.

"If it's that maid, I'm going to scream." Victor opens the door and sighs, relieved that it isn't the maid. It was just the bellman bringing in breakfast.

As soon as he was about to close the door, someone's cheerful voice rings through.

"Good morning, Darlings," the maid sings.

JESUS H. CHRIST! WHY?! WHY?! WHY?! is all Victor screams in his head. Leo cannot hold it in and bursts out laughing, almost tripping over a chair. He doesn't have to hear what Victor is saying in his head. It is written all over his face.

"I can't stay long," the maid says as she proceeds to the bedroom. "I'm here to pick up your suits and get them cleaned before you meet with Ms. Yamada this afternoon." She grabs Victor's suit and is about to walk out when she stops in front of Victor. "There is one more thing . . . " She reaches into her pocket and pulls out a cream-colored envelope with a green wax seal. " . . . this came for you last night."

She hands the envelope to Victor. "I was going to slide it under your door, but I wanted to make sure you got it personally. Something told me that it must be handed off to you. It feels very important. Make sure you read it right away, okay." The maid and the bellman exit, leaving Victor puzzled.

Leo walks over and examines the envelope in Victor's hand. "This envelope looks old. The paper is yellowed."

Victor sets down his mug and holds the envelope in both hands. "Who would send me a letter sealed with wax?"

Leo drops the mug when he notices the seal.

Victor jumps back just in time before his feet are covered in ceramic and hot coffee with cream. "What's the matter? What did you see?"

Leo starts tapping his finger rapidly against the seal. "This . . . this seal. This emblem. It belonged to your grandmother."

The color drains from Victor's face. "W-w-what? How do you know?"

Leo takes a slow breath, trying to keep his composure. "I've never met your grandmother, but during my studies as a young warlock, I was fascinated with symbols and their meanings. Every superior would use a known symbol or create one for their coven, and they had a seal made for them. And this symbol was from when your grandmother was a superior of her coven. *This is her seal!*"

Victor's hands shake, not knowing what's inside. "What if someone else used my grandmother's seal?"

"It's very unlikely," Leo responds. "Your grandmother's coven changed their emblem when your grandmother went into hiding almost 50 years ago. Every seal would have been destroyed."

Victor's legs go weak as he walks over to the couch and sits down. He keeps looking at the envelope. After a few moments, he licks his lips and takes a deep breath. "You open it," he says, holding out the envelope.

Leo holds up his hands, "No, no, no, this letter is for you. And isn't it illegal to open someone else's mail?"

Victor rolls his eyes before he closes them and takes a deep, shaky breath. He looks down at the seal and carefully opens the envelope. When he looks inside, there is only a single tarot card. He pulls the card out and looks at it.

"What is it?" Leo asks with curiosity.

"It's the "King of Swords," Victor answers.

"I'm not familiar with tarot. Is it a good or bad card?" Leo questions.

Victor tilts his head as he studies it and ponders before he answers Leo. After a short moment of silence, Victor says, "It suggests that you should remain open to your current situation. Truth must be established by sticking with the facts handed to you. The king's intellectual power implies that you need to use intellect to make your points across to reach your goal."

Leo looks confused. "Translation."

"Listen to the facts, and you'll find the truth." Victor sits back in his seat. "Why would my grandma save a card for me before I was born or as a child, only to have it sent to me now? In Japan, of all places."

Victor stares at the card some more. Tears begin to build in his eyes. He starts to breathe heavily. With a loud groan, he tosses the card and envelope across the room. "What the fuck are you trying to tell me?" He bends over and rests his head in his hands, covering up that he's crying. "I'm thirty-*fucking*-two-years *fucking* old," he says, muffled in his hands. "Why am I acting this way?"

Leo sits beside him, rubbing his back. "*Shhhh*, it's okay. It's okay. You'll figure this out. You're smart, and you understand Tarot. It'll come to you. You'll see."

Victor sits back up and wipes the tears off his face. His breathing is still shaky, and he tries to take deep breaths to help him calm down. After a moment, he clears his throat. "We need to eat before our food gets cold," he says, getting up from the couch and walking over to the dining table. Leo looks worried as he watches Victor. "Are you going to eat?" Victor asks when he sits down.

Leo stands up and smooths out his robe. "Yeah." He takes a seat, and they eat their breakfast in silence.

It's almost midday, and Victor is looking himself over in the mirror. He starts putting the finishing touches on. A wooden box Victor bought to hold all his artifacts sits on the dresser next to his other larger artifacts. He opens it and puts on his watch, ring, bracelet, and tie clip. The dagger goes in one inside jacket pocket, and his silver card goes in another.

His silver card.

Where's the card? Victor starts to panic. He looks all over his room. "Leo!" Victor shouts as he drops to his knees to look under the bed. Leo comes rushing in. "What? What happened?"

"The card Superior Charles gave me. I can't find it!"

"It has to be around here somewhere." Leo walks in and starts scanning Victor's room.

"Ever since I started getting artifacts, I've been putting them in a wooden box I bought while I was on a layover in Costa Rica. And the card wasn't in the box." Victor starts tossing everything around.

"Found it!" Leo shouts happily.

"Fuck! Where was it?" Victor rushes over when he sees Leo holding it.

"It was in your shoe. It must have dropped there somehow."

Victor sighs in relief as he takes the card from Leo. "Thank you." He slides the card into his jacket pocket and pats it lightly. "Okay, I'm ready."

They walk out of the hotel and head to the water. Victor notices a small boat docked. In the boat are two geishas. "We're going across the lake?" he asks Leo.

"Sort of," Leo replies.

Once everyone is seated, they head out into the water. Victor and Leo have to sit very close to each other because the boat is so small. Leo puts his arm behind Victor and looks out.

Victor's heart races: he likes having Leo's arm around him. Their legs rub against each other as the boat bobs through the water. They hit a little bump, and Victor almost falls into Leo's lap. Leo catches Victor, and they smile at each other. Victor sits back up, clears his throat, and fixes his jacket. He looks over and sees one of the geishas watching them. She gives Victor a little smile.

After twenty minutes on the water, Victor notices something odd directly in front of them. "Leo, do you see what I'm seeing?"

Leo lowers his sunglasses. "You mean the barrier?"

Victor looks forward and sees it's getting closer. Once they pass through the barrier, Victor spots a small island with a temple. "I don't remember seeing this on any map."

"You still have a lot to learn about illusion spells and how to find hiding spots," Leo says, smiling as he leans over the side of the boat, getting a better look at the temple up ahead.

Chiyo greets them as they pull into the dock and step out of the boat. She is wearing a cherry blossom-inspired kimono with a light blue obi belt. Her raven-black hair shimmers in the sunlight and flows by the gentle breeze. She smiles down upon the warlocks with her hands clasped in front of her. "Welcome to Yamada Temple. This has been in my family since the mid-to-late Muromachi Period."

Victor looks around in fascination as Chiyo continues. "We had to use an illusion spell in the middle of the Edo Period to protect the coven and those who sought refuge from those who would harm us." Victor follows Chiyo through the open-air temple grounds to a large open courtyard. "This, my young empath warlock, will be where your lessons on Water Magic will take place."

Chiyo holds out her palm and creates a large ball of water. "You should be able to pick up Water quickly, as many of the spells are similar to Air." She tosses the ball high into the air. It bursts and creates a rainbow as the water trickles down. "First, change into something else you don't mind getting wet in. We don't want Clarence to get upset with you for ruining his suit."

CHAPTER TWENTY- THREE

Three days have passed, and Victor has been excelling at his lessons. He shoots water out of his hands by using the moisture in the air. Victor creates impressively high waves in the lake, higher than Chiyo anticipated. He conjures water bubbles and makes them dance around while one of Chiyo's geishas plays the *koto*. What was most impressive was when he created a dragon out of the lake and made it fly around, combining Air Magic to make clouds emerge from the dragon's mouth for more dramatic effects.

Chiyo is very pleased with Victor's progress. "Karl mentioned you were a quick study, but I must say, you're almost a natural with Water Magic for being an air sign."

"Maybe it's because I'm an Aqueerius," Victor responds.

Chiyo tilts her head to the side, "Aqueerius?"

Victor stops and laughs, "Aquarius. But because I'm gay, I say Aqueerius."

Chiyo busts out laughing, "OH MY GODDESS! That is hilarious!"

After some good laughing to help calm the energy, Victor goes back to his lessons. As he goes through a routine of attacks, Leo sits off to the side, playing Riichi Mahjong with a few geishas. Of course, money is involved, and Leo isn't happy he's losing. When Leo thinks he will win, a basketball-sized water ball drops close to them, splashing everywhere.

"WHAT THE FUCK!" Leo shouts.

Victor has a frightened look. "Sorry about that!"

Leo stands up and uses his Fire Magic to dry himself off. "This is dry clean only, remember. Do you want Clarence's wrath to fall down upon you?" Victor looks more frightened by Leo's remark.

"I wasn't expecting you to be so advanced for not knowing magic," Chiyo states, bringing Victor's attention back to her.

"Thank you?" Victor questions whether her comment was a compliment or an insult.

"I was going to wait until tomorrow, but I think you're ready to learn how to freeze the water using Air Magic." She holds out her palm and creates a ball of water. Within seconds, it freezes and drops into her hand. She holds it out and drops it into Victor's hand.

Victor holds the frozen ball up and examines it. "Karl did something like this when he offered me water. He froze half the ball to make a cup so I could drink from it."

"Who do you think taught him that trick?" Chiyo takes the ice ball from Victor and tosses it into the water. She then creates another ball of water in her palm. "Let's start small. Create a ball in your palm."

Victor holds out his hand and creates a ball hovering over his palm.

Chiyo nods, "Good. Now, I want you to concentrate on the air around it. Make the air move rapidly around the sphere. The faster you move the air, the colder the air will get."

Leo lets out a disgruntled groan as he loses the rest of his money to the geishas. He looks over to see what Victor is up to, then gets up from the table. He brushes off his slacks as he walks over to stand next to Chiyo.

Victor concentrates and watches the air moving around the water. As he begins to focus, his eyes begin to glow **blue** this time.

When Leo steps up to Chiyo, he notices Victor's eyes. "Well, that's new," Leo comments.

"Didn't you mention that his eyes did this before?" Chiyo asks Leo.

"Yes, but they were white last time. Now they're blue," Leo replies.

Victor isn't paying attention to them and remains focused on controlling two specialties simultaneously. A very thin layer of ice forms on top of the water. He begins to feel tired, and the water ball drops to the ground, sighing disappointedly. "I'm sorry, Chiyo."

"It's okay, my young empath warlock. Let's take a small break." Chiyo claps her hands twice, and the geishas set tea on the table. They walk over to the table and sit on the floor cushion.

"I am very impressed with you today," Chiyo says to Victor as she pours tea for them. "I thought I would have to spend more time with you, but I think we might be ready for your test."

Victor looks up, "Does 'test' mean battle?"

Chiyo smiles while pouring, "That's correct, my young empath warlock."

Leo leans back while resting one arm on his raised knee. "But this time, you're fighting a girl."

Victor looks over at Chiyo, "I'm fighting you?"

Chiyo lifts her cup and looks over the rim, smiling ever so slyly. "That's right, along with my geishas."

"Whoa, whoa, whoa. I'm going to fight three of you?" Victor proclaims. "How is that even fair? I barely know how to fight using magic."

One of the geishas places a small tray of tiny Japanese treats to accompany the tea. Leo reaches for a treat and pops it in his mouth. "Fighting is never fair. You must be ready for whatever comes your way, especially if people are after you. This will be good practice for you to defend yourself from multiple attackers."

Victor slumps with disapproval. "I'm not going to like this."

Chiyo sips her tea and looks at Victor, "May I ask you something, my young empath warlock?"

"Sure," Victor agrees as he selects one of the chocolates off the tray.

"How do you make your eyes glow?" Chiyo asks with genuine curiosity.

Victor shrugs his shoulders as he sips his tea. "I honestly don't know. Apparently, it just happens. But I can't feel it happening, nor can I see it. To you, it looks like my eyes are covered in white, but to me, I can see perfectly with no obstructions."

"Blue this time," Leo comments as he pops a treat into his mouth.

Victor gives Leo a puzzled look, "Did you just say blue?"

"He did. It happened when you were concentrating on freezing the water in your hand," Chiyo answers.

Victor puckers his lips as he thinks out loud, "Maybe the color of the glow represents the magic I'm trying to focus on."

Leo and Chiyo look lost.

Victor notices and sits upright. "I can see you two have no idea what I'm saying. Let me try to explain. What if each specialty has a color associated with it? My eyes were white when I was working on Air Magic. And just now, you say my eyes were blue, and I was working on Water Magic. It might mean my eyes glow green or brown when I focus on Earth. And with Fire, my eyes will glow red, orange, or yellow."

Leo scratches at his stubble, thinking about Victor's explanation. "It sounds plausible. We can ask Superior Charles about that. He did mention he saw your grandmother's eyes glowing once before. Maybe he can confirm your theory."

Chiyo claps her hands twice, signaling her geisha to clear the table and take everything away. "Okay, break time is over. Victor, get ready."

Victor gives Chiyo a cheesy smile. "Awww, that was the first time in three days you didn't call me 'young empath warlock.'"

Chiyo stands up and smooths out her kimono. "And if you want to continue that respect, you better win the fight."

Victor cocks an eyebrow. "Challenge accepted."

Leo helps Victor up from the ground and then assists him in putting on his jacket. Leo brushes Victor's shoulders with his hands as he whispers in Victor's ear, "Be careful with the geisha in the dark green. She's a clever little witch." Victor looks over at the two geishas who are joining Chiyo. He spots the one wearing a dark green kimono, and the other is wearing a deep pink kimono.

He turns Victor around to help straighten his tie and smooth down the jacket's lapels. "Try not to use Water Magic all the time. Do your best to combine both Air and Water in your attacks. You'll see why people of magic always make sure they have more than one specialty in their arsenal."

Victor nods.

As Victor heads to the center of the courtyard, the two geishas build a dome of water. The waves in the water sparkle like koi swimming around as the sunlight hits the ripples. Victor and Chiyo, with her geisha, take their positions on opposite sides of the dome. The geisha turn their backs toward Victor. A few seconds later, they turn back around. Their faces are no longer covered in white paint. Their faces are painted as *kabuki*.

Their delicate, feminine features have transformed into bold, exaggerated lines of red, blue, and black. The first geisha in dark green has a fierce, stern glare, outlining her face with thick, angry blue streaks to embody a vengeful spirit. Meanwhile, the face of the geisha adorned in deep pink is painted with vivid red lines on her cheeks and eyes, transforming her serene expression into the passionate, powerful visage of a hero.

"Okay, you have to show me how to do that trick when this is over," Victor comments.

Chiyo lifts her arm and hides her face behind her kimono sleeve. A second later, her face is also painted in a *kabuki* style. Crimson lines fracture across Chiyo's face, transforming her delicate features into the *kumadori* makeup of a *kabuki* hero. The delicate red of her lips is overtaken by thick, dramatic strokes that accentuate her musculature, creating an illusion of intense strength and powerful emotion. A striking gesture, a look of bold courage replaces her once placid expression; her eyes now burn with the theatrical intensity of a warrior ready for battle.

Chiyo responds to him in Japanese, "*If you win this fight, I might think about it.*"

Just as the dome closes at the top, Leo flings a small blue fireball over and through the closing hole. Before it hits the ground, it explodes, signaling to fight—the two geisha charge while shouting a battle cry. Chiyo does not move from where she is standing. Victor looks between the two of them as they head right for him. When they are close enough, he lifts his hands over his head, using the air beneath their feet to hurl them backward.

Chiyo remains in her spot as the geisha quickly recover. The geisha in dark green jumps and throws what looks like a spear made of ice at Victor. Victor uses Air to repel the spear, only to be hit from behind by a blunt object.

As Victor picks himself up, he notices Chiyo's palm is facing out. He looks behind him and sees the dome's wall finish retracting back into itself. "She is using the wall of the dome too? How is that even fair?"

Leo stands at the edge, eating a peach. "I told you to keep an eye on your surroundings." He takes another bite of the peach. "Chiyo, I love how sweet these peaches are. You need to give me some to take back with me."

Victor gives Leo a dissatisfied look. "Whose side are you on?" Victor doesn't pay attention as he's plummeted with a ball of water. Leo shakes his head as he takes another bite of his peach. Victor recovers and is standing too close to the edge of the dome. Suddenly, a sharp icicle pokes him in the shoulder. He turns around, and over half the dome's wall is covered in icicle spikes.

He turns his attention back to Chiyo and the geishas. They have turned the entire dome with icicle spikes facing inward. "Well, this just got more interesting," Victor remarks, wide-eyed.

The geisha start their attacks again, but Chiyo never moves from her spot. Victor has to fight off two feisty Japanese women who are smaller in stature than he is. "How the hell are you so strong for being so small?" Victor remarks, defending himself.

They keep throwing punches and kicks, as well as Water Magic attacks, and Victor does his best to defend and dodge their attacks. He finds an opening to counterattack. Using Water and Air combined, he knocks out the geisha in deep pink. The dome extends to cover the geisha, enveloping her with water, and pulls her outside the dome. As soon as she's outside, she slowly sits up.

Leo walks up to the geisha and looks down at her. But instead of helping her, he hands her something else. "Peach?"

She gives Leo a disgusted look and begrudgingly takes the peach. Leo sits on the ground next to her as they eat peaches while watching the rest of the fight.

The geisha in dark green decides to heat things up . . . sort of. She creates a *katana* sword out of ice. Victor's eyes grow wide. As instinct kicks in, he makes two ice *bo* staffs in his hands. As the geisha wails towards him, Victor does his best to defend himself as he sees ice shards being chipped away from his staffs. He notices her sword is not damaged, which causes him more alarm. The geisha eventually shatters one of the staffs.

Victor starts worrying like he's about to get sliced in half with an ice sword. He swings his staff like a bat, and it connects to the geisha's katana. His eyes widen when he notices he has transformed his *bo* into a *katana*.

The battle continues one-on-one as Chiyo remains in her spot. She raises her arms, causing the icicles to grow longer and sharper. They slowly make their way behind Victor, but he is so engulfed by the geisha that he doesn't realize what's happening.

As Leo watches, he leans to the geisha beside him. "I told him to watch out for her. I also told him to be mindful of his surroundings. I don't think he's a good listener."

The geisha gives Leo a bombastic side eye as she chews at her peach.

Victor and the geisha continue to engage in a sword fight. She eventually finds a moment to kick Victor backward. As Victor stumbles back, he bumps against the ever-growing icicles. He turns around to see that the space around him is getting smaller. He tries to figure out what he needs to do. His thinking is cut short as the geisha advances at him. As they swing, hit after hit, Victor's eyes glow white. He starts using an air pulse to push the geisha back.

Chiyo looks on, lifting her head as she studies Victor's actions. Victor uses a couple more air pulses to push the geisha back, further and further away. He picks up the geisha with his Air Magic and throws her around like a boat in stormy water. The spikes retract so that they do not impale the geisha.

Victor notices this as the spikes start to grow faster. He then creates a gust to pick up the geisha and flings her around the dome. As this happens, the spikes quickly retract. Victor then looks at Chiyo, and his eyes turn from white to blue.

Before Chiyo can react, she's caught in a wave from the dome and is flung around.

Leo and the geisha beside him drop their jaws and peaches in amazement. Victor figured out how to get rid of those damn spikes. He creates water bubbles around Chiyo and the geisha and flings them around like rag dolls. The icicles start to disappear. Once the dome is spike-free, Victor releases them from their bubble.

The two women cough as they catch their breaths and try to wring water out of their kimonos. Chiyo stands up and uses Air Magic to dry her kimono and hair. She waves her hand over her face, removing her ruined makeup. Victor watches, his eyes still glow blue. Chiyo gestures for the geisha in dark green to leave. An opening appears, allowing the geisha to exit. As she walks out, she sits beside Leo, who hands her a peach.

When Chiyo closes the exit, she straightens her poster. "Very impressive, my young empath warlock. But now, playtime is over." She throws her hand up and clenches it into a fist, engulfing Victor in a bubble filled with water. Unable to breath, he starts to panic.

The glow in his eyes begins to fade. His eyes flutter closed as he goes unconscious. His body is now floating inside the water. Then, before Chiyo is about to release him, Victor opens his eyes that now glow bright white. Chiyo holds still, waiting for a reaction.

Victor opens his mouth, and bubbles start forming in front of him. Soon, a giant bubble covers his nose and mouth, allowing him to breathe again. Chiyo scoffs and begins to freeze the water, giving Victor more of a challenge. She twirls her fingers and wrist, causing the air around the water to swirl rapidly. Chiyo slowly walks toward him, watching as he struggles inside the bubble.

As the frozen water starts to close in on Victor, he holds out his arms. His eyes glow slightly brighter as he's about to lose the battle. The remaining water around him starts to swirl around like a whirlpool. The force of the turbulence inside causes the frozen ball to burst. Chiyo goes flying as Victor frees himself from the icy water prison. She rolls around a few times before lying face down.

Leo and the geishas sit in silence for a moment until the geishas jump up to their feet and start applauding. Leo slowly joins in and gives Victor a look of great admiration. The dome begins to retract as Victor walks over to Chiyo. Chiyo looks up at Victor as he extends his hand to help her off the ground. She takes his hand and lifts herself to her feet.

She dusts herself off, takes a step back, and bows deeply. She speaks to Victor in Japanese, "*Congratulations, My Young Empath Warlock.*"

Victor bows in return and responds in Japanese, "*Thank you, Master of Water.*"

CHAPTER TWENTY-FOUR

Victor and Leo prepare for their return to the hotel by boat. Victor notices Leo smiling as he carries a crate of peaches on the boat. Off to the side of the courtyard, Chiyo is kneeling in front of a shrine, offering her evening prayer while the two geishas start packing things up. When Chiyo finishes, she walks over to the boat. She turns around, and with a flick of her wrist, all the lanterns and candles blow out. Leo helps her into the tiny ship, and they sail off.

Victor and Leo sit in the back as they enjoy the sunset. One of the geishas starts playing a *shamisen* while Chiyo plays the *koto*. Victor feels a sense of tranquility as the breeze caresses his face and the water splashes against the boat. Having no motor on the boat helps with the serenity. Leo and Victor kick up their feet while the second geisha uses her Air Magic to move the boat across the lake.

Victor starts to doze off, and Leo wraps his arm around Victor's shoulders, letting Victor lie against him. Chiyo gives Leo a little smirk as she keeps playing music. Looking down at her *koto*, she starts to feel something is wrong. Chiyo stops playing and looks up. The geishas notice her gaze and look behind them.

A massive wave is approaching.

Chiyo jumps up, "Shit! Hang on!" She twirls her arms and wrists to help propel the boat faster across the water. They are still about half a mile away from the shore. Leo and Victor wake up as the boat jerks under them. They turn around and see the wave coming at them.

"What the fuck is going on?" Leo shouts.

"I think someone found our empath!" Chiyo shouts back.

"Why are they coming after me?" Victor asks anyone who will answer.

"We don't know. It might have something to do with your ability," Chiyo answers.

"But why me? Superior Charles is an empath too," Victor questions.

Chiyo looks back at the wave and then down at Victor. "It might have something to do with your grandmother."

The wave is gaining on them. They still have 500 feet to go.

Victor looks back at the wave and then at the shore. "We're not going to make it!"

"Yes, we will!" Leo exclaims.

"We're not going to make it!" Victor shouts again.

"We're almost there!" Chiyo cries out.

The wave's shadow covers the entire boat. Victor stands up and keeps his eyes on the surf as it's about to crash down upon them. He throws his arms out and pulls them back into his center. He uses Air Magic to pull Chiyo, and the two geishas close to him and Leo. Seconds before the water crashes down, Victor spins his arms out in a circular formation. The wave comes crashing down, destroying the boat.

When the ripples start to calm down, bubbles begin to break the water's surface. A giant bubble shoots out of the water, with Victor and the others inside. While floating in the air, Leo notices two figures dressed in black at the dock. A tall warlock and a short-haired witch use their Water Magic to try to drown Victor and the others. Chiyo sees another wave coming at them, but before she can react, the wave crashes down on them.

Victor does everything he can to keep the bubble afloat and to keep it from bursting. As another wave comes their way, Victor watches as it grows taller than the previous ones.

He turns around and starts to focus, causing his eyes to shine a bright blue. Victor looks up as he twists his torso and lowers one of his hands with his palm turned downward. With his other hand, he creates a cloud swirling around, maintaining the bubble's levitation.

Victor scoops his lower hand over his head, mimicking the wave's curve. The witch and warlock look at each other, puzzled, wondering who's controlling the tide. They try to regain their control, but Victor has overpowered them. Victor looks over his shoulder, spins around, and aims the wave toward the dock.

The witch and warlock panic and try to run away. The warlock summons an earth spell as soon as the wave crashes down on them, creating a protective dome from the brick and dirt they are standing on. Victor floats the bubble down on the shore and lets it vanish. He pays no attention to the others as he walks to the dirt dome.

"Is everyone okay?" Leo asks as he helps the women off the ground.

Chiyo and her geisha nod as they smooth out their kimonos. Leo looks around and spots Victor approaching the dome. The glow in Victor's eyes begins to fade. As Victor steps closer, he is knocked back with a chunk of dirt.

"Victor!" Leo shouts as he runs over to him. He helps Victor back on his feet. They look over and notice the witch and warlock dusting the dirt off themselves.

"That empath is coming with us dead or alive," the witch demands. "So, what's it going to be? Are you going to come willingly or by force?"

Victor sneers back, brushing the dirt off his sleeves. "I'm not coming willingly, so it looks like I choose by force."

The witch tilts her head to the side, glaring at Victor. "Have it your way."

The warlock jumps high over the witch and tries to land a punch on Victor and Leo. They dodge his attack, causing the warlock to punch his fist on the ground. The force from the warlock was so strong that it destroys most of the sidewalk.

"It's not safe for you. Go and get help," Chiyo orders her geisha. They nod and scurry away quickly. Chiyo begins hurling ice knives at the witch to keep her distracted. The witch dodges Chiyo's attacks and blocks the blades by making a shield out of concrete.

The warlock throws a boulder the size of a car at Victor. Victor pulls the water out of the boulder, causing it to dry and turn into a big pile of sand. In return, he creates his own ice boulder and flings it at the warlock.

Chiyo and the witch throw makeshift weapons at each other. The witch gives Chiyo a devilish grin. "Let's fight as you're supposed to in Japan." The witch creates a large *katana* sword with earth and concrete.

Chiyo conjures a massive hammer out of solid ice. The ice is so cold that Chiyo's hands turn red from frostbite. Icicles cover her knuckles and the backs of her hands. They charge, ready to hurl their weapons at one another.

As the fighting progresses, Victor gets close enough to the warlock to punch him with a frozen fist, busting open the warlock's lip. The warlock takes his fingertips and presses down on the cut. He looks at his fingertips covered in blood, then proceeds to lick the blood off.

"So, you wanna play like that, huh?" the warlock says to Victor. "All right, then let's play like that." He turns his fists into concrete hammers and starts throwing punches.

Victor remembers his boxing training from his workouts, even though he's not a boxer. But he's able to miss most of the warlock's punches. Leo jumps in and kicks the warlock in the back, causing him to lose his balance and fall forward.

This gives Victor the advantage to uppercut the warlock. The warlock flies backward.

Leo gets distracted when the witch tries to attack him with her sword. Leo sidesteps just before the witch can cut him into pieces. Furious, his hands ignite, and he throws a flame at the witch. She's engulfed in the flame and tries to block it, but Chiyo comes from behind and slams her hammer into the witch's head. The hammer hits the witch so hard that her head is smashed in from the impact.

Blood goes flying, some hitting Chiyo and Leo. The witch's lifeless body falls to the ground.

As Victor and the warlock continue to fight, Victor becomes dizzy. But this time, it's not "going to pass out" dizzy; it's something else. For a moment, he feels something strange entering his body. Victor starts to gain extra energy, strength, and power. His watch starts flashing and vibrating. He glances down and notices a meter rising.

This wasn't any power. It was the power of the dead witch.

The warlock thinks this is an advantage and throws another punch, but Victor grabs the warlock's fist like a baseball. The warlock lets out a painful groan as Victor starts crushing the warlock's hand. He notices Victor's eyes are glowing bright white, which startles the warlock.

"What the fuck is happening?" the warlock cries out.

"You made the mistake of coming after me," Victor responds as he throws a sucker punch.

The warlock blocks the force but is still thrown back several feet.

The warlock snarls at Victor and spits out some blood. "The hell with this," he says, taking a dagger from his jacket. He tries swinging and stabbing Victor, who dodges every move. Leo runs over to help. The warlock spots Leo and then tosses another dagger from behind his back. Leo's side gets sliced open as the blade passes by him. Leo drops down to his knee, holding his side.

Victor watches as Leo drops to the ground. He slowly turns back to the warlock, snarling aggressively. "*That* was a big mistake."

Victor's eyes turn **black**.

The warlock panics and tosses two more daggers. Victor barely moves as the daggers miss. Victor starts to stalk toward the warlock; the warlock's eyes are filled with terror. He keeps throwing daggers, and each one passes by Victor.

The warlock tries to stab Victor in the collar, but Victor grabs his arm, inches away from being struck. The warlock then surprises Victor by thrusting his last dagger into Victor's side. Victor reacts quickly and uses his free arm to knock the warlock's hand away, causing the blade to fly several feet away. Before the dagger touches the ground, Victor uses his magic to catch it and pull it back.

Without skipping a beat, when the dagger reaches Victor's hand, Victor thrusts it into the side of the warlock's head. The warlock's body goes limp. Victor drops the warlock's arm but is still holding the warlock up by the dagger. Victor closes his black-filled eyes and takes a deep breath as if absorbing the warlock's power and soul. He opens his eyes and notices the warlock's eyes have turned completely black.

"Victor?" Leo mentions as he tries to walk over to him. Victor turns and sees Leo. Leo and Chiyo are startled by Victor's eyes. "Victor," Leo carefully points to Victor, "your eyes."

Victor notices Leo is hurt. His expression turns to worry, and he lets go of the dagger, allowing the warlock to fall to the ground. Victor rushes over to Leo to see the damage. Victor doesn't say anything as tears start to appear. He looks into Leo's eyes, but Leo can't return the stare. Victor gently touches Leo's injury, causing Leo's body to jolt from the pain.

Victor retracts his hand quickly but still studies the gash in Leo's side.

"Victor! Leo! Chiyo!" Akisha shouts as she and Madame Jeanette run over to them. Victor turns his head, causing them to stop in their tracks when they see his black eyes.

"Oh, *chéri,* what in the name of *Gran Maître* have you done?" Madame Jeanette says in a low voice.

Victor does not respond and then looks back at Leo's wound. He slowly moves his hand towards the damage. Leo flinches before Victor touches it.

Madame Jeanette cautiously walks over. "Victor, let me take–"

Victor lifts his hand in the air, cutting Madame Jeanette off mid-sentence. He takes his hand and hovers it over Leo's wound. A few seconds later, a dim glow of silver appears. Victor slowly moves his hand back and forth along the injury. As he does, the wound starts to heal. After a few passes, the gash is gone.

Victor smiles and then looks back at Leo, who still can't make eye contact. He looks around, and everyone around him seems worried because his eyes have not returned to normal. When he looks back at Leo, his eyes return to normal, then roll to the back of his head.

"Victor!" Leo cries as he catches Victor before he falls to the ground.

CHAPTER TWENTY-FIVE

Victor wakes up leaning against a tree and notices he's back in the glowing forest. He looks down and sees he's again in the platinum-silver suit. As he looks up at the tree, he doesn't recognize its animals and fruit. Victor looks over to the side and sees a glowing blue stream. He stands up, dusts himself off, and heads toward the creek. When he walks up to the bank, he looks down but doesn't see his reflection. There doesn't seem to be any reflection. He follows the direction the stream is flowing and spots that it leads somewhere.

A small building appears in the distance after following the bank for about a mile. It's familiar; could it be the house he saw before? He continues to walk, watching the building get closer. The closer he gets, the more he recognizes it.

"Am I . . . home?" he says to himself. Victor stops and wonders how he's speaking without moving his lips. He shrugs his shoulders and continues walking to the building.

As before, the building starts to move away when he gets closer. After a few attempts, he decides to stop. *"What if I go around it?"* He turns to walk around, but the building moves along with him. He goes the other way, and so does the building. Victor doesn't know how to react to the situation. He decides to sit down and try to come up with a solution.

"If I can't go toward it, and I can't go around it, then how am I supposed to get inside?"

"You're not supposed to go inside, Victor," a mysterious but familiar voice comments.

Victor looks around. *"Who's there?"* He doesn't see anyone.

"I don't think Grandma would be happy if she found out what you just did. So, let's not tell her," the voice says.

"What did I do?" Victor keeps looking around, but no one is in sight. He stands back up and notices a tree that wasn't there before.

He walks over to the tree and looks up, gently placing his hand on the trunk. *"I used to climb this tree."*

"That's right, and you almost broke your arm. You loved to try to climb all the way to the top, but the branches weren't strong enough," the voice tells Victor.

"You . . . You sound familiar. Do I know you?" Victor asks the voice.

"Of course you do. I am your mother."

Victor snaps back around. He sees a glowing figure that is as tall as he is. He can't make out the face, but he can see a female figure in a flowy, brilliant white dress. She has the same dark, wavy hair as Victor's that falls onto her shoulders. He walks closer to the figure, and her face starts to clear. As he steps closer, his eyes begin to tear up. He brings his hands up and cups her face.

"Mom?"

She places her hands on top of his hands. *"It's me."*

Victor's knees buckle under him, and he drops to the ground. He grabs his mother's glowing dress with his fists and can't hold back the tears. *"I have missed you so much."*

She smiles gently as she strokes his hair. *"I know you have, but I'm here now. Stand up. Let me look at you."*

Victor stumbles as he tries to get back onto his feet. When he does, he looks deep into his mother's eyes. She uses her fingertips and knuckles to help Victor wipe the tears off his cheeks.

"You have gotten so handsome," she says. *"I also see bits of your father in you."*

"*But I inherited your damn stubbornness,*" Victor snickers back.

Victor's mother wraps her arm around his. "*Come, we have much to discuss.*" She turns him around and walks away from the building. They make their way back to the stream and start walking beside it. "*I was hoping to keep you away from all of this.*"

"What are you saying? You knew about Grandma being a witch?" Victor asks.

His mother smiles and speaks again without moving her lips. "*Of course I did. I've known since I was five.*"

"Why would you two keep all of this from me?" Victor asks. His mother just smiles and pats his arms, guiding him toward the stream.

They walk up to a set of rocks. Victor's mother gestures to take a seat as she explains to her son about his grandmother and her decision.

"*Grandma was on her way to become High Priestess. During the trials to test her powers, it concluded that she could very well be the next Grand Witch. There hasn't been any witch or warlock to hold such an esteemed honor in a few hundred years.*

"*There was one more test she needed to accomplish, but it would be some time since it was to be done under a full blood moon during a blue moon month. It was going to be at least a year. But a couple of covens didn't want a Grand Witch running things. They were stuck in their old ways of witchcraft. They hated how modern witches were becoming. So, one witch decided to challenge your grandma.*"

"Do you know who the witch was?" Victor asks.

Victor's mother shakes her head. "*Sadly, I was still young, barely turned eleven. Things got very heated between your grandma and the witch. It got so bad that Grandma stopped me from continuing my lessons. I barely got to learn Air Magic. I didn't know then, but it was for my protection. The witch succeeded in* halting your grandma's final test, and it would be a while before another blood blue moon would happen."

Victor's mother looks off in deep thought. "*My mother began worrying, and when I turned eighteen, she told me I could no longer communicate with any of my friends. I must become mundane. She never told me why. Your uncle was not happy with the news. He wanted to storm into the witch's coven and show them who's who. We struggled to live a mundane lifestyle.*"

Victor lets out a small laugh, "*I was also told to let go of my mundane friends. What happened to Grandma?*"

Victor's mother takes a deep breath, preparing to explain what happened to his grandmother. "*Well, over the years, her body started weakening. Someone created a spell to make her sick. But no one could figure out who. Her coven even went to see the Voodoo Queen for help with answers. Even she had a difficult time. The seers and empaths of other covens couldn't figure out who could have done this.*

"*When I found out I was pregnant with you, a seer sought me out and told me that in order to keep the bloodline safe, you were to be hidden from anyone who could find you and keep you away from this life. But it came with a price.*"

Victor starts to shake his head vigorously. "*No. Don't say it.*"

His mother takes his hand into both of hers. "*It was a sacrifice I would do again if I had to.*"

Victor slides off the rock and drops to his knees. He tries to hold back his tears. "*Why? Why did you do that?*" Victor can't hold back the floodgates anymore. He drops his face into his mother's lap and sobs profusely.

Victor's mother gently strokes his hair. She lifts his head and cups his cheek with her hand. She uses her thumbs to wipe away the tears. "*It was the only way to protect you. They were killing my mother, your grandma. Your uncle became so angry that he left to find the witch who had done this by himself.*

He would show up from time to time, until eventually your uncle disappeared."

"I remember bits and pieces of him as a child. Whatever happened to him?" Victor asks through the sobs.

"No one knows, not even the seers I kept in touch with," his mother responds. "The only thing I had to worry about back then was making sure they wouldn't come after you. I knew it would be a while before my time was up, so I had to make the most of it."

Victor rests his forehead on his mother's knees. She gently combs his hair with her fingertips.

He looks back up at his mother and asks, "Wasn't there another way? Why did you have to sacrifice yourself?"

She lightly shakes her head. "It was the only way, my child. You don't truly understand how powerful you are. It's dangerous and wonderful. Terrifying and amazing. You could be the first Grand Warlock, and because of that, you had to be hidden from those who conjure magic. Some covens want to bring back the old ways of witchcraft. Ways that caused those of religion to fear us."

Victor picks himself up and sits back on the rock. "What am I supposed to do?"

His mother reaches over and fixes the side of his hair. "Well, you're older now. You can make your own choices. You have a good head on your shoulders. You listen and take things into consideration."

Victor comes to a realization. "Like the King of Swords."

Victor's mom sits up straight and smiles fondly at her grown child. "Looks like you've become more familiar with Tarot." She leans over and softly kisses Victor's cheek. When she leans back, she smiles softly while taking one of Victor's hands into hers. "You will figure things out."

Victor jumps up from his bed, covered in sweat, his heart racing, and breathing heavily. He looks around the room and notices he's back in his apartment. He peeks under the sheets. He's out of his suit and wearing just a T-shirt and underwear. Victor looks over to the side of the bed and sees Leo resting in a chair wearing a sweater hoodie, and some workout shorts.

"Leo? Leo," Victor says softly.

Leo slowly wakes up. "Huh, wha . . . VICTOR!" He jumps from his seat and tackles Victor, wrapping his arms tightly around him. "Thank the gods you're okay."

Victor embraces Leo and can still smell the light scent of Leo's cologne. "How long was I out?"

Leo pulls back and looks into Victor's eyes. "You've been out for three days."

Victor seems unsure how to react. "It's been that long?" He looks over at the chair Leo has been sitting in. "How long have you been here?"

Leo makes himself more comfortable sitting beside Victor. "I've been with you the entire time. After you passed out back in Otsu, Akisha, Chiyo, and I rushed you back to the hotel room. When it was obvious that you wouldn't wake up anytime soon, we took a risk and brought you through a mirror and back to your apartment. It was agreed that it would be better to wake up somewhere familiar than in a strange place."

"How did Derek feel about you staying with me this entire time?" Victor asks, looking around, knowing that Derek is someone to watch out for.

"He hasn't contacted me. And frankly, I don't care. I wanted to make sure you were safe while you were unconscious," Leo mentions.

Victor gives a slight smile to Leo, but it fades, knowing that what he wants from Leo won't be able to happen.

Leo reaches for a glass of water on the nightstand and hands it to Victor. "Do you feel strong enough to take a shower?"

Victor looks slyly at Leo, saying, "I might need some help."

Leo chuckles, "Well, we need to head to Texas. We're to meet with Superior Charles. He asked for you to see him once you have awakened and are strong enough. He has a lake house just north of Dallas."

"So, you're taking me to your coven?" Victor asks. Leo nods in response. "Then we shouldn't keep your superior waiting."

CHAPTER TWENTY-SIX

After Victor showers, shaves, and fixes his hair, he goes back to his bedroom and gets dressed. He pulls out his suit and examines it. The suit appears to have been recently cleaned and mended. Victor starts taking each piece off the hanger and tossing them onto the bed.

As Victor prepares his suit, Leo lightly knocks on the door. Leo slowly opens the door and pokes his head in. "No need for your suit. His place is protected, so we'll be safe. Meet me in the living room when you're dressed."

Leo exits, and Victor walks over to his dresser to get something comfortable to wear. As he looks in the drawers, he notices his phone. He picks it up and sees several missed calls from his friends. Victor looks through the texts and notices that Leo responded to everyone.

As he scrolls through, he can't believe how Leo made the texts look like he was sending them. Victor starts to get upset because Leo is pretending to be him. Victor then becomes sad when he realizes Leo could be right. It might be too dangerous to have mundane friends.

Victor still hasn't told his friends that he hasn't been flying since he started his magic training. He isn't sure how much longer he can keep up the ruse. He sets down his phone and drops his towel, then slips into underwear and pair of jeans.

"Victor," Leo shouts from the living room. "Are you ready yet?"

"Coming!" Victor responds as he takes out a shirt to wear. As he puts on his shirt, he notices the wooden box with all his artifacts on top of the dresser. "If I'm not going in my suit, I might as well bring these with me," he says to himself. He starts putting on his jewelry as he walks out of his bedroom.

Turning the corner, Victor notices a large mirror on his wall. "That's new," he states as he ponders why there is a mirror in his living room. "I'm not sure it works with the rest of the room."

Leo uses a small red dagger to etch a rune in the center of the mirror. "You needed something to spruce up the place."

Victor examines the mirror and notes the markings along its length on both sides. "I take it those marks are for protection?" Victor inquires.

Leo steps back from the mirror when he finishes the rune. "That's right. They are protection wards to ensure only those you allow can walk through." He presses his palm over the rune. There is a red glow, then the rune is gone. He turns around to Victor as he wipes his hand on his shirt. "There, I think it's ready."

"Did you just use heat to fix the mirror?" Victor queries.

Leo nods with a smile. "Sure did. This way, no one knows what rune I used. Do you have your dagger?" Victor nods and pulls the dagger from his back pocket. "Prick your thumb and press it against any of the wards on the side."

Victor walks over to the mirror and pricks his thumb. He flinches a little as this is the first time he has had to draw blood. He presses his thumb against a ward and feels the blood smear.

"Now, say your given name," Leo commands softly as he watches on.

"Victor Raymond Russo." The protection wards begin to glow for a moment and then fade out.

Leo holds his thumb up and points it at Victor. "Now, prick my thumb." Victor gives Leo a puzzled look. "I can't do it because these are your protection wards. My blood has to be drawn by you with your dagger."

Victor takes a deep breath and shrugs. "If you say so." As he holds Leo's hand, he starts to shake nervously.

"Don't be nervous," Leo tells Victor with an assuring tone. "I do this all the time." Victor takes a deep breath and pricks Leo's thumb. "See, that wasn't so bad. Now, press my thumb on one of the wards, and then tell me to say my given name."

Victor takes Leo's thumb between his fingers. He notices how soft but firm Leo's hand is. This is the first time Victor has held Leo's hand in his own, but he didn't expect the sensation he was having.

Victor presses Leo's thumb onto one of the wards. "Say your given name."

"Leopold João Oliveira IV." The protection wards glow as before and then fade out.

Victor turns to Leo, asking, "The fourth?"

Leo shrugs. "You can ask my father when you meet him."

"Wait, what?" Victor questions.

Leo presses his palm against the center of the mirror. The protection wards begin to glow a blueish-white hue. The mirror becomes hazy with purples and blues. Leo looks over at Victor and asks, "Ready?"

"Are we meeting Superior Charles or your father?" Victor ponders with confusion. Leo winks over his shoulder and then proceeds to walk through the mirror.

Victor lets out a disgruntled groan. "I don't like it when you ignore my questions, Leo."

Victor steps through the mirror and enters a large rustic cabin-style room. The room exudes a warm, rustic charm with weathered wooden floors and exposed ceiling beams.

Natural light filters through simple linen curtains. A handmade wool rug and a rough-hewn wooden table add character without cluttering the open, minimalist space.

"Nice place," he says to himself.

"I'm glad you like it." Victor looks to his side and sees Superior Charles holding out a glass of bourbon. "Welcome to my home. I'd like to show you around, but we have business to attend to. Follow me." Victor takes the bourbon from Superior Charles and follows him.

They walk down a hallway with floor-to-ceiling windows looking out to the lake. Halfway down the hallway, Superior Charles opens a set of double doors. As they walk in, the room smells of fresh cigars, bourbon, and whiskey.

The room is windowless and lit by a variety of floor and wall lamps. The decor evokes an old-fashioned smokers' lounge. Victor walks further in and looks at a wall covered with various dark liquors. Next to the bottles is a temperature-controlled cabinet filled with boxes of cigars.

Superior Charles makes his way to the center of the room, where six smokers' chairs sit in a circle. Each chair is identical, covered in dark brown leather, with tall backs and thick armrests. Dark brass studs accent the trimming, holding the leather in place. Superior Charles turns to Victor and gestures to an open chair. "Please, take a seat."

The six smokers' chairs have side tables next to each one. There are additional empty chairs and tables against the other walls, presumably for use when there are more attendees. Victor can tell this is where Superior Charles likes to hold his meetings. There is a young warlock walking around, refreshing drinks. As Victor makes his way to an open seat, he looks around the room and only sees one familiar face, Superior Jackie, and three other men in the other seats.

Superior Charles stands in front of his chair, introducing everyone to Victor. "Empath Victor Russo, you already know Superior Jackie. The other gentlemen are elders of my coven. To my right is Elder Jonathan Harps, to your left is Elder Franklin Torres, and to your right is Elder Leopold Oliveira III."

Victor stands by his seat as though he is stricken with stage fright. "Pleasure to meet everyone." He takes his seat between Elders Franklin and Leopold. Superior Charles sits directly across from Victor, with Superior Jackie at his side.

Elder Leopold leans over to Victor. "Hello, young empath. My son has spoken fondly of you."

Victor tries not to smile too much. "Thank you, Sir. He's been a great mentor."

Superior Charles sits back and brings a cigar to his lips. The cigar lights up without the use of a lighter or match. Superior Charles takes a couple of puffs before he speaks. "So," he starts before he exhales, "you've had an interesting turn of events a few days ago."

"You can say that," Victor responds.

"Do you remember everything that happened in Otsu?" Superior Charles inquires.

As Victor is about to speak, the young warlock offers him a cigar. Victor declines before he responds to the question. "I'm not sure where to begin, Superior."

Superior Jackie leans forward, examining Victor's eyes. "How about you start when Chiyo smashed the witch's head in with her makeshift ice hammer?"

Victor rubs the back of his neck, recalling when they were first attacked. "Well, we can start with how those two tried to drown us first."

Superior Jackie waves her hand, dismissing Victor's comment. "We already heard about that from Leo and Chiyo. What happened to you when that witch died?"

"Well..." Victor starts as he ponders how to describe what happened. He knows that as long as Superior Charles was looking at him with focused eyes, he couldn't lie. "I know I was fighting a warlock. Leo tried to help but got turned away when the witch tried to catch him off guard. I remember seeing Chiyo smashing the witch's head in with an ice hammer in the corner of my eye. As I blocked the warlock's punches, things started to feel and look different."

"What felt and looked different?" Superior Jackie asks watchfully, wanting Victor to proclaim that moment.

Victor scratches his beard below his ear, thinking about how to explain what happened. "It just felt like something was being absorbed into my body. Suddenly, I had a new burst of energy."

"And this happened once the witch was dead?" Superior Jackie reiterates.

"I guess so, yes," Victor replies with a shrug.

Superior Jackie twists her neck and looks at Superior Charles. "Looks like our young empath did have a necromantic experience."

Superior Charles takes a puff before asking Victor his question. "Is that when your eyes turned black?"

Victor gives the superiors a confused look. "My eyes turned black? The only thing I remember after the witch being killed was the warlock trying to stab me with his dagger. But when Leo ran over to assist, the warlock tossed another dagger, slicing Leo's side open. That's when it felt like something changed within me."

The superiors and elders look at each other as Victor continues. "I felt angry because someone was hurt under my watch. I could hear myself say something to my enemy, but no words came out of my mouth. I could see everything going on, but my body wasn't mine."

Victor gazes at a spot on the floor as he remembers every moment as though he were in someone else's body. "I don't remember much, but I remember knocking the warlock's dagger out of his hand. Then, when I jammed the dagger into his head, I had the same feeling enter my body. I don't remember anything that took place after that."

The superiors gave each other worried looks. They both knew that what Victor experienced was something beyond the normal means of magic.

"It was a necromantic experience," Superior Jackie conveys with the utmost assurance. She looks back at Victor, asking, "Do you remember healing Leo?"

Victor becomes bewildered. "What do you mean by a necromantic experience?"

"You see, young empath, when those individuals died, you absorbed their life force and power. That's why you were able to feel stronger," Elder Jonathan responds with familiarity. The Elder had witnessed this experience long ago with a witch who was a necromancer. Victor could sense the dark, hooded tone of the memory.

"It's also one of many reasons the second grand witch outlawed all necromancy magic," Superior Jackie adds as she takes a drink. "The third grand witch removed the outlaw soon after she was gifted her title."

"I think I'm going to need more context," Victor remarks as he looks at Superior Jackie.

"You can learn about that during your necromancy lessons," Superior Charles says calmly yet sternly. "If you make it that far. Now, do you remember healing Leo?"

Victor's gaze into Superior Charles' eyes feels cold. The two empaths hold their focus on each other as if they are trying to read each other's thoughts. "I felt some kind of worry, but after I killed the warlock, I don't remember much of anything else." Victor thought he was in the clear but forgot he was sitting before Superior Charles.

"You *do* remember something," Superior Charles says as he brings his cigar to his lips. "What did you see when you passed out?"

Victor thinks to himself, *I guess I'd better tell them.* He exhales deeply before he mentions, "I saw my mother." Superior Charles focuses sharply on Victor, while Superior Jackie and the elders give each other a puzzled look before giving their attention back to Victor. "We were in this glowing forest. There was a house that looked familiar to me, but I couldn't approach it. Every time I tried to get closer, it would move away from me. There was also a glowing stream."

"What color was the stream?" Superior Jackie asks.

"Blue," Victor answers. Superior Jackie lets out a sigh of relief. "Why do you ask?"

"That was the River Styx. It's where the dead go to follow their way to the afterlife." Superior Jackie sits up straight and smooths out her pant leg with her hand. "It's been said that those who specialize in necromancy can travel to the astral plane to find dead individuals and bring them back to the corporeal plane." The superior cups her hands in her lap as she crosses her legs. "If the Styx is blue, it does not find you a threat. If it is green, danger is coming, and you must leave immediately. But if it turns a dark purple, there is no way back to the living."

"This wasn't your first time there, was it, young empath?" Superior Charles remarks as he studies Victor's aura.

"No, this was my second time," Victor responds calmly. "My first time was after I raged out on Karl and Leo."

"Why didn't you tell us this before?" Superior Charles asks in a firm yet scolding voice.

"I didn't know what it meant at the time," Victor replies firmly. "I thought it was irrelevant."

"Nothing is irrelevant around here," Superior Charles responds aggressively. He takes a long drag from his cigar and rubs his temple with his thumb before he continues. "Do you remember the conversation with your mother?"

"I do," Victor nods subtly. "She told me that her life, as well as my own, was in danger. When she was pregnant with me, a seer sought her out to warn her. She didn't tell me who she spoke to, only that she would have to sacrifice herself to keep me safe and off everyone's radar. So, I guess that explains the mystery of how a 30-something-year-old is barely learning how to be a warlock."

Victor looks at Superior Charles and focuses on his aura. He notes both blues and greens intertwining together. He realizes that it was more for fear and guilt. "Tell me about the witch that stopped my grandmother from becoming the Grand Witch," Victor asks Superior Charles.

Superior Charles doesn't flinch and keeps his eyes on Victor. He moves his jaw around as though he's pondering whether or not he wants to tell Victor what he wants to know. They don't break eye contact for a moment, which feels like an eternity.

Superior Charles downs his drink. He signals the young warlock to refill his drink before he responds. "I knew the witch who attacked your grandmother. Her name was Florence Maryweather. She didn't like how witches were becoming so modern in their ways. A few covens preferred more traditional ways and didn't want to mingle with the mundane. Florence was in one of those covens."

Superior Charles knocks back his second drink and sets the empty glass on the table next to him. "When Marie, your grandmother, was given approval from the council to test to see if she would be the next Grand Witch, Florence did not stand by it. She fought tooth and nail against it and postponed Marie's final test. Because a blood blue moon wasn't often, it would be at least another couple of years before Marie could continue. Shortly after Florence won her argument, Marie began to fall ill. Somehow, no one saw it coming, not even the seers."

Superior Charles takes a deep drag from his cigar and exhales a large cloud. "We tried as much as we could but couldn't figure out what curse Marie had. The only person who could have stopped it was Florence. Unfortunately, when we found Florence, she was dead." The superior dabs the cigar ash into a silver tray. "Her death was supposed to look like suicide, but I knew better."

Superior Charles flexes his jaw around as he forces himself to remember the witch he has hated for a very long time. "Florence enjoyed life, which was ironic considering she was a necromancer. Sadly, we couldn't find any notes on what curse had a hold on Marie. It was only a matter of time before she left us. "

Victor sits back in his seat and sets his drink on the table next to his chair. "Did you know about me and my mother?"

Superior Jackie speaks before Superior Charles, "We only knew about your mother. But Marie informed us that she was to go into hiding and to never be found. We honored her wishes and never searched for her."

Superior Charles continues, "Also, we were unaware your mother was pregnant with you. If we had known, we might have taken different measures to save your mother and protect you."

Victor looks around at everyone before looking back at Superior Charles. "My mother told me the seer only saw one way to protect me."

"Seers can see many variations of the future," Elder Leopold explains. "But they can't predict the exact future. So maybe it was a ploy to have your mother sacrifice herself, thinking it was to protect you."

Victor starts to get angry, without knowing his eyes have a slight glow. "I don't believe that."

Everyone starts to adjust in their seats.

"Victor, I think it's best that you calm down," Superior Charles commands in a husky, low tone.

Victor gives Superior Charles a pointed look. Superior Jackie flicks her wrist, conjuring her hand mirror out of her purse to fly over to Victor and stop in front of his face. Victor takes in a sharp breath when he looks at the mirror. He slowly reaches out to bring the mirror closer. Holding the mirror in his hand, he studies his eyes. A moment later, the glow fades away.

Superior Jackie flicks her wrist again, removing the mirror from Victor's hand and returning to her purse. "Looks like we'll need to see how your eyes do that," she notates. "It could be emotions are involved."

Victor sits back, a little embarrassed. "I'm sorry. I didn't mean to."

"It's okay, young empath," Superior Charles remarks. "I can see that talking about your mother brings up many emotions. You were close to her. I get it. I lost my mom when I was young myself. There's not a day that goes by that I don't think about her. But I don't let that emotion get the best of me." Superior Charles stands up, and everyone else follows. "I think you should get back to your lessons. In the meantime, it might be best that we find another mentor for you. I don't feel Leo will be strong enough to continue to be around you."

"No," Victor lets out as he bolts up from his seat. "I mean, please don't. Leo has been great to be around. He's patient with me and has been helping me adapt to this new life I have entered." Victor takes a deep breath and subtly rolls his shoulders back to stand tall. "Would it be improper to ignore the wishes of an empath?"

Superior Jackie gives a little smirk towards Victor before she looks over at Superior Charles, "It seems like our young empath has a point, Superior."

Superior Charles looks at his other elders as they nod in agreement. "Fine. Lieutenant Magi Leopold will remain as your mentor." Superior Charles walks towards Victor but stops in the center of the circle. "*But*, if we feel he can no longer protect you, we will find someone else." He looks at everyone, "Y'all can go. I think we're done here for now." While everyone leaves, Superior Charles puts his hands in his pockets and looks at Victor as he walks closer. "So, have you decided on a coven to join?"

"Superior?" Victor asks as he cranes his head up to look at Superior Charles, who is about a foot taller than he is.

"I'm just wondering if anyone has contacted you," Superior Charles responds.

"No. At least not that I know of," Victor states.

Superior Charles pulls out a maroon square business card with a silver emblem between his fingers. The emblem resembles a horse's head, constructed from geometric shapes. As the light hits the shine of the emblem, it appears as if the mane is flowing in the wind.

"Consider this your first invite," Superior Charles remarks with a smirk. Victor looks at the card before he takes it. "And don't forget, when you're finished with your basic specialties, I want you to come back to see me so we can work on your empathic ability." He pats Victor's shoulder as he turns to leave. "Leo's outside by the stables," he mentions without looking over his shoulder.

Victor watches the superior turn into the hallway and walks away.

CHAPTER TWENTY-SEVEN

Victor walks outside, looking for Leo. He scans the grounds and sees a few dozen people walking around. Others are enjoying the sunny day, lying on a blanket in the grass. A half dozen are windsurfing on the lake. As Victor walks over to the lake, he sees Leo returning a horse to the stables. Leo smiles as he pets the majestic beast, mouthing how handsome and powerful the horse is. Victor smiles, noticing this is the first time he has seen Leo relaxed and enjoying himself.

Leo spots Victor alone in the grassy field when he leaves the stall. Leo sends Victor a smile as he closes the door behind him. He brushes his hands on the sides of his jeans and walks over to Victor. Victor meets him halfway.

"Were you riding around while you were waiting for me?" Victor asks.

"Yes, it's been a while since I rode. We took a lap around the lake," Leo mentions as he looks out to the water.

"It's huge," Victor remarks as he looks around the lake, barely able to see the shoreline on the other side. "How fast were you going?"

Leo smiles ear-to-ear. "She can run on water, so we just went across to the other side and back. You know the saying, 'You can lead a horse to water, but it will just want to run across it.'"

Victor ponders Leo's statement. "I'm not so sure that's how it goes."

Leo laughs and pats Victor on the back. "Come on, let's get something to eat before we head back to your place."

Leo walks Victor over to a large ramada on the other side of the lawn. The coven gathers around several long wooden picnic tables. Several young individuals are helping an older woman bring out the food. As Leo and Victor reach a picnic table, Leo gestures to Victor to have a seat.

"I know you've probably had some good barbecue in Texas, but wait until you've had Elder Maggie's barbecue," Leo remarks.

Elder Maggie starts floating the food around the tables. She has a huge smile as she waves her arms and hands around as if conducting an orchestra. As soon as the food reaches Victor, he goes for a bowl. Before he could take it, a spoonful of green beans plates itself onto Victor's plate.

"Is lunch always like this?" Victor smirks.

Leo lets out a light chuckle, "No. It's only because Superior Charles is trying to impress you."

"Why?" Victor asks, giving Leo a side-eyed glance.

"For one, you're not part of a coven yet. Some young individuals are inherited into a coven when they are born. But if they decide to join another, they must be invited by the superior of that coven," Leo explains.

"What's 'For Two'?" Victor questions while watching the food float around the ramada.

"You're basically a *Solus Warlock*," Leo responds. "A Solus is someone without a coven. That's reason enough for a superior to invite you to join their coven, especially if you impress them. And you're an empath. We don't have many empaths nowadays. That also includes seers and telepaths."

"What do you mean? Have they died off?" Victor ponders as he watches his plate fill with food.

"Or were killed," Leo comments under his breath. "What?" Victor snaps his head to Leo.

Leo puts his napkin in his shirt and picks up his fork. "A little over four decades ago, these dark covens, if you want to call them that, wanted to go back to a traditional way of life. They sought out everyone who was gifted with an ability." He takes a bite of his food before he continues. "You should eat before it gets cold."

Victor pours himself a glass of tea before he takes Leo's glass to pour some tea for him. "What happened to those with abilities?"

"They were told to join those dark covens and help with returning to the ways witchcraft once was, or be killed," Leo responds with a mouth full of food.

Victor drops Leo's glass of tea all over the table. No one around reacts. Leo snaps his fingers upward, lifting the liquid off the table into a ball. Leo then flings his hand over his shoulder, throwing the liquid into a trash can. Victor looks around. Everyone at the table continues to eat and talk amongst themselves while Leo chows down on a couple of ribs.

Victor pours Leo another glass. "How many with an ability are left?"

Leo wipes his face before asking, "Can you please hand me a wet nap?" Victor reaches over to the pile of wet naps until Leo scolds him. "No, with your magic." Victor gives Leo a disgusted look, and Leo gives a cheesy smile in return.

Victor takes a breath and then waves his hand to pick up a wet nap with his magic. As it floats over to Leo, he snatches it before Leo can take it.

"Are you going to answer my question?"

Leo grabs the wet nap from Victor's hand. "About seven empaths are left, including you. Five seers and three telepaths. Only three seers and five empaths are not in one of those dark covens. There could be more, but they have gone into hiding."

"Why were they told to join or die?" Victor inquires.

"Anyone with an ability can perform necromancy perfectly. It's what caused the mundane to fear us, and those dark covens feel that's how witchcraft should be. Darkness and death," Leo informs.

Victor swallows his food before speaking. "I guess that is why Superior Charles mentioned witchcraft is becoming more modern."

Leo shrugs. "You can say that. We're not dressing in black. We're not making sacrifices to please our gods. We aren't using our magic to overthrow the mundane. Because we'd be outnumbered even if we did." He takes a big bite out of a rib before he continues with a mouth full of food. "We use our magic more for good, in a way. We're not all about goat's blood and demons. I mean, there are demons, but we don't use them the way they want us to."

Victor looks around the ramada and notices a diverse mix of people from different walks of life. "Leo, if you're in Superior Charles' coven, why don't you live with him or in Dallas?"

Leo looks up at Victor. Victor chuckles as he commands several more wet wipes over. Leo smiles as he finishes eating and cleans his face.

Leo drinks some tea before he can answer. "Back in the day, covens did live with, or close to, one another. That's why Superior Charles has such a large ranch house. It was only about 20 years ago when his coven decided to live on their own. But they would still serve under him." Leo pauses for a moment to collect his thoughts. "Serve is a strong word."

"I get it," Victor responds. "I take it most of the coven here live elsewhere?"

"Yeah, but most of them live in Texas. I'm one of the few to live out of state," Leo mentions.

"Why do you live in San Francisco if you're in this coven?" Victor asks.

Victor notices his question must have struck a nerve in Leo. But Leo finishes his bite before he responds. "Derek and I were allowed to live outside our covens since our marriage was practically a peace treaty. We chose to live in San Diego because it was closer to his coven. After we broke up, I didn't want to move back to Texas, so I chose San Francisco because my parents live in Santa Rosa. The house they live in was my grandma's on my mom's side. And my parents prefer the weather in California to that in Texas. But there's nothing to do there. So, San Francisco. Also, I got a terrific deal on my apartment."

"How's that treaty now?" Victor questions.

"Since we're still technically married, the covens must keep the peace. I wouldn't look into it too much; it's still confusing. But needless to say, I can still live elsewhere."

"I guess letting you live wherever is one way covens are becoming more modern," Victor remarks. "Are all covens the same way?"

"No," Leo replies. "There are a few covens that still live together. But most live in the same neighborhood or within a mile from their superior's home."

Victor sets down his utensils once he finishes his late bite. He looks over at the table where Superior Charles and his elders are sitting. "He asked me to come back so he could help me with my empathic ability."

Leo looks over where Superior Charles is sitting. "You should take him up on his offer. He's one of the best empaths right now. He's a strong leader, even though he's not the grand warlock."

"Did he go through the trials?" Victor asks, looking back at Leo.

Leo continues looking at his superior. "He tried but couldn't make it past the trials to become the High Priest."

"Speaking of titles," Victor turns in his seat to look at Leo better, "he called you Lieutenant Magi Leo. You didn't tell me you had a title."

"Yes, I'm a second lieutenant. I'm working to become chancellor, but the sheriffs aren't happy that I'm about to out-rank them."

Confused, Victor tilts his head. "Wait, there's a ranking system?"

"Oh yeah. It's a headache to try to understand, but most covens, especially the larger ones, have ranks. It's mostly used for our responsibilities and in battle. Right now, I'm mostly involved with training young witches and warlocks. And being a mentor helps me become chancellor quicker."

"What would your duties be as chancellor?" Victor queries.

"I would be able to represent my coven at the council and have some leeway in the voting process," Leo explains.

Victor leans against the table and ponders, "I didn't picture you as a politician."

Leo snorts in disgust. "Such a nasty word, politician. I would never abuse my power to play my own game."

As Victor snickers, plates of pecan pie with vanilla ice cream start sliding down the table and stopping in front of everyone. "I'm not sure I can eat dessert. I'm full from that brisket." He looks over Leo's shoulder and sees Superior Jackie walking toward them. "Speaking of politicians."

Superior Jackie stops in front of Victor and Leo with a smile. "Afternoon, gentlemen. Before I go, I wanted to give Victor something." She digs through her purse and takes out a round, white business card with a pink emblem and hands it to Victor. The emblem features an elegant design of a rose with the stem forming a subtle "J" shape. "I heard Charles gave you an invite, and I wanted to give you one too."

Leo cocks an eyebrow and looks at Victor. "Two in one day. Very impressive."

Victor takes the business card from Superior Jackie. "Thank you, Superior."

"Think about it," Superior Jackie says with a smile before she turns and walks away.

Victor looks at the business card. He then senses other eyes are looking at him. He looks up and notices the others at the table are giving him a judgmental look.

"Hey!" Leo snaps. "Finish your dessert."

"Whatever," one of the warlocks says under his breath as he rolls his eyes.

Leo leans over to him. "Did you say something? Because I couldn't hear you."

He turns sheepish. "Nothing, Leo."

"Come on, Victor. Let's go for a walk." Leo stands up and throws his napkin on the table as he walks away. Victor wipes his face and follows. Victor looks over his shoulder and sees Superior Charles look at him a few seconds before returning to the conversation with the elders at his table.

Victor and Leo walk along the shore of the lake. Victor takes out his phone when he receives a text message. "*Shit*," Victor emphasizes softly as he reads the message.

"Something wrong?" Leo asks as they stop.

"Amber's birthday dinner is tomorrow night. And I promised Lupe months ago that I would be there."

Leo sighs deeply. "What did I tell you about keeping mundane friends?"

"About that." Victor stops and turns to Leo. "I should be upset with you because you responded to their texts, but I understand why you did it. I was passed out for an undetermined amount of time, and you didn't want them to worry if I didn't respond immediately. You had every opportunity to tell them I can't be their friend anymore, but you didn't."

"It should come directly from you, not me," Leo remarks.

"I can't do that right now. And I knew about this dinner before I met you," Victor says.

Leo scratches his chin and then lets out another deep sigh. "Fine," he says, aggravated. "But I'm coming with you."

"No, they'll start asking more questions and might think we're dating," Victor protests.

"What? You don't want to date me?" Leo gives Victor a cheesy, teeth-filled grin.

"No, I mean, yes. I mean . . . UGH! I don't want to undergo a long interrogation, especially overshadowing the birthday girl." Victor sighs, "I'll be okay. I promise."

Leo puckers his lips, deep in thought. "No, I'm coming with you. But I'll keep my distance. They won't know that I'm there."

Victor looks up at the sky and moans, "Why can't I have a night with my friends alone?"

"You know why. But don't worry, I have an illusion charm I can wear. And I want you to wear your suit," Leo says.

"Seriously? Do I also have to be home by 10 p.m. Dad?" Victor asks, sarcastically.

Leo leans over and whispers into Victor's ear, "I'll tell you when to call me daddy." A chill goes down Victor's spine, and his heart beats faster. Leo pulls away. "Ready to go back to your apartment?"

Victor looks at the time. "Yeah, I should, especially if I'm going to fly back to Dallas tonight."

Leo takes a step back. "Hello! You're already in Dallas. Well, north of Dallas. Why would you need to fly back? You could walk through the mirror."

"Frank and Elliott are flying with me. It wouldn't be right. And our flight is in a few hours, so I need to hurry back," Victor proclaims.

Leo crosses his arms. "Fine, but you better let me know where you're eating and staying."

Victor rolls his eyes. "Okay..." He smirks as he looks into Leo's eyes, "... Daddy."

CHAPTER TWENTY-EIGHT

Victor rushes through the airport, struggling to keep his luggage on his shoulder. When he arrives, Frank and Elliott sit near the podium next to their gate.

"I'm sorry I'm late," Victor says as he catches his breath.

"Don't worry about it," Elliott says as he gets out of his seat to hug Victor. "The flight is delayed. And it looks like we'll get a seat in first class because everyone is going to the next flight, which leaves in an hour."

Frank looks up at Victor with a sly grin. "So why were you late? You're always on time or early. Was it that Leo guy we met the other night?"

"N-No. W-Why would you say that?" Victor stutters.

Frank gives Victor a shit-eating grin, "Elliott, look at him blush. It was Leo!"

Victor glares at Frank as he takes a seat next to Elliott. "Shut your hole, tramp. So, what's the delay?"

Elliott shrugs as he responds, "Mechanical. Crew. Catering. You know how it goes."

Victor looks beyond the podium and sees the flight attendants standing by the door to the jet bridge. "Oh fuck," he groans.

Frank and Elliott look over. Elliott sees who Victor just noticed. "Well, this is going to be an awkward flight."

Frank leans over Elliott and asks Victor, "Isn't that James' sister?"

"Yes, that's her," Victor replies as he tries to hide himself.

Frank leans over more, practically laying on top of Elliott. "Do you think she's going to tell James that you were on her flight?"

"I wouldn't doubt it," Victor responds. "She never really liked me. I think she was just jealous that I took her brother's attention away from her."

Elliott smacks Frank's behind and then Victor's arm. "Looks like you got her attention."

The female flight attendant walks over to Victor and his friends. She stops a few feet away and places one hand on her hip. "Hello, boys. Victor."

Victor tries to hold back how awkward he feels. "Hey, Michele, how are you?"

Michele looks at Victor with an amused expression. "I've been good. I transferred from Seattle last year. How have you been? It's been a while since we last saw each other."

Victor can feel Elliott's and Frank's eyes on him as he maintains his attention on Michele. "Things have been good. Just been busy with work. I see you're working this flight."

Michele turns her head to the departure board behind the podium. "Yeah, we have a mechanical. Should be done in an hour."

"What's wrong?" Elliott inquires.

Michele doesn't look at Elliott as she turns her attention back to Victor. "A flat tire. They are changing it now. It looks like you might be sitting up front with me. I'll make sure to take good care of you."

"Are you staying the night when you get to Dallas?" Frank asks.

Michele keeps her attention on Victor. "Yes, we are. Are you guys staying in Dallas too, or connecting somewhere?"

"Dallas," Elliott answers. "We got a couple of rooms at one of our layover hotels."

"The Grand?" Michele asks, still looking at Victor.

"Yes," Frank replies enthusiastically.

Michele puts a sly smile on her face. She can sense Victor's nervousness. "Well, if you boys want to join my crew in the van, you're more than welcome to." She looks over his shoulder and says, "Looks like I'm needed." She looks back at Victor with a smirk. "See you on board."

As Michele walks away, Frank and Elliott start talking over Victor to each other. "Oh my God, that was so awkward," Frank states.

"So awkward," Elliott replies.

Victor slowly slides down his seat while covering his eyes. "Why am I being tested?"

When it's time to board, Victor and his friends take their seats in the last row in first class. He takes the window seat while Elliott takes the aisle seat next to him, and Frank sits across from them. Victor puts in his ear pods and pretends to take a nap. Elliott tries to get his attention, but Victor ignores him. The last thing Victor wants to do is interact with Michele.

After a silently awkward flight to Dallas, Victor is relieved when they finally disembark the airplane. Victor didn't want an uncomfortable van ride, so he orders an Uber. When the Uber arrives, he spots Michele and her crew loading into their van. She looks around before she gets in and closes the door. Victor sits in the back seat, relieved he won't be seeing Michele again.

A short car ride later, Victor and his friends arrive at the hotel. As they check in, Victor completely forgot that Michele is staying at the same hotel. He freezes when he spots her at the front desk. He tries to find a place to hide, but it is too late; Michele smiles back at him.

Victor stands still as Michele approaches. "It was nice seeing you again, Victor." She turns and walks away.

Elliott and Frank are giggling behind Victor. "Oh, shut up," he snaps to them.

Frank wraps his arm around Victor's shoulder. "This calls for a drink."

"Make it three," Victor suggests.

The next evening, Victor puts on the finishing touches to his suit. He was thankful the vest he ordered from Clarence arrived before he had to quickly pack and leave for the airport. Victor reaches for his jacket and then stops, retracting his hand. "Nah, I think I can do without." As he's putting on his shoes, there's a knock at his hotel door. He opens the door, and Frank is on the other side.

Frank lets out a low whistle. "Damn boy, did you get sex this morning to make you feel sexy tonight?"

Victor rolls his eyes as he walks away. "You're just jealous that I look better than you do."

"Elliott's waiting for us in the lobby," Frank mentions as he steps inside and closes the door behind him.

"Why aren't you down there with him?" Victor asks, discreetly placing his dagger in his vest's upper breast pocket. Victor takes a quick glance in the mirror to ensure it's well hidden.

Frank takes a seat at the foot of the bed. "I wanted to talk to you about something, first."

"What's up?" Victor asks while looking at Frank in the mirror.

"I saw James the other night. He was on a date," Frank says solemnly.

"And why are you telling me this?" Victor asks while looking at Frank in the mirror.

"I mean, I know you two just broke up. And I wanted to tell you before you find out from someone else. Because that's what friends do," Frank remarks.

Victor turns around and leans against the desk, resting his hands behind him. "Thank you for telling me, Frank. But I'm fine. He wanted to break things off with me, and you telling me this just proves he never loved me. If he wants to date other guys, I really don't care."

"He literally broke up with you a few months ago. Aren't you at least a little upset?" Frank asks, stupefied.

"If he was that quick to move on, then so will I," Victor responds as he turns around to retrieve his room key.

Frank stands up and crosses his arms. "If it were my ex, I would slash his tires and set his car on fire."

Victor snickers as he checks himself one more time in the mirror. "I'm going to be the bigger person and pray for him."

Frank laughs, "I think he needs more than just a prayer."

"Like what? A frying pan to the head?" Victor and Frank laugh as they head out of Victor's room. When they reach the lobby, Elliott is waving for them to come outside where their ride is waiting.

Victor and his friends arrive at the restaurant 20 minutes later. He checks them in and the host hands him a buzzer for when the table is ready. Victor thanks him, then orders a round of drinks for the table, to be delivered when they are seated. When he steps back outside with Elliott and Frank, he receives a text.

"They should be here in about five minutes," Victor says after reading Lupe's text message. Seconds later, a car pulls up. Lupe gets out first and then helps Amber out. "Or maybe less," he says in surprise.

"There's the birthday girl!" Elliott shouts out with open arms. He pulls Amber in and kisses her on the cheek. "Damn, you clean up good. I almost didn't recognize you."

Amber laughs, "Ass." She looks over Elliott's broad shoulders and is surprised to see her friend. "Victor! You made it!"

"Of course I did. I wouldn't miss you turning the Big 3-0," Victor remarks as he takes in his friend's embrace.

Frank waves the buzzer in the air. "Our table's ready, guys!"

As the hostess escorts Victor and his friends to their table, Victor stops halfway as he senses something. He looks around to see who it is. He starts noticing the auras of everyone at the restaurant.

"You okay?" Elliott asks Victor.

Victor snaps out of his trance. "Yes, sorry, I was looking for the restroom. I'll be right back." Victor leaves Elliott and acts like he's walking to the restroom.

Victor goes back to focusing on everyone's aura. He passes by a couple and can see that the man is in love and has feelings about proposing. The woman he's with doesn't feel the same. *"Poor guy,"* Victor says to himself as he walks past them. As Victor is about to walk down the hallway to the restroom, he notices a guy sitting alone, not far from where his friends are sitting. The man's aura looks a little off to Victor.

Victor realizes, "Leo." Victor takes out his phone and shoots Leo a text. Victor looks back at the man sitting alone. He turns around and gives Victor a wink. Victor walks back to his friends as he passes by Leo. "That charm really does work," he whispers to Leo.

Victor sits down with his friends as soon as the server brings everyone their drinks. "I ordered the drinks before you arrived so we can have them once we sat down," Victor says, while scooting his chair in. He raises his glass toward Amber, and everyone follows. "Welcome to the Flirty and Dirty 30 Club!" Everyone cheers and clinks their glasses together.

The five friends order their meals, a few more drinks, and catch up with each other. Amber chastises Elliott for talking about a time they flew together that was embarrassing;

Frank laughs. Amber threatens Frank for laughing, but Lupe intervenes. Amber glares at her fiancée, and Lupe glares back. Amber apologizes to Lupe with a smile, and Victor laughs at it all.

Victor feels more like himself again. Not having to worry about his lessons or the fact that there is always someone after him. This is his family. The ones he can always call upon when he needs them. They always have each other's backs. Victor can't give this up, no matter what Leo says.

After everyone finishes their meal, the server comes over holding a slice of cake with a candle. Amber blushes as everyone sings "Happy Birthday." When the song concludes, she blows out the candle.

"PREESSEEENTS!" Lupe sings joyfully. "I hope you like this one, my love."

Victor smiles as Amber opens her gift from Lupe. Suddenly, he starts to feel dizzy. He tries to keep it together. Victor's eyes flutter. It becomes difficult for him to breathe. He feels around his pockets for his silver card.

"Victor, is everything okay?" Elliott asks, concerned.

"I-I'm fine. It's just a massive mi-migraine," Victor responds, trying not to come undone. *Why is it always when I'm eating?* Victor says to himself. *Where is that fucking card?*

"Oh my god, Victor, do you need me to look for a doctor?!" Amber asks.

As Victor tries to look at Amber, he notices a female server in the background holding and shaking his card in her hands. "You bitch," Victor spits.

"I beg your pardon?!" Amber bolts out.

"Not you, her!" Victor tries to point at the server. Victor looks over his shoulder to where Leo is sitting and sees another witch across from him. Victor can't see what spell she's using to keep Leo in his seat, but he needs to do something.

I can't let them do this to me. Not in front of my friends. Not in front of everyone here. Victor tries to figure out what to do before he succumbs to the force trying to knock him out. The server holding his card twists her wrist upward, setting the candle and cake ablaze.

"THE FUCK!" Amber shouts as everyone jumps back from the table. A few women across from them scream and run, causing a mass commotion.

"VICTOR!" Elliott shouts as he tries to pick Victor up from his seat. "We need to go!" The fire starts to grow and get hotter.

"NO!" Victor shouts as he pushes Elliott off him.

Victor regains control and covers his face by crossing his wrists with his index fingers pointing upward. The fire shoots over to the server, and she dodges out of the way. People are running toward whichever exit they can find. They push and trip over each other, trying to avoid the chaos. Victor's friends are stunned as they try to figure out what is going on and what Victor is doing.

Victor stands up, spins around on his heel, and uses Air Magic to pull the witch at Leo's table. "Leo! Get them out of here!"

"Leo?" Elliott questions with confusion. Elliott looks around, befuddled. "Leo's here?"

Leo appears from the charm and runs over to Victor, saying, "You can't fight them alone."

"Get my friends out of here first," Victor demands as he turns his attention to the server. "I'll handle them." His eyes are now glowing white.

Amber notices Victor's eyes and becomes startled. With a shaky finger, she points at Victor's face. "V-V-Victor?"

"Let's go!" Leo shouts at Victor's friends.

"What about Vic?" Frank asks, panicked.

Leo looks over at Victor, watching him take on the witch that bound him to his chair. "He'll be fine. Now let's go!" Leo grabs Amber by the shoulders and turns her toward the exit. Before Leo and the others can reach the doors, two more witches appear, blocking the way out.

"You're not going anywhere," one of the witches snarls. With a flick of her hand, Leo is thrown to the other side of the restaurant. "Now, unless the rest of you step to the side and let us at the empath, you'll end up like him."

Victor's friends turn to look at him in confusion.

Victor tosses the server aside and glares at the two witches blocking their exit. "Do as they say, and get out of here," Victor orders. The witch, posing as a server, picks herself off the ground and throws a flame at Victor, singeing his shirt. Victor holds out his palm and blocks it. He uses his other hand to grab all the liquid around and splashes the server, causing the flame to extinguish.

The witch who was holding Leo in his seat starts charging at Victor. Before he can react, the other two use the wooden chairs to bind him.

"Victor!" Elliott and Frank shout in unison. As they try to reach for him, one of the witches pushes all of Victor's friends aside, knocking them over tables and chairs.

"Leave them alone!" Victor demands, struggling in his wooden restraints. "I'm the one you want."

"I'm impressed you're not raging out," the lead witch comments. "Given the fact that she took that silver card from you."

"I'm getting used to being attacked on a regular basis," Victor sneers, his eyes still glowing. The lead witch approaches Victor. She's wearing a dark green blouse with puffy sleeves, a black satin vest, and oversized black dress pants. "You're still not as strong as you think. We'll be greatly rewarded for bringing you back with us."

One of the witches is shot in the back with a fireball. Leo stands tall, his palm held out. "He's not going anywhere." He throws several more fireballs at the witches.

One of the witches conjures her Metal Magic, lifting her hands as high as her shoulders, then thrusting them forward—every knife in the restaurant rains upon Leo. Leo defends himself the best he can until he's hit in the shoulder.

"NOOOO!" Victor cries out in fury. A bright pulse flies off him, breaking his wooden bind and knocking over the four witches. He drops to the floor on his hands and knees.

The witches struggle to get back on their feet. One looks over at Victor. "Oh, shit," she comments.

Victor is still on his hands and knees, but his eyes are black as he looks up at the four of them.

"We need to get the fuck out of here," the lead witch commands. But Victor has already blocked their path before they can scramble to the door.

"Going somewhere?" Victor says, but not in his voice. As the witches start walking backward, Victor sees his friends slowly getting to their feet. "Guys, get the fuck out of here. It's not safe."

Victor's friends see his black eyes and are unsure of what to do.

"Victor," Elliott says in fear. "W-What's wrong with your eyes? And your voice?"

Before Victor can say anything, two witches fling tables and chairs at him. Victor waves his hand from side to side, tossing away everything thrown at him. The two other witches start flying the silverware at Victor. He holds up his palm, causing the silverware to stop right in front of him.

Victor makes a fist, crushing some of the silverware and binding it together. The witches watch as Victor creates a large, sharp object. As the remaining utensils fall to the floor, the only thing floating is a makeshift spear.

Victor opens his fist, turns his palm outward, then pushes his palm forward, making the spear soar toward the witches. The spear goes straight through the neck of one of the witches, causing everyone to flinch back with a gasp. The spear flies into the wall. The witch grabs her neck as she's choking on her blood. She drops to her knees and then falls to the floor.

Victor closes his eyes and inhales deeply. As he exhales, he opens his eyes and uses a strong air pulse on another witch, causing her to fly back and be impaled by the spear through her chest. The remaining two witches start to shout as their anger grows.

As they charge toward Victor, Leo jumps in front of Victor and blasts a flame into the witches' faces. They scream in agony and stumble backward as they cover their burnt faces.

When Victor starts to lift his hand, Leo stops him and looks into his black eyes. "No! We need them alive for questioning."

Victor looks at Leo's shoulder. The knife is no longer there, but blood is seeping out. "You're injured," he says with a look of concern. Victor places his hand over Leo's shoulder, and a silver glow appears under his palm. He keeps his hand hovering over Leo's injury for several seconds. "How does that feel?"

Leo rotates his shoulder. "Like I didn't have a serrated knife in my shoulder moments ago."

Victor blinks a couple of times, and his eyes return to normal. He looks around at the carnage and how scared his friends are as they help each other off the floor. One of the mirrors on the wall starts to go hazy. Superior Jackie and Akisha come through, with Superior Charles right behind them. Everyone looks outside, seeing flashing red and blue lights.

"Everyone, get out of here. We'll clean up this mess," Superior Charles demands. "Go back to my coven. You'll be safe there."

"Victor, what's going on?" Amber asks, shaken by the chaos.

Victor looks at his friends, "No time to explain. We need to go." Victor and Leo turn their friends toward the mirror. They all stop as they look in the mirror. "Don't worry. It will be fine," Victor says reassuringly. Leo offers to go first, to show there is nothing to worry about. After a bit of hesitation, everyone walks through the mirror.

CHAPTER TWENTY-NINE

Victor and his friends sit around Superior Charles' meeting room. Leo is sitting in a chair, sipping on some whisky. Elliott and Frank are standing by the liquor cabinet, trying out almost every bottle to calm their nerves.

Amber is pacing around the center of the room. "A Warlock! Warlock!"

"Yes," Lupe states while she's sitting in a chair. "We have established Victor is a warlock."

"Why didn't you tell any of us?" Amber asks aggressively.

"Yeah!" Elliott adds as he opens a bottle of bourbon. "I thought we were friends. How could you keep something like this from us?"

Victor massages his forehead. "You have to understand; I was only trying to keep you safe. You saw how dangerous those witches were back there."

"That you murdered," Amber snaps.

"It was technically self-defense, babe," Lupe comments.

"And that justifies what Victor did to them?" Amber retorts.

"This isn't the first time," Victor mentions.

Amber is gobsmacked to hear that her friend has killed before. "You've killed others before?"

"It was all in self-defense," Victor reiterates.

"How can you just stand there and act like it's normal? Do you even sleep at night afterwards?"

"Honestly," Victor pauses, "I haven't had much time to process all of it. I've been getting my eight hours of sleep a night."

"Amber, you have to understand, it was either that or they kill him," Leo states over the rim of his glass.

"I take it you're a warlock too?" Amber asks Leo.

"I am," Leo replies without hesitation.

"You lied about how you met Victor. Is your name even Leo?" Amber questions, crossing her arms as she stops pacing and gives Leo a pointed look.

Leo looks up at Amber and responds, "Yes, my name is Leo. And we only lied because of the way everyone is acting now."

"Guys," Victor interjects as he stands up. "I'll explain everything. I just need–"

Victor is interrupted by the double doors to the room opening. Superior Charles, Superior Jackie, and Akisha walk into the room. Superior Charles has a slight snarl in the corner of his mouth. He marches over to Victor.

"You forgot something at the restaurant," Superior Charles says as he tosses the silver card to Victor. "Try not to lose it again."

Victor catches the card. "I'm sorry, Superior. The witch dressed as a server pickpocketed it out of my vest."

Superior Charles stops in front of Victor and places his hands on his hips. His tall stature gives the impression of a father looking down at his son as he scolds him. "And how did you not know there were a couple of witches at the restaurant?"

Victor feels ashamed. "I guess I was distracted celebrating with my friends."

Superior Charles looks over to Leo. "Have you not talked to him about breaking his ties to the mundane?"

Before Leo could speak, Victor answers. "He did. He's mentioned it to me several times. He even spoke about it yesterday after the barbecue."

"Then why were you with your friends?" Superior Charles demands. He looks at Amber and says, "Happy birthday, by the way."

Victor cranes his neck to look up at Superior Charles. "How am I supposed to let go of years of friendship in an instant?" He looks at Superior Jackie and Akisha. "How are you to expect someone like me to tell my friends, two of whom I've known for over 10 years, that I can't be their friend anymore? It might be easy for you, or you . . ." Victor looks back up at Superior Charles. ". . . or even you, Superior, because all of you grew up in this life. I didn't. I grew up with the mundane."

Victor walks over to an open area where everyone can see him. "I didn't even know witches or warlocks existed until over a month ago. To me and my friends, it was all superstition. Fairy tales. For fuck's sake, we all sat in front of Madame Jeanette without knowing she was a witch."

Frank perks up. "Madame Jeanette is a witch? *I knew it.*"

Victor gives Frank a pointed look before he continues. "These guys are my family. I trust each of them. I love each of them in my own way. How could you ask me to give all that up?"

Superior Charles taps his foot while he thinks. He walks over to his bar and pulls out a bottle from a hidden compartment. "This life is difficult to be a part of. You see, mundane." He turns to look at Victor's friends. "No offense . . . one thing you don't understand is Victor will no longer age with any of you."

Superior Charles pours himself a shot, then downs it. "As Victor continues to use magic, his aging process will slow down. By the time you turn 70, he may still look as he does now." He pours himself another drink. "Look at me. I'm over 147 years old. But I look like I'm in my mid-50s. Are you saying it's okay for him to watch all of you die while he continues to live on?"

"Why should any of that matter?" Elliott asks.

Superior Charles looks over at Elliott. "Did you not see what happened at the restaurant? Your attachment to him put you in danger."

"But we weren't seriously hurt," Elliott responds. "He even protected us."

"And what about his eyes?" Superior Jackie mentions as she walks forward.

"What about them?" Frank asks.

"Did that not startle you?" Superior Jackie responds. "Seeing his eyes change colors or even become completely blacked out?"

Victor's friends look at each other and then over to Victor.

"You see, you all had to stop and think about what you just witnessed. He *literally* had to murder two witches to protect himself and each of you. Do you think you can continue to witness something like that as you stay friends?" Superior Jackie asks Victor's friends.

"It was self-defense," Lupe remarks. "I might have done the same if my life had been threatened. It's a '*mundane*' instinct to fight or flight."

"May I interject?" Leo asks as he stands up. "Victor's friends do care about him. And although I mostly agree that we should not mingle with the mundane, his friends are . . . special." Leo looks over at Victor as he continues. "When Victor was out cold after the attack at Otsu, I responded to all their texts as if I were Victor. I knew if I didn't, someone would be breaking down Victor's door to make sure he was still alive. My bet would be on Amber."

"I would also bet on Amber," Elliott adds, trying to lighten the mood.

"Oh, my money is definitely on Amber," Lupe comments.

Leo rolls his eyes before he returns his attention to everyone in the room. "What we are asking him to do is not as easy for him as it would be for any of us. Look at them now. Yes, they are shocked about what happened tonight, but they trusted Victor enough to walk through a mirror to an unknown location. They could have run when they got the chance. But they stayed, knowing they were in danger, all because they care for Victor."

Superior Charles looks at Elliott and Frank. "Want some from my personal distillery?" Elliott and Frank look at one another, unsure about the request. Superior Charles chuckles as he opens a second hidden compartment. "Don't worry, it's available in stores at $150 a bottle."

"Is that a peace offering?" Victor inquires.

"In a way," Superior Charles responds as he pours two glasses.

Akisha finally speaks up as she walks further into the room. "You know, Superiors, the mundane are right. We are asking a lot from Victor. He has lived among them his entire life." She looks over to Victor's friends. "You four understand that Victor's life will always be in danger? Will you be a support system for him as he learns how powerful he can be? These aren't parlor tricks; this is *real* magic. You saw it with your own eyes tonight. Witches and warlocks are real. We remain in hiding because of the mundane's fear towards us."

Superior Charles turns to Akisha. "Have you forgotten how dangerous the mundane are? Or how many were lost during several riots worldwide that were used to cover up the witch hunts?"

"Excuse me, may I come in?" Everyone turns around and sees an older woman standing in the doorway.

"Elder Maggie," Superior Charles says as he stands up straight. "Yes, please come in."

Elder Maggie slowly enters the room while smiling at everyone. "I don't mean to eavesdrop, but I could hear you all the way in my study. I'm sure by now that the entire coven knows we have non-magic folk here."

"I'm sorry, Elder Maggie, we didn't mean to disturb you," Superior Charles remarks.

"It's alright, dear." Elder Maggie keeps walking towards Victor. She studies him for a moment before she speaks. "I don't know how we lost our ways. If you remember, Charles, I too lived with the mundane. On more than one occasion, I had relationships with mundane men."

Superior Jackie walks closer to the older woman. "Elder Maggie, you know we had to protect ourselves from the religious. Especially after the Salem Trials."

"I remember, dear," Elder Maggie comments. "I was there during those trials."

"Excuse me, Elder Maggie," Lupe interrupts. "How old are you?"

"Young lady, it's not proper to ask a woman her age," Elder Maggie says in a slightly stern voice. "But if you must know, I'm 350 years old." She gives Lupe a wink. "And I must say, this argument is getting tiresome. Everyone is going round and round, and when will it end?"

Elder Maggie turns her attention to Victor. "If this young empath, who could very well be the hope we are looking for to bring order to chaos, can trust his friends, why should we tell him to cut the cord with them?" Elder Maggie turns to walk away. "Besides, if he does become the Grand Warlock, then it will become his word over yours." She winks at Victor as she makes her way out of the room.

Superior Charles walks over to his cigar cabinet and strokes his beard. He lets out a heavy, nasal sigh as he takes out a cigar. As he puts the cigar in his mouth, he turns to look at everyone as it lights up. He takes a couple of puffs before he speaks. "Young empath, if you can vouch for your friends that they won't cause any kind of disturbance, then I'll drop the subject."

Victor looks over at his friends. He can't give up all the moments, all the drama, and all the love. "I can trust them."

"What about Lucas and Jon?" Frank asks.

Victor thinks for a moment. "We don't tell them. At least not yet. I'll tell them when I'm ready."

Superior Charles takes a seat in the circle. "There's a town car outside to take everyone back to the hotel. You'll be safe, don't worry. Victor and Leo will meet up with you later. Akisha, can you please escort the mund–" He catches himself and corrects his question, "Victor's friends to the town car?"

"I need to head out myself. I'll go with you," Superior Jackie offers.

As Akisha and Superior Jackie walk out with Victor's friends, Victor gives them a reassuring nod. When his friends are no longer in the room, he turns to Superior Charles. "Superior, are you sure they will be okay?"

"They will be," Superior Charles replies. "Now, please have a seat, both of you." Victor and Leo sit across from Superior Charles. He looks at Victor and Leo while puffing on his cigar. "There were four witches and one warlock. Did you happen to see where the warlock went?"

Victor and Leo look at each other. "I only saw four witches," Victor responds. "I didn't see a warlock."

Superior Charles holds his gaze on Victor for a moment. As he and Victor maintain eye contact, he asks, "Leo, what happened to you?"

"Somehow, the witch knew I was there," Leo responds. "Even with my illusion charm on, she found me. Before I knew it, she sat across from me and placed this powerful air-binding spell on me. I wasn't able to move until Victor knocked her over."

"How could she have known it was you if you were under an illusion?" Victor asks.

"She knew what charm to look for," Superior Charles states as he turns his attention to Leo. "Where did you get the charm?"

"Derek gave it to me as an anniversary gift eight years ago." Leo pulls out a ring with a small pleochroism sphere gem embedded in the center. "She must have seen the ring."

"When I walked past you, I didn't notice a ring on either of your hands," Victor remarks as he looks at the ring in Leo's hand.

Superior Charles leans over and holds his hand out for Leo to give him the ring. Leo hands it over, and Superior Charles inspects it. He holds the ring close, studying it carefully. "I hate to say it, Leo, but I have a feeling we might have identified the warlock that was at the restaurant."

Leo looks deeply concerned. "I know Derek and I have had our differences, but he wouldn't do something to harm the agreement between our covens."

"I never liked his coven," Superior Charles states as he snuffs out his cigar. "And unfortunately, Leo, I sensed Derek when I arrived." He tosses the ring back at Leo as he gets up and walks over to his liquor cabinet.

"He astral projected into my apartment the other night. What if he's been keeping an eye on you?" Victor asks Leo.

"All the more reason you get a new mentor, Victor," Superior Charles suggests as he pours himself another drink. "I'm going to speak with the council to assign you someone new."

"No!" Victor protests. He pauses momentarily to gather his thoughts. "I think he should remain my mentor."

"Explain," Superior Charles requests as he focuses his eyes on Victor while taking a drink. "Derek won't attack Leo directly. And if he is the cause of all my 'dizzy spells,' then we can use that to our advantage," Victor advises.

"I'm not sure what you're getting at," Leo comments.

Victor looks between Superior Charles and Leo. "If Derek *is* behind the attacks, then we can anticipate he'll try to attack again. Also, I now know what to look for. We could capture Derek and bring him in for interrogation."

"I agree with him, Superior," Leo implies. "I'm willing to be the bait if Derek is the one causing Victor harm."

"And what of your blood oath, Leo?" Superior Charles asks. "You are unable to harm him. Even if a fight breaks out, you cannot go near him."

"He wouldn't be the one harming or capturing Derek," Victor responds. "Derek might be more experienced than me, but if these past attacks on me have proven anything, I always seem to have the upper hand."

"This is a big risk," Superior Charles responds softly.

"Superior, please, have faith in me," Victor begs.

Superior Charles takes a deep breath, cracks his neck, and then nods. "Give me the night to think about this. I want to make sure both of you are not putting yourselves in danger." He points at Victor while holding his glass, proclaiming, "But if this goes sideways, and you die, I'll find you in the River Styx, bring you back, and kill you myself."

"Noted," Victor responds with a leer.

Superior Charles finishes his drink in one gulp, then clears his throat. "Go see your friends. They have many questions to ask you. We'll talk tomorrow."

CHAPTER THIRTY

The next afternoon, Victor is in the shower, trying to recover from a long night of talking and explaining everything to his friends over several adult beverages. He knew spending an extra day to recover was a good idea. As he lets the water pour down on his face, he feels a presence behind him.

"Someone doesn't know the definition of privacy." Victor looks over his shoulder, and Derek, dressed in his suit, stands in the shower behind him. "Are you here to help me wash my back?"

"I just wanted to check out how good your assets are," Derek says as he leans in the corner.

Victor turns around, and Derek can't help but examine Victor's wet and naked body. "If you were physically here, I would have thrown you through the wall into the next room."

"Sounds like a good time to me. I like it rough," Derek taunts.

Victor crosses his arms, not bothering to cover himself. "If you're looking for Leo, you can see he's not here with me. You have no reason to feel threatened."

"He knows better. And if you know better, you should find another mentor," Derek suggests.

"And why would I want to do that?" Victor probes.

Derek places his hands in his pockets and smirks. "Because he's going to be useless to you soon. And then he can come back to me."

"From my understanding, he doesn't want to be with you anymore," Victor jabs.

Derek narrows his eyes. "Unfortunately, that's not his decision."

Victor takes a step forward. "How did you find me?" Derek is around the same height as Victor. Victor locks eyes with Derek, trying to gauge his intentions.

"We've met once before, remember? It was back at your apartment," Derek scuffs.

"I thought for you to astral project to someone, you would have had to be in close contact with that person." Victor notices Derek's eyes shift side to side as he tries to keep eye contact.

Derek finally responds, "And who told you that? Leo? He wouldn't know what he's talking about. That boy can't astral project himself."

Victor steps back into the water, letting it pour onto his shoulders. He studies Derek's aura and can tell he's lying.

"Are you trying to see my aura?" Derek comments with a touch of sass. "You know you can't do that with someone astral projecting. Fuck, who's teaching you all this misguided information?"

Victor keeps his poker face going. *What if Derek is a telepath? Could Derek read his thoughts?* "Why are you here? Besides being a peeping Tom."

Derek stands up straight and smooths out his jacket. "My superior has been informed that you've been receiving invitations to join a coven. He would like . . . " Derek clenches his jaw and tilts his head. There's an expression of discomfort for what he is about to say. "He would like to extend his invitation, against my better judgment."

"What, he couldn't hand me the invitation himself? He has to send his lackey?" Victor pokes.

Derek's nostrils flare, trying to remain professional. "He has more important things to do than send out meaningless invitations."

"And why would I want to accept his invitation?" Victor inquires.

Derek sighs and gives his best sales pitch. "Because our coven would be the best for you. You'll be able to thrive and grow more than you would in other covens." Derek's face returns to annoyance. "You'll get the invite soon. My superior will be expecting a response from you."

"I would rather have my left nut explode than join a coven with an asshole like you in it," Victor declares.

Derek tries to grab Victor's neck, but his hand goes through. Victor feels a slight tingling from Derek's hand. "You're lucky I can't choke you right now," Derek comments as he retracts his hand.

Victor leans forward, almost nose-to-nose with Derek. "I might like it." Derek's face wrinkles with aggression, and then he vanishes like the steam from the shower. Victor watches the vapors dissipate, trying to come up with his own conclusion of this unexpected, and possibly provoked, visit.

Victor turns off the shower and says aloud, "If he is a telepath, I hope he doesn't know what we're planning." As Victor dries himself off, he looks at himself in the mirror. "There's only one way to ensure he doesn't try reading my thoughts if he's close by."

Victor finishes getting dressed and hears a knock at the door. He opens it, and Leo is on the other side. "Come in. We need to talk."

Leo walks into the room with a worried expression. "What's the matter?"

"Derek visited me . . . in the shower," Victor responds while gathering his shoes from the closet.

"What?" Leo hollers in shock.

Victor gets upset as he starts packing his clothes in his suitcase. "You're going to need to have a word with that husband of yours. It was completely inappropriate to show up in a man's shower without an invite."

"He saw you—"

Victor cuts off Leo, "Naked? Yes. I think he was trying to size me up. No pun intended."

Leo walks up to Victor. "I'm sorry. He shouldn't have embarrassed you like that."

Victor moves to the other side of the room to collect his charging cords off the nightstand. "I've been naked with so many guys that I lost count. I'm not embarrassed. I didn't appreciate that he thought visiting me in the shower was necessary."

"What did he want?" Leo asks.

They hear some rustling at the door. They turn their heads when a small envelope slides under. "He wanted to tell me about that." Victor walks over and picks up the envelope. He opens it and pulls out a pentagon-shaped black business card with a gold emblem.

Leo notices the card and is perplexed. "Is that an invite from Superior Tederich?"

Victor holds up the business card and studies it. "It's interesting that Superior Tederich picked a pentagon shape for his invite. It's probably because a pentagon has five points, like a pentagram. How appropriate."

Leo watches Victor put it back into the envelope. "You're not going to consider joining his coven, right?" he asks.

Victor rolls his eyes and tosses the envelope in the trash can. "You really think I would want to be in a coven with that husband of yours?"

"Why are you upset with me?" Leo questions.

Victor spins around. "Because you need to gain a better grasp of your man. It's becoming annoying that he accuses me of keeping you from him."

Leo becomes confused and sits down at the foot of the bed. "What's gotten into you?"

"What's gotten into me? Maybe I don't appreciate someone's jaded lover approaching me while I'm trying to shower." Victor shakes his head as he goes back to packing. "I don't know how to feel about this. We're not even dating, but I'm disgusted that you're still with someone like him."

Leo stands and strides over to Victor. "Victor, please, I would have left Derek years ago if I could. But I'm attached to him because of my ignorance of taking that blood oath. And if he knew that I was planning any harm to him, he could execute that oath. Which would ultimately kill me."

Victor doesn't look at Leo as he stops beside him. "We need to get going. Superior Charles needs to speak to us before we go to Mexico." Leo places a hand on Victor's shoulder. "Please, I don't want you to be upset with me."

Victor barely gives Leo a side-eye glance. "I'm ready to go." Victor shrugs Leo's hand off and walks out the door. Leo lets out a sigh of defeat, following behind him.

A short drive later through the metroplex of the Dallas-Fort Worth area, they come to a building. Victor looks up at a three-story 1950s art deco-style building. The stone exterior has been sun-bleached. Eagles, also made of stone, are perched on top as the building's gargoyles. "Where are we?"

"We are at the library," Leo replies subtly. "We need to get you some books to read."

Victor sighs, "Great, more reading."

Leo gets out of the car first and looks over at Victor. Victor exits through the other side. Leo observes Victor head up the stairs. Victor twists around and gestures to Leo, *Are you coming?* Leo's shoulders slouch as he closes the car door and catches up to Victor.

They walk through a huge, heavy brass door covered with stained glass. When they enter, the odor of old books surrounds Victor's senses. The interior resembles your average library, filled with both wood and metal shelves, covered with books. While walking toward a large circular desk in the center, Leo turns down one of the aisles. Victor follows behind until they come up to a wall of bookshelves.

Victor looks up and notes the signage of the section. "Self-Help?"

"I mean, technically, all the books you've been reading are self-help," Leo comments as he pulls a book down, and a metallic click comes from behind the wall. A narrow portion of the bookshelf jerks backward, allowing Leo to push it aside. Walking through the doorway, it is almost as if they were transported into an entirely different building.

The bookshelves are made of dark-stained oak, with gold trimmings and elegant carvings along the edges. A massive Himalayan pink salt crystal hangs like a pendulum in the center, directly above the librarian's desk. The light coming through the dome above reflects off the crystal, illuminating the library. Five small birds are fluttering around.

Victor and Leo approach the desk, where a single witch sits, reading a book. She has thick, round glasses and short, curly red hair. She's wearing a cream-colored Edwardian-style tea dress with light blue floral prints and a laced square collar. There is a small bird perched on her shoulder as she reads. She's nibbling on the cap of the pen she is holding.

"Ugh, this book has too many plot holes," she says to herself as she begins to write something down on a paper pad. She looks at the little bird on her shoulder, asking, "Do you understand it, Cactus?" As Victor and Leo get closer, she notices them and smiles brightly. "Leo! So nice to see you again. I have the books you ordered."

She turns around to grab a pile of books behind her as Cactus flies over to Leo and lands on his shoulder. As she turns and sets the book in front of them, she looks at Victor. "You must be the empath I've heard so much about."

Leo pulls the books closer to him as he introduces the witch. "Victor, this is Wren Llewellyn. And this little one is Cactus. Wren practically runs this place."

Victor shakes Wren's hand. "Pleasure to meet you. Is Cactus your familiar?"

"You do know about familiars? I like you already," Wren grins happily.

Victor holds out a finger, which Cactus notices and perches on. "I guess your name is Cactus because you're a cactus wren," Victor says to the tiny bird. Cactus flutters her feathers and sings a little melody, as she is pleased Victor knows that.

"Very good," Wren says. "How did you know she was a cactus wren?"

"I'm from Arizona. She's the state bird," Victor explains. "So, I'm familiar with your familiar. And it seems appropriate, since your name is Wren, to have a familiar be a wren."

Wren giggles. "Actually, I have a chime of wren as my familiar." The five birds flying around come down as Wren whistles a bird call. They line up as Wren says their names. "This is Winter, and then this is Sedge. Carolina is a feisty one, so be careful leaving food out. Rock might act tough, but she's a sweetheart. And Song is the baby of the bunch." After they greet Victor in their own way, all of them, including Cactus, fly off.

"So, you're the one I have to blame for providing Leo with all the books I have to read," Victor says to Wren.

"Well, it's my duty to ensure you have the right reading material. If I couldn't do that, then I wouldn't be a good librarian," Wren smiles.

Victor looks down at her notepad. "Looks like that pen has seen better days."

Wren looks down at the pen. "Oh, I like to review the books as they make their way on the shelves. I've read every book in this library and can recommend anything you're looking for. I used to use pencils, but I kept eating the erasers."

"Is this all we need for now?" Leo asks.

"Well, the next lesson is Earth. And from what you told me about how quickly Victor is picking up magic, this should be all he needs," Wren responds.

Victor raises his eyebrow. "I hate to ask, but if I weren't picking up things so quickly, there would be more than three books to read?"

"Seven, to be exact," Wren responds without hesitation.

Victor's eyes widen. "I'm glad I don't have to read seven books in a day."

"Really? Because I can read seven in a day," Wren comments with a cheesy smile.

Leo lets out a low chuckle. "I'll be right back. I need to get something else while I'm here."

As Leo walks away, Wren leans in and speaks to Victor in a hushed tone. "You shouldn't be upset with him."

Victor is caught off guard. "I'm not upset with Leo."

Wren looks at Victor over her glasses. "You can't lie to me. I can see it all over your face."

Victor briefly studies Wren. "You're an empath, aren't you?"

Wren places her finger over her lips. "Not many know that I'm an empath. I've been in hiding for several decades now. Leo and Charles are a few who know that I am one. My superior helped me get this position with the library to keep me off the radar. The wards around this place are ancient, so it offers great protection."

"Leo told me that some with abilities are hiding from the dark covens," Victor says.

"Is that what he calls them? Well, he's not wrong." She pauses for a moment. "You need something from me."

"I guess it is true; you can't lie to an empath." Victor looks over and sees Leo is still looking for a book. "Do you have anything about blood oaths?"

Wren raises an eyebrow. "Blood oaths?" As Victor nods, she looks over at Leo. "Could it be something along the lines of marriage blood oaths?" Victor looks back at Leo as Wren continues, "Let me see what I can find for you." She steps over to a tome and waves her hand over it. The pages flutter rapidly. Wren's eyes shift vigorously side to side as she scans the pages. Once the pages land on what she is looking for, she lets out a *"hmm"* as she studies it. "Most of what I have on the shelves are more current oaths. Maybe I can narrow it down a little. Do you know when he took his blood oath?"

"I think it was back in 1982," Victor offers.

Wren stands up straight and starts tapping her chin with her finger as she gently flips through several other pages. "Most of these oaths were created in the late 1970s, but the oath you're looking for isn't here. My tome would know what oath was used when Leo married Derek. What we're looking for needs to contain old magic. I might have something in the archives. It may take a day or two for me to find it."

"Please. I know Leo is miserable. And yes, I'm upset with him, but I have a reason for projecting my anger," Victor informs.

Wren returns to her seat in front of Victor and gives Victor a slight smirk. "I'll get a hold of you once I find something."

Leo returns with two more books. "I think I'm ready."

Wren picks up the books and starts reading their spines. "If he's going to practice Fire Magic, you'll need a couple more to read."

"I think he'll be okay. He's going to have an excellent teacher," Leo remarks.

Wren packs the books into a small box and slides them over to Victor. "Talk to you boys soon."

Victor and Leo are escorted to a study where Superior Charles sits behind a large wooden desk. Superior Charles looks up over his reading glasses and waves them in. As they walk further into the study, a man sits in one of the chairs in front of the desk. He's clean-shaven, with snow-white hair. He is wearing an all-lavender suit and has a black walking cane with a mother-of-pearl orb on top. He looks up at Victor as he approaches and smiles.

"Victor, please meet Superior Eugene Mitchell. He has come to see you," Superior Charles says while reading paperwork.

Superior Eugene stands up and extends his hand. "Ahh, the young empath. I'm so pleased to finally meet you."

Victor shakes his hand. "Thank you, Superior. It's a pleasure to meet you as well."

Superior Eugene is pleased with Victor's response. "Ah, so refreshing to see such a polite gentleman. And what a nice firm grip you have there." Superior Charles rolls his eyes. "I saw that, Charlie."

"Please don't call me Charlie," Superior Charles says annoyingly.

Victor wonders how much longer he will be shaking Superior Eugene's hand. "So, you're here to meet me?"

"Ah, yes," Superior Eugene releases Victor's hand and digs into his inner jacket pocket. He pulls out a lavender triangle business card with a white emblem. The emblem resembles a staff with a large orb at the top, crowned with thin triangles representing rays of light. "I heard that you're taking invites to join covens. And I wanted to extend an invite to mine."

Victor accepts the business card. "Thank you, Superior. I'll take yours into consideration."

Superior Eugene fixes the buttons on his jacket and stands tall, holding onto his cane. "I would also like to inform you that normally, a new warlock sees me first to do a couple of exams before they are sent off to their studies. But being the empath you are, it can wait until you finish your basic lessons."

Superior Eugene places both his hands on top of his cane. "Now, I know you have many questions, and I will answer all of them for you, but I have a mani/pedi appointment to get to, and you have Earth lessons to go to. So, I look forward to seeing you again soon." He turns to Superior Charles and smiles. "Talk to you later . . . Charlie." Superior Charles ignites his fists into massive fireballs. With a flourish, Superior Eugene walks out of the study, snickering over *Charlie's* reaction.

Superior Charles lets out a deep sigh of relief and extinguishes his fists. "I'm so happy he left. He's a good man, but a lot to take in." He removes his glasses and closes the file he was reviewing. "Word has gotten out that you've been receiving invites to join covens. So, expect to meet many more superiors and receiving more of their invitations. Eugene's coven is in New York, in case you were wondering. Both of you, take a seat."

Superior Charles flicks his wrist and closes the door to his study. Victor and Leo sit as if they were sent to see the principal. "Did you talk with your friends last night?"

"For the most part," Victor replies. "Although we might have more talking to do later on. It was getting late, and everyone was tired. Maybe even a little drunk."

Superior Charles clasps his hands together and leans on his desk. "I thought about your plan, and I'm okay with it. As long as the two of you are willing."

"We are," Leo responds.

Superior Charles focuses his attention on Leo. "Leo, if Derek is the warlock that's been projecting his aura onto Victor, you cannot fight him, per your blood oath."

"I understand, Superior," Leo acknowledges.

Superior Charles leans back in his seat, placing his clasped hands in his lap. "Young empath, I want to ensure you do whatever it takes to keep Leo safe. He's valued in my coven. And make sure he does not, by any means, attack Derek."

"I'll keep an eye on him, Superior," Victor promises.

Superior Charles flicks his wrist and opens the door to the study. "Now go. Chancellor Eduardo is waiting for you two." As Victor and Leo are about to exit the room, "Leo, a word."

Leo nods to Victor. "I'll meet you at the mirror." He walks back up to the desk while Victor exits the office. "Yes, Superior?"

Superior Charles waits until Victor is out of earshot. "He's upset with you. Why?"

Leo takes a deep breath and looks down at the desk. "I think he's more upset over Derek than me. But it's hard to tell."

"His feelings are hurt. Whatever happened, you'll want to fix it. We can't have a young empath-in-training with conflicting emotions. He needs to be focused," Superior Charles suggests.

Leo nods doubtfully. "It's not going to be easy to fix. I thought he was going to melt my face off when he spoke to me before we met up with Wren."

"Then figure out a way." Superior Charles gestures to Leo to leave.

CHAPTER THIRTY-ONE

Victor and Leo enter a small room with windows that look out onto a field. Victor walks closer to the window and sees lines of agave plants sprawling for almost half a mile. He lifts the window open, feels the cool breeze, and can smell the agave roasting in a nearby building.

"*¡Bienvenidos a mi casa, mis amigos!*" Eddie enters the room, holding a bottle of tequila in one hand and three shot glasses in the other. "You're just in time. This bottle is from my latest batch."

"Nice to see you again, Eduardo," Victor proclaims with a smile.

"Please, just call me Eddie. There's no need to use formalities here, my friend." Eddie then walks over and hands Victor and Leo a shot glass.

"No salt and limes?" Leo asks.

Victor chuckles, "Please forgive my friend. He doesn't know how to drink tequila like a Mexican."

Eddie laughs as he pours everyone a shot of tequila. "*¡Salud!*" Eddie cheers. They knock back their shots, and Leo's face goes sour. Eddie pats Leo's shoulder hard and says, "Come now, it wasn't that bad."

Leo can hardly breathe, saying, "Smooth."

Victor hands Eddie his shot glass. "If this is how you greet your guests, I might visit more often."

Eddie pours himself and Victor another shot. "You're welcome anytime, *mi amigo*. Leo, *uno más*?" Leo shakes his head, and Eddie laughs.

Eddie holds up his shot glass for another toast. *"Arriba. Abajo. Al Centro."*

Victor finishes, *"Y Pa'dentro."* Eddie and Victor clink their shot glasses together and knock back their second shot. "Damn! How come I've never seen this brand before?"

Eddie sets down the bottle on a small table and takes back the shot glasses. "Tres Brujos is expensive. You won't see it at normal liquor stores." He claps his hands and rubs his palms together. "So, let's show you to your rooms."

Victor follows Eddie outside and down a sidewalk along the house. He looks out to the field and sees the workers collecting agave to be taken to the ovens. The workers are not using magic to collect and shave the agave for transport; everything is being done manually. As Victor scans the field, he can see their auras intertwining. The workers are enjoying themselves and take pride in their work.

Victor then stops for a moment and takes in the sweet smell of Mexican pastries. He walks up to a doorway and sees several people baking in a kitchen. Tejano music is playing on the radio. Everyone smiles and laughs as they knead the dough or take the bread out of the ovens.

Eddie leads Victor and Leo down another hallway and up a flight of stairs. "I hope you enjoy mi casa while you're visiting," Eddie says as he looks back at them.

"Is everyone here a person of magic?" Victor asks.

As Eddie rounds the banister, he responds, "Almost half of my workers are witches or warlocks. But everything made here is done by hand to keep the tradition alive and proper." He turns around and stops at a door. "Almost everything." Eddie winks at Victor as he opens the door. "Victor, this will be your room."

Victor walks into a room decorated with vibrant Mexican decor. Beautiful tiles cover the wall which his bed rests against. The linen curtains hanging above the balcony door flow in the breeze from outside. He's starting to feel a little relaxed, either from the setting or from the tequila.

"*Buenas Tardes, Señor Russo!*" says a midwestern voice behind Victor.

Victor's relaxation comes to an abrupt end when the maid arrives. "Hello. I didn't realize you work here." Victor notices Leo leaning against the door frame, trying to hide his laughter. Eddie smiles with his arms crossed, amused by the situation.

The maid walks over to a set of suitcases by a tall dresser. "I go wherever you go, my dear. I am, of course, your personal maid. I just want to make sure you have everything here." She looks around and says, "Mr. Leon, I don't see Mr. Russo's suit."

Eddie steps into the room. "His shirt is being cleaned right now. It will be arriving later tonight."

"Okay, well, then I'll just start putting your things away for you, Mr. Russo." As the maid keeps yapping away, Victor starts rubbing his temples.

Eddie chuckles and puts his arm around Victor's shoulder. "Come, let me show you the rest of mi casa."

As they leave the room, Victor stops and says, "Actually, would it be possible to make a trip to Magi Scriptor Sartor in New York?"

Leo and Eddie are taken aback and look at each other. "May I ask why you would like to go?" Leo inquires.

"I wanted to look at something I saw in one of their cases. I've been thinking about it lately and wanted to ask about it," Victor explains.

Leo shrugs. "We weren't going to do any training today, and dinner won't be ready for another couple hours. We can go."

"No," Victor responds a little too sharply. "I mean, I can do this myself. It might be good practice for me to do a few things alone."

"What if it's not safe for you to go alone?" Leo asks, worried.

"I'll be fine and won't take long," Victor affirms.

Eddie holds out his hand. "This way, my young empath." He takes Victor into a room with several mirrors. In the middle of the far wall is a mirror with a gold frame. "This mirror will take you directly to Magi Scriptor Sartor in New York. Just press your palm in the center and walk through."

Victor presses his palm against the mirror, and it goes hazy. He looks over his shoulder, "If I'm not back in 30 minutes, you can come after me. Will that make you feel more comfortable, Leo?" Leo nods, and Victor walks through.

Victor walks into the store, and as soon as he takes his first step, he jumps back when he almost bumps into someone. "Clarence! You startled me."

Clarence has their hands on their hips and a judgmental expression on their face. "And may I ask why you're here to see me?"

Victor looks bewildered. "How–"

"I have my ways," Clarence says as they turn to walk away. "Also, after I saw what happened to your shirt, I figured you'd be coming to see me. Didn't you get the second suit?"

Victor follows Clarence into the main shop. "I don't like how I look in it. The dark blue doesn't bring out the color of my eyes." Clarence smirks as Victor continues, "I wanted to see if you have a shirt and tie in something particular."

Clarence twirls around and places one hand on their hip and the other on a glass case. "How particular are we asking?"

Victor takes a deep breath and licks his lips. *"Platinum Silver."*

Clarence slowly walks over to Victor and crosses their arms. "That is *very* particular." They squint their eyes and start to study Victor. "Are we looking for a full suit?"

"No, just the shirt and tie," Victor answers.

Clarence gets up close and personal with Victor as they look into Victor's eyes. "May I ask why you want to change from blue to platinum silver?" Clarence tilts their head to the side without breaking eye contact. "Could this have something to do with your recent experience?"

Victor inhales sharply in response.

Clarence turns and walks away. "I'll have it delivered with your other shirt when repairs are finished."

Victor chases after Clarence. "I was also wondering if there is an artifact you might have."

Clarence holds out their arms as they continue walking. "Look around. You might find something you like."

Victor rushes past Clarence to stand in front of them. "I need to look for a charm." As Clarence turns down another aisle, Victor speaks loudly, "I need it for protection in the astral plane."

Clarence stops and stands at attention. They slowly turn on their heel and place one hand on their hip. "Now, why would you need an artifact like that?"

When Victor returns to Eddie's home, Eddie greets him. "Did you find what you needed, *mi amigo*?"

"I did," Victor answers. He looks behind Eddie. "Where's Leo?"

"He's in his room, waiting for dinner. But let's talk first. Join me for a drink?" Eddie and Victor head outside on a veranda that overlooks the agave fields. The sun is setting behind the mountains in the distance. "Please, have a seat. I had some margaritas made."

"If you're trying to capture my heart with tequila, you might want to add some chips and salsa to the mix," Victor jokes.

Eddie laughs as he sits and hands Victor a glass. "I'm sure my husbands wouldn't mind adding a fifth into the mix."

"Three husbands," Victor asks, shockingly. "Where do you find the time for them?"

"I've had many, many years of practice." Eddie taps his glass against Victor's. "Tell me, why did Leo mention you're upset with him?"

Victor raises an eyebrow and takes a sip. "I see he is asking his chancellor to find out for him?"

"Well, as his chancellor, I always have concern over anyone in my coven who is upset," Eddie replies as he sits and crosses his legs.

"But I'm not in your coven," Victor says as he takes another drink while looking out to the field.

"Not yet." Eddie sips his drink before he continues. "He mentioned that you're mad at him. He feels that it's all because of Derek."

"I really don't think it's appropriate to discuss this," Victor remarks, still looking out in the field.

"I've noticed how you two look at each other. And I don't like Derek any more than you do. But whatever Derek did shouldn't allow you to stay mad at Leo."

Victor stands up abruptly. "Chancellor Eduardo, please don't take this the wrong way, but what is happening between Leo and me is none of your concern." Victor turns and heads back inside. "If you don't mind, I would like dinner sent to my room. I'll see you in the morning for training."

As Victor walks back inside, Eddie leans back in his seat, stroking his chin.

CHAPTER THIRTY-TWO

The next morning, Leo knocks on Victor's door. "Victor, are you awake?"

"Come in," Victor says softly through the door.

Leo walks into Victor's room and sees Victor standing in his robe on his balcony. "You're not dressed yet," Leo comments.

"I'll be ready in five minutes," Victor informs.

Leo looks around the room and notices two garment bags. "I see you got your shirt back."

As Leo walks over to the garment bags, Victor snaps, "Is there anything else? I told you I'll be ready in five minutes."

Leo looks over at Victor with an angered expression. "Nothing. I'll see you downstairs." Leo is about to walk out when he turns around hastily. "What the fuck, Vic? What is wrong with you right now?"

Victor walks over to the bathroom. When he walks in, he drops his robe, showing off his bare backside to Leo. "I honestly don't want to discuss this right now. I need to get ready." Leo balls his hands into fists, trying to hold back his anger.

Victor pokes his head out. "I can sense you're angry. Maybe you should leave before you rub that onto me." Leo sneers and storms out of the room, slamming the door behind him. Victor's expression goes somber. "Leo, I wish I could tell you."

Victor walks down the stairs, dressed in his suit and repaired blue shirt. Leo and Eddie are standing beside a truck outside in the agave field. Leo keeps a neutral expression, while Eddie's face is curious.

Eddie notices a necklace around Victor's neck. "That's new," he comments.

"I got it yesterday," Victor responds as he stops beside them. "I take it we're going out to the far end of the property?"

Eddie is impressed. "Very good. We'll be far enough away so as not to harm the workers." Eddie hops in the back of the truck and holds out his hand. Leo jumps in first, and then Victor. Victor sits across from them, looking down the trail in the field. Eddie pats the side of the truck, letting the driver know they're ready.

"I was expecting we'd be taking broomsticks," Victor says. Eddie laughs, and Leo rolls his eyes.

A short drive later, they come to an empty field at the edge of the property. There's a small ramada with a couple of chairs and a small fridge in the corner. As the truck drives off, Eddie steps a few feet away and takes a deep breath. "Smell that fresh soil. Perfect for a young warlock to learn how to control."

Eddie takes another deep breath and then turns around, placing his hands on his hips. "I know we're in our suits, but we can have them cleaned later. Leo, I had the fridge stocked up for you. Victor, *ven.*" Eddie takes Victor to a distant spot in the empty field and then sits on the ground, crisscrossing his legs. "*Siéntate,*" Eddie commands, gesturing to a spot in front of him. Victor hesitates before taking a seat in the dirt.

Eddie continues, "All I want you to do is close your eyes and feel the earth beneath you. Clear your mind of all thought and listen to the soil. Listen to the seeds beneath you as they grow."

Victor crisscrosses his legs and places his hands on his knees. He closes his eyes and starts to meditate. He can only hear Eddie's voice and the breeze rustling the nearby flora. As though it were instinct, Victor places his hands on the dirt.

Eddie notices. "Good. Feel the earth in your hands." After moments of silence, Victor tilts his head ever so slightly, eyes remaining closed. "You felt something, didn't you?" Eddie asks.

"Yes," Victor answers. "It is almost like there's something under my hands."

"Can you feel them tickling your fingers?" Eddie smiles. Victor slowly nods. "Help them," Eddie commands softly.

Victor opens his eyes and looks confused. "Help them? Who?"

Eddie closes his eyes and places his hands in the dirt. He takes a deep breath, and as he exhales slowly, blades of grass begin to grow around his hands. He takes one more deep breath, then opens his eyes to look at Victor. He gives Victor a slight smile. "Help them grow."

Victor closes his eyes and regains his focus. He starts to rub his hands slowly in the dirt, taking a deep breath and exhaling slowly. As he opens his eyes, he sees blades of grass growing around his hands. Victor laughs lightly, "I'm sure my dad would like to have fresh grass in his backyard."

Eddie smiles and then lifts his palms upward. When he does, more grass grows around him and Victor. He then holds out one of his hands and focuses on a spot between himself and Victor. Victor sees a small bud grow from the ground. As it grows taller, it blossoms into a red carnation. Victor reaches and plucks it from the ground. He looks at it carefully in his hands.

"Carnations were my mom's favorite flower," Victor mentions, holding the flower delicately in his hands.

Eddie stands up and brushes himself off. "I remember. Your grandmother mentioned it to me one day when your mom was younger."

Victor looks up at Eddie in shock. "You met my mom?"

Eddie shakes his head. He holds out a hand to help Victor off the ground. "I never got a chance to meet her. But I remember it was your mother's birthday, and your grandmother was so busy she almost forgot. She asked me to make a bouquet of carnations as a gift for your mother."

Eddie takes the carnation from Victor. "You'll be amazed by the wonders you can create with this magic. All around you, I have a thriving agave field. All the fruit and vegetables you've eaten have been from the my staff's gardens, who share this magic. We might grow the plants with magic, but there's some satisfaction in harvesting by hand."

"How does Superior Charles feel about you having mundane around?" Victor asks curiously.

"He doesn't like it. But if he ordered me not to hire mundane workers, he wouldn't get any more bottles of his favorite tequila." Eddie places a hand on Victor's shoulder. "I didn't like the conversation with him about your friends. I tried to talk to him about it, but he doesn't like hearing when he's wrong. Plenty of mundane people aren't afraid of individuals like you and me. I wouldn't have that many workers if that were the case."

Eddie looks over at Leo, who is looking at his phone. "Are you going to tell me what happened between you two?"

Victor looks over at Leo, responding solemnly, "Not right now. I'm not ready to talk about it."

Eddie nods. "Then let's continue."

Eddie reaches down and picks up some dirt in his hand. In the small pile of land, he grows a tiny daisy. "We're going to start small and then work on bigger things."

As Victor and Eddie return to the lessons, Leo looks over the tops of his sunglasses with pain in his eyes. Leo doesn't know how to feel about Victor being upset with him. *What did I do wrong?* Leo asks himself. *I thought everything was working out for the two of us.*

Two days have passed by quickly. Victor is standing in the middle of the field, growing two pine trees. As they get larger, he twists the trunks into a spiral. Then, he binds the tops of the trees towards each other and starts curving the tops together.

"Very good," Eddie says proudly. "You have exceeded my expectations these past couple of days, mi amigo. Do you think you're ready for a battle?"

"Already?" Victor asks as he drops his hands to his sides. "I feel like there's still a lot I need to know."

Eddie bends the two pine trees to break at the base of the trunk. "I think some practice will be okay." He uses his Air Magic to toss the trees off to the side. He then lowers his hands to push the tree stumps into the ground.

"You're just gonna leave those trunks there?" Victor asks.

"Nah. My workers will come by and pick them up. They can use the wood for the fire pits." Eddie turns to Victor with a smile. "Ready?"

Victor shrugs, uncertain by this sudden request from Eddie. "I guess, I mean, if you think it's necessary." As he moves to his spot, he looks over at Leo, who's still looking at his phone. He looks back at Eddie and asks, "Are you not going to make a dome?"

Eddie shakes his head. "There's nothing close by that you can damage. I can always regrow and repair any plants that are destroyed. But don't worry, I'll go easy on you."

As Victor and Eddie prepare to fight, a large dirt and rocky wall emerges behind Victor and begins to fall. Victor looks up and splits the wall in two, letting the pieces fall on each side of him. He turns to Eddie with a look of concern and confusion. "What the fuck, Eddie?"

Eddie is just as surprised. "That wasn't me."

Victor and Eddie look over at Leo, who is also bewildered. Distracted, Victor is thrown high into the air on a layer of earth. The layer tosses Victor. As Victor falls, he conjures a gust of wind to help him to the ground. As soon as he lands on his feet, he looks around.

"He's here," Victor remarks, scanning the field. "I can feel he's close."

Eddie looks around. "Who?"

"Derek," Victor responds.

Leo tries to run over to Victor when a rock wall surrounds him. He tries to jump out, but the wall closes the opening.

"Leo!" Victor shouts as he runs over. A vine comes up and twists around his ankle, knocking him down.

Eddie struggles to move as vines wrap around his wrists and ankles. "Damn it!" He burns off the vines, then burns the vines binding Victor.

"Thanks," Victor says to Eddie. "We need to help Leo."

Before they can help Leo, sharp rocks start flying off the wall. Victor creates an air shield to protect himself and Eddie. Eddie stands behind Victor, collecting the rocks with his magic. Eddie shoots the stones back at the wall around Leo. The wall starts chipping away, weakening, allowing Leo to break through his dirt prison.

"Eddie, help Leo," Victor commands as he looks around the empty field. "I know you're here!" Victor shouts out into the open field. "I can sense your presence! So why don't you come out and face me, warlock to warlock?"

Derek appears when he drops the illusion spell. "Looks like you're getting stronger."

Victor turns to face Derek. "That illusion charm must have taken up most of your energy. You're not putting up that much of a fight."

"And you should have listened to me about replacing Leo with another mentor," Derek barks. "Also, my superior is still waiting for your response."

"I'm sorry, I'm not interested in being in any coven you're a part of," Victor snaps back.

"Then I guess no coven will take you if you're dead." Derek starts throwing fireballs at Victor. Victor uses his Air and Water Magic, extinguishing each one flying toward him.

Leo is about to conjure something when Eddie stops him. "Don't! This is Victor's fight."

"But we have to help him," Leo demands.

"I know, mi amor, but the oath." Eddie releases Leo's wrist and says, "He challenged Derek. I will step in if I need to. *Comprende?*" Leo nods and watches on.

Victor lifts Derek high into the air on a layer of earth. He then causes a microburst to slam Derek to the ground. Derek reacts, breaks himself free, and turns the layer of soil into a fiery ball of dirt. Victor jumps and rolls to the side before it crashes down on him. When Victor looks up, Derek is hurling down at him, holding his dagger.

Victor covers himself with a thick layer of dirt. Derek lands on top and starts stabbing away at the earth, trying to dig his way to Victor. When Derek stands up, Victor explodes his earthy cover, sending Derek backward.

"Enough of this!" Victor shouts. As Derek stands, Victor shoots roots up from the ground and starts to bind Derek. Derek struggles to break free. Fireballs go flying out all over the place. Eddie helps block the attacks from hitting anyone.

"Let me go!" Derek demands. "Stop fighting like a little bitch!"

"He's not a bitch, *chéri.*" Madame Jeanette and Superior Charles suddenly appear behind Derek. Eddie and Leo are confused about where they came from, not seen in the middle of an agave field.

Derek snarls at Madame Jeanette as she slowly steps beside him. "What? The wannabe empath had to call for reinforcements?"

"No, *chéri*, I'm here because of this . . ." Madame smiles fondly as she opens her palm. *"Bòn nwi."* She blows black sandy dust into Derek's face. Derek coughs until he passes out.

Superior Charles shakes his head as he approaches. "Jeanette, you know I don't like it when you use Voodoo magic."

Madame Jeanette flicks her hair back and grins at Superior Charles. "Then how was I supposed to knock him out, Charlie?"

Superior Charles flares his nostrils. "You know I don't like being called *Charlie*," he groans through his teeth.

Victor frees Derek from his bindings, letting him drop to the ground with a thud. He looks back at Eddie and Leo and asks, "Are you two okay?"

Leo sneers at Victor. *"Now* you care?"

Victor walks over to Leo and says, "Please, listen to me. I had to project my emotions so a telepath couldn't read my thoughts."

Leo is taken aback. "What?

Victor looks down at Derek. "He is a telepath, Leo. And his mistake was when he talked to me in the shower."

"He what?" Superior Charles responds shockingly.

Victor waves off Superior Charles's concerns as he continues, "In one of the books Leo gave me after the first time I astral projected, it mentioned that you must be in close proximity to the individual. I never met Derek in person, so that meant he was close to me at some point. Without knowing, Derek's been using an illusion charm to get close to me, which is probably why Superior Charles sensed Derek at the restaurant."

Victor continues explaining as he walks closer to Derek. "The mistake he made was when he mentioned I should get another mentor. He wouldn't have known that if he were with you. You two always bicker, which distracts some of your thoughts from him. You would always bring up something he did. But when he met me in the shower, I was thinking about the conversation in Superior Charles' study.

"Only those with an ability can continue using it while projecting. Hence, he was aware of the suggestion to have a new mentor. I needed to test my theory. The only way to do that was to get angry. Anger is one of the most powerful emotions that can trick a telepath. So, unfortunately, I had to remain angry around you, just in case he was close by."

Victor's expression becomes somber as he turns to look at Leo. "The distraction of you being upset with me would be the only thing on your mind. He wouldn't have shown up in person if he had ever discovered our plan to capture him."

Leo looks down at Derek. "I've been with him for over 30 years, and I didn't even know he was a telepath. I can't believe he kept that from me."

Superior Charles steps forward, commenting, "I had a feeling Derek was a telepath, but I could never figure out how to force it out of him. Telepaths can mask themselves when hiding, and illusion charms can help them. Also, telepaths are best at pushing their auras onto empaths, making them the best at poisoning an empath's emotions."

Superior Charles snarls as he looks down at Derek's unconscious body. "Derek could be the reason behind Victor's rage episodes. He didn't anticipate that Victor would recover so quickly at the restaurant, which is why I sensed him. He was probably trying to make Victor rage out before the cops arrived."

Leo walks over and stops beside Victor. "To protect me from him, you had to cover your tracks with our plan."

As Victor takes Leo's hands, Superior Charles clears his throat and jerks his head, letting everyone know to give Victor and Leo some privacy.

"I hope you understand I didn't mean to hurt you, Leo," Victor says softly. "But I needed to keep you out of the loop to find and capture him. I'm just happy it didn't take long. The dude has a real hard-on for me. Lucky for us, he's not as powerful as he says he is."

Leo looks down while he rubs the pads of his thumbs on top of Victor's hands. Leo takes a deep breath and looks into Victor's eyes. "I should be angry with you but keeping me in the dark was smart." Their eye contact burns between them. "I wish I could kiss you," Leo says softly.

Victor mouths *"Me too"* as he swallows his feelings. Victor shakes himself out of the heated emotion. "He should be out for a while. We only have tonight to do what I have planned."

"What do you have planned?" Leo inquires.

Victor turns to look at the others. "Is there a mirror that can take us to *Teotihuacán*?" Victor shouts over to Eddie.

Eddie looks at Superior Charles, who looks back suspiciously. "Yeah, there is one that leads into the gift shop," Eddie replies.

"What's at *Teotihuacán*?" Leo questions.

Victor looks down at Derek. "It's where I find out why someone is after me."

CHAPTER THIRTY-THREE

Three days ago...

Victor is nervous as Clarence saunters over to him. "It's because... umm."

Clarence places their hands on their hips, stopping just inches from Victor. "You're not planning on another attempt to visit the astral plane, are you?"

Victor swallows dryly. "It would be better if I had one, just in case I happen to visit there again."

Clarence squints their eyes as they study Victor. "Follow me." They take Victor into a back room. As they are about to pass through a second set of dark curtains, Clarence holds out a hand and places it on Victor's chest. "What you're about to see cannot be discussed with anyone. These artifacts can only be seen by those who are empathic. If your ability is not strong enough to walk past that curtain, I cannot help you."

Victor nods and proceeds to walk through the curtains. He enters a small room with three crystal cases against the walls. The cases contain various artifacts, including rings, wands, belts, and daggers. Victor can feel the energy in the room change as a glow surrounds each artifact.

Clarence walks up behind Victor and softly says in his ear, "Can you feel them?"

Victor nods slowly. "Yes. It's almost like they are trying to speak to me." He looks over to Clarence, who stands between two cases. "Are you an empath?"

"No," Clarence responds coyly.

"Then how were you able to come through the curtains?" Victor asks as he continues looking around the tiny room.

"I created the wards in this room; that's why," Clarence responds with a hint of snark. They slowly walk around the room, inspecting everything in the cases. "I wanted to make sure anything empaths can use was protected. Especially after what happened when empaths were being killed off."

"Leo mentioned that. He said it wasn't that long ago," Victor remarks.

Clarence slides a hand across a case and looks inside it. "Anyone with an ability was targeted and demanded to help change things back to the traditional ways of witchcraft. It's also written that those with abilities can easily become the next Grand Witch or Warlock."

Clarence glances at Victor's reflection in the case as he examines a small dagger. "Others don't want to be ruled by someone who could be more powerful than them. The survivors are protected, but if they try to excel more with their powers, it will put a larger target on their backs."

Victor becomes worried. "I already have a large target on my back, and I'm not even that powerful."

"You're more powerful than you think." Clarence opens the case and pulls out a silver necklace with a charm. The charm has five circles lying unevenly on top of each other. The points where each circle overlaps another resembles a pentacle. "If you are anticipating or planning on revisiting the astral plane, you'll want to ensure you are wearing this."

Victor takes the charm in the palm of his hand, letting the necklace dangle down. He notices small symbols etched on the bottom of each circle. "*Slán leat*. It means 'Safe Journey' or 'Safety with you' in Irish. It's written in the Theban alphabet as it was commonly used among the Wiccans," Clarence explains.

"How much for it?" Victor asks as he gazes at the swirling aura coming off the charm. Light blues and soft silvers intertwine against one another as they swim around the circles.

Clarence closes Victor's hand into itself and places their other hand on top. "No cost for it. It was meant for you. Just be careful."

Two nights ago ...

Victor is sitting up in bed, reading a book Leo gave him. His dirty dishes from dinner are sitting on the table. There's a knock at his door. "Come in."

The maid enters the room. "Oh, Mr. Russo, please pardon the interruption. A letter came for you. It's from the library."

"Thank you."

She picks up the dirty dishes. "Good night, Sir."

Victor sees it's a message from Wren.

Victor,

I might have found something for you. Meet me in Eduardo's mirror room in five minutes after you read this letter. It's important.

-Wren

Victor folds the letter and gets out of bed. He hides the letter in his suitcase and gingerly walks over to the mirror room. When he enters, Wren walks through a mirror.

Wren is holding a small, worn book. "I think I found what you are looking for, but you're not going to like what it says," Wren says softly. She opens the book and holds it out for Victor. "The blood oath Leo and Derek took can only be broken by either trial by the High Priest or Priestess or blessed by the Grand Witch or Warlock. Unfortunately, neither of those exists right now."

"Are you sure it's safe to speak here?" Victor asks.

Wren brushes off the question. "Eduardo has wards placed around this room. He's had many private conversations here."

Victor takes the book from Wren. "How are you sure this was Leo's oath to Derek?"

Wren takes out her phone and plays a video of Leo and Derek taking the blood oath. Victor takes the phone and watches closely. Leo starts to speak in Latin. As he speaks, a younger version of Superior Charles slices Leo's palm with a dagger. Derek places his hand on top of Leo's cut. When Leo finishes, Derek begins talking. Another warlock slashes Derek's palm. While Derek continues, Victor notices a change in Derek's voice.

"I might not be able to speak Latin or Spanish, but I have some idea of how the words are enunciated. He's pronouncing the words in a Spanish dialect while the oath is in Latin."

Wren nods. "That's right. The only person who took the oath was Leo. I'm surprised he didn't notice it right away." Wren makes a disgusted face as she watches the video. "I've never liked Derek."

Victor hands the phone back. "Get in line. Where did you find the video?"

"Superior Charles had a copy saved in the archives. Most covens need a safe place to keep their files, so they bring them to the library's archives."

"Do you think you could find anything on my grandmother?" Victor asks.

Wren shrugs. "I can take a look. But I can't promise anything."

Victor looks at the page Wren opened the book to. "I take it even though it was a marriage, it doesn't matter if only one person took a blood oath?"

"You'd be shocked how common it is for only one to take an oath. Yes, you are correct."

Victor's eyes move across the page. "How do we break the oath?" Wren points to the bottom section of the second page. "I have to go to the astral plane?"

"And I guess it's a good thing you got that charm yesterday," Wren comments nonchalantly while looking over the page.

Victor looks bewildered. "How did you know?"

"Clarence likes to keep records of every artifact purchased at the library. They know it's the safest place to keep all their records," Wren states while still glancing at the book in Victor's hands with her hands behind her back.

Victor raises an eyebrow. "Noted."

"Were you planning on revisiting your mother?" Wren questions slyly.

Victor turns sheepish. "N-N-No. I wanted to make sure I had something on me if I went back. I've been there twice already."

Wren grins while looking at Victor from the corners of her eyes, "*Mmhmm.*"

Victor brushes her remark aside and returns to the book. As he scans a section, his expression grows somber. "It says here that in order for the oath to be broken, the one who spoke it has to die. Then, they can be retrieved from the astral plane." Victor looks up in shock, and Wren nods. "I don't accept that."

Wren places a finger to her lips. "Not so loud." She looks over at the door. "There *is* something else you can do in the astral plane." She hands Victor another book, which is already open to a page Wren wants to show Victor. "If you take Derek there with you, you can find out who is after you."

"It has to be his superior who—" Victor cuts himself off and gives Wren a suspicious glare. "How did you know I was going after Derek?"

Wren smiles wickedly as she takes back a book from Victor. "There's a rumor through the grapevine that he was after another empath several years ago and pulled the same tactics as he did on you." She changes her demeanor to be more subtle. "And as for Derek's superior, it wasn't him. Superior Tederich might be a complete dick, and his coven prefers the traditional ways, but they were never involved in any of the senseless killings of anyone who has abilities. It has to be someone much more inclined to stop you for some reason."

"Why me?" Victor asks.

Wren shrugs and shakes her head quietly to say, *"I don't know."*

Victor ponders, moving his jaw from side to side. Then, something dawns on him. "Have you heard of Florence Maryweather?"

Wren tilts her head to the side as she ponders the question. "That name sounds familiar. If you give me some time, I'll see what I can find for you. In the meantime, I've compiled a list of things you need to complete your task. As soon as you get Derek, you must ensure he's completely knocked out."

Victor points to a line on the page. "What's this about '*going to a place where two of their ancestors met?*'"

"You'll have to ask a seer for that help," Wren suggests.

One day ago...

Victor takes off his dirt-covered suit after a hard day of lessons. He groans from the pain. As soon as he senses someone's presence, he turns to the door to his room. "Come in, Superior." Superior Charles and Madame Jeanette walk into the room. "I'm glad you two could make it. Did anyone see you?"

Superior Charles shakes his head. "Eduardo doesn't know we're here. Your letter sounded important."

Victor gestures for them to sit at the table. "I was given some information last night that I wanted to go over with both of you." As he takes his seat, he hands Superior Charles the book Wren gave him. "It seems like we can find out who might be after me."

Superior Charles' eyebrows pinch together. He seems very concerned about what he's reading. "You want to visit the astral plane?"

Madame Jeanette gives Victor a shocked and worried look. "Victor, you know visiting the astral plane is dangerous."

"I've been there twice already. Both times, I was safe," Victor remarks, trying to give them reassurance.

"*Oui*, but you were invited. You did not go there on your own," Madame Jeanette advises.

Superior Charles lifts his hand, commanding attention. "It says here that you need to visit a place where your two ancestors met and need three necromancers." He sets the book down in his lap and looks up at Victor. "How would you accomplish this?"

"Can you view images from the past?" Victor asks Madame Jeanette.

"Of course," Madame Jeanette affirms with a coy smile.

"Could you help me find where two of our ancestors have met?" Victor asks.

Madame Jeanette nods and sits back in her seat, sighing, "If I use my pipe, the others will know we are here."

Victor twists his wrist while pointing a couple of fingers into the air. The air starts to swirl above them, causing an inward suction.

Madame Jeanette raises an eyebrow. "Impressive." She pulls out her pipe and looks at Superior Charles. "Would you give a lady a light, *mon ami*?" Superior Charles snaps his fingers and lights the pipe. She looks over at Victor and studies him as she takes several puffs, preparing the tobacco. She inhales deeply and exhales the smoke onto the table.

Madame Jeanette slowly places her hands on the table as she gazes into the smoke. "I see pyramids. They are here, in Mexico."

"There are at least 10 places, maybe more," Victor informs.

Madame Jeanette slightly tilts her head as she continues to examine the smoke. "I see two, close together. One has a sun over it, the other a moon. And there is a street with dead souls."

Victor perks up as he understands what Madame Jeanette is seeing. "That sounds a lot like *Teotihuacán*." He sits back in his seat. "I always wondered if my family genealogy went back to the Aztecs. But now, discovering Derek's ancestors could have intermingled with mine makes my skin crawl."

"Maybe you're cousins," Superior Charles says with a sneer. Victor gives Superior Charles a pointed look, and Madame Jeanette giggles as she whips the smoke away.

"You take that back," Victor demands in a low tone.

Superior Charles lets out a husky chuckle as he looks back down at the book. "Now, where are you going to find three necromancers, as the book says?"

Victor looks at both of them. "Well, there are the two of you, and I know where I can find a third who can help."

Madame Jeanette clasps her hands and leans on the table. "How did you get your hands on this book?"

Victor brushes off some dirt from his sleeve. "Someone told me about it."

"Was it Wren?" Madame Jeanette probes, lifting an eyebrow.

"Maybe," Victor responds secretively. "Also, I'm starting to get tired of this target on my back. If I'm anything like my grandmother, then I'll do whatever it takes to find out who's trying to harm me."

Present day...

It's late into the night, and the gift shop is dark. A mirror on a wall starts to glow and go hazy. Eddie steps through and looks around. "All clear."

Superior Charles and Madame Jeanette come through, each holding a box with ingredients. Victor and Leo are carrying Derek.

"Fuck, he's heavy," Victor says as he's adjusting Derek's weight.

"Try having him fall asleep on you," Leo responds as he sets down Derek's legs. "Okay, we can stop carrying him." Victor sets Derek on the floor, and Leo lifts Derek off the ground with his Air Magic.

Victor gives Leo a disgruntled look. "You couldn't do that to bring him through?"

"I didn't want my magic to trigger anything in the mirror realm," Leo replies. "Now, where are we exactly taking him?"

Victor gestures to head out. As everyone walks outside, Victor looks at the dark figures of the pyramids in the distance. "The road between the two pyramids. *Avenida de los Muertos.*"

As they make their way down the trail, several people start to appear, holding candle lanterns. The flicker of the flames reflects on their faces. The people watch in observance as Victor and the others walk toward the pyramids.

"Who are these people?" Victor asks softly.

"They protect this land. And they want to see who the new empath is," Eddie explains.

Victor notices two tall, muscular men wearing Aztec garments and feathered headdresses several feet in front of them. An older woman, holding a wooden walking stick, stands in front of the men. Eddie holds out his hand, gesturing for everyone to stop. He walks up to the three Aztecs and speaks to them in Nahuatl, the language of the Aztecs. When he finishes, they turn and walk away.

Eddie turns around and waves for the group to follow. "They will take us to the spot that will work for us."

After ten minutes of walking, the muscular men split and walk a few feet in opposite directions. The woman turns to Eddie and stomps the ground with her walking stick before walking away.

"Place Derek here," Eddie tells Leo.

Leo places Derek on the spot while Superior Charles and Madame Jeanette set down the boxes. Once Derek is in place, Eddie is handed a jar of salt. He creates a circle around Derek.

Leo takes a jar of black sand and creates another circle next to Derek. Victor takes the bones from a snake and places them between the two circles.

Superior Charles lights three large candles and places them around while tracing a triangle with the melting wax.

Madame Jeanette begins to burn sage in a bowl and uses a large eagle feather to waft the smoke over the two circles before placing the bowl at the head of the circles.

"Is that everything?" Leo asks.

"Almost." Everyone turns around and sees Superior Jackie carrying four large rose quartz crystals. She hands them to Superior Charles and Eddie. "These need to be placed at the edges to create a square." As Eddie and Superior Charles carry out the task, Superior Jackie turns to Victor. "Are you sure about this?"

Victor looks down and examines everyone's work. "Not really. But if this is what needs to be done to get answers, then I'll do it."

"Who's the third necromancer?" Superior Charles asks as he places a crystal into position.

"Sorry I'm late," Wren says as she walks up. She's wearing her blue suit with high-water slacks, a teal blouse, and a matching teal tie. She has a pocket watch in her vest and wears black-and-white loafer-style heels. As she approaches Victor, she hands him a garment bag. "I got what you asked for."

Eddie looks at the garment bag, slightly confused. "You need to do a wardrobe change?"

"Yes. Be right back." He walks behind one of the small buildings off to the side. A couple of moments later, he's changed into his new platinum silver shirt and matching tie. As he walks back, everyone but Wren is surprised by what he changed into.

Superior Charles crosses his arms, scrunching his face as he disapproves. "As if you don't have a large enough target on your back right now, you're going to light a beacon, allowing everyone to see you with this new color."

Victor walks past Superior Charles, handing Leo his blue shirt and garment bag. "I'm very aware. But if I plan on being safe in the astral plane, then this is what I need to wear." Victor steps into the center of the circle of black sand and pulls the charm necklace from under his shirt. He looks at everyone and notices the Aztec men and the older woman walking away.

"Is everyone ready?" Victor asks. Everyone nods.

Victor takes out his dagger and slices his hand. He balls his hand into a fist, dripping his blood along the bones. He then takes a deep breath and lies down in the circle.

Superior Jackie steps over to Victor, placing a black tourmaline gem on his heart and an amethyst on his mind's eye. Superior Charles, Madame Jeanette, and Wren take their position behind a candle. As Superior Jackie, Leo, and Eddie step outside of the square created by the quartz, Superior Charles, Madame Jeanette, and Wren hold their hands out to their sides with their palms upward and start to chant in Latin.

While they are chanting, Victor looks up at the stars. He slowly takes a breath. Then, he closes his eyes as he exhales.

CHAPTER THIRTY-FOUR

Victor opens his eyes and looks around. He sees he's sitting on the rock where he and his mother last spoke. As he continues to look around, everything seems to be in order. The stream is blue, the plants are glowing, and he's in his full platinum silver suit.

Victor sits and ponders what he's doing there. He knows that there is a reason he's here. Suddenly, Victor hears rustling in the background. He turns around to see where it's coming from. Victor scans around the forest but doesn't see anything. As it continues, he decides to walk around and investigate. When he turns to round a tree, he sees Derek trying to break out of a thorny bush.

Derek struggles to break free, but it is of no use. He looks up and sees Victor. *"Where am I?"* Derek pauses and feels his face. *"Why can't I speak?"* He becomes confused. *"I'm speaking, but my mouth isn't moving."*

"You're in the astral plane," Victor replies as he remembers the reason he is there.

Derek looks around and is unimpressed. *"It looks like a normal forest to me. And why are you wearing that godawful suit?"*

Victor looks around as he approaches Derek. He looks up at a tree and tilts his head. *"You don't see the forest glowing?"*

Derek jerks his neck back, giving Victor a grimace. *"Glowing? What are you, high? And what did you do to my powers?"*

"Our powers don't work on the astral plane." Victor looks around the forest. *"Strange. I can see everything glowing, but you can't. Maybe I'm more powerful than you. Maybe that's why your powers don't work."*

"I don't believe you," Derek sneers.

"Of course, you wouldn't because you can't read my thoughts. But I'm telling you the truth," Victor claims as he crosses his arms.

Derek stands up straight and lifts his chin. "You figured out that I'm a telepath. What gave it away?"

"You did," Victor responds without hesitation. "You made a couple mistakes while trying to apprehend me. First, it was when you visited me in Japan. When you came to see Leo, it was actually to see me. Yes, I heard you and felt your presence in Leo's room."

Derek rolls his eyes as Victor continues. "The second time was when you visited me at my apartment, trying to scare me away. After you left, Leo told me that you two hadn't been together for a couple of years. But I don't think you left. While Leo was talking about his broken relationship, I could sense someone's annoyance. I couldn't figure out where it came from because I focused on Leo's sadness."

"Maybe it was your neighbor."

Victor just ignores Derek's remark and keeps explaining. "The last mistake was when you visited me in the shower. You could have only done that if you had been in close contact with me. Superior Charles mentioned he sensed you when you and those witches tried to attack me and my friends. Then, to discover that telepaths can project their emotions onto empaths, causing them to rage out, I knew it had to be you."

Derek looks unamused. "I don't know who told you about how astral projecting works, but–"

Victor holds his hand up, cutting Derek off. "You can stop with the dramatics. Leo didn't tell me anything. Superior Charles did. Leo gave me a little insight and a book to read. But Superior Charles went into great detail. He is the author of two books on the subject." Victor studies Derek for a moment. "Something tells me that my apartment and my friend's birthday weren't the only times we've met."

"No, it wasn't," Derek says.

"When was the first time we met?" Victor orders.

Derek fixes the cuffs of his sleeves. "Well, it looks like I have underestimated you. If you must know, I was there having dinner when Magenta came for you. I was there to knock you unconscious, but I was surprised at how strong your empathic ability was. And I was also caught off guard by how much stronger Leo got."

Victor lowers his arms to his sides when it dawns on him. "You were the witch Leo went to talk to. He said it was another empath who detected danger. But it was you. I take it when you finally linked our emotions, you weren't expecting something, which caused your surprise to be misinterpreted by Leo. And when he went over to speak to you, you lost focus."

Derek smiles sadistically with the corner of his mouth. "Very good. You're not as stupid as everyone thinks you are. Even though I saw his smug face, I wasn't expecting Leo to come talk to me. That asshole threw me off my game and somehow your emotions fought back. But if I revealed who I was, I would have been bombarded with Leo's questions. He's a complete pain in the ass, I don't know what the fuck I was thinking marrying him."

Victor narrows his eyes and places his hands on his hips. "Are you done with the insults, Derek? Because I'm the one who's free to move around, and I would hate to keep you here."

"Oh, I'm shaking in my bush," Derek says sarcastically.

Victor steps closer to Derek. "I think the biggest mistake was outside Superior Charles' ranch. You knew you couldn't enter his property without setting off any alarms. Were you trying to see if we figured out you were hiding in plain sight at the restaurant?"

Derek's eyes widen. "How in the world could you have picked up on that?"

"My empathic abilities have been improving daily since I began practicing magic," Victor remarks. "And Superior Charles knew you were close by. You were trying to make me rage while I was inside his coven. But you were too far away for me, and your powers were too weak even to work properly." Victor takes another step closer. "But there is one more mistake you made."

Derek crosses his arms, cocking an eyebrow. "And what's that?"

"Letting me know that Superior Tederich is the one who's after me," Victor responds.

"Please, I didn't tell you that," Derek snorts.

"Of course you did. Why else would you tell me about his invitation to be part of his coven?" Victor smirks.

Derek rolls his eyes. "You're an idiot. I didn't tell you that Tederich is the one after you. He doesn't give a shit about you. That's why I've been trying, for years, to get into Superior Audrey Brook's coven."

Victor gives Derek a neutral expression. "You really think I don't know when you're lying? I know Superior Tederich is interested in me. Why waste the effort of sending me an invitation? Also, how else did he know where to send the invitation? He must have known your 'husband' was my mentor and asked you to find out for him."

"How would you know if I'm lying or not? As you said, our abilities don't work here." Victor points down to the bush. The bush crawls up Derek's legs like a snake wrapping around an animal. "What's going on?" Derek panics.

"This bush is tethered to my empathic ability in the corporeal plane. The more you lie, the more that bush grows. A loophole, if you will," Victor explains with a sneer.

Derek grows angry and balls his hands into fists. He throws up his hands as if he's trying to throw fire at Victor. Victor takes a few steps back so as not to get hit by Derek's hands. After several attempts, Derek pants as he regains his breath. He stands straight, fixes his tie, and smooths his hair. *"So, it looks like there's no way of getting out of this."*

"Oh, there is a way. You answer my questions honestly. The sooner we get this done, the sooner we get out of here." Victor puts his hands in his pockets. *"Who's after me?"* Derek turns his head and looks off into the forest, snubbing Victor's questions. *"Well?"*

Derek lifts his chin as he takes a deep breath, then turns his attention back to Victor. *"If I tell you, I'm dead."*

"You'll be dead even if you don't answer me." Victor points to the stream. *"What color do you see?"*

Derek squints to see the stream Victor is pointing to. *"It looks blue, I guess."*

"Then you're safe. So, who's after me?" Victor reiterates.

Derek takes a moment to answer. *"Superior Florence Maryweather."*

Victor looks down at the bush. It doesn't grow. *"Florence Maryweather took her own life years ago."*

"You would think that. But she's still alive. She fooled your grandmother, didn't she?" Derek comments smugly.

Victor remains calm at Derek's remark. *"For some reason, I don't want to believe you."*

"You shouldn't believe him."

Victor and Derek look around to see who said that. They turn their heads when they hear someone approaching.

"Mom?!" Victor exclaims. *"Why are you here?"*

Victor's mother appears behind a tree. *"Florence Maryweather is dead. I see her all the time trying to walk upstream."*

Derek becomes upset. *"What's going on here? You knew I wasn't lying. The bush didn't grow. And who's this?"*

"This is my mother, and it seems you're not telling the truth," Victor responds.

Derek starts worrying. *"But I am telling you the truth."*

"Then why are you worried?" Victor questions.

Derek points to the stream. Victor turns around and sees it's now green. Victor looks down and notices he's no longer wearing his full platinum silver suit. He's wearing the black suit he has on in the corporeal plane. He turns to his mother and asks, "What's going on?"

She places a hand on Victor's shoulder. "You've been here for far too long. You need to wrap this up before it's too late."

Victor steps up to Derek. "Listen to me; if you want to get out of this alive, you need to tell me the truth."

"I am telling you the truth," Derek says aggressively. "The person who is after you is Florence Maryweather."

Victor's mother steps closer. "My dear, the person after my son is not Florence. That person is an impostor."

Derek becomes more worried. "Look, I don't know what to tell you."

"Then you're going to take me to her," Victor demands.

"Impossible," Derek refuses.

Victor takes out his dagger and points it at Derek's throat. "I beg to differ."

Derek shifts his eyes between Victor, Victor's mother, and the stream. "I don't know where she is, and I've never met her in person. She gives my orders to my contact. Just like when she told me to take care of the witch that cursed your grandmother."

Victor presses the point of his dagger slowly into Derek's neck and draws a little blood. "What did you just say?"

"You heard me," Derek snarls. "I knew the witch who cursed your grandmother, Marie Russo. She was the one who messed up when covering her tracks."

"What was her name?" Victor demands.

"I don't know," Derek states.

"Yes, you do!" Victor pierces Derek's neck, allowing more blood to protrude.

"Honestly, I don't know. Florence just told me where to find her." The bush doesn't grow up Derek's leg.

"YOU'RE LYING!" Victor shouts, causing a white glow to pulse off him, shaking the trees and disturbing the animals.

Derek's eyes grow wide as he looks at the stream. The forest slowly fades into darkness.

Victor's mother begins to worry as she looks around and slowly pulls back Victor's hand. *"My love, you need to go."*

"Not until I get him to tell me the truth," Victor says aggressively. Loud moans come from behind him. Victor slowly turns and sees dead souls climbing out of the dark purple River Styx.

Derek starts to struggle. *"Get me out of this!"*

Victor turns to his mother, asking, *"Mom, how do we get out of here?"*

Victor's mother shakes her head. *"I'm not sure. You've been here for too long. Your friends are the only way you can get out of this."*

Victor, his mother, and Derek watch as the dead souls slowly walk toward them.

"Guys, blood is starting to come out of their noses." Leo panics as he and Eddie rush over to Victor.

"Watch out with the circle!" Superior Charles commands.

Madame Jeanette opens her eyes. *"O Bondye! Sa pa bon!"* She rushes over and places her hand on Victor's cheek. "They are in trouble. We need to act quickly."

Leo drops beside Victor. "How do we get them back?"

Wren starts to assess the situation. "Give me a second. I'm trying to think."

"Make it quick," Superior Charles demands.

Wren paces side to side. She keeps looking down at Victor and Derek.

Eddie looks at Wren. "Hurry, the bleeding won't stop."

Wren stops and perks up. "I can do it." Everyone looks at her. "I need to go get them."

"No! I'm not letting someone else go to the astral plane. Especially if they are in danger," Superior Charles protests.

Wren takes the jar of black sand and makes a circle above Victor. "If you recall, Charles, I am older than you and more experienced in necromancy." She looks down at Madame Jeanette, "No offense."

"None taken," Madame Jeanette replies.

Superior Charles gives Wren an aggravated look. "You're only two years older than me."

Wren plops the empty jar in the box. "I just need two minutes." She sits down in the circle and crisscrosses her legs. As she closes her eyes, she starts to whisper a chant.

Victor and his mother are as far back as they can go as the dead souls get closer.

"*This is all your fault!*" Derek shouts.

A flash of light appears out of nowhere. As Victor's vision refocuses, he sees Wren making circles with her hands and arms. She creates a barrier, blocking the dead souls from approaching further.

Wren turns to everyone once she completes the barrier. "*We need to get going.*" She looks at Victor's mother. "*Are you Marie Russo?*"

Victor's mother shakes her head. "No, I'm his mother, Theresa Russo."

Wren curtsies. "Pleased to make your acquaintance, Mrs. Russo."

Victor rushes over to Wren, explaining, *"We can't leave yet. Derek is lying about something, but he won't admit it."*

"I'M NOT LYING!" Derek shouts as he desperately struggles his way out of the bush.

"What are you lying about?" Wren asks Derek.

"Florence Maryweather," Victor responds.

Wren gives Victor a confused glance. *"That's impossible. She's dead."*

Derek becomes furious. *"NO, SHE'S NOT! She ordered me to kill the witch who cursed his fucking grandmother! Now, she has me trying to kill him too!"* Derek turns his anger on Victor. *"But for whatever **fucking** reason, you just **WON'T DIE!**"*

"He mentioned he gets his order from his contact," Victor informs. *"But he won't give me a name."*

Wren holds Derek's face in her hands. *"What is the name of your contact?"*

Derek tries to break free from her hold. *"I already told you, I don't know."*

Wren's hands start to glow. *"You do know. You just don't remember. That memory was taken from you."*

"What are you doing?" Derek demands as he struggles in Wren's grasp.

"I'm linking our abilities together," Wren responds. She looks at Derek's left hand and notices a tan line on his finger. *"He's missing his wedding ring."*

"So. Why does that matter?" Victor comments.

Wren lets go of Derek's face. *"The memory of his contact's name is in his wedding ring. His ring is a focus."* The dead souls are pounding away at the barrier. The barrier's glow starts to weaken.

Victor holds his dagger to Derek's neck. *"Where's your wedding ring?"*

"I don't know," Derek says before shouting in agony. The thorny bush is halfway up his thigh. *"FINE! Fine."* Derek

sighs deeply and places his hand in his left pant pocket. He pulls out his wedding band and places it back on his ring finger.

"*The name,*" Victor demands.

"*Superior Morgana Crimson,*" Derek responds.

As soon as Derek answers, the dead souls break the barrier. Victor's mother jumps in front, and a flash of light emerges from her hands. "*I can't hold them for long. You need to get out of here.*"

Victor looks worried at his mother. "*Will you be okay?*" She turns her head to look at Victor and gives him a wink. Victor holds up his hands and pauses. "*Fuck! I forgot the words. We've been here too long.*"

Wren holds up her hands and chants in Latin.

Victor and Derek simultaneously open their eyes, gasping for air, and start coughing as they regain consciousness. When Victor sits up, he opens his eyes again, and they are black. Quickly, he pounces on top of Derek and holds his dagger to Derek's neck.

"VICTOR!" Leo shouts as he leaps over to try to get Victor off Derek.

Derek looks determined as he stares into Victor's black eyes. "Do it. You know you want to."

Victor doesn't blink as he looks back into Derek's eyes. He takes out a bracelet and slaps it onto Derek's wrist. Victor stands up, hovering over Derek. Derek tries to kick Victor but hurts himself.

"That charm prevents you from hurting anyone," Victor comments. "Any attack you try, the effects harm you instead. Also, if you try to run, I can pull you back with a snap."

Leo looks at the bracelet. "Where did you get that?"

Victor blinks a few times, and his eyes go back to normal. "Wren. She placed it in my pocket while everyone was getting things ready."

Superior Charles walks over and stops above Derek's head. He looks down at Derek's aggravated glare. "Derek Hernandez, you will be sent to trial with the council for the crimes you have committed."

Derek looks at the bracelet and tries to pull it off. "Looks like I don't have much of a choice."

Victor steps away as Superior Charles and Eddie pick up Derek. Eddie performs a binding spell on Derek. Derek snarls at Victor but Victor remains focused in case he tries to do something to escape. Eddie lets out a sharp whistle. Out of the darkness, the two muscular Aztec men appear to assist Eddie in taking Derek back to the mirror.

As the others watch Derek being taken away, Superior Charles looks at Victor and asks, "Did you get the information you needed out of him?"

Victor nods. "Derek said that Florence Maryweather is still alive."

"That's impossible," Madame Jeanette proclaims. "She's been dead for almost 30 years."

"He claims she is still alive and hiding. He receives orders from her from his contact, Superior Morgana Crimson. If we find Morgana, we'll find Florence."

CHAPTER THIRTY-FIVE

Victor sits with Leo and Wren at the island in Eddie's kitchen. Victor hasn't washed the dried blood off his face. They sit in silence, munching on chips and salsa. Victor is exhausted. He begins to drift off but is woken up when Eddie returns. Everyone looks to the door as they hear footsteps outside. Eddie, Superior Charles, and Superior Jackie walk into the kitchen.

"Derek won't be bothering us anymore," Superior Charles says as he grabs the bottle of tequila off the island. "He's behind wards and in a secluded room until his trial with the council."

Eddie walks up and stands next to Leo. "Sadly, even though he's locked up, there is still the blood oath."

Leo slouches his shoulders and sighs. "I know. And I'll have to accept it."

Eddie reaches out for Leo's hand. "Don't worry, *mijo*. We'll figure something out."

"Where's Madame Jeanette?" Victor asks.

"She's working on something for me." Superior Charles responds, knocking back a shot of tequila.

Victor grabs the bottle and pours himself a shot. "It's about Morgana, isn't it?" Victor downs his drink and slams the glass on the counter. "I want to help her find that cunt."

Superior Jackie touches Victor's shoulder and gently squeezes. "No, young empath." She takes the bottle from Victor and pours herself a drink. "If she is working with Florance, then she is much too strong for you." She drinks her shot and then pours herself and Victor another. "And to add salt to your wound, she won't be easy to find. She's been in hiding for a very long time."

Victor knocks back his shot and then stands up. "I'm going to wash this blood off my face and go to bed." He walks out of the kitchen with his head low as if he's been defeated, even though he won tonight.

Leo stands up and calls out, "Victor, wait. I'm going to head to bed too." When Leo reaches the door, he turns around and says, "Have a good night, everyone."

When Victor and Leo are out of view, Superior Jackie looks at Superior Charles and asks, "Do you think those two will ever get a chance to be together?" Superior Charles shrugs his shoulders.

"I think when Victor accepts that he'll be the next Grand Warlock, then he'll be able to break that oath and finally move on with Leo," Eddie comments, holding his shot glass close to his lips.

Wren rests her head on her fist as she leans on the island. "We could always execute Derek." Everyone turns to Wren with gruesome faces. "Oh, don't tell me none of you thought about it."

"I have thought about it once or twice," Superior Charles admits. "But I'm not going to kill someone out of spite."

"We all have, *amigo*," Eddie says as he pours everyone another drink. "I just wish those two the best for now." They each take a shot glass and clink them together.

In the middle of the night, Victor tosses around in his bed. He keeps adjusting his pillow, rolling side to side. But his thoughts are running rampant. He sits up and brings his knees to his chest. He looks at the wall, knowing Leo is on the other side. Victor wants to be with him, but he knows the consequences if Leo commits adultery. But they cuddled the other night, and nothing happened. That should be okay—just two friends consoling each other.

Victor gets out of bed and puts on his robe. He peeks his head out and looks around the dark atrium. Quietly, Victor walks over to Leo's room. He's about to knock on Leo's door when Leo opens it. As Leo is about to make a sound, Victor presses his fingers against Leo's lips. Leo and Victor stare into each other's eyes as Leo embraces Victor's fingertips. Leo closes his eyes, takes Victor's hand into his own, and holds Victor's hand to his face. Leo looks back at Victor and pulls him in for a deep embrace.

"We can't do anything that could violate this oath I'm bound to," Leo whispers into Victor's ear.

"I know," Victor whispers back. "But that doesn't mean two friends can't keep each other company."

Leo pulls back and gives Victor a little smile. "You're a bad influence."

"And you don't like it?" Victor smiles back.

Leo pulls Victor into his room and closes the door behind them.

The following day, Victor and Leo slip into shorts and shirts and walk into the kitchen. Eddie is the only one standing at the stove. He dances around to the salsa music playing on the radio. Victor and Leo walk over to the kitchen island and sit, enjoying the view of Eddie dancing around while paying no attention.

Eddie turns around and smiles. "*Buenos días, mis amores.* Breakfast will be ready soon."

"Where are your husbands?" Victor asks.

Eddie turns back to cooking eggs. "Jorge and Miguel are out of town on business, and Fernando is working at night while we prepare for an upcoming event. You just missed him as he went off to bed." Eddie conjures his Air Magic, lifts three plates off the shelf, and plates food on them. He plucks the plates from the air and carries them over to Victor and Leo.

"*Huevos Rancheros y Chilaquiles.* Oh, I forgot the fruit." Eddie looks over to the far counter where the fruit is and flicks his wrist to bring three small bowls to them.

Victor digs into his food. "Did you give your staff the day off?"

Eddie takes a bite. "No, they will be here later today." He swallows and drinks coffee. "I wanted to give the three of us time to talk before you two leave today."

"I forgot to tell you, we're leaving today and moving on to your next lesson," Leo tells Victor.

"Already? I like it here," Victor comments with a pouty face.

"You only like it here for my tequila," Eddie winks at Victor over his coffee mug. "Victor, I just want you to know that you no longer have to worry."

Victor gives Eddie an unamused gaze. "Are you trying to lie to an empath?"

"Someone's starting to get a little cocky with his ability," Eddie snickers.

Victor takes a bite with a sly look. "There's nothing little about it."

Eddie smiles and gives Leo a wink. Leo blushes. "Well," Eddie pauses as he takes a bite. "Like I said, you shouldn't have to worry any longer. Morgana doesn't like to get her hands dirty. She will eventually find someone else to come after you. If she fails, then Florence will have to come out of hiding. That's if she is still alive. But by then, you'll be stronger than you are now." Eddie sets down his fork and looks up at Victor. "If you ever need a place to escape, you are welcome here anytime. *Mi casa es su casa.*"

"Thank you, Eddie," Victor says with a smile. He turns to Leo and asks, "So, where to next?"

"I'm going to keep that as a surprise," Leo comments as he hops off the stool. "I'm going to start getting ready." Leo gives Eddie a big hug. "Keep out of trouble while I'm gone."

"I make no promises," Eddie responds. Once Leo leaves the kitchen, Eddie turns to Victor. "If you two aren't careful, you could hurt or even kill Leo."

"Yes, I know about the blood oath," Victor sighs deeply.

"If you keep cuddling in bed with him, one thing will lead to another. How else do you think I ended up with three husbands?" Eddie chuckles as he collects the dirty dishes.

Victor raises an eyebrow. "First off, I know that's *not* how you got three husbands. And secondly . . ." Victor lets out another deep sigh and looks at a spot on the island. ". . . I just needed him last night. After what happened, I was feeling distraught. Yes, I was able to get answers out of Derek, but it felt like I could have gotten more out of him. And seeing my mom again, it just made me miss her even more."

Eddie nudges Victor's shoulder with his own as he walks over to the sink. "Don't worry, mijo. She's watching over you. But it would be best if you were careful with Leo. I was his mentor when he started his warlock lessons. He's like my baby brother, so I always look after him." Eddie turns on the sink and starts soaping up the dishes. "Now, get ready. I'm looking forward to seeing how powerful you will become."

Victor turns in his seat to get a better view of Eddie. "Everyone keeps saying I'm going to be powerful. And that's not helping because if I fail, I'll feel like I failed everyone."

Eddie shrugs a shoulder as he washes. "You should believe in yourself, young empath. Because if you are anything like your *abuela* . . ." Eddie glances over his shoulder. "You will become the Grand Warlock."

Victor ponders this for a moment as he watches Eddie washing the dishes. He looks out the window at the agave field as the workers begin to start their day. To think, one day, those workers will be looking up to him. Even Eddie will be looking to him for guidance and strength. Victor takes one more look over at him before he heads up to his room.

As Victor makes his way up the stairs, he notices the door to his room is open. He can hear shuffling inside. He carefully walks to his room, slowly opens the door, and peeks inside. The maid is packing everything away.

"You don't have to always pack for me, you know," Victor remarks as he steps into the doorway.

"Nonsense, Mr. Russo. That's what I'm here for." She walks around the room, humming away. "I took the liberty to send off your suit and dirty clothes to be washed and delivered to your next destination."

"You make it sound like you won't be at the next stop," Victor comments as he leans against the doorframe.

"Mr. Oliveira asked me to take some time off. I won't see you for about a week," the maid mentions as she continues folding and packing the clean laundry.

Victor walks over to the nightstand beside the bed and picks up his phone. He has several messages from his friends. "You know, you've been my maid for a few weeks now, and I don't know why I never got your name," Victor remarks as he responds to his friends' messages.

"It's not necessary, Mr. Russo. I'm only in and out, so there's not much time to chit-chat." She stops packing and turns to Victor. "Plus, I can see that same look on your face that your grandmother had when I was her maid."

Victor snaps his head up in shock. "Wait. You knew my grandma?"

The maid smiles softly as she returns to packing. "Yes. I have been with the Russo family since 1946. It was such a shame when she passed. She was an incredible witch."

Victor crawls into bed and sits against the headboard. "Can you tell me about her?"

She looks up in thought as she folds the shirts. "Marie Russo was very kind. Had a wonderful heart. Hell, she might have been annoyed by me, but she appreciated me and what I did for the family." She smiles softly as she places the folded shirts in the suitcase. "I was still a young witch myself when I was hired. Before I was hired, the Russo family was much larger. They were also very powerful and very wealthy many, many years ago. But that was no hindrance for them helping out their fellow witch."

"There were more Russos?" Victor inquires.

"Oh yes. But I never got a chance to meet all of them," the maid explains as she finishes with the laundry and moves on to remove any clothing from the dresser. "I think it was sometime after 1931 when things started to go awry within the covens. It was almost like a civil war. Witch against witch. Coven against coven. It was because your great-grandfather was showing potential to become the first Grand Warlock, but there were other reasons, too.

"It lasted a good part of a decade until your grandmother, and several other covens made a truce. By the time a truce was made, it was only your great-grandmother, Carmela Russo, and your grandmother, Marie. Sadly, Carmela passed away shortly after I was hired."

The maid stops for a moment as she goes over the memory. "I was supposed to be Carmela's caregiver, but Marie knew that I didn't have a coven to fall back on, so she allowed me to stay as a housekeeper. The house might have been filled with members of her coven, but Marie felt lonely until she finally remarried and had children."

She resumes packing and continues her story. "It wasn't until 1961 that your grandmother started showing signs that she might be the next Grand Witch. The fighting almost started up again before her grand trials. Luckily, plenty of new superiors were elected to the covens. They were able to prevent another civil war; however, it put Marie's grand trials on hold. But that didn't stop one particular witch from putting a curse on Marie twelve years later, just before Marie could retake the trials."

She zips up the suitcase and takes it off the chair and onto the floor. She takes a moment before she looks over at Victor. "When it was certain that Mrs. Russo would perish, she asked me to keep things in order for her family. I gave her my word that I would return to assist her family with their needs, even though I didn't know if any other Russo would return. But something told me I needed to keep my promise. As soon as it was known that you had survived, I was contacted by Madame Jeanette. She was one of only a few witches Marie asked to find me."

She steps closer to the bed, giving Victor a somber expression. "I just wish I were there to help your mother, but when Mrs. Russo took her children into hiding with her, I was asked never to come looking for them, for everyone's protection."

"With everything that's happened to a family I never knew about, I don't know if this is something that I want," Victor says as he brings his knees to his chest.

The maid takes a seat at the foot of the bed. "What do you mean?

"It just feels like people have high expectations of me. I know nothing about my mother's side of the family. Maybe I should just go back into hiding."

"You mustn't think that way, Mr. Russo," she declares.

"How can I be a powerful warlock when I never learned to be one at a young age?"

"Your grandmother's blood flows through your veins. Just like in your mother's and uncle's."

His eyes shift around as he goes into thought. "I remember seeing my uncle a few times when I was little, but I don't remember much after that. Have you heard anything about him? Where he might be by chance? Maybe if I could reach out to him, he could help me with my training and understand what's at stake."

She places her hands in her lap and slouches her shoulders. "I haven't seen or heard anything from your uncle since he found out your grandmother was cursed. I thought he just disappeared off the face of the Earth."

"Do you remember my mom or my uncle?" Victor asks, crisscrossing his legs.

The maid lets out a light laugh as she thinks about Victor's mother. "I do remember your mother. Such a sweet young lady. It was a shame that she had to stop her lessons. I could tell she too, had great potential. Your uncle, on the other hand, was a stubborn boy. He was a ladies' man, always showing off his powers. He didn't like it when your grandmother told him he needed to go into hiding and stop using his powers. But then he left in a rage, looking for whoever cursed your grandmother. I haven't heard from him since. I could have been working for him if he stuck around, keeping the Russo household going."

"Do you think things would be different if my grandmother were still alive?" Victor ponders.

"Oh, most definitely, dear. She would have brought order to chaos," the maid responds.

"Were you part of her coven?" Victor asks.

The maid smooths out her outfit. "I'm a solus witch. No coven wanted me."

"Why was that?" Victor inquires. "Surely, you must have gotten an invite."

She shakes her head subtly. "No, my magic isn't that powerful. Especially during those dark times, I wasn't fit for battle. But your grandmother knew that if I couldn't defend myself, I should be somewhere I could be protected. She had a few on her staff whose magic wasn't very, well, magical."

The maid pauses. "I guess you could say that your grandmother made a coven for those who had magic, just unable to wield it." She stands up and brushes out her skirt. "Well, your bags are packed, and your suit will be delivered to your hotel later today."

"Thank you," Victor says as he gets up from the bed. "Umm, I guess it's been very rude of me never getting to know your name."

"Annabelle," she mentions before she walks out the door.

"Thank you, Annabelle," Victor reciprocates.

Annabelle curtsies. "You're welcome, Empath Russo." She takes her leave and closes the door behind her.

After Victor has showered and changed, he grabs his small bag and heads to the door. When he opens it, Eddie holds a bottle of tequila and a tray of shot glasses. "FUCK ME!" Victor shouts as he jumps back, grabbing hold of his chest.

"Now? I think Fernando would get upset if we didn't invite him," Eddie says with a grin. "I can't let you leave without one more shot."

Victor takes a shot glass as he shakes his head with a smile. "I'm definitely going to miss this."

"As I said, you're welcome to visit anytime." Eddie leans in and gives Victor a small kiss on the lips. Victor is a little caught off guard, but he shrugs it off when Eddie pulls back. They cheer as they take their shots. "So, you ready to learn how to control fire?" Eddie asks.

"We'll see. Leo still hasn't told me where we're going or who will teach me," Victor responds.

Leo slides up next to Eddie. "The honor has been placed on me to teach you Fire Magic." He smacks Eddie on his shoulder. "And why didn't I get a kiss goodbye?"

"*Oh, diculpame, ¿dónde están mis modales?*" Eddie gives Leo a small kiss on the lips.

"Is this how you always say goodbye to all your guests?" Victor asks with a raised eyebrow.

"Only the cute ones," Eddie says with a cheesy grin and a wink.

Victor rolls his eyes and follows Leo and Eddie to the mirror room. He looks at their belongings and wonders, "How exactly are we going to take all this through a mirror?"

"We're not," Leo informs. "A carrier is coming to pick up our things. I already have everything we need at the hotel." Leo gives Eddie a tight embrace. "Thank you again for the hospitality."

"Of course, *mi amor*," Eddie responds in Leo's ear. "Let me know if you need any help." Eddie turns to Victor and pulls him in and wraps his strong arms around Victor. Victor embraces Eddie even though he can hardly breathe. "And don't be a stranger, okay, *mijo?*"

"I promise," Victor answers as he pats Eddie on his back, hoping Eddie will let go so he can breathe.

Leo presses his palm onto one of the mirrors. When the mirror goes hazy, he turns to Victor and holds out a hand. "You ready to go?"

Victor takes Leo's hand into his. "You still haven't told me where we're going." Leo smiles and pulls Victor through the mirror with him.

CHAPTER THIRTY-SIX

Victor emerges on the other side of the mirror, and it looks like he's back in New York or Chicago. As he follows Leo to the elevators, he feels an ocean breeze coming up the stairs, and a light scent of tropical flora tickles his senses.

As the elevator doors open, a woman in Hawaiian garb greets them. "Aloha, Mr. Oliveira. Your room is ready."

"We're in Hawai'i?" Victor asks as he steps into the elevator.

"Yes, we are," Leo smiles.

"Which island?" Victor asks.

"You might recognize it when we get to the room." Leo glances over to Victor and gives him a wink. "You could say I did some research when I selected this place."

"Are we on the 13th or 14th floor?" Victor jokes.

"This hotel only has 10 floors. We're on the 10th floor," Leo answers.

They step out of the elevator and make their way down the hall. As they approach the door, two other women are there to greet them. "Victor, meet Makana and Nali," Leo introduces. "I helped both of them with their Fire Magic back in the day."

Makana is holding leis, and Nali is holding a tray with drinks.

Makana approaches them first. "*Aloha*, Mr. Oliveira, Mr. Russo, welcome to Hawai'i," she says, placing the leis around Victor and Leo's necks.

Nali walks over to hand them their drinks. "Mai Tai, anyone?"

"*Mahalo*, Makana, Nali," Leo smiles. "It's always a pleasure being here."

Makana waves a key card across the sensor on the door behind her and pushes open the double doors to the room. "Please, come in."

The spacious suite is a tropical retreat, featuring rich, dark *Ko'a* wood furniture accented with woven rattan and bamboo details. The cushions are patterned with hibiscus, plumeria, and lush foliage. The walls are adorned with vibrant, original paintings of the Hawaiian waters with the sun setting. On the private lanai, there are teak chaise lounges.

To the left is a small kitchen with open cabinets for easy access to dishes and glassware. A variety of small appliances sit on the countertop. A basket of fresh tropical fruits, adorned with a big red bow, welcomes guests to enjoy a taste of Hawai'i.

Victor walks further into the living room, over to the large window. Looking out the window, he can see the beach. A couple of dozen blue and white beach umbrellas are placed neatly next to each other with a set of chairs under each. Further in the distance, he can see Molokini Crater.

"We're in Maui," Victor says with amazement. "How did you know this was one of my favorite places in Hawai'i?"

"You mentioned how you enjoyed your layovers here. Lucky for you, we *also* have a hotel here," Leo replies.

Nali walks over to the kitchen. "We have the kitchen fully stocked for you, and your massage appointment has been scheduled for later today on the lanai."

Makana walks over and opens the double doors to the bedroom. "Your belongings will be here shortly, and your suits can be picked up at the cleaners in an hour."

Nali and Makana walk to the front door. Makana turns around and says, "Please let us know if you would like anything else."

"The luau is at 7 p.m. I made sure you got your favorite seats, Mr. Oliveira," Nali mentions.

"*Mahalo*," Leo says as the women leave the room. "So, what do you think?" he asks Victor.

Victor looks around and notices there is only one bedroom in their suite. "Are we sharing a room?"

"Yes. Will it be a problem?" Leo questions.

"I mean, we've always had two rooms everywhere we went. You don't think it won't be tempting to sleep together?" Victor asks.

Leo shrugs his shoulders as he puts his hands in his pockets. "I mean, yes, it's a considerable risk. However, we've slept in the same bed many times already. Also, it's a massive king-size bed. And, if I have to, I'll sleep on the couch."

"I'm not going to let you do that," Victor remarks.

Leo walks past Victor to the bedroom. "Fine. Then you can sleep on the couch."

Victor's jaw drops. "Ouch." He follows Leo into the bedroom. He stops once he walks in, amazed at the size. "I didn't realize how large this room is. It's almost as big as my apartment." He looks out the window with an unobstructed view of the sapphire waters below. Victor walks over to a small silver suitcase. "Is this one mine?" Leo nods in response. Victor opens it and examines its contents. "Looks like you packed light. There's no swimsuit."

"We don't need one," Leo responds as he draws back large curtains on the other side of the room, revealing a balcony with a raised hot tub, perfect for soaking in. A set of chairs and a small table sit in the corner.

"But what if we want to go snorkeling?" Victor inquires.

"If we have time for snorkeling, then I'll get us some swimsuits," Leo comments.

"So, are we just here on vacation, or is this a business-slash-pleasure trip?" Victor asks as he unpacks.

"Well, practicing your magic with a large source of that element is best," Leo explains. "And Hawai'i sits in the middle of the Ring of Fire that circles the Pacific. Plus, I enjoy feeling that the goddess Pele is helping provide the source."

"Is Pele real?" Victor asks with skepticism.

Leo looks back at Victor. He gives him a wink before walking back into the living room.

Victor follows a few steps behind.

Leo walks into the kitchen and collects some fruit from the welcome basket and a knife from the counter. "Today, and maybe tomorrow, we will just relax, my young empath. You have been through a lot, and I think you deserve a break." Leo starts cutting up fresh pineapple. "Would you like a drink?"

Victor plops down on the couch and turns on the TV. "Sure."

There's a knock at the door.

"The massage therapist is here," Victor mentions without looking to see who's at the door.

Leo gives Victor a stunned look. "You can sense her?"

Victor hops off the couch and walks to the door. "Him." Victor opens the door, and a very handsome, toned man is on the other side wearing perfectly ironed light-tan slacks and a simple white polo. *"Aloha,"* Victor says under his breath as he takes in how stunning this man is.

"Aloha," the handsome man says with a gorgeous smile. "I'm here to give you gentlemen a massage out on the lanai. May I come in?" Victor steps to the side, allowing him to enter. "It will take me a few minutes to get set up. Who would like to go first?"

"I volunteer as tribute," Victor blurts out before Leo can get a word out. Leo laughs as he turns the blender on to make the drinks. The man smiles back at Victor as he heads to the lanai.

A few minutes later, the man walks back inside. "Okay, I'm ready." Victor doesn't hesitate, taking his shirt off before stepping outside. Leo chuckles as he sips his freshly blended cocktail.

After a much-needed massage and nap, Leo and Victor walk hand-in-hand to the luau on the beach. Nali greets them again, waiting for them with fresh leis. She escorts them to their seats close to the stage. As they take their seats, two servers set a drink and a basket of sweet breads in front of them.

"I have never been to an actual luau," Victor mentions as he picks up his drink.

Leo leans over and gives Victor a peck on the cheek. "You're in for a treat."

Victor does his best not to blush. "Are you sure you're not in danger with what we are doing?"

"What do you mean?" Leo ponders.

"Holding hands, kisses on the cheek, sleeping in the same bed?"

"Nothing bad has happened to me yet," Leo says as he sips his drink. "Also, the definition of adultery is slightly different in witchcraft than in the mundane. We would have to engage in intercourse without the other spouse's consent. All these other gestures are harmless and friendly."

"If you say so," Victor worries. However, his worry dissipates when the food arrives. A server sets a silver platter featuring generous portions of *kalua* pig, slow-roasted until tender, alongside *lomi-lomi* salmon and moist chicken long rice. Sides of sweet *poi*, *haupia* coconut pudding, and fresh tropical fruit traditionally accompany the main dishes. They enjoy their meal and the show as the sun slowly lowers into the water, turning day into night.

In the middle of the night, Victor tosses and turns. His facial expressions show he's having a bad dream. Leo is on the other side of the bed and doesn't move when Victor sits up abruptly, breathing heavily. Victor is covered in sweat, and his hands are shaky. He looks around the room to get his bearings.

Victor looks over at Leo, who is sound asleep. He tries not to disturb him while quietly getting out of bed and heading to the bathroom. Halfway there, Victor stops and stands straight up. A chill runs through his body, causing his skin to break out in goosebumps and his hair to stand on end. He takes in a slow, deep, and shaky breath. There is a feeling that someone else is in the room with him.

Victor slowly examines the room and cannot see anyone. He opens the door to the living room; he doesn't notice anything. He slowly walks over to the window, placing his hand on the curtains, trying to hold back his nerves. Before Victor opens them, he closes his eyes and takes another deep, shaky breath. He swallows dryly, opens his eyes, and slowly pulls back the curtains.

The bedroom fills with the bright light from the full moon. As Victor looks around outside, his scans bring his attention to the water. There is a figure of someone standing on the shore. The figure has a dark glow to it. Victor can't make out whether it is a man or a woman. The waves crash against their feet. As Victor focuses on the figure, they look back up at him.

Their eyes glow a lime green.

"LEO!" Victor shouts as he runs to the bed.

Leo is startled awake. "What! What is it?" Victor abruptly pulls Leo out of bed and over to the window. Victor rips back the curtains, but the figure is gone. Leo looks outside and then over at Victor. He can see Victor is frightened. "What did you see?"

Victor looks down at the spot where he saw the figure on the beach. "I think she found me."

Leo grows concerned. "Who? Morgana?" Victor slowly nods. Leo turns Victor to face him, but Victor doesn't stop looking towards the beach. "Are you sure it was her?"

Victor licks his lips before he responds. "I-I don't know. Someone was down there. I couldn't make out who it was. They only had this dark glow to them. And when they looked up, I could see a green glow coming from their eyes, just staring right back at me."

Leo pulls Victor in for a tight hug. Victor buries his face into Leo's shoulder as he returns to shaking. Leo lightly rubs the back of Victor's neck. "*Shhh*, it's okay. You're safe and with me."

Victor shakes his head on Leo's shoulder. "You don't get it. I sensed so much fear. It manifested in my dreams. Whoever was out there projected fear onto me." Victor pulls away from Leo. "Look. I'm still shaking."

Leo goes over to the nightstand on Victor's side of the bed. "Where's your silver card?"

"It should be with my jacket in the closet," Victor responds.

"You should be keeping it close to you," Leo mentions. Leo rushes to the closet and rummages through Victor's garment bag. He finds the silver card and hurries back to Victor, who hasn't moved from his spot. Victor clasps the card in his hands and holds it against his chest. Leo pulls Victor back in for another hug. Victor's heart rate begins to slow down, allowing him to relax in Leo's arms.

"Well, isn't this touching?" a mysterious voice comments behind them.

Victor turns around abruptly to the voice. He sees the figure from the beach standing at the bedroom door. Leo jumps in front of Victor and creates a red fireball in his hand.

"Who are you?" Leo demands.

An older gentleman appears from the dark glow, dressed all in black. He stands with his hands clasped in front of him. His hair is gray and silver, neatly trimmed and combed back. His goatee is well-groomed and shaped around his sharp chin. A small, charcoal gray pendant of a raven's head is pinned to his lapel. He stands a little taller than Victor and has a lean, toned figure. His eyes are the same dark brown color as Victor's.

"Did I interrupt the two of you? You must have been doing something since you're both in your underwear," the warlock comments.

Leo makes his fireball brighter. "I asked, who the *fuck* are you?"

The warlock waves a hand and extinguishes Leo's fireball. "Young Warlock, has anyone told you you should respect your elders?"

"You're no elder of mine," Leo sneers through his teeth.

Leo and Victor keep their eyes fixed on the older man as he steps forward. "I just wanted to check out the new empath," the warlock remarks.

Victor lowers Leo's arms from blocking him and steps forward. "Well, you've got to check me out."

"In more ways than one, to say the least," the older man says sarcastically as he raises an eyebrow. "Now, I'm sure Derek would *love* to hear that his husband is half-naked with the warlock he's supposed to be mentoring. And I'm sure the council would have a field day if they found out one of their prized mentors is fraternizing with a student."

Leo grows angry. "Derek can't do anything where he is. And the council already knows about this relationship."

"Do they now?" the warlock questions. "Well, I guess I'll have to have a long discussion with them."

Victor holds back Leo before he charges. "Who are you?" Victor asks calmly.

The older warlock takes a step closer. "That's not important, young empath." He looks deep into Victor's eyes. "You have your mother's spirit. Your grandmother's too." He leans in closer, placing his hands behind him. "Hell, even your uncle's. The Russo line flows within you." The man turns and walks away. "We'll see each other again."

He stops and glances over his shoulder. "Don't worry, it won't be anytime soon." The entire room goes completely dark. When the moonlight slowly appears again, lighting up the room, the mysterious warlock is gone.

Leo rushes to the nightstand to grab his phone. "We need to get Superior Charles here now. Maybe even Jeanette."

Victor keeps looking at where the man stood. "Don't bother. There's nothing they can do."

Leo looks up at Victor with a look of shock. "What are you talking about, 'don't bother?' They need to investigate who he was."

Victor walks over and stops next to where he last saw the mysterious man. "I already know who it was," he says, looking forward as though he is still looking at the man who was once there with him.

"Who was it?" Leo questions.

Victor remains quiet, still gazing at the blank space in front of him. "That was my uncle," he finally says.

Leo drops his phone and his jaw. "Are you certain?"

Victor nods slowly in response. "Quite. I could see my mother in his gaze. They both have the same twitch with their left eyebrow when judging someone."

"All the more reason to get Superior Charles involved," Leo suggests as he walks over to Victor.

"No," Victor speaks sharply over his shoulder.

"Why not?" Leo demands.

"This isn't something a coven can take care of. And last time I checked, I'm not part of any coven," Victor responds calmly.

"What are you talking about, Vic? Why does it matter if you're part of a coven or not?" Leo questions as he walks around the bed.

"This is a family matter," Victor proclaims. "Getting a coven involved, especially anyone I'm not incorporated with, will only worsen things."

"And how do you know all this?" Leo questions.

"Because I just do," Victor snaps back. He takes a deep breath, calming his emotions. "I can't explain it, Leo. I just know." Victor walks over and takes a seat at the foot of the bed. "It's something that my mother told me before she died. I never quite understood what she meant until now."

Leo takes a seat next to Victor and places his hand on top of Victor's. "What did she say?"

Victor takes a deep breath and licks his lips. "When it comes to family matters, no other family can get involved." Victor places his other hand on top of Leo's and looks into Leo's eyes. "Your coven is your family, not mine. I have to face him alone."

Leo shakes his head in disagreement. "Victor, you're not strong enough. Fuck, he extinguished my fireball as he was astral projecting."

"He wasn't astral projecting," Victor comments.

Leo's face turns white, and his eyes grow wide. "Are you telling me he was physically here? In our room?"

Victor nods slowly. "I've been quickly picking up on when someone is physically with me or not." Victor looks back at the spot on the floor. "My uncle paid me a visit."

CHAPTER THIRTY-SEVEN

The following day, Superior Charles, Superior Jackie, Madame Jeanette, and Akisha sit around the living room with Victor and Leo. Superior Charles looks out the window with his arms crossed.

"Are you certain it was your uncle?" Superior Charles asks.

Victor rubs his temples and moans. "For the last time, yes. I know it was my uncle. I don't know why it's so difficult for you to comprehend."

"It's just that no one has seen your uncle since he disappeared in 1975," Superior Jackie comments.

Victor sighs and gets up from the couch. "Let me get my phone." Victor walks into the bedroom.

Superior Charles turns around and looks at Leo. "Leo, I need you to get a second room. It's not safe for you two sleeping together."

"Everything is fine," Leo responds. "Nothing has happened to me."

"Leo, just beca—" Superior Charles stops talking when Victor returns to the living room.

"I know what you're talking about," Victor explains as he sits back on the couch. "Not only could I hear you in the other room, but your auras changed since I've returned."

Superior Charles cocks an eyebrow. "I see your ability is growing stronger." He clears his throat, "Well, as I was saying, just because nothing has happened doesn't mean that temptation won't arise."

"We appreciate that you care about us, but we will figure this all out," Victor affirms.

"The affection between the two of you is all over your auras," Superior Charles remarks. "Everyone can see it, even if they aren't empathic."

"Then we'll be extra careful," Victor says, annoyance evident as he scrolls through the photos on his phone. "I think there has to be a reason why you haven't heard from him since 1975." He holds up his phone for the others to see. "Because who is this on my fifth birthday?"

Everyone is shocked by the photo.

Akisha takes Victor's phone out of his hand. "That's . . . How? He's been in hiding ever since."

"There are a few more pictures of my childhood," Victor elucidates. "He stopped coming around when I turned eight. Around the same time . . . my mother got sick."

The front door opens, and Wren walks in. "Sorry I'm late. I got tied up looking for some books for Tabatha. She's got a witch who's having issues with Water Magic." Wren is holding a tome in her arms, the size of a large laptop and five inches thick. "I overheard your question, Akisha, and I think I discovered why we haven't seen him."

Wren plops the heavy book onto the dining table and waves her hand over it. The cover flips open, and the pages flutter until they stop on a page Wren wants. "According to some records I found, Michael Russo died in 1972, which is weird that he would disappear three years later. So, either that man in Victor's pictures isn't Michael Russo, *or* he changed his identity."

Superior Jackie sets her wine glass on the coffee table. "Do you think you could find out if any warlocks somehow appeared unexpectedly in the records?"

Wren shakes her head. "Whatever he did, he did an outstanding job covering his tracks. Even my spells can't find any discrepancies in the records. And I'm still waiting to hear back from Europe to get access to their records."

"You only found out about this. How are you so fast looking for shit in a massive library archive?" Victor asks Wren.

"Oh, I'm very thorough," Wren subtly responds as she closes her tome with a thick thud. "And I already have access to every record around the globe except for Europe. You can thank the EU for their restrictions to grant access." Wren turns to Madame Jeanette and asks, "Jeanette, did you see anything?"

"No, I'm sorry, chérie," Madame Jeanette answers. "Everything Victor told us about last night doesn't appear in my visions."

"Victor, could I please talk with you on the lanai for a moment?" Wren asks.

"Whatever needs to be said to him, you can tell everyone," Superior Charles remarks.

Wren stands tall to Superior Charles, even though she's the same height as Victor. "With all due respect, Superior, Victor is not in a coven, and you are not my superior. Now, after I speak to him, he can decide whether or not to share this information."

Victor and Leo are surprised at how Wren just spoke to Superior Charles. Superior Charles squints his eyes and flares his nostrils. Wren makes her way to the lanai, giving no fucks. Victor stands up and follows after her.

Victor closes the door behind him and meets Wren at the far end. "So, what's up?"

Wren pulls out a small, worn-out book from her back pocket. "I have something you should see."

"Is this the book about older blood oaths?" Victor asks, taking the book from Wren.

"It is. I dog-eared the page for you," Wren informs.

Victor opens the book and studies the page. "There is a loophole of sorts. But it won't be easy since Derek is currently locked up."

Wren takes a very deep breath as she prepares herself to tell Victor some news. "That's why I wanted to talk to you in private first."

"WHAT THE FUCK!!" Superior Charles shouts, startling Victor and Wren.

"Well, looks like someone else just found out," Wren comments as she walks over to the door.

Victor looks at Wren from the corner of his eye. "What just happened?"

Wren slides the door open and says, "Derek broke out."

"WHAT THE FUCK!!" Victor bellows out.

When Victor walks back inside, Eddie and Chiyo have arrived. Victor looks at everyone and says, "Tell me this isn't true."

Eddie steps forward. "Yes, Derek broke out yesterday morning. We don't know how he was able to break through the wards."

Victor is befuddled. "But the bracelet that I placed on him. Can't I send him right back?"

Eddie and Chiyo look at each other before Eddie looks back at Victor. "He chopped off his hand."

Leo jumps up from his seat. "He *WHAT?!*"

Eddie walks over to Leo, holding up his hands. "You don't need to worry too much because he inflicted this injury on himself. You will be fine with the blood oath. Also, he'll have to use a significant amount of healing with whatever magic he's using. Derek won't be able to astral project to see you anytime soon."

Victor pinches the bridge of his nose. "So not only do we have to worry about my uncle returning for whatever he could be planning, but now we have to deal with Derek coming after me again?"

Chatter engulfs the room. It becomes a white nose as Victor walks to the couch. The noise grows louder around him. When he takes his seat, it becomes louder and louder, to the point where he can't take it anymore.

"QUIET!" Victor roars. A flash of light with a green hue pulses off Victor. Everyone in the room immediately stops talking and becomes calm without realizing what happened.

Victor stretches and rotates his neck and shoulders, keeping his eyes closed. When he opens his eyes, everyone is looking at him, stupefied. "What?" he asks, shifting his eyes between everyone.

Superior Charles walks over to Victor. "Outside. Now."

Victor moans in aggravation as he follows Superior Charles through the bedroom and out onto the balcony. "Why didn't you want to go out to the lanai?"

"There's more sunlight here. And I need to look at you with natural light." Superior Charles closes the sliding door and turns around. "Plus, there's more privacy." He walks over to the railing overlooking the waters. "Your ability is growing. And it's growing rapidly. Do you know what you did just now?" Victor looks at Superior Charles with skepticism as he shakes his head. "You pushed your aura off you, which caused everyone to calm down. Even me."

Victor is dumbfounded. "I'm sorry? I caused you, a warlock more powerful than me, an empath, a superior, to calm down. Just by pushing my aura off me and onto you?"

"That's what I said. And not many empaths can do that to me," Superior Charles states.

Victor looks away as he ponders.

"What is it, young empath?"

"I can't do this," Victor says as he walks to the railing overlooking the bay.

"What can't you do?" Superior Charles says sincerely as he looks down at Victor.

"All of this. It's just so much pressure now," Victor claims as he leans against the railing.

"What pressure are you talking about?" Superior Charles probes.

"Don't do that."

"Do what?"

Victor glances sideways at Superior Charles. "You know exactly what I'm talking about. I know you're reading my feelings. I can sense it."

Superior Charles places his hands on the railing and looks out at the water. "I want to hear it coming from you. What pressure are you talking about?"

"THIS!" Victor exclaims as he turns around with his arms open as if he's expressing everything around him. "All of this. You! Them! Those goddamned invites you have in the inner breast pocket of your jacket."

Superior Charles pulls out an envelope. "I'm surprised you knew I had these," he says as he opens the envelope, filled with business cards of various shapes and colors. "Thank God we switched to business cards. We used to use gemstones back in the day. That shit gets heavy to carry around."

Victor crosses his arms and leans back against the railing. "I could sense the emblems. They embody the superiors of each coven. I didn't tell Leo this, but ever since what happened at the restaurant and after I took Derek to the astral plane, my empathic ability has grown. I haven't been able to make heads nor tails of it, but it's been causing me to sense more than just the feelings of those around me."

Victor nods to a couple of surfers wading in the water at least 100 meters from the shore. "I can tell those two are enjoying their vacation." He doesn't look down during his following example. "The couple to the right, three floors down, sitting and trying to enjoy lunch. She isn't happy that her friend didn't invite her to the inauguration dinner of the new superior of her friend's coven."

Superior Charles looks over the railing and sees two witches eating in silence. He focuses on them, "My God." He looks back at Victor. "You're right. And I know the superior you're talking about. Are you sure you're not also a telepath?" Superior Charles' humor does not amuse Victor. Superior Charles notices and places a consoling hand on Victor's shoulder. "I know this pressure seems tough right now. But you'll be amazing."

"If I were a telepath, I would understand why you think I'll be the first Grand Warlock," Victor retorts. "So, tell me, Superior, why are you interested in me? A warlock that has just dived into the deep end, not knowing any of his family's history. Not having any family member to help him understand what's going on."

"Why am I interested in you?" Superior Charles asks, trying to understand the question.

Victor looks up into Superior Charles' eyes. "Yes. You were the first to show clear interest in me and invited me to your coven. Now, I have at least what, 30 more invites? Five are in Europe. But you, out of every superior, have more interest in me. Why?"

Superior Charles moves his jaw around, pondering his answer. "It's what Jeanette showed me."

"Explain."

Superior Charles sighs as he takes out a cigar and lights it without even snapping his fingers. "Normally, we are not supposed to discuss strong premonitions." He takes a deep puff before he continues. "But Jeanie is cautious about your ability as an empath. Additionally, I am one of the few empaths who are not in hiding and strong enough to guide you in the right direction. And everyone inside, including me, wants you to succeed."

"Succeed to be the Grand Warlock," Victor comments softly while looking out at the bay.

"For the most part, yes," Superior Charles remarks.

"I just don't understand why," Victor states as he looks back at the Superior.

"Because it's what else she saw." Superior Charles goes quiet for a moment. "Something is coming. We don't know who or what it is. But it scared her familiar as well. Unfortunately, no one was powerful enough to stop it." He turns his attention back to Victor. "But you are. Your mother could have been; rest her soul. Even your grandmother would have been powerful enough. What wasn't said is that Florence was your grandmother's half-sister. If she is still alive, as Derek claimed, she has something planned—and you're in her way."

Victor pinches the bridge of his nose. "I swear to God, or Goddess, or whoever you pray to, if there is anything else you're not telling me, I'm going to jump off this building."

Superior Charles turns around to look at the door. "Well, then, I guess this is goodbye," he says sarcastically.

Victor perks up at a familiar presence and spins around, seeing them stepping out onto the balcony.

"Lucas?"

CHAPTER THIRTY-EIGHT

Victor stands in utter silence, his mouth slightly open, watching his childhood friend walk outside, holding a drink in each hand.

Superior Charles snuffs his cigar at the edge of the lap pool before walking to the door. "I'll give you two some privacy."

Lucas doesn't say much as he stands by the door. Victor is still trying to process what's going on. Lucas walks over to the chairs and places the drinks on the small table. "Why don't we have a seat?" Lucas suggests.

Victor slowly walks closer to Lucas. "What the fuck is going on here?" Victor looks over Lucas' body. "Is there an illusion charm or something?"

Lucas laughs, "No, no. It's me. Your best friend, Lucas." Victor wraps his arms around Lucas, nearly knocking their drinks off the table. Lucas laughs some more. "Sounds like you're having some issues grasping what's happening around you."

Victor pulls back with a shocked look on his face. "Wait! Does this mean . . ."

Lucas nods. "Yes. I'm a warlock."

Victor punches Lucas in the arm. "What the fuck, dude! We've been friends for years, and you never told me?"

"You still punch like a bitch. And you know the first rule of fight club," Lucas jokes as he rubs his arm.

Victor dramatically cocks his head. "Don't start with me right now. I don't think you understand what I'm going through."

"You mean the whole Grand Warlock thing? Yeah, I'm aware," Lucas mentions as he takes a seat.

Victor is thunderstruck, plopping down in the chair next to his best friend. "How do you know about all this?" he questions loudly.

"Because my superior is interested in you. She gave Superior Charles her invite to give to you," Lucas responds.

"First question, because I need to know . . . how old are you?" Victor asks.

Lucas laughs, tossing his head back. "Out of all the questions that must be going through that pretty little mind of yours, that's the first question you ask me?"

"Well?"

"I'm still one year older than you," Lucas replies, setting his drink back on the table. "And to follow up with your next set of questions: I started training at eight. Jon is also a warlock and is 30. He and I were inherited into our covens by our parents. Jon and I have been invited to join a coven together, but we are happy being a part of two separate covens. We do not have any abilities like you. And I specialize in Water, Air, Fire, and Light. While Jon specializes in Fire, Earth, Air, and Shadow."

Victor looks at Lucas with astonishment. *"WHAT THE FUCK IS GOING ON?"*

Lucas' laughs echo around the walls. "You have no idea how good it feels to tell you finally. Well, you're an empath, so I'm pretty sure you know." Lucas gives Victor a perplexed look. "Which is surprising that you never picked up on any of this all these years."

Victor shrugs his shoulders as he reaches for his drink. "I mean, I never really thought about it. I always was drawn to you when we were teens, and I knew we would be great friends. But it never dawned on me that you were a warlock."

Victor pinches his eyebrows together, pondering, "So you weren't pressured to not mingle with the mundane?"

Lucas shakes his head as he swallows his drink. "Nope. My superior doesn't give a crap about all that. She's only concerned that we don't expose our magic. Come to think of it, I don't think she approves of romantic relationships with the mundane. Unless they are trustworthy."

"Frank, Elliott, Amber, and Lupe know about me," Victor mentions over the rim of his glass.

"I heard about what happened at Amber's birthday. It caused a huge uproar with many covens," Lucas explains. "Some covens won't come forward to take responsibility for those witches who attacked you. But I haven't told our friends I'm also a warlock. Don't want the whole, *'Ohhh, you should have been there for Victor. Why didn't you know Victor was in trouble?'* talk with our friends."

"So, why are you here?" Victor explores. "And the timing of it all?"

"Superior Charles contacted me shortly after the attack on Amber's birthday. He wants you to see a familiar face to help you discuss this. I was busy substituting some young water witches, but I didn't want to distract you with your own training. After your encounter last night, he called me to come over as quickly as possible," Lucas explains.

Victor perks up when he remembers the events from their time in New Orleans for his birthday. "Wait a minute. Did you know about the test Madame Jeanette was doing? Did you lead me to her when we were in New Orleans for my birthday?"

"Actually, no," Lucas responds. "I wasn't aware of any of that. I was there under the pretense of celebrating your birthday, especially after your break-up with your asshole ex-boyfriend. But then, you discovered Jeanette's shop. Jon gave me this look as though he knew this would happen. He told me after the trip that he saw Jeanette watching us as we were bar hopping. When we walked inside, we worried our covers would be blown. But Jeanette knew to play along as if she had just met us."

"When did you find out?" Victor asks.

"It was after you agreed to talk with Leopold," Lucas answers freely. "Jeanette contacted Jon and thanked him for bringing you to her. I didn't understand what she meant until I realized she had a vision, and it came true. I then realized the whole endeavor was to test you to make sure you were the one they've been looking for."

"And the reason you're coming forward now?" Victor asks as he looks into his empty glass with a sad face.

"I wanted to surprise you after you finished the first part of your training. It's been concentrated, and I didn't want to disturb you," Lucas mentions. "It's a big deal when empaths have learned the common specialties for whatever reason; don't ask me why. I was hoping to be the one to teach you Light Magic. But I was told no. However, I can be there when you learn. And Jon has permission to be there when you learn Shadow."

Victor looks through the window and sees everyone sitting around in the living room. "Everyone in there wants me to become this Grand Warlock. What are your thoughts?"

Lucas looks inside and studies the crowd. "Honestly, I wouldn't know anyone else qualified," Lucas says sincerely as he turns his attention back to his friend. "I've seen how good a leader you are. Remember when we used to work together in the theme parks during parades? You were always on it with getting things ready in the area you were assigned to lead, and made sure everyone understood their tasks. And let's not forget all the times we played paintball. You always had a strategy ready, and almost every time, we won."

"Three times we lost, and that's because the bitch thought I was an ass giving orders and didn't know what I was talking about. And she was always the first one to get shot. Who invited that trollop anyway?" Victor and Lucas snicker at the memory before Victor sighs and becomes serious. "But this isn't paintball. This is real. And I don't know what the fuck I was thinking. I literally came into all of this without a thought in the world. It was as if I knew I was supposed to be here without question. But now, everyone expects me to become this person when I don't even know if I could become that person."

Lucas pats Victor's leg. "I believe in you, Bestie. And I will always be by your side. And now that you know I'm a warlock, you can always come to me if you need to talk."

"Thank you, my friend." Victor hugs Lucas. They squeeze each other tightly.

Victor and Lucas pick up their drinks and walk back inside. When Victor walks into the living room, everyone goes silent and looks over at him. It was almost as if they sensed that Victor wanted their attention. He takes a deep breath before he speaks.

"We cannot allow what has happened in these last twenty-four hours to cloud what's in front of us," Victor proclaims as he looks around the room. "If we are to be ready for what comes next, I need to keep up with my training. Regardless of what dangers may come my way, I must be prepared. I don't know what my uncle wanted last night or if he is behind any of this. We don't know what's going on with Morgana or Florence, and I don't give two shits about Derek."

Victor takes a slow breath as he looks around at everyone. "I'm still coming to terms with what I am supposed to do. And that's become the warlock that you need me to be."

Superior Charles smiles as he raises his glass. "To our young empath and his journey." Everyone raises their glasses and repeats after Superior Charles.

Lucas leans over so only Victor can hear. "That's the leader I remember at paintball."

The next day, Victor stands by the dresser, putting the finishing touches on his suit, while Leo walks out of the closet holding an oblong box. Victor senses Leo admiring him.

"My eyes are up here," Victor says to Leo without looking.

Leo chuckles as he walks over to Victor. "You're starting to enjoy your empathic ability. I guess talking with Lucas yesterday put you in better spirits. And I see you're going to start wearing your silver shirt and tie."

"Platinum silver," Victor smiles as he looks himself over in the mirror. "And talking with Lucas for a while did help me. I could always confide in him when I needed help figuring things out." He turns and sees the box in Leo's hands. "What's all this?"

Leo smiles and places the box on top of the dresser. "Well, I was going to give this to you after you finished your basic lessons. But after your uncle's unexpected visit, I felt it was necessary to give it to you now."

Victor steps up next to Leo, gazing at the box. "Wow." He gently slides his hand across the box. "I feel . . ." Victor opens the box and is mesmerized by the beauty of the small black sword. He gently hovers his hand over the length of the blade. He stops when he reaches the pearl embedded in the black metal.

"What do you feel?" Leo asks.

Victor looks up at Leo. "Hmm?"

"You said you feel?" Leo repeats.

Victor grips the blue handle and picks up the sword. "The magic in this sword."

"That's interesting because I could barely feel any of it," Leo mentions.

Victor gives Leo a cocky look. "Because this sword is made for an empath." Victor moves to an open area of the room and starts swinging the sword around.

"Have you handled swords before?" Leo asks, impressed by Victor's skills.

"Besides the one between my legs?" Victor jokes as he gazes at the blade's beauty.

Leo laughs, "Yes, besides the sword between any man's legs."

Victor extends his arms out, pointing the sword at the wall. "No." He pulls the sword back and inspects it. "For some reason, it feels like I've handled a sword before. Maybe it's the connection I have with it. I'm not sure. Maybe you can explain how magic like this works."

"Sadly, describing magic could take more than just an afternoon." Leo moves some tissue and pulls out a sheath harness. "Come here." Leo helps Victor place the harness straps over Victor's shoulders. Once Leo gets the harness fitted just right on Victor, Victor twirls his new sword around and places the blade into the sheath flawlessly.

"Okay, now you're just showing off," Leo remarks as he steps back and admires Victor.

"I'm not sure I'll be able to wear the blazer. The handle is poking out too high above my shoulder," Victor mentions as he picks up his blazer off the bed. He looks back in the mirror after he slips his blazer over his shoulders. "Whoa! It's like I don't have a sword at all. How?"

"Magic," Leo jokes as he sparkles his fingers around in a circle. "You ready?"

"Where are we going?" Victor asks.

Leo walks over to a mirror on the opposite wall. "Time for you to learn Fire Magic. And the big island has the best source of fire."

CHAPTER THIRTY-NINE

Victor and Leo walk through a mirror into a tiny shop. Half of the store resembles a convenience store, offering food and drinks, while the other half serves as a gift shop with a wide selection of Hawaiian-themed items. The shop owner sits behind the counter on a tall chair, reading his magazine while listening to the radio. He doesn't bother looking up when they arrive.

"*Aloha*, Koa," Leo says as he and Victor approach him.

Koa doesn't look up and gives Leo a little wave. If you would call raising your hand off the counter and fluttering your fingers in the air a "wave." As soon as Victor is about to step outside, he stops suddenly. He turns around and begins scanning around the shop.

Leo is already walking away from the shop. He turns around when he notices Victor is not next to him. He looks back and spots Victor looking around. Leo walks back up to the entrance. "What is it?"

Victor looks around the shop until he notices a rack of necklaces and bracelets against a wall. When he walks over, his vision begins to blur. This time, he focuses on the energy given off by many of the items in the shop. One in particular catches his attention. A red hue surrounds the small charm hanging on a hook.

Leo steps up beside Victor, asking softly, "What do you see?"

"This charm," Victor responds as he points to it. A Hawaiian fishhook made out of lava rock from the island. It is an inch and a half long, and gleaming. Unlike the other charms, it is not attached to a necklace.

"Pele must like you," Koa says. Victor and Leo jump out of their skins because they didn't hear Koa walk up behind them.

"DON'T DO THAT!" Victor shouts as he holds onto his chest. "Why does everyone have to sneak up on me?"

"And you're the empath," Leo jokes.

Victor fixes his breathing as he returns his soul back into his body. "What do you mean by 'Pele must like you?'" Victor asks Koa.

Koa takes the charm off the hook. "Pele is the Goddess of Volcanoes and Fire. She does not allow anyone to remove native pieces from these islands, like the lava rocks or sand. If you do, you will be cursed with bad luck until you return it."

Leo gives Koa a skeptical look. "That's just a myth."

"I would trust what Koa is saying," Victor says as Koa hands him the charm. "I've been on flights to Hawai'i, carrying mail and boxes filled with lava rocks being returned because someone started having bad luck when they got home from their holiday."

"Seriously?" Leo questions.

"Don't tell me that Mr. Leo over here doesn't believe in superstitions," Victor jokes. "I'm sure Brazil has a few, like if someone sweeps your feet with a broom or if you leave your flip-flops upside down."

Leo gives Victor a pointed look. "Don't you dare joke about those things."

"So, will this charm be for you?" Koa asks as he studies Victor.

"What kind of charm is it?" Victor inquires as he examines the charm in the palm of his hand.

"This charm is perfect for those who are gifted with Fire. It helps it burn hotter and brighter." Koa leans in, speaking in a lower register, "It is also said that if it is a gift, the receiver will have a strong bond with the one who offered it to them."

Victor studies the power stored inside the tiny fishhook made from lava rock. "I'll take it."

Moments later, Victor and Leo walk out of the shop. As Victor looks at the charm, he purposely walks slower than Leo. Once Leo's in front of him, he says, "Hold on. Let me fix your tag. "

"My tag?" Leo questions.

Victor walks up behind Leo and pretends to fix Leo's shirt tag. With quick hands, he unclasps Leo's necklace and slips the charm on it. He attaches the chain and allows the charm to drop forward.

"What the . . ." Leo is startled when he feels the charm fall down his chest. He looks down, holding it with his fingertips, and says, "I should have known you were up to something."

Victor leans in and kisses Leo on the cheek, barely touching the corner of Leo's mouth. "I think it suits you. So, where are we heading?"

As the words leave Victor's mouth, a black 1979 Lincoln Continental town car pulls up as if on cue. And surprise, surprise—it's the same driver from New York and Kyoto.

"How much longer is she going to be our driver?" Victor queries.

"I think for a few more weeks," Leo mentions as he opens the door for Victor.

A 20-minute ride later, they pull into an empty field, half of which is covered with dry lava. In the distance, Kīlauea, an active volcano, is visible, with a light plume emanating from it. After Victor and Leo walk a few feet from the town car, the driver takes off, only to park under a tree.

"What? She's not going to leave us behind this time?" Victor asks sarcastically.

"Nope, because she has nowhere to be. Also, she has all our food and drinks, so she can't go anywhere." Leo walks forward onto the dry lava. "Welcome to your Fire Magic training, young empath. And just because I'll be your instructor for this doesn't mean I'll go easy on you."

"Do I get a passing grade for sleeping with the teacher?" Victor jokes with a devilish grin.

Leo shakes his head and laughs. "What am I to do with you?" Leo twirls his wrist around, making a makeshift coat rack out of the lava rocks. He slips off his jacket and tosses it onto the rack. Leo moves further into the field while flicking his wrist and conjuring a blue fireball in his hand. "If you haven't already noticed, I have conjured fire in colors other than your typical reds or oranges. That's because the color depends on the intensity."

"So, kind of like how hot a star is based on its color. Red stars aren't as hot as blue or white stars," Victor suggests.

Leo nods as he processes Victor's response. "I think that's one of the best analogies that has been said. In this case, it's the opposite; red is more intense, and blue is less intense." Leo flings the fireball at Victor.

Victor blocks it with little effort. "Seriously, Leo?"

Leo ignores Victor's response as he continues. "The most commonly used are red, orange, and blue. You will sometimes see yellows or greens. But you'll only see that for those with more Fire Magic experience because they use more magic. Let's say if I want to burn down Derek's house, I would simply use a red fireball. But if I need to break through three feet of steel, I would need to use a yellow flame thrower."

Leo shoots his palm above his head, and a yellow flame blasts up at least ten feet. Victor has to cover his eyes from its brightness. The heat from the flame causes him to sweat instantly. "Fireballs and Flame Throws use different forms of energy and intensity. You need to be careful when using either." Leo cuts off the flame and dusts off his hands.

Victor takes off his jacket and places it on the coat rack next to Leo's. "Why are you telling me about this first?"

"Because just like actual fire and its intensity, if you cannot keep it contained, it can grow out of control," Leo explains. "I've seen some 'know-it-all' witches that claim they are experts in Fire Magic. They ended up with severe burns on their hands. Some can't grow their eyebrows any more like a Kardashian."

Leo conjures two small fireballs in one hand. They slowly circle each other like two stars caught in each other's orbits. "When learning Fire, you should always master other specialties first, even if your first specialty is Fire. If you can control the other specialties, you will understand how to control Fire. It's also beneficial if Air is one of your other specialties. It helps fire breathe, and it helps snuff it out."

Leo balls up his hand, snuffing out the two fireballs as he walks a few feet backward. "Take off your sword and come stand over here."

Victor removes his harness and hangs it with their jackets. He walks over and stands a couple of feet from Leo. The uneven ground makes it appear as though Leo is taller than Victor.

"Now, hold out your hands with your palms raised. Almost like you're praising a god." Leo motions his hands as mentioned.

"Like Pele?" Victor grins slyly.

Leo giggles and loses focus. "Yes, like you're praising Pele." He clears his throat and straightens his stance. "Now, I want you to feel the heat beneath your feet. Feel the flow of the magma under you. Focus on the fire burning the ground. When you feel that, take hold of it and bring it up and into your hands."

Victor raises his palms and closes his eyes, focusing on his breathing to open his mind. He turns his attention to the energy below him. He could feel the heat rising. A warm sensation begins crawling up his legs. It warms his torso and continues up to his shoulders. The sensation extends down his arms and into his hands.

Victor suddenly hears clapping.

As he slowly opens his eyes, a tiny orange flame dances around in each hand. It's not quite a fireball, but the fire spins in the ocean breeze. They cover his entire palms and are about six inches tall.

"Wow," Leo exclaims proudly. "Many who start learning can't do this for at least a week."

"Maybe it's because of the connection from the charm I got you," Victor winks.

Leo snickers as he rolls his eyes. "Now, drop that energy back into the ground." Victor closes his eyes and starts to feel the warmth in his body fade away.

"Good," Leo remarks. "That's really good. I'm impressed. Now, bring back that energy. Only this time, I want you to focus on how much of that energy you want. Try to make the flames blue." Leo holds out his hand and conjures a blue flame in his palm.

Victor nods and returns to focusing on the fire below. After a moment, he stops, opens his eyes, and starts shifting them around as he wonders what to do.

"What is it?" Leo asks curiously.

Victor thinks for a moment. "I'm trying to figure out how to control the amount of energy. I can feel it in my core, but it feels too hot for some reason."

"So, what would you do if your body is too hot?" Leo probes.

Victor deliberates on what Leo is asking. "You would try to cool it down."

Leo nods in agreement. "And how would you cool it down?"

"By turning on a fan or drinking some water," Victor replies. Leo gives Victor a smile and a wink.

Victor has an epiphany. "Ahhhh, I get it now." Victor starts focusing again, this time on the air around him to help cool him down. He can feel the air being absorbed into his pores and notices the change in his body's heat. Soon enough, blue flames dance around in his hands.

"*Perfeito!*" Leo cheers. "Now, this is the tricky part. Do you remember how to focus on creating a water ball?"

"Yeah?" Victor responds.

"Use that same thought process—only this time, with fire," Leo orders.

Victor focuses on the fire in his hands. He can feel that the fire doesn't want to become a ball. He takes a deep breath and keeps trying, but the fire doesn't want to listen. Victor's hands begin to shake, and the flames extinguish as he drops his hands.

"It's okay," Leo says as he gently rubs Victor's arms. "Let's try again."

After several more attempts, which felt like several hours had passed, Victor could finally create a fireball in each hand. He lets out a sigh of satisfaction with a huge smile.

"Very good. Only took you an hour," Leo jokes. Victor sticks out his tongue at him. Leo chuckles before continuing. "Now, let's see how long this will take you. I want you to make your blue balls bigger."

"Phrasing," Victor says sarcastically.

Leo throws his head back in laughter. "I'm sorry, my English no good," he says in a thicker Brazilian accent.

"I think when I met you, my blue balls got bigger," Victor adds. Leo keels over and loses it.

Victor loses focus and joins Leo in the laughter.

Once Leo finally calms down, he shakes off his giggles and returns to his posed stance. "Okay, let's get back to focusing on creating larger *fireballs*."

"I'm sorry, but I think I need to take care of my blue balls first," Victor snickers.

Leo rolls his eyes. He's beginning to regret teaching Victor. "Fine, let's take a break. Can you finish in less than two minutes?"

Victor clutches his imaginary pearls around his neck. "Excuse me. What little faith you have in me. I can be finished in 45 seconds."

They both break into laughter as they make their way to the town car to get lunch.

CHAPTER FORTY

four days have passed since Victor started practicing Fire Magic. Eddie is standing off to the side, conjuring earth-made targets for Victor to hit. Leo stands just behind Victor, commanding what he wants Victor to use on the target.

"Red Ball. Blue Ball. Red Flame. Orange Ball," Leo commands. Victor throws one attack after another.

"Red Flame," Leo orders.

Victor throws a blue flame, missing the target. He hunches over from exhaustion and is covered in sweat from working hard. It also doesn't help from the heat of the fire and the humidity.

Leo pats Victor on the shoulder. "Let's break for lunch. Eddie made chicken *katsu*."

"Oh, I love chicken *katsu*," Victor mentions cheerfully. As he turns around, wiping his sweat-drenched face with a towel, he sees Wren preparing a stone table Eddie created. "Wren? What are you doing here?"

She looks up and smiles at Victor. "Hey, hot stuff." She giggles, "See what I did there? Get it? Get it?"

Victor laughs as he shakes his head. "Funny. What are you doing here?"

"Well, I'm here in an official capacity," Wren mentions as she sits daintily. "Since you're finishing the first part of your training, I'm here to review the exam with you."

Victor plops down on the stone bench beside Leo and gives him a confused look. "You didn't tell me there was an exam."

Leo places his napkin in his lap and piles food on his plate. "The exam is based on everything you learned in the past few weeks."

"How come it's taken you longer to learn Fire Magic than any of the others you've practiced?" Eddie comments as he stuffs his mouth full of food.

"I didn't realize how intense Fire Magic was going to be," Victor replies.

"Told you," Leo remarks immediately.

Victor gives Leo a side-eye glare. "If my teacher wasn't a dick about it, I might have been able to finish sooner. Or it could be because he wanted to be alone with me for as long as possible."

Leo gives Victor a shit-eating grin without looking at him.

"You've been tough on him. Maybe I should have done that so you guys could have stayed longer," Eddie winks at Victor.

"You'll do anything to get me to stay with you," Leo comments without looking at Eddie. He takes another bite before he continues. "And try to get me drunk from your tequila at the same time."

Everyone at the table snickers.

"What does this exam entail, Wren?" Victor asks as he's chewing his food.

"It's the same thing Leo was doing with you just now. I'll be calling out commands as you attack your targets. Then you will battle it out so I can see your fighting skills," Wren explains.

"The targets will be moving as well," Eddie adds with a mouth full of food.

Victor raises an eyebrow. "Moving targets? And a battle?"

"Well, if you had stayed longer, I could have shown you how to make moving targets with your Earth Magic," Eddie winks.

Leo leans over to Victor, still chewing his food. "It's so easy. You already know how to do it. Just flying chunks of earth in the air."

"He doesn't know how to make the targets walk," Eddie grins cunningly. Everyone looks at him with skepticism. He leans back dramatically, clutching his imaginary pearls. "I'm sorry that you can't fathom my awesomeness."

"Victor did the same pose to me a few days ago. Is it a Mexican thing?" Leo asks with a mouth full of food.

"No, just a gay thing," Victor responds.

Wren adjusts her glasses, then puts her clasped hand in her lap.

Victor is about to take a bite when he feels Wren's eyes on him. "What?"

"I'm ready," Wren responds.

"Well, I'm not," Victor remarks as he puts another bite. "Leo hasn't been feeding me because he's a horrible teacher and won't let me eat unless I perform an attack perfectly." Victor looks over and sees Leo's narrowed eyes.

"Keep it up, and I'll make sure you don't eat again for a week," Leo declares.

Victor points his thumb at Leo with exaggeration. "See! This is how it's been for the past week with this guy."

Leo leans into his index finger and massages between his eyebrows. "I would *sooo* like to set you on fire right now."

Victor leans into Leo and whispers, "I like it when you put your heat all over me."

"Is that a euphemism?" Wren asks with a confused expression.

Leo gives Wren a side-eyed look before he turns to Victor. "Are you finished yet? The sooner we finish this exam, the sooner we can head back to the hotel and get in the hot tub."

Victor gives Leo a look as he takes the last piece of chicken from Leo's plate. After a few chews without breaking eye contact, he says, "Now I'm ready."

Everyone chuckles as they stand up and walk to the open field. Victor takes his spot next to Wren. Wren hands him his jacket. He thanks her and puts it on. Eddie starts creating stationary targets of different sizes and distances.

Before Wren starts giving commands, three black SUVs arrive. Everyone turns around, confused, as the vehicles park. Superior Charles steps out first, then holds out a hand to help Superior Jackie, while Superior Eugene walks around from the other side. Akisha, Madame Jeanette, Lucas, and Jon start to climb out of the second SUV. Everyone is dressed in their suits for the ceremony.

Lucas is wearing his gray suit with a light blue shirt and deep blue tie. On his lapel is a small brass shield pin with his coven's emblem engraved in the center. The shield resembles a coat of arms than a coven emblem. Jon is wearing a dark blue suit with a simple white shirt and a solid black tie. On his right wrist is a small silver chain with a charm linking the chain together.

When the third SUV turns off, Victor's eyes light up with joy when he sees Elliott, Frank, Amber, and Lupe hopping out. Although they are not dressed up in suits like all the other magic wielders, they are dressed in simple business attire. Victor walks over in astonishment.

"What is everyone doing here?" he asks his friends.

Amber and Lupe run over to Victor to hug him.

Superior Charles walks over to Victor with his tall demeanor. "Well, this is kind of your big day, young empath. It's not every day we have an empathic witch or warlock complete the first portion of their training. Chiyo sends her regards. She just started training a group of young witches." Superior Charles puffs his chest out and places his hand on his hips. "You know, the last empath to finish this part of the training was me. Before that, it was your grandmother."

Wren raises an eyebrow, knowing she passed the exam after Victor's grandmother and before Superior Charles. Wren takes a few steps forward, focusing attention back on the exam. "I don't mean to put a damper on things, but we need to finish this exam before it gets too late. Especially if we are to make the celebratory luau tonight. Now, please keep your distance so no one gets hit by projectiles when the targets explode."

Eddie creates chairs out of lava rocks for everyone. As Superior Charles steps up to his seat in the first row, he looks at it, waves his hand around a couple of times, and adds some more elegance to his chair using nearby plants, leaves, and tree branches. As he's about to take a seat, he sees that Superior Jackie has done the same thing, only more elegantly, with native Hawaiian flowers blossoming before her.

"Show off," Superior Charles comments in his low husky voice. Superior Jackie gives him a wink before they both sit down.

Eddie rolls his eyes at the spectacle.

"I saw that, Eduardo," Superior Charles says as he lights up his cigar. Even though he didn't physically see it, he's known Eddie long enough to know when he makes gestures behind his back.

Leo sits behind Superior Charles with Lucas and Jon. "So, Lucas, I see that you finally told everyone."

"Well, I figured since we were all invited, I might as well tell them," Lucas remarks.

"Hey Leo, thanks again for inviting us," Frank mentions from behind.

Leo turns and looks at Victor's mundane friends. "I didn't invite you."

"I invited everyone," Superior Charles comments over his shoulder. "Now, will the peanut gallery please quiet down?" Superior Charles turns back around and nods at Victor to begin.

Victor steps next to Wren and takes a deep breath. He stretches his neck and rotates his shoulders, getting loosened up for the physical intensity he's about to endure. As he closes his eyes, he starts to feel this energy flicker around his chest. It starts to spread throughout his body. This energy feels familiar. It's as though he's been touched by it before. As his fingertips begin to tingle, he begins to see an image.

A glow starts to appear. It's dim and hazy at first. Then, it starts to get brighter. As he focuses on this glow, he can make out a figure. He smiles when he realizes it's his mother. She is smiling proudly back at him.

"Are you ready?" Wren asks softly.

Victor opens his eyes. This time, he knows his eyes are glowing white. He can feel the energy coursing through his veins. "Ready."

Wren notices Victor's eyes but doesn't flinch. She knows this is the untapped power Victor didn't understand. He now has control over it. She looks over at Eddie, standing on the sidelines, giving him a nod to begin.

"Let's start with some Air Magic," Wren commands.

Wren starts giving orders on where to direct the attack. Victor is cool as a cucumber, consistently hitting his targets. One after another, Victor doesn't miss a beat as Wren speeds up the attacks.

Wren switches things up and throws in Water Magic. Victor complies without any hesitation. A hint of a blue hue appears in his eyes as he goes back and forth between Air and Water Magic.

"Tidal Wave," Wren commands.

Victor looks over to the ocean and reaches out with his hand. His eyes turn blue from the intensity of his magic. As he moves his arm in a sweeping motion, he pulls water from the ocean over the cliff and crashes it into the targets. The help from the currents pulls his targets back into the water. Plumes of steam emerge in the distance as the water hits the lava flow.

"Were his eyes glowing blue just now?" Lupe whispers to Amber.

"Yes, they were," Lucas answers.

"Does that not bother you?" Jon asks Lucas. Lucas shakes his head.

Madame Jeanette turns to Victor's friends and places her index finger against her lips.

Wren keeps giving out commands. She has now added Earth and Fire into the mix. As she keeps giving Victor commands, she looks over at Eddie. Eddie nods, confirming he understands the silent request. He begins making the targets move around in the air. Eddie begins chucking the targets at Victor. He goes slow at first but then starts to pick up speed.

Wren takes a few steps back to avoid getting hit but doesn't stop giving commands. Eddie gets a little too excited, and a large chunk of earth flies past Victor, heading toward the audience.

The first row doesn't flinch. But the back row starts to get nervous as they witness a large piece of earth flying toward them.

Victor twists and flings his arm out as if holding a whip. He wraps the boulder using Air Magic, stopping it inches away before hitting Superiors Charles and Jackie. A breeze comes off the large rock and brushes against their faces. As Victor retracts the target, he flings it against another moving target.

Superiors Charles and Jackie turn their attention to Eddie, narrowing their eyes at him. Eddie blushes a little but doesn't make eye contact as he does some light whistling.

"We're going to talk about this later," Superior Charles says in a low voice.

After a few more minutes, Wren gives one last command. "Red Flamethrower. All Targets."

Victor sees six moving targets in the air and three walking towards him. He looks at his targets, takes a deep breath, and turns his eyes bright red. He slowly raises his arms as though lifting a heavy object, causing the ground to shake. Everyone starts darting their eyes around, unsure as to what is going on. Victor pushes his arms into the sky, creating his own miniature volcano. Everyone looks on, feeling the heat radiating from it.

Wren raises her eyebrows. "I did ask for a flamethrower, but I guess I'll count this."

Victor turns his head to Wren. She doesn't notice him giving her an annoyed look, but she can sense it. He drops his hands, causing the lava to return to the ground. As one of the targets starts to fall, He raises his palm and throws a red flame, causing it to incinerate. He doesn't stop looking at Wren when he finishes and drops his hand.

Wren turns to Victor and gives him a neutral expression. "Show off."

Victor chuckles as his eyes return to normal. When he turns around, everyone starts to cheer.

Wren spins around to the audience, hands clasped in front of her. "Now, it's time for the battle portion of the exam," Wren expresses loudly over the excitement. "Is Victor's opponent ready?"

Superior Charles stands up and fixes his blazer. "The real question is, is the young empath ready?"

Victor's mouth drops. "I have to battle against you?"

Superior Charles fixes the cuff of his jacket while giving a sly grin as he walks over. "Don't worry, I won't go easy on you."

"This battle will be simple. It is based on a point system," Wren explains. "The stronger the attack or defense, the higher the points. If you can make it to 100 points in five minutes, you pass." Wren gestures to the empty field. "Warlocks, take your positions."

Victor and Superior Charles walk to their spots across from each other. "Was this your idea to be my opponent?" Victor asks Superior Charles.

Superior Charles grins. "I've been hearing how well you fight. I wanted to see it for myself."

Wren creates an air dome in the field. Once completed, she proceeds with the second part of the exam. "Warlocks, ready?" Victor and Superior Charles nod. "Begin!"

Superior Charles effortlessly sends a volley of fireballs. Victor sees them coming and tries to focus. Without knowing, he creates a large water barrier that engulfs all the projectiles. Victor then pushes his hands forward, thrusting the barrier at Superior Charles. Superior Charles blocks the attack with his own barrier using lava. Superior Charles doesn't let up on his attacks. Victor does his best to keep up but can't dodge all of them. Victor sends his counterattacks, but that barely fazes the superior.

Victor becomes exhausted. He doesn't know how many points the attacks are because Wren never mentioned the point matrix. Victor starts thinking to himself, *Is it a point per attack I send? Do I get more for larger-sized attacks? What if they don't hit Superior Charles? Does that even count?*

"TIME!" Wren shouts. She makes circular motions in the air to lower the dome. Superior Charles brushes his sleeves while Victor tries to regain his breath.

Wren walks over to Victor with a towel. "Good job," she remarks.

Victor takes the towel and starts drying off his forehead. "So, did I get 100 points?"

"247, to be exact," Wren replies proudly.

"You mean I got 100 points in less than five minutes? Why did you keep me going?" Victor demands.

Superior Charles claps Victor on the back. "I asked her for the full five minutes. I didn't want you to give up so easily when you reached 100. You don't get that in the real world."

Wren turns to the audience. "It's with great pleasure to announce that Victor Raymond Russo can now officially hold the title of Empath Warlock."

Wren holds out her hand to Victor. "Congratulations, *Empath Warlock Russo*." Victor smiles, taking her hand and shaking it with pride.

Victor's friends rush over to him and get into a group hug, congratulating him. As the cheering calms, everyone starts to hear slow clapping from a single individual. Victor's smile slowly disappears as he senses who's behind him.

He slowly turns around, spotting Derek in the distance.

CHAPTER FORTY-ONE

Derek slowly walks toward Victor, clapping and giving him an evil smile. Victor notices Derek's left hand has a slightly darker skin tone. Derek got a new hand from somewhere, but Victor doesn't understand how.

"Bra-Va! Bra . . . Va," Derek exclaims as he concludes his clapping. "You should be feeling so proud of yourself. Empath. Warlock."

Victor and Leo step in front of Victor's friends. "What the fuck are you doing here?" Victor demands, keeping his focus on Derek.

"I feel like Maleficent for not receiving an invitation to this *soiree*. I'm here to bestow a curse on your firstborn." Derek looks at Leo with disdain. "Unfortunately, his firstborn won't be with you. Although it would be funny, cursing my husband's child."

Leo narrows his glare at Derek. "We're no longer together, Derek."

Superior Charles steps in front of the group with his fists balled to his sides. "I think you'd better consider that you're outnumbered here, Warlock Hernandez. You better get your sorry little ass out of here before I make sure you cannot break out again."

Derek holds out his new hand and shakes his index finger. "Tsk tsk, that's not how you're supposed to talk to me." Derek looks back at Victor, presenting his newly acquired hand. "You like what you did to me? I had to get a new hand because of you."

"Fuck off," Victor calls out. "You did that to yourself."

Derek holds up the bracelet Victor placed on him. "If you didn't put this piece of shit on me, then drastic measures wouldn't have occurred." Derek tosses the bracelet to the ground. He conjures a large rock, smashing the bracelet. "I don't want you to get any dumber ideas."

"How did you get a new hand?" Victor asks with curiosity.

"He got it from a necromancer," Madame Jeanette responds as she walks forward. "Who did you have to kill to make sure you got a new hand? I can smell it's still fresh."

Derek buffs the nails of his new hand against his chest. "A young warlock was willing to sacrifice his hand for me. He didn't need it anyway because he can't conjure magic with it." He holds his hand as if admiring the nails. "Such a shame too. He was great at buffing out my shoes. Now, he can only scrub the coven's floors with one hand."

"You make me sick," Victor expresses with a disgusted look.

"No, you're the one that makes me sick," Derek spits back. "Trying to act like you're better than everyone. That's why your grandmother was killed. And your mother."

"Don't listen to him," Leo whispers to Victor, placing his hand on Victor's arm, hoping it will keep Victor calm.

"Why don't you tell everyone not to listen to me, Leo?" Derek taps his temple with his new index finger, "Telepath, remember. Oh, wait, you don't remember. Because you were too stupid to figure it out. Gods, what the fuck did I ever see in you?"

"Enough of this!" Superior Charles shouts. He tries to bind Derek with his Earth Magic. As the earth grows up to Derek's neck, Derek lets out a diabolical laugh before breaking free. Eddie, Victor, and Leo throw up an air barrier to protect everyone from the flying debris.

Victor narrows his eyes and tries to focus on Derek's aura.

"I would caution you, Empath Warlock. You won't like what you see," Derek warns Victor with a demonic smile.

Victor notices a dark glow radiating off Derek's chest. But he can't pinpoint where it's coming from. "He's got an artifact on him," Victor mentions to the others. "But I don't know what it is."

"That's probably how he was able to break out of his bind," Superior Charles explains. "He's connected to someone who's sharing their magic."

"No one is sharing their magic with me," Derek mentions viciously. "Fuck, how are you even a Superior? And don't you know it's not polite to talk about someone behind their back? Especially a telepath?"

Victor becomes annoyed and barks back. "We get it. You're a fucking telepath. Shut your face already." Victor begins to sense something, which makes him nervous. "He's not alone."

"I sense it, too," Superior Charles says. He narrows his eyes, focusing on the horizon behind Derek. "Shit," he hisses through his teeth.

A large, shadowy cloud appears behind Derek. People dressed in black outfits start to emerge from the anomaly. When the cloud disappears, at least 30 people are standing behind Derek. Victor recognizes two witches who attacked him during Amber's birthday dinner.

Derek tilts his head, cracking his neck. "Either you come with us willingly, Victor Russo . . . " Derek pauses for dramatic effect. ". . . or you die today."

Victor straightens his posture and puts his fists on his sides. "I'm not going anywhere today. Wren, take my friends to a safe location," Victor orders while keeping eye contact with Derek.

As Wren gathers Victor's mundane friends and scurries away, a giant wall of fire bursts out of the ground, blocking the road to exit and shooting one of the SUVs into the air. Everyone but Victor reacts. Victor does not want to give Derek the satisfaction of a sneak attack if he looks away.

Derek smirks vindictively. "Guess that means everyone dies today." He points to Victor, and everyone behind him starts running and shouting a battle cry.

Wren looks around and finds a good spot to hide Amber, Lupe, Elliott, and Frank. "This way, into the forest!"

Everyone else steps forward, standing side by side with Victor in the middle. "Wait for it," Victor commands.

The enemy gets closer. "Wait for it."

The enemy is about 50 feet away. Victor's eyes turn red. He pushes his palms forward, causing lava to shoot out of the ground, and directs it toward the rushing enemy. Three are engulfed in the lava before five witches use Water Magic to hold it back. Eddie takes the opportunity to lift the ground under them, causing them to fly backward.

Eight hostiles, holding daggers, jump over everyone with their Air Magic. Superior Eugene holds up his walking cane. Using his Light Magic, the mother-of-pearl orb shines brightly. The enemy is blinded and falls to the ground.

Akisha and Leo conjure flames from their palms, at least 20 feet long, trying to keep the enemy back. One of the warlocks flings his arms up, sending a gust of wind from the ground, sending Victor and others soaring backward.

Wren takes Victor's mundane friends to a secure area in the forest. She quickly starts drawing wards on the trees around them. As she steps out, she presses her hand on one of the trees and whispers a chant. The wards glow in bright blue when the chant is complete.

"You'll be safe as long as you remain within these wards," Wren explains. "Do not, by any means, leave this area."

"How is this going to keep us safe?" Elliott asks as he walks up to Wren.

"Nothing and no one can enter this area without my permission," Wren clarifies.

"DUCK!" Lupe screams.

Wren ducks down as a fireball flies over her head, crashing into the barrier. She flings a large tree branch, smashing it into the witch's head, killing her instantly.

Wren turns around and tugs firmly on her blazer while letting out a huff. "See. Nothing and no one can enter without my permission." She points her finger at everyone and orders, "Do not leave this area." Wren spins around and runs back into the battle.

Victor and the others try to get back onto their feet as the enemy rushes toward them. Victor starts fighting off two warlocks that try to get the jump on him while he's down. One swings his dagger at Victor, but Victor blocks the attack and kicks him back. He hits the second warlock's nose with his palm, blasting a fireball in his face, setting his face on fire. The warlock stumbles back, screaming in agony.

Madame Jeanette kneels and digs her hands into the ground. She begins to chant in Haitian Creole. The ground starts shaking and breaking apart; a green glow emanates through the cracks. Decrepit hands start emerging from the earth. As they claw their way through the cracks, the bodies of the dead island natives look at the enemy in black.

Madame Jeanette raises her purple glowing hands. She shouts to the dead in her Haitian dialect, *"Attack the ones dressed in black! Protect the young empath warlock!"*

The necromancers try to gain control of the dead. Madame Jeanette's power is stronger. Several foes try to fight off the deceased but are outnumbered and torn apart.

After Victor fights off two more witches, he looks at Derek, who hasn't engaged in the battle. As Victor tries to focus on Derek, a warlock rushes at him with a sword.

Victor dodges the attack. "Oh, you wanna fuck around like that, huh?" Victor throws off his jacket and pulls out his sword from its sheath. Victor's sword is smaller than the warlock's.

The warlock cocks an eyebrow. "That's a pretty small sword for being black."

"Is that supposed to be a euphemism?" Victor says snarkily.

The sword-wielding warlock charges at Victor, swinging violently. Victor blocks all of the attacks with ease. Victor can tell that his sword was meant for him. He can feel the power and draws from it. Victor counterattacks effortlessly as the warlock starts launching fire attacks, slicing the fireballs into pieces.

A witch with a couple larger daggers tries to catch Victor off guard. She swishes her blades around, trying to take a slice from Victor. Victor now has two enemies with weapons trying to skin him alive. He blocks their moves while fighting them off, throwing some trick shots with his Air and Fire Magic.

When the witch falls back from a fireball, Victor turns his attention to the warlock. As Victor fights off his enemy's attacks, the witch tries rushing from behind. Without looking, Victor flings his elbow back, connecting to the witch's nose. A dagger goes flying out of her hand. In a seamless motion, Victor catches the blade and hurls it right between the warlock's eyes.

The witch tries to rush at Victor from behind again. She didn't learn the first time: *you shouldn't sneak up on an empath.* Especially an empath with a sword. Victor slams his sword into the witch's stomach. As he turns around, he twists his sword. He slams the witch with an air pulse to the chest, releasing her from the blade.

Leo and Superior Charles are occupied with three warlocks trying to use their Air Magic on them. It backfires on them when Superior Charles uses their magic to lift them all from the ground. The five of them are now levitating in the air. Leo opens the ground below, conjuring a pool of lava under them. Superior Charles creates a microburst to rush down, slamming the warlocks into the lava. Superior Charles closes the lava pit as the warlocks scream in misery, allowing him and Leo to land safely on the ground.

It narrows down to one-on-one combat. Derek decides to send a massive fireball toward Leo. After Victor stabs a warlock in the heart, he notices Leo isn't paying attention to the meteor flying directly at him.

"NOOOO!" Victor flings his sword at the fireball. Victor watches the sword soar through the air as if it were in slow motion. The tip of his blade connects with the fireball, causing it to explode. Everyone, including Derek, is flown back by the force. Victor's sword lands a few feet away from him. Victor stumbles back onto his feet and picks up his sword. Everyone around him groans while getting back onto their feet.

"DEREK HERNANDEZ!" Victor shouts as he points his sword toward Derek.

Derek stands up and brushes himself off, giving Victor a repulsed look. "What the fuck do you want?"

Victor's eyes turn black.

"*Challenge et tua est pietas in coniuge. Ad mortem.*"

CHAPTER FORTY-TWO

Leo is shocked at what he just heard. "Victor! What the fuck are you doing?"

Superior Charles finishes binding the remaining enemy. He looks over at Wren and storms over to her. "What the fuck did you tell him?"

Wren binds a witch before she responds, "I gave him a loophole."

Lucas and Jon rush over to their mundane friends to make sure they're not injured. "Are you guys okay?" Lucas asks.

"We're okay," Frank answers. "What is going on? Why is everyone looking either worried or pissed at Victor?"

Lucas looks back at Victor, still pointing his sword at Derek. "He's challenging Derek."

"To what?" Frank questions.

"Challenge et tua est pietas in coniuge. Ad mortem," Jon says to his friends before he looks back at Victor. "I challenge your devotion to your spouse. To the death."

"What does that even mean?" Elliott questions.

Lucas keeps looking at Victor as he responds, "He's going to try to break the blood oath between Leo and Derek. Unless that oath is broken, Leo will never be able to fall in love with anyone else."

Superior Charles, furious, barks at Wren. "Why the fuck did you tell him that's how to break the blood oath? Do you not understand what you just did?"

"I completely understand!" Wren hollers back. "And you and I know that if that oath isn't broken, Leo will die at Derek's hands."

"It's the only way, *chéri*," Madame Jeanette comments. Superior Charles spins around, only to see her crossing her arms. "Leo needs a challenger. Victor accepted his fate."

"We're all going to have a conversation *once* this is over," Superior Charles snarls as he looks back at Victor. "You both better hope Victor wins."

Derek slowly walks over to Victor. "Did you seriously invoke a challenge? With me?"

"You heard me." Victor opens his arms wide. "Look around, your coven lost."

"They weren't part of my coven," Derek notes smugly.

"Of course, they weren't," Victor remarks, lowering his hands to his sides. "That's because all of you never denounced your covens. You've been secretly involved with another coven. A coven of extreme traditionalists. A coven that killed my grandmother, chased my mother into hiding, perverted my uncle into Dark Magic, and has stopped at nothing to come after me."

Victor's black eyes remain focused on Derek as he gets closer. "And this is all because you know I'm your biggest threat."

Derek pulls a sword from under his jacket. "I will never bend my knee to you, and you will never become the Grand Warlock."

"'Nough talking," Victor orders. "Prepare to die, you piece of shit."

Derek snarls as he ignites his sword on fire. Derek and Victor charge at each other. The first clash of their swords rings out.

Akisha and Superiors Jackie and Eugene gather the remaining enemy and bind them with wards so they can't use their magic and try to escape. Akisha looks on as Victor fights Derek alone. She is worried about what will happen if Victor loses.

Superior Charles walks up to Leo as they listen to the swords clashing. He places a hand on Leo's shoulder and asks, "You understand what will happen if Victor loses?"

Leo takes a moment before he responds. A single tear runs down his cheek as he fears the outcome. "If Victor dies, Derek can do whatever he deems fit to me, even if that means killing me without any repercussions to him."

"You better hope Victor is strong enough," Superior Charles mentions.

"He is strong enough, Superior," Leo affirms.

Superior Charles lets go of Leo's shoulder. "He might not be."

"What do you mean?" Leo asks as he looks up at his superior, eyes wide.

"Victor hasn't been able to break the connection from the artifact Derek is wearing. Until Victor does, Derek is the stronger one right now," Superior Charles explains.

Victor and Derek continue clashing swords. Derek kicks Victor in the stomach and then tries to kick Victor in the face. Victor blocks Derek's kick and grabs his leg. He flings Derek onto his back and then attempts to stab Derek in the face, but Derek rolls out of the way. They continue to attack, block, and counterattack. Derek finds an opening and knocks Victor to the ground.

Derek brings his fiery sword down upon Victor. Victor places his sword over his face before he's sliced in half. Victor uses an air pulse, sending Derek backward. Derek recovers quickly and rushes after Victor, tackling him to the ground. Both swords fly out of their hands, landing several feet away. Derek aggressively tries attacking Victor with his magic, but Victor blocks everything thrown at him.

Derek lunges and grabs Victor's head between his hands. Victor shouts in agony as Derek tries to use his telepathic ability to scramble his mind. Victor's eyes and mouth start to glow brightly. Victor places his hands on Derek's face, trying to push him back. But Victor is unaware he's intertwining their abilities. A bright flash comes off them, and they fall to the ground.

"VICTOR!" Leo shouts, running to him.

"DON'T!" Madame Jeanette grabs Leo and pulls him back. Superior Charles assists, wrapping his arms around Leo.

Leo struggles to break free. "He needs my help!"

Madame Jeanette places her hands on Leo's shoulders. "We cannot get close to them, *chéri*."

"Why won't you let me help him?" Leo cries out, still struggling to escape Superior Charles' grasp.

"Leo, you can get hurt." Madame Jeanette looks back at Victor, lying on the ground. "He is alive. I can hear his heartbeat. But he is not on our plane right now."

Victor and Derek are in a dark, unknown place, shooting Fire Magic at each other. Victor doesn't stop to think about what's going on as he tries to defend himself. Victor tries to look for Derek's aura and realizes that he can't sense anything. Could it be because Derek learned how to hide his aura from empaths?

Derek occasionally presses his finger against his temple. It's as though Derek is trying to read Victor's thoughts. Victor realizes that neither of their abilities are available wherever they are. Victor can't think about it now; he must stop Derek.

During their battle in their new environment, Victor notices Derek patting his left breast. There must be something Derek has on him. But Victor can't figure out what it is. He tries to bind Derek with Air Magic. For a brief moment, Victor can see a glow from an artifact that Derek keeps touching. He tries to grab it, but Derek casts a flamethrower spell at

Victor. Victor uses an air pulse to send him backward, avoiding getting torched.

The glow is dim because of where they are. Whatever it is, the artifact is becoming weak. And Victor can tell Derek is getting weaker. Victor tries to go after the artifact, but Derek keeps defending himself from Victor's advances.

Victor's friends follow Lucas and Jon back into the open area. They notice Victor and Derek are on the ground while everyone keeps their distance.

"What's going on?" Lupe asks as she wraps her arm around Amber's.

"Victor's consciousness is in another realm with Derek," Wren explains. "Derek is a telepath, and he connected his ability to Victor's. Unfortunately, we have no idea where they are or how long they will be this way. But we can't get close to them because when they return, there is a possibility that an orb will appear. Your consciousness will be lost forever if you are within that orb."

Lucas spins around in shock. "Are you serious, Wren?"

Wren nods. "It's a very rare occurrence. But it's been known to happen. And it is very, *very*, dangerous if we try to intervene."

Victor's body starts to twitch. His head turns towards everyone; blood is coming from both nostrils. His friends gasp and hold each other. After a moment, a bright orb starts to appear between Victor and Derek. As the orb grows, two shadowy images move around within it. The orb crawls outward, rushing toward everyone.

"Get back!" Superior Charles shouts. He grabs Leo and pulls him along as the group rushes to find cover. Some run into the forest, some hide behind the SUVs. Superior Charles stands behind a tree, observing. If the orb gets closer, they will have to run even further away.

The six attackers in bindings remain on the ground. They struggle, trying to move as the orb approaches them. They become engulfed by the bright light, and then it vanishes. Their bodies lay there, lifeless.

Everyone emerges from hiding to see Victor and Derek still on the ground. "Can you still hear Victor's heart?" Superior Jackie asks Madame Jeanette.

"*Oui*, he's still alive, as well as Derek," Madame Jeanette responds.

Victor starts fluttering his eyes open. His eyes are back to normal. He shifts his eyes around, remembering where he is. Victor snaps his head over and spots Derek struggling to get up. Once Victor remembers the artifact inside Derek's jacket, his eyes return to black.

Victor pounces on top of Derek and grabs hold of the part of his jacket where the artifact is hiding. He rips a vast chunk of Derek's jacket and holds it above his head.

"GIVE THAT BACK!" Derek shouts as he tries reaching for Victor's hand.

Victor holds Derek down by the throat, keeping him firmly on the ground. He sets the object in his hand ablaze. Victor opens his hand when the flame vanishes, letting the ash fall.

Derek is enraged and hurls Victor several feet through the air. "YOU SON OF A BITCH! YOU'RE FUCKING DEAD!" Derek charges after and grabs Victor's sword off the ground.

As Victor regains his balance, he sees Derek charging at him. Before Victor can conjure his magic, Derek swings Victor's sword, decapitating Victor.

Everyone screams in horror. Leo is so angry; he is about to conjure his Fire Magic. "The blood oath!" Superior Charles shouts, grabbing hold of Leo's arms.

Derek starts to laugh hysterically. "What a worthless piece of shit. He couldn't even stop- " Derek looks back and notices Victor's body hasn't fallen to the ground. ". . . The fuck?"

Victor starts laughing, a deep, echoing sound that reverberates through the battlefield. Derek looks back and forth between Victor's head and Victor's body, his confusion turning into horror. Victor's hand shoots out, grabbing Derek by the neck and lifting him effortlessly off the ground. As Victor's laughter fades, his severed head on the ground begins to pixelate, disintegrating into tiny shards of light that swirl into the air before reappearing seamlessly atop his shoulders.

Victor's eyes are solid black, with a dark, shimmery glow that extends outward. The glow resembles smoke. Derek is dumbfounded by what has taken place.

"What type of fuckery is this?!" Derek shouts, thrashing in Victor's iron grip, desperately chopping at Victor's shoulder with Victor's sword.

Victor catches Derek's fist with ease, wrenching the sword from his grasp. "This sword belongs to me. And as long as it has a connection with me, I cannot be harmed by it." With a casual flick of his wrist, Victor sends Derek hurtling backward, crashing into the ground several yards away like a rag doll.

Victor strides purposefully towards Derek, who struggles to his feet, only to be knocked aside again by a swift swipe of Victor's sword. As Derek rises, Victor calls upon his Earth Magic. The ground beneath Derek trembles and shifts, throwing him off balance. Massive walls of lava rock erupt from the earth, forcing Derek to bounce between them, each impact leaving him more battered.

Victor raises his hand, and Derek is lifted into the air, invisible forces tightening around his neck like a noose. With a disdainful flick, Victor sends Derek crashing through the nearby trees. Derek's body snaps branches like twigs as he plummets to the forest floor below. Blood trickles from his nose, and multiple gashes cover his face. He rolls off his back, coughing, and gets to his knees, glaring at Victor with bloodshot eyes.

Summoning every ounce of his remaining strength, Derek charges at Victor, screaming in defiance. Victor doesn't flinch. With a mere flick of his fingers, a torrent of enormous fireballs rains down upon Derek. Derek tries to shield himself, but the force of the impact slams him into the ground, leaving him groaning in agony.

Victor's shadow looms over Derek as he approaches. Derek, lying in a crater of scorched earth, turns and looks up at him. "There's only one way to kill me in the challenge, and your sword won't work because it's too short."

Victor raises an eyebrow, a smirk playing on his lips. "I'm a grower, not a shower."

"What?" Derek gasps, grimacing in confusion.

With a flourish, Victor twirls his sword, and with a jerk of his arm, the blade extends, doubling in length. Black flames burst from the blade, and the embedded pearl glows with an eerie light. Derek's eyes widen in terror.

"Fuck me," Derek mutters.

Victor swings the elongated sword over his shoulder, the black flames dancing along its edge. "You're not my type." With a swift, backhanded strike, Victor decapitates Derek, sending his head flying toward the lava flow. The head lands with a sizzle, and Derek's body erupts in flames, a piercing shriek of agony escaping from the burning neck. The body burns intensely, turning into a pile of ash within seconds.

Victor drops his sword after it returns to its smaller size, and the flame is extinguished. Victor stumbles backward, exhausted from the fight. He blinks a few times, allowing his eyes to return to normal.

Before Victor could react, Leo wraps his arms around him. After a moment of shock and awe, Victor smiles as he returns Leo's tight embrace. Leo pulls back and looks at Victor in the eyes. He cups Victor's cheeks, pulling him in for a deep, passionate kiss.

After a moment has passed, Leo pulls away and slaps Victor in the face.

"The fuck was that for?" Victor asks as he rubs his cheek with a bewildered, yet cheerful expression.

"Don't you ever pull that shit again," Leo demands before pulling Victor in for another kiss.

As they break apart, Victor says sarcastically, "Then maybe next time, don't do a blood oath while getting married."

They laugh as they walk hand in hand back toward the group. Victor is covered with everyone's embrace. While Victor is enjoying the attention, his smile fades away. His eyes turn black as he scans the area.

"Now what?" Leo asks with annoyance, knowing something else is about to happen.

"Why is everyone trying to disrupt our enjoyment?" Wren states aggressively.

"What's going on?" Superior Charles questions as he scans the area with Victor.

Victor doesn't respond as he continues scanning the energy in the area. He's drawn to something on the volcano. "Everyone, stay here," he commands before breaking away from the group.

Using his Air Magic, he quickly bounces around through the air as he makes his way to the side of the volcano. When he comes to a landing, he slowly walks around to see who's there. He knows there's a presence but doesn't see whose it is.

"Congratulations, Empath Warlock Russo."

Victor spins around, making eye contact with the figure behind him. "Uncle Michael."

They silently stare at each other for a moment. Victor's uncle nods while sneering as dark cloud appears behind him. Before Victor can do anything, his uncle disappears into a dark cloud. Victor's eyes return to their normal dark brown, knowing he won't see his uncle again anytime too soon.

Late into the night, Victor and many of his crew sit around a bonfire on the beach while still wearing their leis from the luau and comfortably dressed in Hawaiian shirts, chinos, or flowy sundresses.

"It's a shame Jeanette and Eugene had to leave and miss this beautiful evening," Superior Jackie says as she sips away at the straw in an empty glass. She drunkenly slides off her seat and lands in Superior Charles' lap. "Damn it, Charles, I'm married. Stop trying to get me in your lap."

Everyone laughs.

Once Superior Charles helps Superior Jackie back into her seat, he turns his attention to Victor. "I have a question for you, young empath. You mentioned earlier today that you knew about this secret coven Derek and those others were a part of. How did you know they were part of a second coven?"

Victor looks around as everyone's eyes are on him. "Well, I didn't realize it at the time. I didn't know what to look for until I was at your home during the barbecue. When I started noticing everyone's auras, I also spotted another glow coming off them. I didn't know what it was because it was a different color from their aura, smaller too, and was in random locations.

"I would see it on a wrist, over the heart, even on their earlobes. I saw it on Leo's wrist, Superior Jackie's chest, and your arm. When you handed me your coven invite, I realized I was looking at your coven's emblem. Then, when Superior Jackie handed me her invite, I confirmed that the emblem on her invite was also a charm on her necklace."

As Victor continues to talk, he picks up a stick and starts drawing symbols in the sand. "When Derek attacked us at Eddie's, I noticed he had two emblems on him. I recognized one was for Superior Tederich's coven, but the second was different."

Victor focuses on what he's drawing in the sand as he continues. "It gave off another energy that was there, but then again, it wasn't. It had an aura, but it's hard to put into words. It then dawned on me that the four witches who attacked me at Amber's birthday dinner had the same emblem in addition to their coven's emblem. When I thought back to Japan, it was the same thing with the two who attacked me. I knew there had to be a connection; I just couldn't put my finger on it."

Victor repositions himself as he continues drawing. Superior Charles listens on as he watches. Eddie leans over to get a better view from his spot around the fire.

"The day after my uncle invited himself into my hotel room, I pulled Wren aside as everyone was leaving," Victor informs. "I sat down with her to review all the coven invites you gave me from the other superiors. I wanted to get to know who these superiors are. As I looked through her tome, there was a list of the more traditionalist covens."

Victor leans back to inspect his work before he goes back to adding more details. "While going through the list, the second emblem never appeared. When remembering my uncle's visit, I saw nothing on his person. He knew how to keep it hidden, or he was not involved. It's tough to say at this time."

Victor gets up and walks over to the other side of his drawing. "Now, fast forward to today's fiasco. As soon as all those witches and warlocks appeared, I could scan them all, and they all had the same second symbol. I called Derek out for denouncing his coven for this second one. The way he didn't deny it confirmed my suspicions." When Victor finishes talking, he also finishes a symbol he drew in the sand.

The symbol is a pentagram. Directly below the pentagram, a crescent moon turned downwards with the points twisted into a braid. In the center of the pentagram was a simple, upside-down Celtic knot.

Superior Charles walks behind Victor and looks down at the symbol in the sand. "Wren, have you ever seen this symbol before?"

Wren shakes her head. "No. And I don't think I've ever seen an aura coming off our charms representing our covens. I've seen a glow, but never an aura."

"Same." Superior Charles pats Victor on the shoulder. "You are something special, young empath. And if this is what you saw, we should send it around and inform the council."

"No," Victor states firmly. He then looks up at Superior Charles. "Let's keep this between ourselves for right now."

"Why would we want to do that?" Superior Charles questions.

Victor looks around the bonfire as he explains, "If they know that I know what to look for, then they might change how they operate or recruit."

"He does have a point there, Charles," Eddie says as he examines the symbol closely. "We should wait before we tell the council."

Superior Charles crosses his arms. He hums in the back of his throat as he ponders the request. "Well, the council already knows what happened today." He looks back down at the mysterious emblem. "But if our empath warlock suggests keeping this between us, then we'll keep it between us." Superior Charles sighs heavily as he walks back over to his spot in the sand. "So, Victor, have you thought about which coven you wanted to join?"

Victor looks up from his thoughts. "No, not yet. I haven't had any time to think about that."

"You'll have to decide soon. The council would like to know when you speak to them. It's better to have a coven sponsor you for the second part of your training," Superior Jackie remarks as she starts a new drink.

"What about my mentor?" Victor asks, looking at Leo.

"I was only your mentor until you completed this part of your lessons," Leo mentions. "I will most likely be given a new assignment soon."

Victor pierces his lips together. A mischievous expression appears on his face. "I think if I'm going to be the Grand Warlock, I should decide who my mentor is."

Eddie laughs heartily. "This guy barely received the title of empath warlock, and he already acts like he can do what he wants."

"That's because he will be able to do what he wants soon," Superior Charles comments.

CHAPTER FORTY-THREE

A month has gone by since Victor's encounter with Derek. Victor shifts around in his sleep. His facial expressions look as though he's having a bad dream. Victor wakes up abruptly in his bed. He looks around and remembers he's back in his apartment. The TV is still on, playing a crappy nighttime show with the volume down low. He looks over and sees Leo curled up with a pillow. They're lying on the comforter after falling asleep from an evening run and are still in their jogging clothes. The room starts to flash around as a storm builds up outside.

Victor shakes Leo awake. "Babe, wake up."

Leo swats Victor's hand away. "Five more minutes."

"Come on, I'm hungry," Victor pouts.

Leo sighs as he removes his shorts. "Fine, but you'll have to do all the work this time."

Victor laughs, hitting Leo with a pillow. "I'm talking about getting dinner. Go take a shower."

Leo turns his head to look at Victor with a sly smile. "You're not going to join me?"

"I'll join you in a minute," Victor says, leaning in to kiss Leo.

As Leo undresses, Victor slaps his ass. "That's gonna cost you $2," Leo says with a wink.

Victor waits until Leo gets in the shower before he picks up his phone. He notices Wren sent him a couple of messages and a missed call.

"About time you call me back," Wren says when she answers the phone.

"What's going on?" Victor responds quietly.

"I overheard a couple of the council members talk about you while they were in the library today," Wren informs. "They are planning to have a couple of the members meet up with you. I think they're not happy with you not joining a coven. And also want to go over how you knew about the secret coven."

Even though Wren can't see it, Victor looks perplexed. "How? How did they find out?"

"I honestly don't know," Wren responds. "I know none of us told them. But somehow, the council knows that you're keeping it a secret from them."

"Babe! Are you going to join me or not?" Leo shouts from the bathroom.

"In a minute," Victor shouts back.

"That's another thing too," Wren continues, "I don't think they are happy that you and Leo are together, even though it's been a month since you killed Derek."

"I didn't kill Derek. He got what was coming to him," Victor protests.

"Regardless, I think some council members are unhappy with you. It would help if you tried to lay low as best as possible. And don't be surprised if you meet another mentor to continue your lessons," Wren informs.

"VICTOR!" Leo shouts.

Victor sighs, "I'll give you a call tomorrow. Let me know if you find anything else about what we discussed."

"I got my chime flying around, feeling things out," Wren responds. "Just keep a low profile for now."

Victor ends the call and puts his phone on the dresser. He doesn't look behind him when he senses Leo's gaze. "Don't give me that look," Victor says to Leo. He turns around and sees Leo standing naked at the bathroom door. "You're getting water everywhere," Victor states.

"Get your ass in the shower with me now," Leo demands. Victor snickers.

As Victor steps into the shower with Leo, Leo slams Victor's naked body against the cold tiles. "Now, time for your punishment," Leo comments, pressing his lips against Victor's.

They kiss under the rushing water. Leo grabs the soap and starts lathering Victor's chest and shoulders. Victor smiles as he kisses the man he can finally be with.

Victor senses someone is at the front door but tries to ignore it. "I'm coming," he says as he presses his lips against Leo's.

"Already?" Leo questions against Victor's mouth. The person at the front door keeps knocking.

"I SAID I'M COMING!" Victor shouts.

Leo stops and jerks his head back. "What the fuck? I heard you. You didn't have to yell in my ear."

Victor lets go of Leo and pushes himself off the wall. "I'm sorry, someone won't stop knocking at the door." Leo lets out a groan of annoyance as they quickly rinse off and turn off the water. Victor steps out and dries off as the knocking continues.

"I SAID I'M COMING, GODDAMNIT!" Victor lets out as he hobbles around, trying to put on some shorts.

The knocking doesn't stop.

"FUCK! I'LL BE RIGHT THERE!" Victor shouts. He storms over and flings open the door.

"WHAT?!"

There is no one there.

"The hell?" Victor questions with confusion.

Victor looks around until he feels something pawing at his foot. He looks down, and a standard schnauzer looks up at him with puppy eyes. The poor thing is dirty; its gray hair matted around its paws and stomach. The hair around the snout is muddy as if he were rummaging around in the dirt, looking for something to eat. The dog starts to whimper and shiver from being cold and wet from the rain.

"Who is it?" Leo asks, still drying his hair with a towel. Victor steps to the side, letting Leo notice the helpless schnauzer at the door. "Did someone leave him at your door?"

"I don't know. He has no collar, no note." Victor leans down to pick up the schnauzer. The schnauzer lifts his front legs, allowing Victor to pick him up.

"Poor thing looks like he's had better days," Leo comments.

"Poor thing is cold. We should wash him and try to brush out this matted hair. After the storm passes, we can try to find his owner tomorrow." Victor walks back into the bathroom and turns on the water. "Leo, could you please grab a couple of towels for me?"

Victor kneels down against the tub and starts washing the dog. As Victor starts cleaning the dog's snout, the dog begins licking Victor's hand. The schnauzer keeps licking Victor as though he's thanking him. Leo sits down next to Victor and helps with the shampoo.

After a few minutes of washing all the dirt away, Victor wraps a towel around the poor animal. While Victor dries the dog's head, he makes eye contact. Victor pauses, mesmerized as if the two are making some connection. Victor and the dog do not look away from each other or blink. Victor can feel something building up inside of him, but he doesn't take his eyes off the schnauzer.

"Victor?" Leo questions, lightly shaking Victor. "Babe?"

Victor shakes his head, snapping back to reality. "I... I..."

"You what?" Leo looks down at the schnauzer. His eyes slowly open wider at what's before him. "Babe, um, I don't think he has an owner."

"Why would you think that?" Victor asks as he brings his focus to Leo.

"Look at his tail," Leo suggests, pointing down.

Victor looks where normally a small nub of a tail for a schnauzer would be. Instead, there is a shadow of a cat's tail flinging around. It disappears, and the small schnauzer tail returns. Victor becomes confused, looking at Leo, who grins.

Leo looks back at the dog. "I think you are now the proud owner of a familiar."

"Really?" Victor is perplexed. "I didn't ask for a familiar."

Leo shakes his head as he warps the dog in a towel. "It doesn't matter. Sometimes familiars will show up when you least expect it."

Victor slumps down on his knees. "But you don't have a familiar."

"I never asked for one, nor did I feel as though I needed one," Leo explains. "Familiars are very picky with who they select. I've even heard familiars leaving their witch if they become bored or deem them unworthy to keep them."

"They can do that?" Victor asks.

Leo shrugs his shoulders. "Familiars are weird." The dog looks at Leo, letting out a little growl. Leo is taken aback. "Not all familiars are weird."

The dog huffs.

Victor giggles as he lifts the small familiar up, giving him an Eskimo kiss. "Looks like you and I are going to be great friends." Victor is attacked by doggy kisses. "Let's get into bed so you can be nice and warm. But don't get used to it because you're getting your own bed tomorrow."

"You know he won't listen; he'll just end up sleeping with you. And then I'll get jealous because you'll be sleeping with him more than me." The dog sticks out his tongue at Leo and pretends to lick his nose. "I swear, he just stuck his tongue out at me."

"So, what are we going to name you?" Victor asks his new familiar. "How about Guapo? Because when I'm done cleaning you up, you'll be *muy guapo*."

Guapo licks Victor's face as fiery doggy kisses. "Guess he likes the name."

"He's a dog; they like anything," Leo comments. Guapo lets out a slight growl and a soft bark at Leo. "Victor, if he bites my face off, this is all on you."

Victor laughs as he hands Guapo to Leo. "Hold him for a minute. I'm going to get some water. Poor guy must be thirsty." Leo heads to the bedroom as Victor walks to the kitchen.

"Thirsty?" Leo comments while looking at Guapo, unamused. "He was out in the rain. There was plenty of water outside." Guapo growls at Leo, exposing his little teeth. "Okay. Okay. I'm sorry. Babe might as well get him some food." Leo has to hold Guapo back, trying not to be licked. "None of that, mister. The only tongue I want on me is your master's."

Victor rummages in the kitchen. He gathers a bowl of water and a small plate of lunch meat, then heads back to the bedroom. As he makes his way back to the bedroom, he drops everything out of his hands in shock.

"Mom?! Grandma?!"

Two glowing women sit at the dining table.

"Victor, we need to talk."

ACKNOWLEDGEMENTS

I hope you enjoyed the read, because I plan to continue Victor's adventures throughout five more books. I started writing The Warlock Series in 2020, while on a voluntary leave from working as a flight attendant. During that time, I planned out each part of the series. From the storyline to character development, I have spreadsheets and documents detailing every idea and aspect I imagined. Dry-erase boards, Post-it Notes, and red string are too cluttering for my taste.

When I returned to flying almost a year later, I made sure to carry my laptop and tablet with me everywhere. Between my trips, on layovers, and during those long flights where I had to stay awake all night, I finished the first draft of *A Warlock's Beginning*. From then to now, there are so many that I would like to thank for being a huge support during this journey.

I would first like to thank my biggest cheerleader, my cousin Rachel. She's loved the idea, the characters, and the story. She has also expressed how much she despises cliffhangers. She has been impatiently waiting for me to finish writing the second book.

My dearest friend, Isabelle. She is the inspiration behind Wren Llewllyn. She contributed her ideas about how Wren would speak and act, and helped with editing the very first draft. It was also a pleasure and an honor to be her Flower Girl (or Flower Gay) at her wedding. Isabelle has also been a great help when I can't seem to find the right words to say, because sometimes, my mind is a jumble.

My BFF Eddie for helping with some proofreading. We have been friends for twenty years and have always been there for each other, even though we no longer live in the same state. Here's to twenty more years of friendship.

A big thank you to my Aunt Heidi and my buddy Benjamin. These two found the time to help with some light editing as I finished the first draft of this manuscript. They helped me cross my I's and dot my T's, as well as making sure I used the correct punctuation,

My cousin Cruzito for being the photographer who took my author headshots for my portfolio.

A huge shout-out to Ayda Rose for creating the cover illustration. Her talent cannot go unnoticed. I look forward to working on more projects with her.

Another thank you goes to my friend and fellow author, David Wichman, for introducing me to JuLee Brand. David literally pulled me along with him to find JuLee at the Tucson Festival of Books. JuLee provided me with a bundle of knowledge to help turn my manuscript into a published novel.

There is also a long list of friends who live in another state or even another country and have supported me during this journey. They have always provided their positive energy, their drive for success, and their excitement to help keep this empath's personal battery charged. I am grateful to have them in my little coven.

And finally, my parents. My father, John, and stepmother, Elsa, have always supported me and believed in me throughout the years. They were just as excited as I was when I told them my book is going to be published. Now they have bragging rights, telling everyone their son is an author.

Victor's journey isn't over, and I'm looking forward to sharing it with you. Make sure you keep an eye out for announcements on the second book in my Warlock Series, *The Making of a Warlock: A Warlock Reborn.*

ABOUT THE AUTHOR

Dominic Anaya was born and raised in Arizona and currently lives in Texas. *The Making of a Warlock: A Warlock's Beginning* is his debut novel. Besides sitting in front of his computer, he is flying all over the USA and to other parts of the globe. Some of his favorite destinations have been Iceland, Italy, Japan, and the United Kingdom. Dominic's travels inspired many of the destinations Victor has been to and will go to as his journey continues in Book Two of his Warlock Series: *A Warlock Reborn*.

Follow Dominic online and on social media @domanayabooks

Made in the USA
Coppell, TX
21 February 2026

72490708R00236